Ember

By

Madison Daniel

Ember

This book is sold subject to the condition that it shall not, by way of trade or otherwise, be lent, re-sold, duplicated, hired out, or otherwise circulated without the publisher's prior written consent in any form of binding or cover other than that in which it is published and without similar condition including this condition being imposed on the subsequent purchaser.

Published by
Crushing Hearts and Black Butterfly Publishing, LLC.
Algonquin, IL 60102
ISBN-13: 978-0615605975

ISBN-10: 0615605974

This is a work of fiction. All characters and events portrayed in this novel are fictitious and are products of the author's imagination and any resemblance to actual events, or locales or persons, living or dead are entirely coincidental.

Edited by: V. Blondell Williams
For Crushing Hearts and Black Butterfly Publishing

Cover by: Para Graphic Designs

"For my forever muse.

Hand on heart."

~M.D.

Prologue: Nightmares

~Stop Crying Your Heart Out: Oasis~

"Hold on."

"Hold on. Don't be scared."

Please don't let go. The pain is dizzying. Just do not let go of her. This is my fault, I'm sure of that now. Look her in the eyes and don't let go of her. Whatever happens, don't let her be scared. Be stronger, for her.

Nothing else matters now. Not the pain. Not my mistake. Not the taste of blood in my throat. Not the smell of ash all around us. All that matters is her...just her. Hold on.

"Hold on a little longer!" I scream. I'm starting to panic. Stop it! You know what happens when you panic. I have to calm down. Just breathe. Stay calm. Do it now, for her!

"Max I'm slipping!" she screams.

"No! I won't let it happen!" I say focused. But she was right. I was losing her. I'm heating up again. Try harder and focus.

"Help me Max! My hands hurt...it burns! Help me! Please!" she cries louder. I'm so dizzy now. It's too hot. I'm too hot now. I can't hold her. She slips away and my heart breaks.

"Noooooooo!!!" she wails but her voice sounds so far away now.

Slow motion again. The dark pulls at the sides of my eyes and they burn something awful. Fight it. Fight the darkness. I reach out in front of me as far as I can. My eyes burn and I cannot see through my tears. But I can still see the look of terror on her face. I can still see her tears and her burnt and broken hands.

"Please no!" I beg. The world grows heavy.

"Don't go...don't go away..." Now I was screaming. She falls away.

I fade away...blackness.

"Love at first sight. I've always heard that said in movies or my favorite books but I never believed in it for a second. Death at first sight. That was much more my style. You know, the whole James Dean kind of thing. Live fast, die young sort of culture. Soon enough I would have experienced both." - Max Valentine

Ember

~Cruel Summer: Bananarama~

Saturday morning – 9:27 a.m. – August 12th.

"Easy Max," I warned as my airline food turned over in my stomach when the wheels of the plane first touched the ground. I rubbed my hands along my temples to sooth the throbbing building in my head. My temples filled with warming heat and the dull ache faded as the plane finally skated along the landing strip, safe and sound. I sighed with relief before being nudged by the person next to me to move out of his way. That settled my stomach as my anger awoke from its slumber.

"I hope this was the right choice..." I mumbled to myself and grabbed my things.

"Enjoy your stay," a stewardess said blankly. She didn't even make eye contact as she spoke. I shook my head and made my way into the airport. At least check out would only take an hour and was basically painless...this time.

"All right, calm down Max," I told myself as I stepped out the front doors. This was supposed to be my new start and this was not the way I should go about it. My temper was legendary and it had a way of getting the best of me. That was one of the many reasons I was here, on this island. My last chance at redemption on this tropical paradise they call Hawaii. Well, not exactly the big isle but one of her little sisters, Maui.

I had spent the last eight years running from the past, from my many mistakes and now I was at the end of my rope. I needed to make it work this time. I needed to

1

try harder this time and I needed to do it while controlling my famous temper.

The city of Kahului would be my savior or my nail in the coffin. And with the exception of the miserable flight, I think I was on the right path. As my eyes filled with the exotic landscape, it was love at first sight. The smell of the air hit me as soon as I walked out the doors of the airport. It was thick and sweet with an amazing floral smell that intoxicated my senses immediately. Fluffy grayish blue storm clouds in the distance brought the familiar smell of rain through my pores. Being the end of summer, it was hot and sticky from the humidity and those distant thunder clouds called to me. Ominously they seemed to taunt me but I have always enjoyed the ominous. Some would describe my childhood the same way.

A little yellow and red cab pulled up beside me with a honk of its horn, startling me from my daydream. I threw my bag into the back seat and quickly slid my six foot frame next to it. My guitar case followed with a thud. I snapped my seat belt on and handed the man behind the wheel a piece of paper with my destination on it.

"Do you know where this is?"

He said nothing...not a single word. His dark brown eyes only glared at me from the rear view mirror. I sat there silently as he shrugged his shoulders and slowly pulled away.

"Good...I guess you know the way," I smiled and he didn't even acknowledge me. Nice, I thought to myself sarcastically. I gave him one last glance before pulling out my shiny black mp3 player, quickly placing the tiny ear buds in my ears. I scrolled through my playlists of music to find the perfect antidote for my rude chauffeur.

A light and poppy tune which always put a smile on my face and reminded me of my summers growing up in the desert. I had found that music was one of the few things that truly soothed the inner demons in me. It kept me sane through some of my toughest trials and I treated it as if it were my own brother. That was the worst part of relocating here; I had given up the local band I had created back in California. Music was my life and lately I had been ignoring it.

"Just breathe," I told myself as I rolled the back window down. The island air swept inside my lungs, sticking there as I sung along with the music.

The cab ride only lasted twenty minutes and I tossed the mute cabbie a twenty dollar bill.

"Keep the change my friend," I smiled. He looked at the toll, $19.35 and his brow furrowed in annoyance. He didn't appreciate the joke, so I tried another one.

"So…how do you make a dead cat float?" I asked and stepped from the back seat. His eyes pulled down in disapproval and he put the car in gear.

"Two scoops of ice cream…one scoop of dead cat!"

Nothing again…not even a smile. He drove away quickly and I shrugged it off with a laugh. Stretching my arms I inhaled another breath of the tropical air and glanced around at my new surroundings. I was on a lone street that curved and faded away in the distance. A single house stood alone with tall trees on the right side and a bigger than normal driveway along the front. The house wasn't small and it wasn't big. It was tucked away under the shade of the trees, cozy and modest. It reminded me of a post card I had once seen.

The sun faded away behind the building sky and the smell of approaching rain snuck up on me. The thunder clouds were definitely headed my way…almost as if they were following me. My uncle warned me about how much it rains here on the islands. He told me that if I could stand the rain that I would do just fine living with him on the isle.

My Uncle Frank hasn't had much contact with the family since the accident but he always did his best to send me a post card or late night phone call, once in a blue moon. The accident drove a wedge between him and my dad, his brother. I always felt guilty for that. I think that was one of the reasons he ended up so far away from us. That and the brutal divorce from my Aunt Sharon didn't help much either.

But that was then and this was a new day. So when my favorite uncle offered me a place to stay and finish out my last year of high school, I couldn't say no. The sad fact was that I didn't have anywhere else to go after my father's funeral. Now here I was standing in front of his house enjoying the view. I walked up to the mailbox, slowly running my hand over the top of it. It was black with faded yellow numbers painted along the side, 214. Our last name Valentine was written underneath them in bold red letters.

I checked my watch to find that my Uncle Frank was running late as usual. I didn't have too many memories of his habits but I did remember that he wasn't a big fan of keeping a schedule. I think I inherited some of that gene too. He had told me to keep an eye out for a large truck with the words Lava Landscaping on the sides, but like him, it was no where to be found.

It's been ten years since I've seen him but I could still remember almost every detail of him. His hair was light brown like my fathers, his eyes were dark brown like mine and I had grown into a similar build. I was just a little skinnier I suppose. He stood almost 6' 2" but when I was younger I would have sworn he was 7 feet tall easy. He had the best sense of humor back then and was quite the practical joker. That used to drive my dad crazy, probably because he was the victim of most of Frank's pranks. He was my hero back then and now he was the only family I had left. If my dad was still alive I think he would have wanted it this way...I mean, his older brother watching over me. I think Frank was his hero too.

I was so lost in my trip down memory lane that I didn't even notice the tiny audience I had attracted. A little stray dog stood on the other side of the street, staring at me with wide eyes.

"Woof," he gently announced. I snapped from my daze to find the dirtiest little long haired Dachshund puppy I'd ever seen. His reddish brown fur was covered in a mix of mud and grass but from his posture I would say that he was proud of his camouflage.

He couldn't have been more than 2 years old, give or take a few months. With the exception of needing a bath he looked to be in great health. His little torso hovered only inches from the ground and he had no tags that I could see. Obviously someone didn't want him anymore. When our eyes met I could tell he was sizing me up and he didn't seem to be scared in the least. So I decided to test that theory.

"What do you say big guy..." I knelt down slowly in front of the mail box and pulled out a small bag of peanuts I had been given on the plane. "...You hungry?"

His little brown eyes looked down at the shiny green bag in my hands and then back to my eyes. He then slowly stretched his front paws forward, taking a couple steps toward me but he never moved his hind legs. He just crept forward until his back legs were sticking straight out behind him. He picked up his pace as his eyes focused back on my hands and after a couple feet he brought his hind legs up. He looked so silly as his back legs caught up with the rest of him.

MADISON DANIEL

He bobbed across the road with this silly little confidence and without hesitation he snapped up the peanuts, crunching them down quickly. A rumble came from his throat as his tail wagged waiting for another one. So I fed him another and another. A soft thunder rumbled above us and the sun was totally gone now as I heard the sound of an approaching engine. I just assumed it had to be my uncle and kept feeding my new acquaintance the rest of my snack. When I finally did look up I found a newer Jeep bearing down on us. I stood up motioning with my leg for the dog to get behind me and he did cautiously.

The next few seconds blurred into slow motion as I took in every detail. The Jeep was jet black and finely detailed, with big expensive off road tires and had been equipped with every bell and whistle. It had a removable top, which was off at the moment and a sport rack on top. A long purple and black surf board was strapped to the top and slightly shaded the driver. That's when I first saw her.

Her hair was dark deep brown, almost black, with slight wavy curls at the ends. It was just long enough to settle past her shoulders comfortably and was barely blowing in the wind. I found that weird because of the speed she was traveling at it should have been a mess of tangles swirling around her face. I didn't have time to think about that because that is when I noticed her eyes: those haunting, crystal blue eyes that would later invade my dreams and fill my nightmares.

Those eyes weren't particularly happy to see me. She focused them right through mine, which were probably bugging out of my head by now. She glared at me as if I were bothering her in some way. They closed slightly, never looking away from mine as the truck sped up and finally disappeared around the bend in the road.

"Whoa..." it slipped from my lips as time began to speed back up to normal.

Ember

"I'm a little dazed." My new buddy just sniffed the passing air, ignoring my words. Just then the back of my sneakers caught the edging of the street, sending me falling backwards. My arms flailing about me as my legs flew in the air as I hit the ground in a thud. My head was still spinning as my body came to a rest in the dirt and grass. So I gave myself a minute to remember every inch of her face as I caught my breath again. That was a mistake.

As I lied there laughing at my amazing grace I didn't even see or hear the motorcycle heading right for me. One of those small foreign bikes that were usually referred to as 'crotch rockets.' It was white with red and blue streaks along the sides. But my new friend had seen it coming and without any hesitation he was leaping over my body and growling in mid air at the stranger on the bike. His growl grew deeper as his paws found their footing and his tiny furry chest stuck out like a shield. The strip of fur on his back was standing at attention. I was in awe of how fearless he was but the man on the bike was not. I'm not even sure he saw us at the speed he was moving at or if he just didn't really care. The whine of his engine squealed louder as he gave the bike more gas. My little bodyguard stood his ground as the bike raced toward us.

The world came back into focus as I heard the painful yip from the dog as his body broke under the power of the motorcycles back tire. The man on the bike didn't even glance our way as he sped off down the road. The dogs twisted torso tumbled through the air behind me. Climbing to my feet I could already tell he was in bad shape. His body lied broken and bloody as his breathing became shallow and slow. A faint whimper was all he could manage but that was fading also. I had to act fast.

Quickly I scooped him up in my arms, glancing over my shoulders to be sure there were no witnesses. A gasp escaped his dry throat and his eyes began to glaze over.

"Hang on little hero..." I said as I brought him to my chest. "...I gotcha...don't move." I took a deep breath and concentrated. My body temperature began to warm under my tee shirt, filling my flexing arms with unnatural heat quickly. Faint steam escaped my hands and billowed around my face. The smell of singed fur filled my nose and the air around me, causing my eyes to water. A whitish orange glow pulsated from inside my arms as the first snap of his spine cracked back into place. The heat poured from my shoulders as my hands squeezed tighter and burned hotter. The glowing embrace throbbed back and forth as I pushed harder.

"Stay calm Max...stay focused...don't over do it," I warned myself out loud. There was more cracking as the bones set themselves and his front paws slowly began to move. His little chest filled with air and a tiny whine slipped from his mouth, only this time it was a soothing whine. Then, before I was ready for it, he was licking and pawing at my face. The steam faded into thin air as the glowing inside my grasp disappeared.

"You're welcome little one," I grinned. I felt a little winded and let my grip on him ease. He leapt from my arms to the ground and began jumping up and down in a dizzying display of joy. As he began to run around my legs in a thankful hysteria, a voice startled me.

"Well, that's a new trick."

I turned to find my Uncle Frank exiting his old truck with a bag of groceries in hand. His face was as calm as could be.

"You saw that huh?" I winced.

"I saw the whole thing. Just another magical day in paradise." He smiled and I felt at ease. Frank still looked the same. Just some gray on the sides of his head and a handful of wrinkles filling in his face. He was in good shape still, though he didn't seem as tall as I remembered. His eyes still held that same light in them that they had when I was younger.

"It's good to see you Uncle Frank," I said with relief.

"Max I'm so glad you took me up on my offer."

"I can explain..." I tried to say.

"Later my boy..." he said as he hugged me. "...Lets get you settled in first." He grabbed my bag as I slid my guitar behind my back. Together we walked to the front door of the house and my newest buddy followed close behind with a bounce in his resurrected step.

MADISON DANIEL

2000 Miles_02

~(Sittin' On) The Dock Of The Bay: Otis Redding~

Walking into the house I felt instantly at ease. It was exactly how I had pictured it. A modest 2 bedroom, 2 bath home that looked like it was about twenty years old. There were more windows than you'd expect in such a small house. Two large ones in the living room over looking the front yard and four more in the little kitchen that let the natural sun light wash over the tiles. The kitchen led to a decent sized patio with a grill and a place to eat. The living room was simple with a medium sized TV at the back wall and two small couches surrounding it.

"So Max...what do you think? Do you approve?" he asked excited.

"Not bad uncle..." I said quietly. "...But it's obvious that Aunt Sharon got all the money," I teased. He laughed and tossed me my bag.

"Your room is on the right...smart ass," he teased back and pointed down the hallway.

"Thanks."

My room seemed awfully big for the size of the house and surprisingly much cleaner than the rest of the place. He must have really wanted me to feel at home. There was a large window behind my bed with an amazing view of the distant mountain lines. An endless shower of sunlight lit every corner of the room. There was a small closet by my door and a desk next to the bed with a newer laptop computer on top of it. A small dresser on the opposite wall with a few framed pictures strategically placed along it.

One picture was of my dad and my uncle standing together, arms locked around each other as if they were caught off guard during a wrestling match. They looked like they were in their early twenties and both seemed as happy as I have ever seen them. Another picture was of my mom and I. I was about eight or nine in it and so happy. My smile was huge and looked just like my mother's. I had inherited that and her playful laugh. We also had the same dark brown hair.

The third and final picture I only glanced at quickly and reached out and flipped it face down so I couldn't see it. I closed my eyes and inhaled a long deep breath, trying with all my might to make the image disappear. It did after a few seconds and was replaced with darkness. I shook my head and opened my eyes.

"Do you like it?" Frank asked from my door way. It startled me.

"The rooms perfect...more than I deserve." I ran my hands through my bangs and they quickly fell back into my eyes.

"Thanks uncle." As I spoke his eyes glanced over at my dresser and the over turned picture frame. His face filled with a grimace and he understood completely. I never could hide anything from him. We've always had this weird connection since I was born. I think my dad was a little jealous of that bond we shared.

"Thank you for the bed and computer..." I was changing the subject. "...I'll take the best care of them."

"I know you will," he smiled.

Suddenly with the force of a rocket, the little stray wiener dog came bounding through my door and launched his dirty body into my arms. I almost dropped my guitar from the impact. His head turned toward Frank and he barked as if to say hello with his tongue hanging from the side of his mouth. He was as happy as could be and Frank and I looked at each other and laughed.

"You ever seen something so small act so big before?" he asked curiously.

"I know, he has absolutely no fear," I added. Frank walked over and put his hand on the dogs head and patted softly. The little bodyguard was enjoying all the attention.

"When that jackass on the bike hit him he spun so high in the air, like a little top, I thought for sure he was heading to Oz," he laughed hearty at his joke.

"That's perfect," I said cutting him off.

"What?"

"Oz!" I snapped. "I think that's what I'll call him." I was proud of myself and looked down to see if he approved of his new call sign but he was much more interested in rubbing his filthy back all over my fresh blankets. My eyes shot over to my uncle and he nodded in approval.

"Oz it is," he agreed turning to the door. "I'll see if I can find him something to eat, you see how well he takes to a nice, hot bath." Oz's head whipped around at the word and his ears folded back.

"Ah...it seems he is familiar with the procedure," Frank chuckled.

I grabbed him gently and felt where I had burned his fur away, under his left front leg. Picking him up he began to lick my face in a last attempt to change my mind about the impending bath of doom. I smiled and tucked his long torso under my arm like I was holding a football and walked to the bathroom.

"Sorry about the fur little man..." I ran my hand along the faded fur. "...But I'd say that it was a fair trade though," I smiled and placed him in the shower. He just sat there pouting as I began scrubbing the earth from his hair. After about ten minutes of scrubbing he was good as new. His reddish brown coat filled with a shiny glow. He quickly jumped from my hands and ran through the house like a dog possessed. I let him be and made my way back to my room and unpacked.

As I finished up, I went to the window and opened it letting the fresh air rush in and intoxicate me once again. Oz ran back in the room and onto the bed. One, two, three turns in a little circle and he plopped down right in the center. He fell asleep almost like someone had pulled out his batteries. Snoring was only minutes behind and it made me laugh inside. While I stood at my window a thought crossed my mind, a thought that hadn't done so in a long time. Maybe I could be part of a family again.

"Maybe," I whispered out the window.

4:17 p.m.

Home...that is what my uncle was offering me, a place to call my own. A second chance at making things right and maybe even being happy again. I personally didn't think I deserved the chance, but he did. I would always be grateful to him for the unconditional trust. The truth was that I was alone and my uncle Frank was the only family I had left. Now I know that sounded bleak but I felt like I had won the lottery.

The smell of the barbecue firing up filled the air through the house, grabbing my senses. Frank was grilling some kind of meat, I think pork and it smelled delicious. I changed my shirt quickly and ran out on the back patio to see if I could help with anything. Oz was right beside me as I walked with his little stomach already growling.

Ember

"Well uncle, how can I help with dinner?" I asked slapping my hands together in a loud clap. He smiled and slowly looked around the backyard.

"For starters...I'm having a little trouble with this darn grill. I can't seem to keep this right burner lit," he said annoyed. His eyes grew big watching me as he leaned over the burner.

"Do you think you could give me a hand?"

"Let me see," I said gently nudging him out of the way. My eyelids pulled together as I leaned over the grill and began to concentrate. I could feel Frank's stare intensify.

"Well?" he asked impatiently.

"Stand back a little," I warned. The fumes from the grill were already making my eyes water so I decided I better make this quick. My chest filled with heat and my neck covered with tiny goose bumps. I snatched a quick breath and exhaled in one fluid motion, letting a thin reddish orange flame spring from my lips. It stretched like a stream of water, flipping and twisting through the air. The burner popped with a burst of fire, igniting instantly. Quickly the flame settled into its new home and I let my body power back down.

"Ta da!" I said turning to Frank. His eyes were wide and I don't think he was breathing but he stepped closer to the grill again, letting out a long relieved breath.

"I'll never get tired of watching you do stuff like that. You've really learned how to control your gift haven't you?" he asked proudly. I shrugged a little embarrassed.

"Anything else?" I asked quickly. He went back to flipping the meat on the grill and pulled a new piece of meat up, placing it on the empty burner.

15

"Grab us a couple cold ones and I'll handle the rest."

"Got it...but I don't drink alcohol, so I hope you have something other than beer," I smiled. He looked at me surprised.

"There are some sodas in the fridge too." He paused and smiled. "I wish I had that kind of will power when I was your age. I mean, what kind of eighteen year old doesn't drink?" he said to himself.

"I'm not like most eighteen year olds," I called from the kitchen.

"I guess I shouldn't be surprised though, you were always a pretty good kid." He quickly placed a couple pieces of meat on a plate, watching me as I walked back out on the patio with two cold drinks.

"That is except when it came to that famous temper of yours," he teased. My hands began to heat and I looked at him wincing. Please don't say it...please.

"Isn't that right...Mad Max?" he said with a huge smile.

"Ugh," I groaned.

In a full blown laugh now he sat down at the patio table and handed the plate of meat to me. I placed the dish next to a fresh bowl of salad he had already prepared. Oz sprang from the kitchen door and slid right beside me with his tail wagging. I sliced him a chunk of pork and sat it in front of him.

"You know Frank...I haven't been called that in a few years," I was annoyed. His laugh faded as my tone changed.

"I wasn't trying to get a rise out of you son..." he paused. "Well, maybe a little."

16

Ember

"I guess I have earned the name though." I let a small smile return to my face.

"My abilities kind of make it easy to be a hot head...so to speak." I reached for the salad bowl.

"I've known about the fire starting stuff for years, ever since you purposely burned my carton of cigarettes when you decided it was time for me to give up the habit," he winked. I blushed when I remembered the scene.

"I think you were around seven," he thought out loud. He was right. He leaned in and whispered in a serious tone.

"Now what's the story with that neat little trick you did out front this morning?" And if on cue, Oz's tiny head popped up from his piece of meat. He licked his mouth quickly and wagged his tail gently.

"About two years back I was stringing my guitar one afternoon and I accidentally jabbed the end of one of the strings into my palm." I held up my right hand. "It hurt something awful and blood gushed from it everywhere. It got all over my clothes, making me mad of course..." Frank's eyes filled with the glee from before when he mentioned my old nickname. "...My hand quickly ignited into a flame and slowly it healed beneath the flame...I was shocked." I sipped a drink from my bottle of soda and continued.

"No matter what I did to myself it healed and every time it seemed to speed up. So that made me wonder if it only worked the one way or if I learned to control the flame, maybe I could do the same for others." I sighed lightly and Frank's face filled with cautiousness.

"I haven't had too many opportunities to practice on others," I said glancing down at Oz. He barked at me as I patted him on the head.

"But it seems to be working fine."

"How far do you plan on pushing this…gift?" he asked bluntly.

"I don't know…" I sat silently for a second. "…I just figured if I could make up for my past mistakes…maybe I'd be forgiven. Maybe the nightmares would finally stop."

"You still have that same nightmare huh? About that day? About her?" he asked cautiously. I nodded yes.

"Almost every night." My eyes fell to my hands as I began to rub them together nervously.

"I don't sleep that well. I hope that won't bother you too much?"

Smiling he said, "I'm a pretty heavy sleeper. No worries my boy."

He fell silent pondering what to say next and I just watched him waiting.

"No matter how many stray animals you save Max, it won't change what happened that horrible day." His words hurt a little. "And it will not change the truth," he added. I was scared of what the truth was and Frank knew it.

"Mia loved you…and your gift."

Ouch. I was right to be afraid.

"And she forgives you son," he said with a heavy tone. I was absolutely speechless. I hadn't heard her name spoken out loud in a long time and it hit me like a sledgehammer. I felt sick inside. My fingers fell across my right inner wrist where I had her name tattooed in black and red lettering.

"My beautiful Mia," I spoke under my breath.

Ember

Frank saw the rawness in my face and he felt bad for bringing her up. He took another minute to pour himself another drink as I squirmed in my seat.

"You ever hear anything from your mother?"

"Not a peep," I said through my teeth and shook my head in disgust.

"When she left after the accident years ago, she cut all ties...forever it seems," I said angry.

"I don't even know if she heard about dad's heart attack. Even if she had, I'm sure she would have just blamed me anyways," I squeezed my drink and it began to bubble with heat. "...Just like last time!"

Frank slid the bottled drink from my hand with a napkin in hand. His face winced from the heat of the glass but he said nothing.

We sat for a few minutes saying nothing and finished our dinner. Finally he spoke up.

"This islands awfully beautiful, don't you think?" he was changing the subject but I was glad he did.

"From what I've seen...yes," I said as I started to feel settled again.

"I know every inch of the island. If you have any questions just ask," he said with a grin.

"I like my privacy sometimes...any secluded beaches or coves I could have to myself?" I had already begun to feel happy just talking with him. I lit my finger with a snap of my wrist and a flame reached for the sky. His eyes grew bigger.

"You know...for practice," I finished.

"Hmmm...I think I know the perfect spot." His eyes relaxed as I let the flame fade away.

"Really?"

19

"Very secluded, very private," he smiled.

"Where?"

"Not too far from here. Mokule'ia Beach." His smile wilted slowly. "But the kids have a newer name for it though."

"What's that?"

"Slaughterhouse," he groaned.

"Nice."

"It's just some stupid name that seemed to stick for some reason. Most Maui locals call it by its true name." He stretched his back. "Anyways, it will probably be exactly what you're looking for. It used to have a steady stream of visitors but that's changed in the last couple of years."

"Why's that?"

"I'm not sure. It's a great place to surf but a little dangerous. You might encounter a stray surfer with a death wish but it's secluded enough for what you're asking." He paused again. "Most of them can't stand it anymore."

"I'm not following," I said and in the distant background more thunder rumbled again. He smiled and looked off in the direction of the storm.

"The weather. It always seems to be raining at that beach. Big thick dark rain...all year round." He leaned across the table "Some of the locals say that it's cursed." He contorted his face in a sad attempt to be scary but he failed miserably.

"It should be perfect," he finished.

"Sounds like a plan," I said excited. I've always been attracted to the rain...every aspect of it. The coolness of the drops on my skin. The smell as the first raindrops touched the desert floor. The breeze that seemed to carry every smell it passed over. I loved all of it. So the haunted beach sounded just fine to me...ghosts or no ghosts.

Back in my new room I felt spent. My weary eyelids were growing heavier by the minute. Just before I gave into the sandman I spied on my desk a small blue and white pamphlet. It was folded neatly next to my computer. I opened it up and pulled another folded piece of paper out.

"Maui High...home of the mighty Sabers," I read aloud. It didn't look like it was that big of a campus, only 1700 students total. Most of the schools I had attended had at least 1000 kids in each grade.

"Sounds fun." I leaned back on my bed, sliding my ear buds in and turning on my music. My eyes closed as the days events ran through my head. The miserable flight, the gorgeous landscapes and the mysterious girl behind the wheel of her truck and then I remembered the man on the motorcycle.

I wasn't sure why I thought about it but I did. As he drove away, after crushing my little friend without a single glance, I notice his back. Well, not his back exactly but the back of his pullover. It had two words scrolled across it...'MAUI HIGH.'

"Great," I sighed. Monday should be fun. In a school that small, running into him shouldn't be too big of a problem. I felt my anger rising and took a couple deep breaths until I was calm again.

I thought it would take me hours to fall asleep with all the thoughts running around my skull but I was wrong. Sleep fell on me like gravity and I faded into my dreams. I was also hoping that in my tired state I wouldn't dream this night but I was wrong...again.

MADISON DANIEL

The nightmare came harder and faster than usual that night. I had been through this many times before but tonight was different. This time, as I watched Mia catch fire and fall away from me over and over again, her screams were drowned out by the pounding thunder above us. I couldn't see any clouds or rain, just the slow rolling thunder. It turned out to be a very long night.

Broken_03

~Time Is Running Out: Muse~

Sunday morning – 10:03 a.m. - August 13th.

My plan for getting up early didn't quite pan out. I woke up to Oz jumping on my head. His warm little paws scratching at my fore head.

"Ow...quit it," I slurred from the corner of my mouth but he only bounced harder when I resisted. He was ready for his next adventure and my lazy butt wasn't going to slow him down today.

"All right, you win," I groaned as I stumbled to my feet. I found my way to the bathroom and took a quick shower. As I walked to the kitchen I realized that Frank had already left for the day. On the kitchen table was a glass of juice that sat on top of some cash and a piece of paper. I stuck the cash in the pocket of my board shorts and read the note out loud.

"Max...I'll be back this afternoon. Enjoy your first full day on the island. I hope the map's enough to get you there? If not...just follow the thunder. Be safe...Frank."

Scribbled below his writing was a simple map that he had drawn up himself. It was clear and easy enough to read. I stuck the map in my other pocket and glanced down at Oz.

"Well little man, you up for an adventure?" I asked and he danced in place. "Some lions, tigers and bears!" I sang to him. He jumped straight up, front paws reaching out and barked twice. It almost sounded as if he were singing along with me. I swung my guitar behind my back, stepped out the front door and inhaled the morning air.

"We're off to see the wizard!" I teased.

Sunday afternoon – 2:33 p.m.

Frank was right about this beach, it was totally empty and completely overcast. I thought that was strange because there wasn't a cloud in the sky when we left the house. It seemed even darker over the water, giving the ocean a menacing shade of black.

"...You're something beautiful...a contradiction...I want to play the game...I want the friction..." I sang out loud as my feet first touched the sand. A small wave crashed against the sand, signaling our arrival. A cool breeze hit us and the sun was nowhere to be found.

"...You...will be...the death...of me..." I sang softly and a shiver danced down my back.

The beach was quite breath taking in its own morbid way. There was a thin stretch of sand shaped like a crescent, with yellowish brown highlights and sprinkles of black peppered throughout it. Dangerous, sea carved rocks stuck from the ground and ocean on both sides of the beach. The largest cluster resided at the back, where the sand met the pavement of the road. Some were in the shapes of miniature mountains, while the others resembled daggers peaking from the earth. The image of a human shish kabob popped into my mind. Softly something rattled my nerves.

"Whoa...do you smell that?" I asked Oz as the mysterious new scent hit me. He grunted, lifting his snout into the oncoming breeze. It was a familiar smell to me but I stood confused by its presence here.

Ember

"Cherry blossoms," I whispered. How is that possible? I asked myself. Oz shook his head gently as I tried to ignore the overwhelming scent and continued inspecting the beach.

The waves rolled in faster then the wind was letting on and they rolled back out with hardly a sound. The only real noise was coming from the blowing wind as it rushed through the tropical vegetation. Instantly it fell even colder, sending a whine from Oz's mouth and a quiver along his body. He also seemed uncomfortable with the uneasy vibe of the ocean.

The faintest of sprinkles began to fall on us and I felt like maybe this wasn't the best spot to have brought my guitar. So I wrapped it up in the towel I had brought with us and carried it to the edge of the trees, where it could have some coverage from the rain. Oz looked up at me shivering and the damp sand had begun to cling and clump to his fur. No matter how hard he shook it just wouldn't let go of him.

"Sorry big guy...I guess you weren't really built for the beach," I joked. I felt my temperature drop now too but all I had to do was heat myself from within. I was fine but that didn't help Oz at all, so I devised another plan.

"Maybe we could get a small fire going," I said petting his head. I was sure it wasn't aloud but from the seclusion of the beach, I didn't think anyone would throw too big of a fit. Besides, this would give me a chance to practice one of my tricks I had been working on.

"Okay, prepare to be amazed!" I called to Oz. He had begun to sulk and huddled his wet torso next to my guitar. I swiftly snagged one single stick from the pile of wet kindling I had gathered, bringing it inches from my face. It was only a foot long with a slight bend at the top of it.

"Now focus," I breathed harder. As I exhaled, steam rose from the hot slit of air escaping my lips and quickly burst into a slice of fire. The thin flame jumped to the tip of the stick and danced around. It only managed to last for a few seconds before surrendering to the building rain.

"Damn it." I thought I had it. I inhaled deeper this time and forced an even bigger flame onto the stick. It ignited easily and I was happy with myself. I glanced over at Oz for approval who just sat with his front paws tucked under his chin with a worried stare on his mug. When my eyes turned back to the stick the flame had burned out again, this time making a wet sizzling noise.

I was officially annoyed now and could feel my chest filling with disgust. Steam slowly swept from my shoulders to the air as the cold rain began to feel like falling pieces of ice against my burning skin. My temper began to flair and that's probably why I didn't notice the pair of curious eyes watching me from the waves.

"Stay where you are Oz. Don't move," I warned. The steam was coming off of me thick now as the raindrops increased in size and strength. From behind my dripping bangs I concentrated my anger on the drenched pile of wood and tossed the stick into it hard. My core was burning now and felt as if it wanted out from inside me. Within seconds a white and orange flame covered my hand while the rain pushed down harder on me.

"Just let go a little more," I told myself. The flame flared up and grew, twisting in the storm. It slithered up my arm, stopping just before my steaming shoulder as my muscles clinched tightly. The thunder rumbled over the top of me in defiance, making me smile.

"You're gonna have to try harder than that Mr. Rainmaker," I boasted. I could hear Oz whine from behind me as the wind increased too. I sucked in a breath and pushed at the building fire in my arm. In a burst, a ball of fire escaped my hand, slamming itself into the kindling. Sand and sparks scattered as the trail of smoke withered in the rain back to my hand. The pile of wood burned hot with the sound of the raindrops dying inside it.

I let the remaining fire flicker along my fingers as lightning flashed above me. It was so close that I thought if I reached up I could grab it out of the sky. The sight of lightning that close should have scared me something awful but it didn't. What did send chills down my fiery spine was the flash of white fire above me made no sound at all. It was accompanied by something much more startling....the sound of someone screaming. I wasn't alone.

Oz started barking as I whipped my body toward the sound of the scream. My eyes searched the breaking waves as time started to slow back down to a crawl. That is when I saw her, the girl from the day of my arrival. The one in the Jeep with the haunting blue eyes.

I found that I could not speak, I could not move as my body had frozen stiff as stone. Locked in her gaze, I stood there with my left arm ablaze in the pouring rain. Smoke danced off my silhouette like a ghostly ribbon and trailed off into the sky.

She was twenty yards from the beach and even from that distance her features were intoxicating. She stood like a statue at the front of her surf board as it slowly cut through the black water. Her legs were long and tone, like an athlete. Her black bikini hugged her fit torso, exposing her stomach and tone arms. The menacing water barely touched her, only peppering her skin in soft delicate bursts. Her hair fell with dark beads of water trailing through her soft curls. The ocean was a beast now but her hair hardly moved, it cradled and shaped her shocked face.

The flickering lightning revealed every line of her face and exposed her full lips pulled together in a serious pout. Her eyes were glowing blue and sparkling, like two jewels on fire. How could someone's eyes burn so bright from so far away? It didn't make any sense.

As I stood burning on the beach, the sea became tiresome of our time bending interlude. It swelled up and began to rise behind her and I could feel time pulling at my body again, speeding back to normal. My eyes pulled from hers and focused on Oz who was running back and forth in hysterics. My flames disappeared as I looked back at the girl and the wall of water building behind her. She didn't seem to notice the danger, even when the waves began to tilt the back of her board up and out of the water. She continued to stare at me with those angry eyes in some kind of quiet calmness. Thunder seemed to rattle the surf over and over again, shaking my bones in the process.

I tried to scream to her but nothing came out of my mouth. The dark wave stood up behind her like a monster rising from his grave, covering her in an icy shadow. It hung there just long enough for her to snap back to reality and realize that she was in trouble. She broke off her stare just as the wave crashed down over her and buried her in darkness. Lightning split the sky with the force of an explosion, almost knocking me off of my feet. She was gone now and the sea quickly began to settle itself, satisfied with its latest meal.

Oz and I ran to the edge of the water in a panic trying to see any sign of her but it was nearly impossible to see anything. The water was much too dark and the rain was falling too thick now.

"Oz...do you see her? Do you see anything?" I screamed. Nothing...only water. Water that seemed to be settling itself down as quickly as it had grown angry. The waves faded to what looked like ripples and the rain began to stop. That didn't make any sense.

Ember

"Don't panic Max. Stay calm," I tried to convince myself but it was too late, I was losing control of my emotions and the steam poured off of my shoulders again. I filled with anger as I started to blame myself for not warning her sooner. Heat was pulsating from my body in waves as I tried to keep myself under control. That's when Oz began barking feverishly from the end of the beach. I knew exactly what he was saying...he had found something.

Her surf board had washed up on shore in two pieces. I ran to them hoping that she wasn't far behind but she never appeared, sending me back into my panic. My hands fell onto the two pieces of board, quickly burning into them as I threw them behind us. I was so angry now that I tore my shirt off in a fit, readying myself to jump in the water. I knew I wouldn't be able to swim against the current, even with it calming down now but I had to try. That's when I felt something hit my shin. It was her hand followed by her broken body.

I calmed myself as best as I could, trying to cool my hands and gently picked her up. I raced her limp body to the middle of the beach where my bonfire had burned out. In my arms I could already tell that she wasn't breathing or at least not strong enough for me to tell. As I lied her down Oz rushed to her side with a soft whine in his throat. I could see how bad she really was now.

Her body was twisted and bloody with her color fading fast. Her back looked broken, with many gashes along her left side where she must have collided with the sharp rocks. Her left leg looked even worse. It was fractured in at least three places. One of the fractures was so bad that the bone had torn through the skin, completely exposed. She had been bleeding heavily but now it was beginning to slow.

"Not a good sign," I told nobody. I lowered my head to her mouth and listened for any sign of breathing.

29

She had the faintest pulse but it was almost gone now too. I was out of time. There was only one thing left to do. I closed my eyes and tried centering my racing thoughts and focused. This was probably not a good idea; I had never attempted something like this before. There were so many questions. Would this kill her? Would this kill me? How do I explain this to her if I was actually able to do this? Too many questions.

"Never mind!" I scolded myself as my hands made my mind up for me and filled with burning heat. Oz leaned his head down, whimpering in confusion and fear.

The steam came in waves again, blowing off of me in the breeze. The rain had faded to a mist now and the clouds had pulled back enough for the sun to peek through. Its warmth was welcoming and soothing. I slid my left hand under her head on the curve of her neck. Her hair felt soft and cool on the back of my hand. My right hand followed the length of her left side, down to her hip and small of her back. That is where the most damage had occurred.

My palm settled around her hip as my fingers traced themselves down her spine and the fresh wounds. Her skin was pasty white now...I needed to hurry. So I let go and fire filled my every pore, followed by my hands glowing with hot fire. The smell of burning hair filled my nose but only for a moment and nothing happened as I pushed.

"What's wrong?" I asked the fire inside of me. As I grew frustrated I dug my knees into the sand and tried again. I pushed the fire much harder this time and my head spun like a top for a second but I shook it off quickly. My chest felt like burning razors while my mouth gasped puffs of hot steam as I tightened my grip on her.

Ember

The gashes on her side started to close, pulling themselves together and fading away. Slowly at first but then in a blink her wounds were gone, leaving only goosebumps covered in smeared blood. Her color started to return as her breathing grew from nothing to very strong. Her chest filled with air and her back began to arch and twist with the sounds of bones cracking and snapping back into place. The sound was too familiar for Oz and he turned and ran but stopped himself a few feet away.

More bones set as the sound of rumbling thunder replaced the cracking. Her breathing was almost back to normal when the last few bones healed themselves. Her skin filled with heat and she lurched forward. It took all my strength to hold on to her as her eyes peeled open. She ripped her head from my grip and sat up dazed. A scream tried to escape her mouth but was drowned out by the crashing thunder around us. Fresh new drops of rain started to fall on us, washing the blood into the sand. I let my free hand find the other side of her hip to hold her steady in place. As my hand found her skin, her eyes filled with confusion and anger. She reached out and slashed her fingernails across my face, drawing blood instantly.

"Ouch..." I said through gritted teeth. Four bright red streaks glowed through the rain on my face and my temper flared again. I held steady, never easing up my grasp and looked her directly in those hateful eyes. She kept up her struggle until she watched the four bloody scratches vanish as if the rain had washed them away.

"Don't," I warned her. "I'm not finished." My voice was calm and she stared as the steam billowed away from my mouth as I spoke.

I slid my right hand along her devastated leg, being careful not to touch the exposed bone. My left hand lowered to her stomach and gently held her in place. She fought this at first but stopped as she watched the steam escape my burning hands. I was in the zone now and her leg healed itself quickly with a snap, crackle and pop. The rip in her flesh sealed closed in one swift motion as the excess blood washed away, leaving her leg good as new. Her hands reached out to her leg and traced themselves down to my hand that was still wrapped around her ankle. She had a tattoo of flowers circled around it and it was almost glowing as if she had just had them inked.

The rain fell silent again and the sun forced its way through the dark sky, showering us with its warm rays. As the light washed over us, I found it hard to see and my eyes hurt from the light. Oz stretched his head toward the rays and shook the excess water off his body. My silent angel just sat there staring up at the sun like she had been living in a cave for the last ten years. My eyes fell from the sky and back to her face, her features were striking. I could feel my pulse quicken and my hands heat again as I realized I was still holding her stomach and ankle firmly. She was so soft and so smooth that I didn't want to let go of her. I didn't even know her name but I felt the strongest connection with her, almost like I was whole. That scared me immensely.

I let go of her and stood up slowly with her eyes falling upon me again. We were both frozen again when Oz barked, yanking her hypnotizing stare at him and I was able to breathe again. She stole a glance at the sun again and then back at me. Her eyes were full of anger and I thought she might get up and clobber me but I summoned every ounce of courage I had left and extended my hand down to her. She ignored the polite jester and hopped to her feet with a kick of wet sand.

"You're welcome," I quickly said. I tried to sound like I was half joking but I don't think I pulled it off too well. She saw the pieces of her busted surf board lying in the sand behind me and her face tightened in more anger.

Ember

She pushed past me and scooped up the two halves. I tried to help but she stepped away from me as if I was still on fire. My chest burned with uneasiness and I kept my distance.

She stepped forward as if she was going to say something but stopped herself at the last second. Her eyes fell to my hands and the thunder returned, this time with less intensity. The sun was pushed back behind the weary clouds, bringing the waves to life again. She turned and walked toward her truck which was parked behind some trees on the other end of the beach. I felt stupid that I hadn't noticed it before and hung my head in disappointment.

Her pace quickened as she stomped closer to her Jeep and the rain began to fall again. I wanted to call to her but I couldn't think of anything to say. I wanted to chase after her but my legs would not move. I could think of only one thing at that moment. I had been on the island for little more than twenty-four hours and had already given away my secret to a complete stranger.

She threw the broken pieces in the back of her truck and climbed behind the wheel. I waited for her to drive off but she didn't. She just sat quiet and still, gripping the steering wheel tightly with her blue eyes burning into mine again. I could feel my hands fill with the fever to burn again but I held back the urge. She drove away in anger and the thunderstorm seemed to follow shortly after. I watched petrified.

"...You...will be...the death...of me."

4:45 p.m.

The journey home was a long one. As we walked in the house I tossed my guitar on the couch and collapsed right next to it. Oz ran for the kitchen and his water dish.

"That bad huh?" Frank asked from above me laughing.

"Not now uncle...I'm exhausted," I said with my face buried in the cushion.

"I'll grab you a drink." With a laugh he walked into the kitchen.

"Thanks."

"How was the beach?" he called from inside the fridge.

"Hot," I yelled back.

"That's funny, it looked like it was storming like crazy that way to me." He shrugged and handed me a bottled water. "Oh well, I know of some other beaches..."

"No! That one was perfect."

"So you were able to get in some practice?"

I looked at Oz and then back to him.

"You could say that."

Ember

Morning Glory_04

~Amber: 311~

Monday morning - 7:27 a.m. - August 14th.

First days at a new school are supposed to be exciting and unforgettable. A scary mix of nerves and shame that help shape the person you are destined to become one day. I've had enough first days at new schools, that I was an expert in the trials of being the new kid. Every other semester I found myself in a fight with the school bully, causing me to lose control of my famous temper and making my father freak out. Or, if I was getting too close with my friends or girlfriends that they might find out my little secret, he would pack us up and find somewhere new to start again. No matter how much I kicked and screamed about leaving again. Unsurprisingly at each one of those places was another school, another first day, another batch of glares and stares. Thanks dad.

I had high hopes for this coming school year, it being my last one. No more running and no more hiding. Just finish the last couple credits I needed and graduate. It was time to make something of myself and I was excited at the thought of my future and the fact that it would unfold on this tropical paradise. One of my uncle's favorite quotes was, "Knowledge is power." He was right. He's always right...almost.

A knock at the front door startled me from my rambling thoughts. I quickly threw on my faded tee shirt and ran for the door. I had to jump over Oz, who had now stretched his little frame across the living room floor. Sleeping away, with his tongue sticking from the side of his mouth. My feet hit the floor with a dull thud.

"Hang on," I called out. As my hand found the door knob I gave Oz one last glance and saw that he hadn't moved an inch. Heavy sleeper. I opened the door not ready for what was on the other side. I found myself face to face with an angel.

Her hair was blonde with slight hints of red streaming through it, as the morning sun radiated from behind her petite frame. Her blonde locks fell almost half way down her back and a hint of her sweet shampoo filled my nose. She couldn't have been much taller than 5' 2" but she gave off a much larger radiance. She looked up at my eyes with a quiet confidence I had never seen before. She was smiling slightly with an inquisitive look in her eyes. They were jade green and reflected her golden locks inside of them.

She was dressed in a white tank top that exposed a cluster of freckles that resided on her round shoulders. Her blue jeans were snug and her car keys dangled from her right pocket. They would jingle with every slight shift of her hips. She looked casual yet proper. She was beautiful. Not the drop dead, gorgeous supermodel beautiful, but the girl next door beautiful.

"Aloha," she said smiling. "I'm Sam. Are you ready?"

I was lost. I tried my hardest to focus and say hello back, but I think the most I was capable of spitting out was...

"Alo..." At which point I closed my eyes and hoped I was still dreaming away, safely in my bed. A gentle laugh came out of her lips as I cracked open my eyelid and dared to sneak another peek at her lightly freckled face before I decided to run and hide. My face felt hot with my burning embarrassment.

"Wow...you're pretty good with first impressions Max," she teased. Now I was falling deeper into my confusion. I had never met her before, yet she seemed to know me quite well. I shook off the embarrassment and willed myself back to reality.

"Um...good morning," my voice almost cracked but I stood firm and held out my hand to shake hers and smiled. She took my hand and softly shook it. My hands were warmer than normal and she noticed but only tightened her grip.

"I'm Samantha Summers," she said and looked for any sign of recognition. "I'm here to take you to school," she continued but I only stared at her dumb founded.

"Didn't your uncle tell you?" she asked. I stared some more.

"You're uncle asked me to pick you up this morning," she tried again. I turned and looked around the house for any sign of Frank "the matchmaker" Valentine but of course he had already left for work. Funny how he hadn't mentioned any of this to me during the many hours of catching up we had done.

"Uh...no. He didn't say a word," I said coyly. She paused for a moment then tilted her head slightly and a grin grew across her lips.

"Surprise!" she burst out and before I could make any sense of what was happening, she reached past me and scooped up my school bag. She turned and walked quickly toward her car. I just stood there with my hands on my hips stunned. Swiftly she entered her car and waved to me.

"Come on Valentine...I won't bite." She winked and slid behind the wheel. I grabbed my guitar and tucked my mp3 player in my front pocket. A smile filled my face as I ran out the front door and the slam from it woke Oz from his morning slumber. He bounced to his feet annoyed, looked around and let out a sigh. He ran to my bedroom, jumped up on the bed and plopped himself down, falling quickly back to sleep.

Samantha's car was small and compact, like her. A little, silver Toyota hatchback that my guitar almost didn't fit in. It was maybe ten years old, give or take a year, but in good condition. She had a simple chain hung around the rear view mirror and it gently swayed back and forth as she drove off. The reason I noticed it first was because of what was hanging from the end of it. A tiny silver charm, shaped like a mask from the theatre. It was suspended inside a tiny oval and spun around easily when moved. One side was a mask with a giant smile and the other a mask with a depressive frown. It reminded me of an album cover I once saw. I liked it instantly. The rest of the front seat was very clean and smelled like her...strawberries.

The engine purred along and she turned her radio to a local station that pumped out some poppy music. Her eyes watched the road and then found my hands. She stared at them for a second and then the tattoos I had on my arms. She only seemed to glance at the one on my left forearm before concentrating on the one on my right inside wrist. It made me uncomfortable, so I turned my hand away from her view.

"So you have absolutely no idea who I am, do you?" she asked playfully.

"Not a clue." I smiled at her. "Samantha was it?" I asked playing dumb. I knew exactly what her name was and I would never forget it.

"That's right. You may call me Sam if you want." She paused then found my eyes with hers. I let out a slow sigh.

Ember

"So...do you make it a habit accepting rides from people you've never met before? Or is this a first?" Her hand pulled her bangs behind her ear and I felt my pulse quicken slightly.

"Nah...I do it all the time." I leaned back in my seat. "I usually only accept rides from sane people though," I smiled.

"Are you saying I'm crazy?" she asked flustered.

"No, not at all," I continued.

"Then what are you saying?"

"Look, most sane people don't kidnap innocent young men they've never met before," I said full of cockiness. "No matter how good looking they might be," I added and her mouth fell open with a laugh.

"Kidnapped?" she spit out.

"Yup," I said a little too cocky and she glared at me.

"You got in my car willingly. I did not make you do anything." Her voice was rising now but she still sounded playful.

"First of all, let's get things straight. I had to come along for the ride...you had my bag. So either I call the police and report that I had just been violated by a cute little blonde or I let you kidnap me." I sounded so arrogant but she didn't seem to mind the "cute" comment. I smiled even bigger.

"I was kind of leaning towards option one."

"Oh really," she smiled.

"Yeah, but then I figured, if she really is some kind of sicko I could probably handle her," I said and checked her face for the recognition of my cynical humor. Her eyes seemed to laugh but her smile had faded a little. So, I stupidly continued.

"I mean, you're barely four feet tall...I think I could take you." I laughed and realized I was the only one laughing. Uh oh.

"You'd be surprised...things aren't always what they seem." Her tone was softer now but had a hint of seriousness. "I could be a raging ax murderer for all you know."

"Nah...You're a good girl. I can tell," I said. Instantly I could tell she wasn't a big fan of those words, "good girl."

"Oh...am I now?" she spoke politely even though her face looked defensive.

"Of course you are." I decided to push a little more. That probably wasn't the smartest decision based on the fact that all I knew about her was that my uncle knew her.

"And I'll tell you why."

"I'm listening," she huffed politely.

"Your car is simple and clean, very clean. That means you care about yourself and whoever might be in the passenger's side. A bad girl wouldn't care what other folks think." I reached out and touched the necklace that dangled from the mirror.

"You are an artist, or have a very artistic side. That's why you like this necklace so much. You probably were given it by some great aunt or maybe a grandmother who was in the theatre herself and just as artistically driven as yourself." As I paused to take a breath, I noticed her eyes were pulling together as if she was staring into the sun.

Ember

"And the fact that it's a pair of masks and not some bloody cross or skull tells me that you prefer the light and not the dark, another sign of a good girl." I was on a roll now and felt more confident than usual. "And finally, my uncle wouldn't trust you if you weren't...a good girl." I crossed my arms and sat back as far as I could in my seat.

"You done?" she asked quietly. I smiled and nodded yes. She looked at me and I suddenly became very uneasy.

"My turn?"

"Shoot," I said.

"So...if I'm such a good girl, then I guess that makes you the typical 'bad boy'...huh." Her smile was completely gone now. "A big tough guy with his guitar in one hand and tattoos in the other." She was upset. I covered my wrist with my left hand to hide the three letters inked across it.

"The look in your eyes like you don't care..." a wicked smile crept back on her face. "The smugness in your posture as if you've already got everything figured out. This island, this situation, this...girl." Her eyes snapped back to the road. "You're just too cool for all of it, aren't you?" she finished.

"Wow..." I felt stupid. "Tell me what you really think." My sarcasm couldn't hide that her observations were dead on. I was acting like a know it all and she called me on it. The fact was, I didn't know a thing about her, just that I already liked her. She watched as I fidgeted in my seat.

"Sorry Max," she apologized. "Too much coffee this morning."

"It's okay," I said.

41

"I don't usually drink coffee in the morning. Only when I'm nervous about the day I have ahead of me," she continued blushing.

"It's all right," I said flattered. "But you don't need to be nervous around me...I'm actually a 'good boy' trapped in a 'bad boys' body."

A laugh came out of her mouth so loud it scared me for a split second. "I meant nervous about the first day of school..." Her laugh grew louder and I started to heat up with embarrassment.

"Oh," I spoke softly as my face continued to change different shades of red. Her eyes watched me closely as I withdrew and she seemed to take comfort in my vulnerability. We rode in an awkward silence for a moment and then a new upbeat song began on the radio. Without even realizing it, I was singing along.

"...Amber is the color of your energy..." I sang under my breath. Her smile returned as I sang.

"It was my mother," she said softly.

"What?" I was caught off guard.

"My mother gave me the necklace." Her face brightened as she spoke the words and I could actually see the confidence wash over her.

"Oh." I began to compose myself. "I have done everything BUT figure out this island." My thoughts quickly jumped to the previous afternoon on the beach.

"And you're right, I shouldn't judge you so fast..." I said and she listened closely. "But I think I'm right about you...at least a little. You are a good person. I can already see that." I looked her in the eyes and she turned her eyes to the road. She was still a little upset.

"That's why I got in the car so easily."

"I'm glad you did."

Ember

"And what exactly is this situation? How do you know my uncle?" I asked. She relaxed a bit and smiled at me again.

"My dad, Tim Summers, works with your uncle. They've known each other since your uncle moved here," she explained. "I've known Frank since I was little," she said and a tiny giggle escaped my mouth. She looked over at me as a giant smile grew across my face. She still was...little.

"I meant when I was younger and obviously smaller. Smart ass!" She was embarrassed now too.

"I didn't say a word," I tried to convince her. Her face was red now.

"I know I'm short," she snapped with anger rising in her throat. I burst out laughing and she smacked my arm playfully.

"You're not short, just vertically challenged." I couldn't stop the laughter and she seemed less than amused.

"Anyways...Frank asked my dad, to ask me if I would pick you up for your first day of school and make sure you made it on time," she paused. "I take it you inherited your uncles sense of punctuality?" I nodded in agreement.

"And on behalf of all the vertically challenged people in the world, I'm thinking about making you walk the rest of the way." Her tone was playful again. I liked her voice when she was teasing me. It made me feel at ease for some reason. I barely knew her and I felt comfortable and safe.

"I'll be good," I promised.

Her tiny car rounded a corner and the school came into view. The parking lot was only half full. She made her way to the front of it and pulled into a spot slowly.

"Thank you Sam," I said as I opened the door and stepped out.

"For what?" she asked curiously and turned the car off. I only smiled at her and reached in and pulled my guitar and bag out. She quickly followed my lead and exited the driver's side.

"Well?" she asked impatiently.

"For the morning kidnapping," I said from across the car. "For the ride, for your honesty..." I said and then paused. I swung my guitar around my back and turned and walked away. She seemed flustered and I turned back to her a few steps away and said.

"For your smile."

I walked away towards the closest building, not having any idea where I was headed. I was trying to be cool and mysterious, the 'bad boy.' So I kept walking, not looking back. I rounded the corner of the building and pulled out the map of the campus Frank had printed up for me and tried to find my bearings. I set my school bag down and reached into my front pocket and pulled out my mp3 player. Quickly shoving the ear buds in my head and scrolling down my playlists to find a track to settle my nerves. Click.

Ember

~Island In The Sun: Weezer~

"Ah...much better," I said as I caught my breath. I pushed myself forward and started my journey to the administration office. As I walked, I noticed that the campus wasn't too large. The buildings were older but in decent condition. The school colors, blue and white, covered almost every wall. I crossed an open court yard with benches that a few students were scattered throughout. It had a snack bar at the far end and was surrounded by trees. I made my way through it without too many glances and rounded the corner to find the office.

I walked through the doors cautiously and found a boy in some kind of distress. He was tall and a little gangly, with long dirty blonde hair pulled back in some strange version of a ponytail that I had never seen before. His skin was tan and I could barely make out his eyes, but they looked brown. He had a pair of drumsticks on him, one in his shorts back pocket and the other in his hair, behind his ear. It was slid in there like a number 2 pencil.

He was jerking around in a crazy motion as if someone was shocking him with a taser gun over and over. Now normally I would be on the floor laughing in hysterics at the sight of this, but being the new kid, I thought I'd play things more reserved. I approached him slowly and found that one of his tangles of long hair had gotten caught in the zipper of his blue pullover. He was grunting and cursing under his breath. At least I think it was cursing. His lips were held so tightly together that not much sound could escape. I almost lost it again and covered my mouth with my hand so I wouldn't laugh. As I did, I looked around the office and noticed that everyone was quite aware of the boy's dilemma but was ignoring him. This must not be the first time they had witnessed this show.

I took a long deep breath, sat my bag on the floor and let my right hand heat up a little. I took a couple steps forward and found myself right in front of him. He looked up at me and nodded as if to say, "What's up" and then continued his alien cursing.

"Here...let me try," I said while reaching out my hand. He froze instantly, staring at my hands with this curious blank face. A smile escaped my mouth finally as I got my first look at the tangle he had made from his lunatic dancing.

"You know I should just grab some scissors and start hacking away," I said kidding but he didn't move. He just kept staring at my hands. I already had a hold of the zipper and it was quickly heating up inside my palm. Not a lot though, just enough to soften the metal. I had to make this quick before the smell of burning hair got too strong. I pried the front of the zipper slightly open and jerked the wad of hair out as fast as I could. It only seemed to singe the ends slightly. He never wavered, never flinched; he just kept inspecting my hands. Even when a tiny string of smoke danced faintly off the zipper for a split second and faded away. I was sure he had seen this but he would not look away from my hands. It was starting to creep me out.

My voice cracked with nerves. "There you go my friend. No problem." His searching brown eyes finally rose and found mine and it was hard to read his expression. He looked as if he might be thinking really hard and that it might be a touch painful for him to be doing so.

"The names Max," I quickly threw out there and he cut me off.

"You play guitar!" he shouted. Confusion filled my face and the rest of the office personnel seem to come to life as well.

"You play music!" he shouted again and I couldn't help but laugh. So I decided to have a little fun with him.

"What gave it away? The concert tee I was wearing? The headphones I have sticking out of my ears?" I leaned into him a little. "Or was it the giant guitar I have strapped across my back?" I finished with a polite wink. He stood there pondering what to say for a moment.

"Your fingers. I know an ax man's fingers when I see them." He was quickly and easily excited.

"You any good?" he asked but before I could answer he kept up his inquisition. "Please tell me you're good...please! My band needs a decent guitar player." He reached for his drum sticks and began whipping them around in the air, above his head.

"I play drums."

"Wow...really?" I said sarcastically.

"Best on the island. My band 'NEON CRUSH' are a sonic explosion! I bet you'd fit right in," he said as he spun the sticks between his fingers.

"A band?" I asked.

"Well, it's just me and my friend Marcus...but we kick ass!" he boasted.

The language was finally enough to get the office secretary involved. She walked up and broke into our conversation.

"Mr. Kadooka, that will be enough of that language, thank you," she sounded impatient. She turned her attention to me, with a polite smile.

"And how may I assist you?"

"I'm Max Valentine." I handed her my registration papers. "I'm new."

"Mr. Valentine, welcome to our school. Your uncle said you would be joining us this semester." She pulled a slip of paper from under the counter. "Here are your classes."

"You know my uncle? Wow, small world," I grunted.

"Everyone knows Frank," she said with a big smile. "He's what you call, good people," she paused and then continued. "He was in here just last week preparing your enrollment. And if you don't mind me saying...he was right."

"About what?" I asked.

"Those are the biggest brown eyes I have ever seen." She winked and from behind me I heard the drummer boy gasp with laughter and chuckle loudly. I turned red instantly.

"Um...thanks...I think." I shrank behind my dark bangs.

"Relax Mr. Kadooka," she scolded. "You have the privilege of showing Max and his eyes around today. Do you think you can handle it?" her tone turned negative.

"As long as I keep my attention on the task at hand and not those big puppy dog eyes..." he smiled. "I should be fine!" He nudged me with his arm and my eyes rolled around my head in embarrassment. She did not seem to share his taste in humor and stared blankly at him.

"No worries," he smiled wildly and dragged me out of the office by my arm.

Outside he stopped me and glanced at my guitar.

Ember

"That sure is a beautiful instrument." He extended his hand. "Kai Kadooka, thanks for the help with my pullover."

"Anytime."

"New to the isle huh? Where you from?"

"Southern California."

"Cool...I hear they have some of the best bands out there," he gushed.

"NEON CRUSH was it?" I asked and swung my guitar around into my hands. "So when are try outs?"

"How about now?" he smiled. I strummed a couple chords to warm up. Instantly, I started to play the song that was popping from my ear buds that dangled at my shoulders. As soon as I did, he pulled his sticks out again and started clicking them against any surface he could find. First the wall, then some windows and finally some railing along the side walk. It startled me at first but it only took a second to realize that he was playing right along with me, and his technique was rather good. He knew the song as well as I did.

"Ah, what the hell..." I said to myself and started to sing. Without the slightest hesitation he joined in and we sounded all right.

"...When you're on a golden sea...You don't need no memory...Just a place to call your own...As we drift into the zone..." we both sang.

We carried on like that for a couple minutes before I realized that we had already drawn a little crowd. To my surprise, the crowd seemed to be enjoying it. We came to the end of the song and the crowd cheered wildly and thunder rumble from somewhere in the distance.

"That was phenomenal!" Kai screamed in triumph. I just nodded in agreement. That is how I became the newest member of NEON CRUSH. I wasn't too crazy about the band name but it felt good to find a kindred spirit so soon. He shook a few hands and a few people greeted me with an "aloha." Nervously I glanced down at the time on my mp3 player.

"What's next Max? You know any Smashing Pumpkins?"

"Well, seeing as how we only have a few minutes until the first bell, can I have the two minute tour?" I slid my guitar back behind me.

"You got it." He grabbed my schedule and glanced over it for a moment.

"Well, your first three classes are over there in that building." He pointed north of the court yard. "And the rest are over there." He pointed again in the opposite direction with a goofy smile.

"Okay," I was less then excited with his navigational skills and he could see the worry on my face.

"Max my friend, I've got your back. You see, we have four out of six classes together..." He spun a stick around his fingers and slid it behind his ear. "Just follow me bro."

"Thanks Kai," I said and then did just like he said, I followed his lead. Unfortunately, he led me right into my first complication. Right into the last person I expected to see.

My temptress from the beach stood silently watching me. In the morning light she was even more breath taking. My feet stuttered below me and I almost walked into Kai as the world seemed to slow down again. Slow motion set in as the sun ran behind some building grey clouds and the campus filled with a cool shade. Thunder broke off from the clouds and I couldn't breathe. Kai noticed immediately.

Ember

"Earth to Max...come in Max..." he teased but I couldn't hear a single word he was saying.

She shifted her posture uncomfortably and her short black summer dress clung to each move she made. It seemed to move along her shape like the ocean had done. Her hair was blowing in the breeze that had suddenly filled the campus and it carried her scent right through me. Her eyes looked even bluer then I had remembered and they still were very angry with me. Kai smacked my shoulder and it took me a few seconds to realize that he was talking to me.

"Ouch man...I have never seen her look at anyone like that," Kai said stunned. "Well, at least not until they had hit on her or teased her about her life style..." he stopped as the first drops fell from the sky but her gaze stayed locked on mine. Just like before at the beach.

"Who is she?" I managed to squeak out. Kai looked back at me with half a smile.

"It doesn't matter," he was coy. That brought me out of my daze a little. I looked at him confused.

"What? Please. I need to know."

"Boy, it didn't take you long, did it?" he joked. "Most guys make it at least a week before they fall for Asia." Asia, her name was Asia. But that wasn't enough, I needed more information. I stared at him trying not to lose my temper.

"Asia," I whispered and her face hid behind her falling curls of dark hair as if she heard me speak her name but that wasn't possible. Was it?

"Asia Lyn Michaels has broken enough hearts on the island that she's become a legend. As notorious as any one of our major volcanoes," he laughed proud of himself. I stood in complete silence.

"Only more dangerous."

51

The thunder rumbled above and time seemed to speed up again. "You're not making any sense Kai," I snapped.

"Trust me...she's not right for you," he said softly. "For any man..."

"For any..." I started to ask when my attention slammed back into focus as I noticed the girl standing beside Asia. Standing beside her wasn't the right way to put it though. It was more like standing with her. Together.

Asia's friend was small and petite, with short black hair. It was cut in an edgy bob and had bright blue streaks scratched through her bangs. The blue accentuated her big brown eyes that were full of worry. Piercings filled her lips and nose and she was dressed like a lost school girl from outer space. A shiny buttoned up top and plaid skirt with torn up leggings and combat boots. It was hard to tell under all her makeup but I was sure she already hated me. Her hand was locked around Asia's and she was glaring at me through her blue bangs.

The rain started peppering the ground and the kids that were gathered around started running for their classes but I couldn't move. I was frozen again but this time it wasn't because of Asia's intense stare. It was because of the words I saw the little brunette say. I couldn't hear them but I think I was able to read her lips.

"Is that him?"

My heart crashed inside my chest and the fear paralyzed me. I wasn't sure if it was fear that she may have told someone my secret or the scary fact that Kai was right. I was 110% head over heels, infatuated with Asia Lyn Michaels. Asia glared at me harder when her small friend asked the question and then she turned away from me and pulled her away quickly. I took a step forward before stopping myself. The two girls ran to the parking lot and Asia hopped in her Jeep. Her eyes found mine again and the thunder crackled all around. The tiny brunette leaned in and kissed Asia quickly on the lips, but Asia never took her eyes off of my confused stare.

"Whoa!" Kai exclaimed.

"What in the blue hell is going on?" I asked him.

"Parts is parts my friend..." he chuckled and put his arm around my shoulders. I felt my inner heat build.

"And you are carrying the wrong ones if you want to take that ride bro," he teased. "If you catch my drift?"

"You mean she's a les..."

The thunder cut me off as her Jeep pulled away, leaving the little brunette standing in the drizzling rain.

"That's no man's land my friend," Kai laughed. The first bell rang and he shook his head at me.

"Come on lover boy." He gave me a good shove in the opposite direction. I lunged forward still lost in confusion.

"I'll explain everything in first period."

MADISON DANIEL

Ember

~Dig: Incubus~

First period – Algebra II – 8:36 a.m.

Class started with a bang as I found myself at the front of the classroom, with twenty pairs of eyes watching my every move. The teacher, Mr. Holgate, sat patiently at his desk, waiting for me to begin my introduction but I was still reeling from my close encounter of the female kind. Kai shot me a glance followed by a thumbs up as I quickly gave everyone a short background about myself. You know, the usual, where I was from, last school I attended...I was on auto pilot.

My speech only lasted two minutes but it felt like an eternity, and I couldn't remember a single thing I had said. The hundred questions I had for Kai clouded every waking thought I had. Walking toward my desk, I could tell that he knew exactly what I was thinking about. He grinned at me as I sat down next to his desk and the teacher began his lesson.

"Hope this helps Romeo," Kai said as he handed me a folded piece of paper. I took it and mockingly laughed silently. I quickly unfolded it and found his hand writing almost illegible. It read...

"She's a rich and spoiled drop out who would rather surf and shop, than study. Everyone around her seems to get hurt or worse. Some say she is CURSED. Her "friend" is Lucy Zhang: a Chinese art student who hardly talks to anyone but Asia. They grew up together and are as close as...well, you saw them. You helped me

55

out this morning, now it's my turn...leave her alone. You saw the way she was looking at you...Just give up bro!"

I was officially losing my temper now and my palms started to heat around the edges of the paper. I crumbled it slightly in my hands and leaned into Kai.

"What the hell does this mean?" I whispered.

"I can tell you're a good guy Max...you don't need that walking tragedy," he whispered back. My eyes pulled tight and he continued.

"We've got all year to find you a girl."

"That's not what this is about Kai," I said a little louder than I should have and the teacher turned a disapproving glance our way. A moment passed and Kai leaned in closer.

"She's out of your league bro."

My temper grabbed a hold of my better judgment and I started smoothing out the crinkled paper.

"Oh yeah?" I questioned under my breath and quickly scribbled on the paper and handed it back to him. He opened it with a wry smile and it faded slowly, leaving only a confused, hurt look.

"FOR YOUR INFO...WE MET ON THE BEACH THIS PAST WEEKEND AND I HELD HER IN MY ARMS!...HA!"

I waited for him to get angry but he didn't. He just frowned and shook his head a little. My anger turned to guilt. I wasn't upset with him, so I shouldn't be taking it out on him. Besides, I was the new kid on the island; he understood how things worked around here, not me. I was being an arrogant jerk.

"Look Kai, this isn't some silly crush..." I started to say but stopped when I realized maybe that was all this was. First day of school crush.

"It's all good friend," he said as his smile returned.

"When do I get to meet the rest of the band?" I asked lightening the mood.

"Soon." He smiled and shook my hand and like that we were good again. I sat back and let the remaining hour tick away but couldn't stop thinking of the way Asia had looked at me. It was crazy, just by seeing her again my cage was completely rattled. Kai could tell I was still dwelling on the morning's events but he let it be and never brought it up.

The class ended and we gathered our gear and headed out to the hallway.

"It looks like you're gonna have to go solo in your next class." He patted my back. "But I'll make sure you get there in one piece," he joked.

"And I thought chivalry was dead."

As we walked down the hallway I caught a quick glimpse of Lucy. She was watching me closely and chewing on her hair. When she saw me find her stare she vanished into the crowd. My thoughts swirled around the mysterious Asia again.

"You said something about Asia being cursed. What did you mean by that?" I asked. Kai looked at me curiously.

"You don't want to hear this. It's a long story."

"Sure I do. I know we don't have much time before next class, but give me the short version."

"It's kinda dumb but Hawaii has these stories...more like superstitions. They're very old, you know, like folk lore and that kind of stuff." He shifted his books around in his arms.

"Well, one of those old stories talks about the balance."

"The balance?" I asked puzzled.

"Yeah, the life force that helped create the islands. All the elders talk about it, the first inhabitants...our ancestors. If you abuse the land, the life force will eventually return the favor." He stopped me with a cautious hand and looked at me seriously.

"Asia's great, great, great grand folks did many things to the land in pursuit of the all mighty dollar. And it worked...maybe too well. Many of the locals hate her family for what they had done in the past and they probably always will." He winked.

The bell rang through the halls, signaling the start of second period and Kai looked at his watch and scratched his head.

"So what does all that mean?"

"Gotta make this quick bro...I don't wanna start the year off with a tardy my first day. I usually save that for the second week of school," he laughed. "Anyways, the story is that the spirits of the island made good on the legend and the Michaels fam started dropping like flies as soon as she was born," he made a serious face and finished.

"Some say that's what happened to her parents. She turned eighteen and BAM! They vanished like ghosts."

"Ghosts," I said annoyed.

"That's when her inheritance kicked in…and man was it a lot of deniro!" He stood there waiting on my reaction but I wasn't sure what to say. I opened my mouth to say something when we were suddenly interrupted by my second period teacher, Ms. Snyder.

"Excuse me boys but you have thirty-seconds to find your seats," she said snotty. With that said Kai bolted down the hall for his classroom and I turned to walk in the Biology room. At the last second, in mid sprint, with his messy ponytail bobbing around his head he shouted out.

"Spooky huh!" He disappeared into his class and I managed a worried smile, and then walked slowly into my class.

I was in no mood to go through the whole class introduction thing again, so I handed Ms. Snyder my schedule and ran for a desk. I did everything I could to not make eye contact with any of my fellow classmates as I walked toward an empty desk in the middle of the room. I sat down and slid my head into my hands, to help hide my sudden shyness and could feel my hands had already warmed from my fluctuating emotions. Controlling my emotions was the hardest part of having my particular abilities. But unless I wanted the schools emergency sprinklers kicking on from the new guys freak show hair do of flames, I needed to relax. Easier said than done. That's when I felt the tap on my left shoulder from behind me.

"Not so cool now, are we Valentine?"

I recognized the sarcasm instantly. Samantha, my morning therapist. As I sank into my chair she gathered her stuff and slid into the empty desk next to me before I could respond.

"Is this all right?" she asked but the look in her eyes already told me that she knew the answer.

"Does the confidence come from somewhere deep down or are you just making up for the lack of height?" I didn't realize at first but I was smiling when I said it. Her eyes flashed with shock and then back to their calm jade hue and she giggled softly.

"There's that smile again." She nudged me with her elbow. She seemed to be taking credit for my new found happiness. "If you plan on sitting by me the rest of the semester, you better get used to it," she teased. And just like that, I was completely calm again.

"And why should you be so lucky?"

"Because, I will be the one that you'll want to copy off of when this course becomes too difficult for you," she teased back.

"That wont be necessary Sam...I can make my own way."

"Oh really, is that so?" she asked with an eyebrow raised. She was so confident.

"Yes...but if you ask me nicely, maybe I'll let you cheat off of me." I knew I sounded cocky but it felt almost natural around her. She seemed to make my confidence bloom. Part of me took a liking to her immediately and then we were snapped back to reality when Ms. Snyder stepped into our view.

"That will not be necessary Mr. Valentine," she said loud enough for the whole class to hear. I thought to myself, "How long had she been standing there?" but she continued on. "I am assigning biology partners first thing this year and you two have made my choices that much easier this time. You and Ms. Summers will be team one."

She continued down the line, pairing student with student. Sam and I looked at each other smiling, when she leaned even closer to me.

Ember

"You just won the biology partner lottery Max," she said so soft that it took me a second to focus. At that moment, I wanted to know her. I wanted to laugh with her. I wanted to kiss her. I slowly leaned back in my chair and thought to myself, I had won...in more ways than one.

I spent the rest of class watching her every movement. The way she held her pencil, her posture and her delicate movements. The way she slid her bangs behind her ear and tilted her head. That one was my favorite. I was finally relaxed and didn't think once about folk lore or dangerous mysteries and that felt good.

Third period English was shaping up to be one of my favorite classes so far. Not only did I get to sit and flirt with Sam, who just so happened to sit next to me in this class also, but my newest best friend Kai, sat on the other side of me. All three of us talked about silly things we all enjoyed or disliked when we had a moment or two. I found that Sam and Kai had known each other for their whole lives. Kai seemed to notice how at ease I was with her and kept nodding to me when her attention was focused elsewhere. He had that look on his face as if to say, "See, I told you there was plenty of fish in the sea." I would only give him a small smile and pretend I didn't understand his shenanigans.

Third period went by quickly and I had hoped for the same in fourth period, Computers 101. The fact that they were both in the class too led me to believe it would be. I was sorely misguided in my enthusiasm.

The first real sign that this coming school year might be a little rocky popped up in this hour. This sign was named Devon Wahlberg. I earned his disapproving gaze as soon as Sam said hello and sat down next to me. The kind of gaze reserved for rival gang members and convicts. The unmistakable gaze of an ex boyfriend, current boyfriend or just plain over protective psycho. I wasn't sure which of the categories to lump him in yet, but I knew we were destined to clash. I could actually taste it.

Sam hadn't noticed his glare at first or just pretended not to. Maybe I should have been ignoring it also but I hadn't earned the name "Mad Max" for keeping my cool. I spent my first moments of class staring right back at him. He wore his smugness with ease. His hair was bleach blonde and spiky. It sat atop his hazel grey eyes. He was in good shape, very athletic build and his skin was dark tan. So dark, it looked fake. His clothes were casual yet extremely expensive. All well-known brands. He sat at attention, like a king on his thrown and watched me while he smacked his gum on the side of his mouth. If I was told to sit down and build the perfect asshole, he would be the end result.

Sam finally let herself realize his stares and excused herself and walked over to him. I didn't like it one bit. As she left I leaned over to Kai and asked the obvious question.

"Who is that?"

"Devon Wahlberg," his tone was annoyed.

"And?" I insisted.

"He's the king ding-a-ling around here. His family is the richest on the island...that is with the exception of a certain blue eyed she-devil we're not going to discuss right now." He was joking but I was not.

"And?" I repeated.

"And let's not start your first day of school making enemies bro. He's not worth it," he warned.

"If Sam has to go out of her way to handle him on my behalf, then he is completely worth it," I said through my teeth and my gut heated with a fire. Kai only stared at me, hoping for me to understand and heed his warning.

Ember

"Just try and not make it worse...for her sake," he pleaded softly. I watched as Sam strolled back to the desk next to me. Her face looked tight and nervous but I decided not to push my luck...for her.

"Okay," I whispered to Kai.

I managed to make it through most of the class without incident. Sam was quieter now but still managed to flirt with me. I found out that her favorite color was green, like her eyes. Kai on the other hand seemed more nervous than he should have been. His leg kept bouncing under his table and he didn't say much. I had almost forgotten about the earlier stand off when it happened. Devon and I made eye contact and without any hesitation he gestured to me with his right hand. A gold bracelet dangled from his wrist, as his hand slowly folded into the shape of a gun that he pointed at me and pulled the trigger. He continued smacking his gum from the corner of his mouth that was now curved up into a smug smile, and lowered his hand back down. I waited for the anger to build inside my chest. I waited for the fire to tickle my hands but it never came. Instead, I broke out in laughter. Loud and uncontrollable, it startled the class but I couldn't help it.

The mere thought of his gesture made me think that I was in some crazy dream, as if I had flown across the world, to this amazing island to live out some horrible eighties movie. I have nothing against those movies; I rather enjoyed most of them but the idea that I might be living one, was to me...hilarious.

"Did that actually happen?" I asked Kai as I wiped the fresh tears from my eyes. He was laughing too but it seemed more of a nervous laugh. Sam, on the other hand, was far from amused. She looked angry and if I was reading her signals right, she was mad at both of us. That made things much less funny and I found that feeling...awkward. She spent the final moments of class silent and annoyed and so did I.

The bell rang again, signaling lunch time, so Kai and I gathered our things and walked into the hallway. We waited for Sam but she quickly stuffed her books in her back pack and raced past us. She ran up to Devon and they both started to argue. That sent my calmness far away. As my brow fell down across my eyes and my muscles tensed, Kai grabbed my arm and pulled me the opposite direction. A laugh filled his chest and I was starting to think that he didn't take anything seriously.

"If this is the kind of reaction you bring out in the opposite sex Max...then this is gonna be one painful year." He shook his head and pulled out one of his drumsticks.

"Don't get me wrong." He began to twirl it in his fingers. I began to pout.

"You just need to know who's fair game and who isn't," he quipped as we walked out onto the grass of the lunch court yard. Only a few students had gathered so far.

"That could be one of my first favors to our budding friendship." He looked at me with the patience of a three year old on Christmas Eve. I shook my head, giving in.

"Alright...lets hear it."

Iron Jaw_07

~Somewhere I Belong: Linkin Park~

We sat down on a bench, under a large tree, farthest from the school and he handed me half his lunch. I had left so quickly this morning, I didn't even think about what I was doing for lunch. I took it even though I wasn't in the mood to eat and he inhaled his half.

"So you say I need your advice with the ladies...shoot."

"First off, I really like Sam, I always have. She's smart and cute and as sweet as they come but she also comes with baggage. You have already met that baggage." He continued eating as he counseled me.

"They grew up together. Their families have been close their whole lives. Sam and Devon have been on again, off again since the sixth grade," he said catching his breath and I interrupted him.

"And what are they now?"

"Off again...I think. It's hard to tell these days. Things haven't been good with them two since his family came into money. Lots of money," he shrugged. "It changed him for the worse. There was a time when he was a pretty stand up guy."

"Yeah right," I snapped.

"I know it's impossible to believe with the way he carries himself now...but it's true." He finished his food.

"So you think I shouldn't even bother?"

"Not exactly."

"Then what are you saying Kai?" I was feeling a headache building behind my eyes. Partly from the stress but mostly from not eating much.

"If Sam is who you want, then go for it...but with Devon lurking in the shadows all the time, it could get messy." He nudged me.

"Messy..." I let a grin fill my face. "It's not worth fighting for if it's not messy. Besides, a little drama is the best inspiration for song writing." My confidence was building back up. Kai smiled in agreement.

"No doubt."

"Friendship was all I was offering her anyways." My confidence wavered when I said it.

"I'm just getting to know you Max, but I can already tell when you're lying...or at least lying to yourself." He was right.

From across the yard, I watched as Sam and Devon entered the lunch area. Neither one of them looked very happy. They were being shadowed by four other boys who looked as if they shopped at the same clothing store. I recognized them from computer class. The closest boy to them was also the biggest. He was easily six and a half feet tall and in better shape then Devon. His hair was light brown and just long enough to pull into a ponytail. His brown eyes seemed to search the court yard, as if he were on patrol. The second boy had short curly black hair and dark brown eyes. He was a little shorter than Devon and not in as good of shape as him. He seemed quiet and kept to himself. The final two boys were obviously twins. They looked identical, down to their hair cuts. Both had short blonde hair and blue eyes. They were tall and skinny and seemed to walk as if they were one person. It was kind of creepy.

Ember

Sam looked my way and waved a quick hello as she sat down with them. I wanted to wave back but I thought it would be best for everyone if I didn't push my luck. So, I turned my attention to Kai and she seemed hurt by that. A few moments passed and I found her watching me. Devon and his crew were watching her watch me and then they were quickly focused on me. All five of them. Kai noticed immediately and grabbed both our gear and stood up.

"Come on bro...I'll show you the rest of the campus."

I wasn't a fan of running from a confrontation but I reluctantly followed behind Kai with my guitar in hand. I gave Sam a quick smile and wave just before we disappeared. She returned the smile and looked happy when she did. Kai just rolled his eyes and picked up his pace.

"So what's the story with Devon's posse back there?" I asked when I caught up with him.

"That was the four horsemen."

"But there are five of them?" I chuckled.

"I meant Devon and the four horsemen."

"You can't be serious?" I gasped.

"That's what everyone calls them. They're Devon's right hand men." He rolled his eyes.

"I'm listening."

"Well, the big one is Jason Mahikoa. Devon's second in command. He's big and dumb and totally loyal to Devon."

"You sound like you're describing a gang Kai..." I laughed.

"I am. The shorter one with the dark hair is Brian Olohana. He's kind of the brains of the outfit. And the twins, Eddie and Alex Hansen, well they're just bottom feeders, sucking at the power tit." He winked but his face was dead serious.

"Okay...I'll bite. So what does this gang do?" I chuckled to myself at how silly this all sounded.

"Anything they want." Kai's tone was ominous and dark.

The lunch bell rang and we walked to our next class, Civics and Social Studies. I was hoping to talk to Kai more about Devon and his circle of jerks but our teacher Mr. Hahn was not a fan of our new friendship, and we quickly found ourselves on opposite ends of the classroom. The class went by slowly but it wasn't too painful. My last class of the day, Music Appreciation, was my only class by myself. No Kai, and no Sam. But I did have the music and that put me in a good mood again. I had finally convinced myself that the day would end on a high note as the final bell rang but I was wrong.

As I walked out the doors a small, nervous girl with bobbed black and blue hair was waiting for me. Lucy did not look happy. Her arms were crossed and her boots were tapping away with nervousness. She quickly stepped in front of me and pointed her neon blue fingernail in my face. This was going to be bad.

"Asia wanted me to warn you not to bother her again. Ever! This is your one and final warning newbie!" she growled through her pierced lips. Her face was red and hard with anger and I didn't know what to say. I stared at her motionless with my bangs dangling in front of my eyes. I was trying to hide behind my hair. It was a technique I picked up early in life but it never seemed to work very well.

Ember

"Lucy..." I tried to say but she stepped forward and put her hands on my chest. A crowd had already started to gather around us and in the crowd were Devon and his boys. They quickly pushed their way to the front. The fury in Lucy's eyes pulled my attention back to hers and she leaned closely into me.

"She is mine." Her nails pushed into my chest like knives, first through my tee shirt and then piercing my skin.

"Only mine!" she yelled. I could feel the blood wetting my shirt now and it was hot and thick. She kept her grave eyes locked on mine and slowly let go of my chest. Just in time too, because my core temperature was starting to build above normal. My back filled with sweat and my hands began to burn hot. She quickly wiped the blood from her nails on her skirt and took a step back from me.

"Message received," I grunted but my attention pulled to the cuts in my chest. They were so hot now that they were glowing under my shirt. I could feel them healing easily and I brought my left arm to my chest to prevent anyone from noticing. That's about the time Devon decided to introduce himself.

All five boys lined up behind Lucy, with Devon directly behind her. All of them with their arms crossed over their expanding chests. Lucy seemed to change her demeanor from hate to terror in a matter of seconds and I found the look on her face devastating. My blood began to boil. Devon just smiled at me arrogantly and tapped her on the shoulder.

"Lucy, Lucy, Lucy...you can run along now. I'll take it from here," he laughed and she shivered under his shadow.

"Run and find your bitch and tell her that she has the worst taste in lovers..." His smile grew even bigger.

"Or whore or mail order bride, whatever it is you call yourself." Her shiver turned into a full tremble and a single tear fell down her cheek. My eyes locked onto his and my hands balled into fists.

"That's enough Devon," I warned. The growing crowd winced in disbelief.

"Besides...if Asia was ready to play for the other side, I'm sure she wouldn't waste her time with this piece of..." I stepped forward and he stopped in mid sentence. That was all I had to hear, his smug voice speak Asia's name and I was ready to end him. His eyes seemed to light up at my advance and he clamped his hands around Lucy's tiny shoulders. He winked at me and leaned down and kissed the top of her head, taunting me. It was working.

"Let her go," I demanded and the crowd started to get excited. The four horsemen dropped their arms to their sides and began laughing from behind Devon. I never broke eye contact with Devon, not even when Kai came running up.

"Whoa!" he said as he slid between Lucy and I. "Devon lets think about this for a second," he sounded uncertain of what exactly to do or say next. Lucy used the moment to break Devon's grip and run off into the crowd, but his eyes never fell from mine.

"Your boy is not starting off this semester too wisely Kai," Devon threatened.

"Nah, he's cool." Kai turned and shot me a dirty look. I gritted my teeth together and pushed forward into Kai's back and realized just how much heat I was generating. I was worried that he could feel the heat I was creating, so I pulled myself back and turned toward the wall. It took everything I had to concentrate hard enough to power back down, but I did it. Everyone in the crowd took that as a sign that I was backing down from the fight.

The students sighed in disgust and moaned as they went on their way, most of them heading for the parking lot or school buses. But Devon and his boys stood strong, like statues and continued to glare at me with smug smiles.

"You see...all good on this end. No worries Devon," Kai said full of nerves. The tension seemed to fade but I was furious. Furious at Devon and his crew, furious at what Lucy had said and furious at Kai for stopping me.

"All...good..." I spoke slow and through my clinched teeth. I was so mad at everyone but mostly I was angry with myself for letting this loser make me lose control so easily. Mad Max strikes again. Our eyes found each other again and he nodded to his boys to stand down. He then reached into his pocket and pulled out a stick of gum. He peeled the wrapper off and slid it between his lips.

"Welcome to Maui High," he said and then flicked the gum wrapper at my chest with a sigh. As I watched it fall to the ground, they all strolled off with their eyes still on me. Kai let out a deep breath and flipped his finger along the rips in my shirt and smiled.

"Messy," he whispered.

"My bad," I agreed.

"Can't wait for tomorrow's adventure," he said and grabbed my bag. "Come on Mad Max, I'll take you home," he teased. I froze from his words.

"What did you just call me?" I asked petrified. How could that name follow me all the way over here?

"I was just messing around." He looked at me surprised.

"Oh," I said bummed.

"You have got to admit, it kinda fits ya brother."

I just shrugged my shoulders and followed him to his car.

It was an old American muscle car in poor condition. The paint was faded and it needed new tires. As I slid into the passenger seat I noticed the inside resembled the outside. There was one silver lining though, the stereo. It was new and top of the line. I was drained and in no mood to talk and he knew it. So he slid a blank CD into the stereo and turned the volume up. He smiled and drove off. It was a demo of the great and powerful NEON CRUSH. The music was average alternative rock and entirely too loud but at least I didn't have to talk about my day. I closed my eyes and enjoyed the ride to my house.

"Thanks for everything today, Kai," I said as we pulled into my driveway.

"My pleasure," he smiled.

"You mind if I catch a ride with you in the morning?" I asked him.

"No worries bro," he said and pulled out of the drive way. "Mahalo!" he yelled out the window as he drove away. I waved as he rounded the corner and disappeared. My uncle suddenly pulled up in his old Ford truck and honked the horn at me. He hopped out and walked with me to the front door.

"So...how'd it go big guy? It's a beautiful school isn't it?" He was so excited despite being exhausted from work.

"Well, I made it home in one piece." I wanted to smile but it felt like too much of a struggle to do so.

"And your ride this morning?" He was a little too giddy when he asked. No need to fill him in on all the details. I'll just give him what he wanted to hear.

"She's sweet," I tried to keep it simple.

"And?"

"And she's easy on the eyes." I smiled at the thought of Sam's hair behind her ear.

"And?"

"And what?" I sounded more annoyed then I should have. He looked at me worried.

"I'll fill you in at dinner...okay?" My tone was much nicer that time. A tiny grin crept back to show that I hadn't hurt his feelings too badly.

"Sounds good son," his voice was full of pride. He almost seemed proud of me. No, he was proud of me. That's when it hit me. This felt like home. He felt like home.

I was home.

MADISON DANIEL

Ember

~Monsoon: Tokio Hotel~

Monday afternoon – 4:29 p.m.

In my room, I lied across my bed face up, staring at the ceiling fan thinking over the days events. It turned out to be quite a first day. I didn't want to tell Frank about my problems, I was still too upset. I was sure the almost fight would only make him angry. If only there was some way to put off our talk. Not forever, just until the morning. And with a rumble of thunder against my open window, my wish was answered.

Oz came to life from his afternoon nap as the whine of an engine outside rattled to a stop. A door creaked open and closed with a thud shortly after. The wind pushed itself through my window and carried with it the smell of cherry blossoms. Oz and I both ran to the window and my heart stopped as I watched Frank approach the black Jeep. My hands gripped the window sill tightly and Oz's tail shuffled back and forth.

"What brings you this way Miss Michaels?" Frank sounded suspicious. It seemed that her presence was not welcome. I had never heard him that way before.

"Is Max home?" she asked politely. Time slowed as I realized that she knew my name.

"Oh crap...she knows my name," I said out loud. Oz tilted his head as he watched from the window with me. His nose lightly sniffed the air and a low growl shook within his chest.

"What business do you have with Max?" he was cold and defensive. Her body language made it clear that she did not enjoy his tone.

"We bumped into each other this past weekend...on the beach," she said with almost no emotion. Frank stared at her for a long moment, trying to read her expressions. She folded her arms and stared back.

"Max..." he shouted with a hint of annoyance in his voice. "You have company." By then I was already walking out the front door. She turned her attention to me as soon as my first step fell on the ground. I found my cheeks burn with heat from her stare. I stood next to Frank and he looked displeased. He let a sigh fall from his mouth and handed me a folded piece of paper. It was a letter but I didn't recognize the hand writing.

"I found this in the mail box. We'll talk later," his voice was very serious. "It was nice to see you again Miss Michaels." He never even looked back at her as he spoke. Casually he walked back to the house and closed the front door behind him but within seconds I could see his shadow through the living room curtains, watching us. Trying to get my nerves under control, I turned to her slowly. I made a point not to make eye contact too quick for fear of being paralyzed again. When I finally managed to look up at her, my head had already started spinning from her intoxicating scent. I waited for her to say something...anything, but she just stared at me not moving.

"Hello...I mean aloha," I said clumsily. "I'm Max." But she already knew that, you big dummy. A tiny sliver of lightning flashed behind her in the far off distance. She ignored it and continued to watch me. Her eyes searched my face and then down to my hands. It made me uncomfortable, so I slid the piece of paper in my back pocket and rallied up some courage.

Ember

"Looks like rain." I figured I'd lighten the moment. Her eyes pulled quickly back to mine and her right eyebrow rose a little. I nodded to the clouds brewing in the distance behind her. She didn't respond. I felt my temper roll over in my chest. Enough with the small talk, this was my chance to set things right.

"Are you okay?" I tried to sound relaxed when I asked but she only glared at me harder. A tiny glimmer of hate spun inside her sapphire pupils. I pushed my feet forward.

"I mean...are you feeling better?" I said it soft and polite. Her mask of hate cracked open just enough for me to steal a glimpse of what lied deep within those eyes. Her head fell towards the ground and then quickly back up to my face.

"Come on," she demanded. I ran my hand through my hair as she turned toward her truck and walked back to it. I just stood there watching her walk away, in awe of how naturally she could make my pulse race. I followed behind trying not to make it obvious I was in a hurry. As I jumped in the passenger side, the thunder thudded above us and the lightest of sprinkles fell all around.

"Where are we going Asia?" I startled her when I used her name for the first time.

"You'll see," she said quickly and with that she was done talking. Her hand reached for the stereo and she clicked it on. Music filled the air too loud to talk. This should have bugged me more than it did but I wouldn't have known what to say right now anyway. I relaxed a bit and stretched back in my seat and enjoyed the ride.

The views on our drive to the mysterious destination were nothing short of amazing. So many different shades of green flickered by as we raced along the road. The feeling of the island air was fantastic. It felt cool and moist against my skin. I watched as the dark skies rolled above us, hiding the direct sunlight whenever it dared to shine through.

After about fifteen minutes, she pulled off the main road and onto a dirt road. It wasn't very smooth and it took us up, along the side of a small mountain. The smell of the ocean was close and the air grew cooler. A few moments later she veered off the path entirely and rushed up and out a clearing. It was massive and took her about two minutes to reach the end. You could see the ocean in the background as the clearing ended with a dangerous cliff. A dozen jagged boulders peeked from the earth and hung themselves over the edge.

Asia turned the truck off and hopped out immediately without even a glance my way. That's probably because she knew I'd be watching her. I stepped out too and inhaled the ocean air. I wasn't even at the edge of the clearing and I could tell from the sound of the crashing waves below, that it had to be easily a couple hundred feet down. The ocean looked black again and the smell of rain was building. That smell was one of my favorite things in the wide world and she seemed to always smell like a mix of it and cherry blossoms.

"This place is amazing," I said quietly. Her head turned my way and then back to the edge of the cliffs. She hopped up on one of the largest rocks and stood facing the blowing wind. Her hair danced along her tone shoulders as I walked closer to her. As I approached, she turned toward me and the wind seemed to increase. Her eyes watched me through her brown tangles and I stopped where I was. Her black skirt rustled in the breeze just above her knees and her stylish string tank top filled with air. It quickly spat out the air and then filled again and again. Back and forth it flickered, exposing her fit stomach and lower hips. Then something unexpected flashed in view. A scar that looked remarkably like my hand was peaking from her skirt, just above her left hip. It crept over and around to the back. She was completely aware that I saw this but did nothing to stop my wandering eyes. I probably would have stared all afternoon if she hadn't spoken up.

"Admiring your handy work, I see," she said bluntly. I was flustered by her tone. She ran her hands along the sides of her hair and slid her hip to the side.

"Or are you just enjoying the view?" she said more like a fact than a question. I think I blushed. The fact was she had spent her whole life being admired for her physical beauty, so why should this silly boy be any different. At least in her mind, that was probably how she saw me, another boy chasing her around the playground. But I was different...and I would make her see that.

Reaching out my right hand, I asked softly, "May I try something?" She seemed puzzled by my question or at least her eyes did. I took a breath and forced myself not to lose eye contact with her. She searched my face for a second and then bit her lower lip. She gently put her left hand in mine and her fingers were soft and cool.

"Who is Mia?" she asked point blank but she did it in a soft tone. Either way, I wasn't expecting the question and it knocked the wind out of me. I held strong ignoring her question and stepped up to her on the giant rock.

"How did you know my name Asia?" I felt proud for pulling myself out of the shock from her speaking Mia's name. A lightning bolt struck over my right shoulder, distracting me for a second as her left hand squeezed tighter around my fingers.

"I dreamt it," she almost whispered. I wasn't expecting that. I looked deep into her eyes and slowly reached down and slightly tugged her top up. Just enough to expose the scar as my fingers grazed over it.

"Please don't be scared," I told her.

The thunder grew all around us and I let my body heat up. I gave her a quick glance to show her that things would be okay, and then knelt down in front of her. She had become as still as a statue when my hands warmed and fell to her hips. I tried my best to concentrate, which was almost impossible at this distance. I was so close that I could taste her goose bumps.

"I dreamt of your name the night you healed me," her voice was shaking. "And many other things," she stopped. My mind wanted to race from the words she had just spoken. Keep your head in the game Max. I had never tried this before but if I could pull it off, it just might be the ice breaker I needed with her. Her eyes watched closely as I inhaled a long breath and exhaled slowly. My breath grew hotter and steam twisted off of it in tiny ribbons. The hot air slid across her scar like smoke and her hands fell to my shoulders. I continued blowing and the hand print faded a little more with each breath. Finally, it faded to nothing and was replaced by her almond skin and some mighty large goose bumps.

As I stood back up her hands fell to her hip and quickly inspected it. Her eyes found mine with intensity and I braced for her impending anger but no anger appeared. Her hands reached for my right hand and she pulled it up to her face. She stared at the three letters tattooed across my wrist and turned my hand outward, exposing them clearly in the light falling rain.

"That night...I saw your name. I saw your childhood." Her eyes watched me closely for a reaction. I felt my body pull away a little but she just leaned in closer, never letting her grip loosen a bit.

"I saw the flames..." she continued and started tracing the letters with her finger. "And the last thing I saw was the name Mia." She was caressing my wrist now and my head felt dizzy. The rain began to fall harder and ribbons of steam started floating up off of my shoulders and for the first time in my life, I didn't feel like I had to hide it.

"Who is she Max?" Her voice was sweet. I pulled myself from her grasp and turned toward the oncoming rain and let myself go. The flames started at my fingertips with a pop and slowly swirled around my forearms. My arms glowed a deep vivid orange and red as the fire washed up to my shoulders. The heat pulsated off of me and I felt safe. The sound of crackling rain bounced off the flames as the drops tried their best to put me out. I brought my right hand up as the rain fought harder against my abilities.

"My sister," I said as I stared at the flames dancing around the three letters on my wrist.

"This gift of mine can do amazing things..." I paused and looked at her glowing blue eyes. "But sometimes it can be a curse."

"Where is she now?" She stepped toward me and I could smell her familiar scent of cherry blossoms.

"Gone." I gritted my teeth. "Because of this," I said full of anger. I created a ball of fire above my right palm. It was the size of a softball and burning with white and yellow flames. The raindrops drilled tiny spinning holes into its surface as it spun. Her eyes became sad and fell to the ground. I squeezed my hand around the ball of flame and it burned out into a cloud of black smoke.

"Some people say that I'm cursed." Her face looked hard again with pain and sadness. I slowly powered down and shook my dripping bangs out of my face.

"That's what I hear." My response was quick and she seemed to bring her guard back up.

"And what exactly have you heard?" She was angry again. I took a step toward her and the sky rumbled slow and soft.

"Everything," I smiled. Her eyes dropped from mine and I watched as a tiny bead of water slid down one of her curls. It dropped to her chest where a dozen other drops glistened at me and slowly rolled down beneath her top.

"And I don't care," I continued. She looked back up at me scared and it looked like she was holding something back.

"You should," she snapped.

"Why should I care what other people say?"

"Because they might be right."

"And they might be totally wrong Asia," I said and stepped in closer. "Your friend is not too fond of me," I continued. From the look on her face, I had gone too far now.

"Friend?" she asked but I could tell she knew exactly who I was talking about.

"Lucy," I said softly. "She had a few words with me today."

"What did she say?" she demanded.

"Does it matter?"

"Tell me what she said Max." The thunder crackled behind her and her body tensed up.

"I don't care what she said!" I snapped back. "There is something going on here between the two of us. Something powerful and I think you can feel it too." My confidence was growing stronger with every heart beat. Worry settled on her face and she stepped back from me.

Ember

"I think we were supposed to find each other on that beach."

"Max...I think I better get you home." She had put her walls back up.

"You don't have to push me away," I said with my confidence fading. She turned and started to walk to the Jeep.

"Yes, I do."

"Okay," I agreed.

The sun had just finished setting and a fresh blanket of stars was spreading across the sky. As we pulled into my driveway I was sure that Frank would be upset that I had missed dinner and denied him the events of my first day of school. I could hear Oz barking from inside the house. Asia never even turned the engine off, she just glanced my way.

"I'll see you around Max." But her tone made it sound like the opposite.

"Good night Asia," I smiled even though I didn't feel very cheery at the moment. She only took a deep breath and quickly drove off. As she disappeared around the corner, thunder rumbled in the distance and my head felt light. I was beginning to feel the day and needed to eat and get some rest.

I walked in to find Frank at the table reading a magazine. On the edge of the kitchen table was a plate of food wrapped in tin foil. Without looking up from his magazine he slowly pushed the plate my direction and smiled. I picked it up exhausted. Oz was already at my feet dancing in circles.

"I'll expect a full report tomorrow after school. Okay son?" He looked at me from behind his glasses with affection and I felt relief wash over me. He was so good at making me feel welcome, no matter what. I guess I needed that after the day I had just finished.

"Promise uncle," I agreed and ran off to my room, with Oz following right behind me.

The meal didn't last long between the two of us and I started to get myself ready for a shower. I took my shirt off and dragged my weary body to the bathroom for a much needed scrubbing. I turned the water on hot and let my muscles relax and tried my hardest not to think about anything that happened today. It almost worked...but the flowing water only reminded me of the rain on Asia's smooth skin. I could almost feel her touch through the water. This was not helping. I had to focus on what was important, school, my music, and starting over. Anything but girls! I turned the faucet handle to the coldest setting I could and cleared my head.

10: 39 p.m.

Later that night I found myself still restless, as I lied in my bed in my favorite pair of old blue jeans. Oz was asleep next to my ribs and his paws would scratch at my exposed skin as he ran in his sleep. I was exhausted but could not fall asleep. That was one of the side effects of letting my power out. It would keep me going like caffeine. So I reached over and picked up my guitar and played for a few minutes. The thunder rumbled outside my window and my thoughts fell under her spell again. So I sat the guitar down and turned out my bedroom light, angry with my lack of will power.

"She's just a girl," I tried to convince myself. Then from my window came a tapping. I woke from my daze and fumbled over my bed to reach the window and just like that...she was there.

Ember

Asia was standing outside my window with her hands gently pressed up against the glass. Her breath softly filled it up with a delicate fog and lightning flashed far away. Quietly I opened the window, being extra careful not to startle Oz or wake my uncle. The breeze swept inside my room like a serpent and the chill made my skin stand up at attention. Her eyes filled with the light from the moon and seemed to glow even bluer now. Little curls of neon yellow danced off the highlights in her hair and it softly swayed around her shoulders. She looked like a dream.

I waited patiently for her to say something but she didn't. She only stared at me closely, first my face and then my chest. I was confused but growing excited when our eyes locked into another stand off. Her haunting face seemed happy to see me and a little smile curled at the side of her mouth. She slowly bit her bottom lip and lightning flashed across the horizon but it made no sound. I started to smile and she leaned in quickly and pressed her lips into mine. I froze for an instant until my instincts took over and my lips followed her lead. Slowly and completely her kiss devastated me. I was now lost in a dizzying smell of cherry blossoms.

The kiss was electric and her full lips tasted like rain. I knew that sounded crazy but they did. Everything was in slow motion and my insides felt hot as my power filled every pore I had. The kiss couldn't have lasted for more then ten seconds but it felt like ten minutes. I couldn't breathe and I thought that my heart might burst from my chest. I was in ecstasy.

As we pulled apart the thunder shook my room from above us and the rain started to fall slowly. Big fat drops fell against my skin and my head felt dizzy. That's when I realized that Asia was smiling and her face looked radiant. The new rain drops peeked out from her hair like stars and my hands started to steam a little bit.

"Thank you Max..." her eyes sparkled with tears. "Thank you for saving me." And with a toss of her hair, she was gone. She ran toward her Jeep that she had parked down the street. The rain began to pour, making it hard to see but I watched her until the tail lights from her truck vanished in the dark. As I closed the window I could still taste her lips. Her hand prints were still smeared along the glass, gently fading away. I fell backwards on my bed with my mind racing.

"Uh oh..." I said to myself. My pulse was still racing.

"I am in trouble," I warned as the truth set in. Asia Lyn Michaels had just carved her initials into my essence. I could feel the fire call to her...for her. There was only one thing to do. So I jumped from my bed, grabbed my still damp towel, raced to the shower and turned the water to the coldest possible setting.

I didn't sleep much that night. I spent most of it tossing and turning on my bed. When I finally fell into my dreams, there were no nightmares to live. No screaming, no fire, no little sister. Only the rain and Asia's soft kiss.

Crush_09

~# 1 Crush: Garbage~

Tuesday morning – 7:59 a.m. – August 15th.

Kai was running late to pick me up, of course, so I had a few minutes to kill. That's when I remembered the note Frank had handed me the day before. I ran to my room and dug the jeans out of the dirty laundry pile, by my closet. I turned out every pocket but found nothing. There was no note, not even pocket lint. I checked the rest of the pile of clothes. Nothing. Did Frank find it while I was asleep? Did it fall out of my jeans on my tour of the island last night? Oh well, I'm sure Frank will remember what it said. He was awfully upset about it. Or was he just not a fan of mysteriously stunning girls in little black Jeeps?

I could have spent the rest of the morning pondering this. It seems my mind was still racing from the night before when Kai pulled up and honked his car horn. BEEP! BEEP!

"Lets roll Max," he called from the car. "Come on rock star! Let's do this!"

I laughed as I ran out the door, stopping only to give little Oz a pat on the head. I tossed my guitar and school bag in the back seat and jumped in.

Algebra II – 9:05 a.m.

"So I was thinking...maybe we should consider playing the 'Lolo Bash' beach party this weekend?" Kai asked.

"First off...we haven't even had a practice yet. Hell...I haven't even met the rest of the band yet and second...the "Lolo what?" I found his positive attitude infectious but insane.

"If we put in some hours practicing after school, I'm sure we could be ready in time. I mean, you saw how quickly we clicked yesterday morning." His smile was huge.

"Don't take this the wrong way Kai, but you're out of your mind," I teased.

"But the 'Lolo Bash' is the biggest party of the year. It could be amazing," he squealed as his eyes stared off into space.

"Relax." I patted him on the back. "We will be amazing one day, trust me."

"You're right..." he conceded. "...But we have to make an appearance. Everyone will be there."

"Okay," I said not excited at all. I'm not a huge fan of parties and an even lesser fan of drinking but I didn't want to bring him down any more than I already had. His giant smile returned and I was beginning to realize that I was so lucky to have found such a good person so quickly. I'd known him for only a little over a day and it already felt like we had been friends for years. I hoped I'd never lose that.

Biology – 9:45 a.m.

As I sat down next to Sam I could tell that something was wrong. Her eyes were big and nervous to see me. She must have heard about the altercation between Devon and I. And I thought I'd be the one nervous to see her after yesterday. It was hard to be nervous around her. She made me feel so comfortable.

"Morning Sam," I said quietly, trying to feel out her expression. She smiled up at me nervously and continued sitting there silent. She must be extremely upset with me about yesterday.

"You okay?" I asked.

"Fine," she said. When I tried to find her eyes they trailed away from me with disappointment. Now I was completely baffled. Ms. Snyder watched us closely with an inquisitive grin and the final bell rang, signally the start of the class. Without a warning, Sam exploded with guilt.

"Max I'm sorry..." she inhaled a long deep breath. "I should have told you about Devon. You know...him and I...our history." She was twisting her pen in her hands.

"I mean there is no more him and I...not now...not again." She was ranting in one long monologue at barely a whisper. I just sat back and held on.

"That's why I wrote that note for you..." Holy crap...the missing note was from her.

"I just wanted to apologize for not speaking up sooner," she continued but now I was lost in my own guilty thoughts. I can't believe I had already lost that note. This also probably meant that she hadn't heard about the ruckus after school yesterday. That was hard to believe, as small as the school was. Gossip has a magical way of spreading through school hallways at the speed of light.

"Max...please don't ignore me. I feel bad enough already," she interrupted. I couldn't believe she was beating herself up for nothing. She didn't owe me an apology for anything. She didn't belong to me and I was not her property either.

"It's okay...there is nothing to apologize for." I smiled and I realized what a good and sweet person was beside me.

"Now stop being silly and let me copy off of you today...because I was totally lying yesterday..." I teased and a smile filled her face again. "I suck at science," I joked. We both laughed and attracted the grumpy glare of the teacher.

"So you got my letter?" her voice was warm. I shifted anxiously in my chair.

"Um, yes," I lied.

Computers – 12:01 p.m.

There was a half hour left in fourth period when my stomach started to knot up with tension. Sam spent the class right next to me, avoiding Devon's stares, which were often. Kai spent it between Devon and I, trying his best to prevent another incident. It wasn't working too well, because every chance Devon had to get a rise out of me, he did. I had the strangest feeling that this was how my semester was going to be. Everyday.

"Just ignore him," Kai whispered in my ear when Sam wasn't paying attention. Devon smiled from across the room at me. A smarmy, used car salesman smile.

"I'm trying," I grumbled. Actually, I wasn't in the least bit trying to ignore him. I almost wanted the attention but I wasn't sure why. I needed him to be the bad guy, so that I was the good guy...I guess. Either way, this would make for a long and trying school year. I looked at Sam as she ran her long blonde hair behind her ear, exposing the lines of her neck again and I thought.

"That would be fine with me..." I didn't mean to say it out loud, but I did and Kai looked up at me like I was half crazy.

"What?" he asked.

"Nothing," I groaned. Sam winked at me as if she knew exactly what I had been pondering and I cleared my throat nervously. A few minutes later the bell rang and we gathered our stuff and headed for the door. Devon watched my every move as we did and Sam noticed his disturbing stare. She shot him a disapproving look as we passed through the door and into the hall. That made me smile...big.

Lunch – 12:35 p.m.

Kai had the notion that lunch would be the perfect time to work on our set list. He told me that the rest of the band would meet us at the table under the tree, where we ate the day before. As we approached the bench at the back of the court yard, I could only see one kid waiting on us.

He was short and skinny, with a small red Mohawk stitched down the middle of his head. He looked unsure as we walked up to him. His big brown eyes focused on my every step. In his right hand was an old beat up, acoustic guitar. The paint and finish were worn and it was covered in stickers, mostly of different band names and according to his decorations, we had the same taste in music. That made me feel at ease. Kai ran up to him, spinning his drumsticks in his hands.

"Noggin bro!" Kai called out for all to hear and the two proceeded to bump foreheads with a dull clunk. The sound of their heads colliding together made me smile and made Sam roll her eyes.

"I'm glad to see you back friend," Kai said. "What took you so long?"

"My family and I kind of got stuck in Australia over the summer. Just got in late last night," the boy said with a pleasant temper.

"Better late than never!" Kai sang and turned his attention to Sam. "You remember Sam don't ya?" he asked.

"Of course." He and she exchanged a soft glance. It was obvious that they were familiar with each other, but no where near as close as Kai and her.

"And this must be the infamous Mad Max." His voice was cheerful but cautious. I cringed at the fact that my old nickname had officially caught on. Sam seemed to be the only one who noticed my discomfort.

"Marcus Allen, I'd like you to meet are savior and future chic magnet...Max Valentine." Kai slowly bowed as if we were in a cheesy kung fu movie. "Or as the locals have come to know him...Mad Max."

"Please to make your acquaintance," Marcus said extending his hand. I shook it firmly.

"Pleasures all mine Marcus." I was trying my best not to blush and forget about that stupid name. I was noticeably uncomfortable now and Sam stepped in and made it worse.

"It hasn't even been two days and you have a nickname already," she teased. "Oh sorry, I meant Mad Max." She laughed out loud and Marcus and Kai followed her lead. I loved the sound her voice made when she did, so I held my building frustrations in and didn't let myself get annoyed too much.

"Yeah…I guess," I said.

"You should be proud Max…you earned it," Kai shrugged with a laugh. Sam looked at me confused.

"No…I didn't." I tried to correct him but it was too late.

"You are way too modest." Marcus added. "The way you stood up to Devon and his cronies yesterday…awesome," he gushed and I felt Sam's stare on me.

"Five against one! Man you've got some big balls dude!" he continued in awe. The green flecks in Sam's eyes only seemed to brighten with her disapproval and to add smoke to the fire, Marcus wouldn't shut up.

"And Lucy…man was she lucky you were there to help her." He shook my hand again with more conviction this time. "You sir, have my respect."

Kai had finally noticed the anger on Sam's face and tried his best to get Marcus to stop talking, from behind her, with hand gestures. It was in vain though. My right hand found the back of my neck as Sam stepped closer to me.

"Hey Marcus," Kai called to him.

"What man?"

"What's the first rule of fight club?" Kai asked as he motioned with his fingers to zip his lips. Instantly, Marcus understood that things might not be as cheery as he had thought.

"There is no fight club!" Sam snapped and pulled me away by my hand. The wonder twins looked at each other and sat down quickly on the bench. They both started playing the first song they could think of and pretended they didn't see us.

"All right Max...spill it," she demanded. Her face looked more serious then I had ever seen her. I wouldn't say she was furious, but close to it. I took a breath and looked around the court yard to find Devon and the horsemen watching with smiles. He sat with his arms crossed and an alligator smile.

Sam put her hand on my cheek and pulled my wandering eyes back to hers and I could feel them burning right through mine. In the distance a storm was approaching, with its cool winds already flowing into the lunch area. It felt good against my body which had begun to warm slightly.

"Lucy Zhang stopped me to talk..." I started slowly and her face changed to a questioning glare. "And Devon decided to make his presence known." I was praying that I had said enough. The last thing I wanted to do now was go into details.

"And?" she asked direct but not pushy.

"And nothing happened. Lucy had her feelings hurt a little..." I paused. "Devon made his feelings clear about how he felt about our new friendship." I was so convincing that I almost believed my half truths. Her eyes searched mine for a moment then turned and found Devon watching us. She let a gasp of tense air out and turned back to me.

"Okay..." She smiled as she found my hands with hers. "Friends," she said with a strange little smile. It made me feel like this conversation was far from over. Then, out of the blue thunder rumbled around us. It seemed to take most of the students by surprise, as they all shuffled and chatted nervously. Some with there eyes toward the sky.

At that moment, the smell of cherry blossoms filled the air, triggering my hands to pop with heat. Sam felt this too and I pulled my hands away and shoved them in my back pockets. Her eyes looked on in surprise but I wasn't sure if it was from the sudden rush of heat that she had felt or my reaction to that burst. The breeze picked up and the smell faded lightly and for a second my hands cooled.

A hush seemed to sweep through the crowd as if the whole student body had simultaneously choked on their lunches. My mind wouldn't let me understand at first, I was still busy trying to shake that familiar scent from my nose. Not when the crowd fell silent. Not even when Kai and Marcus stopped playing their instruments. They sat motionless with their mouths open, staring directly behind me. Only when Sam took a step backwards and that smell returned with a vengeance, did I let myself understand.

I turned around slowly and found Asia not more than twenty yards away, strutting toward us. And I do mean strut. She was in a thin black and white summer dress that accented every curve she flaunted. She seemed to move in slow motion and in unison with my heart beat. Her walk was primal and she was completely aware of the attention she was commanding. Her eyes locked onto mine and I could feel time slipping away again. It only took a moment for her to reach me and notice I was frozen again. She seemed to enjoy that.

"Max..." she purred. My hands were so hot now I was sure that they would ignite in my back pockets. "I do believe this is yours." She slowly handed me the note I had misplaced. I was afraid to take it from her for fear that it would turn to ash. I couldn't move and I definitely couldn't speak. That brought a devilish grin to Asia's lips as she stretched out her arm past me towards Sam. Her haunting blue eyes never looked away from me.

"That's funny, you didn't seem to have a problem talking last night Max." Her tone was sinister. She let the piece of folded paper fall into Sam's hands. Sam took it and looked down at my hands. The thunder grumbled and Asia walked past us, making sure to slightly graze her body along mine as she did. When she did, it felt electric and the fire in my chest screamed to get out. As she walked away her hair whipped behind her like a dark flame, and every boy watched her slither away. Every last one of them...except me. I was staring at the hurt look on Sam's face as she stared at the note I had lied to her about. I waited for her to yell or hit me but she did neither.

"Sam," I choked out finally. The thunder faded as she looked up at me with her bleeding eyes and I felt my head start to pound. Why should I care what she thought? I barely knew her but it crushed me knowing I had hurt her. She shook her head and walked away. I watched as she left me standing alone. I watched in silence as she disappeared around the corner and Devon followed swiftly.

"What the hell just happened?" I asked myself. I was still in a fog. I had never felt anything like that before. I felt like I was being pulled in two directions emotionally and it was numbing. I felt like a candle flame, flickering alone in the middle of a hurricane. Afraid to bend, afraid to move either way for fear of being blown out. I felt safe...yet trapped.

Had Asia read the note? The way she had carried herself suggested that she had. What did the note say? Damn it! Why didn't I read it before I left with Asia? You big dummy. Should I go after Sam? Should I try and find Asia? I was confused. I wanted to do both.

"Did that just happen?" Kai bellowed. "That had to be the greatest thing I have ever witnessed bro!" He slapped me on the back and jumped up on the bench and threw his arms into the air. His hands clenched around his sticks.

"Mad Max! Mad Max!" he chanted. Marcus followed right behind him, jumping to the top of the bench in one giant leap. He chanted right along as the crowd quickly joined in. Marcus even added a little dance while he pumped his fists in the air. It had a tribal vibe to it and he looked awfully silly…kind of like a drunk gecko walking over fiery hot coals.

That was enough to offend me back into the moment. Embarrassed, I gathered my things and scurried to my next class. I was a few minutes early, but I didn't care. I wanted to be alone. As I walked past the chanting crowd and into the school, I felt the curious eyes of someone following my escape. They were big, brown and stared at me through bright blue bangs. I pretended not to notice Lucy's prying stare and continued to my classroom.

My last two classes went by at a crawl as I couldn't stop myself from thinking about the scene in the court yard. The scattered chants of my new nick name, between classes didn't help either. Patiently I made it to the final bell and was relieved to find Kai and Marcus waiting for me at his car. As I strolled up, something familiar caught my attention. I almost didn't see it at first but when I turned and confirmed my suspicions, I almost lost my cool. A blue hoodie with the words Maui High pasted across the back was sitting atop a white motorcycle. I knew immediately who was wearing the gaudy thing, even before he turned and winked at me. Devon smiled at me and started his bike and four other engines revved to life with the same familiar squeal. All five of them quickly drove off and I felt my head begin to pound as I remembered the sound of Oz's tiny frame breaking under his wheels.

"Come on brother," Kai interrupted and opened the door for me. He and Marcus both bowed as I got in the front seat.

"Easy fellas...I'm in no mood," I warned.

"I know exactly what you need my friend," Kai said with absolution.

"Sleep and a shower," I barked. Marcus jumped in the back seat and Kai revved his engine, mocking Devon and his gang of crotch rockets. I let a small smile out and he nodded. He twisted the knob of the stereo and let the music wash over us at its loudest possible volume. It hurt my ears at first but as I slowly let the music heal me, I found my smile returning and my headache fading away. Just like that I was healed...for the moment at least.

My partners in crime had a surprise in store for me, as they drove past my house and to Kai's garage, in his back yard. This was where all their musical equipment was kept. As I walked into his garage for the first time I was struck at how professional everything was packaged.

A full drum set with all the bells and whistles a drummer could ask for. It was deep red with tiny flakes of black that seemed to twinkle under the right light. There were three amps on the right side of the drum kit and one on the left. A couple microphones stood up front; in their long black stands. The walls of the garage were sound proofed and covered with all kinds of posters. Mostly centerfolds and concert memorabilia.

We didn't even exchange words; we just picked a spot and an instrument and started jamming. It was almost like magic how well we connected on a musical level. Especially Kai and I. This went on for hours, with only a few breaks for some water. As the sun fell and the stars flashed, we played and I forgot about everything. That was not a good thing. I had forgotten about my promise to my Uncle Frank about our talk. I hadn't even called to let him know I would be late. He would surely be upset.

Eventually we called it a night and Kai rushed me home. I tried to sneak into my house quietly but Oz's welcoming bark ruined the effort. The clock said 11:17 p.m. and I cringed as I picked up Oz in my left arm. He licked my face wildly.

"Calm down Oz...I missed you too," I whispered. Frank never woke up. He had left me another dinner wrapped in foil. As I slid it toward me along the kitchen counter I noticed a note taped to it. It read...

"Maybe next time, Mr. Popular. Enjoy the food. We'll talk tomorrow. Samantha called around 7. It sounded important. Sweet dreams, MAD MAX!"

I crumbled up the piece of paper and threw it in the trash.

"Frank's gonna ring my neck," I said to Oz. His tail wagged and he growled playfully. I grabbed something to drink and carried my cold dinner into my room. I ate quickly and fell to sleep even quicker. I was completely drained.

I didn't dream of anything that night.

MADISON DANIEL

Temptations_10

~Flutter Girl: Chris Cornell~

Wednesday – 9:40 a.m. – August 16th.

Second period Biology, I was dreading this class all morning but here I was, standing before the door that would lead me to my judgment. My judgment from Sam, on how much of a jerk I was for lying to her. I was just starting to get to know her and lying wasn't the best way to build a real friendship. Or was it more than that? Maybe the reason I felt so awful was because we were building a relationship. The silly thing was that if I had just told her the truth about the letter, she would have been fine with it.

"Just breathe," I whispered. I focused my nerves and there she was, watching me from inside the classroom. I made sure to not make direct eye contact, at first. I stood there silently as my fellow classmates pushed past me and giggled as I hovered around the door way.

As the song changed on my mp3 player and filled my head with a haunting groove, a thought fell upon me. We barely knew each other and I hadn't felt this comfortable with anyone since my sister Mia.

I turned up the volume of the music and used it for strength as I stepped through the door. With cautious emerald eyes she watched me patiently. I slowly crossed the room, using every bit of strength I had, not to look at her. I slid into my desk and from the corner of my eye I could see Sam's finger tapping nervously on her desk.

All the kids in front of me had turned around to look at me with giant grins painted on their faces. It scared me at first and puzzled me even more. That's when I noticed Ms. Snyder at the front of the classroom, flailing her arms wildly in my direction. Her agitated face was mouthing something, but all I could hear was the pounding music pouring around my cerebellum. I smiled slightly as my cocoon of sound was about to be popped.

I felt a tiny elbow stick in my side like a knife and the pain shot through my ribs and stomach. Before I could react, Sam's other hand wrapped itself around the wires dangling from my ears and with a quick tug they were rolling along the top of my desk.

"Ouch," I snapped. It didn't really hurt as much as it startled me but I was over compensating for my embarrassment. The class was all laughing at me. All except Sam. She only glanced my way once and then turned her attention to the teacher, who was glaring at me.

"So nice of you to join us Mr. Valentine," she scolded. "May I start my class now or do you have more entertainment for us today?"

"Sorry," I said blushing. Sam leaned away from me and the gesture made my hands burn with frustration. Ms. Snyder turned and began the day's lesson and I sat there quietly thinking for a few moments. Why was I letting this little blonde affect me this way? I was stronger than this and it was time to embrace that.

"That's it," I said under my breath. Time to make a move. I quietly slid a folded piece of paper across her desk until she gently picked it up. As she started to read it I pretended to start my studies and patiently awaited her reaction.

"100 WAYS TO SAY 'I'M SORRY' BY MAX VALENTINE.

SORRY, SORRY...FRIENDS?"

It felt like she had been reading the letter for hours now. Holy crap...was she actually counting every sorry?

"Sam?" I began to ask and she quickly tucked the piece of paper in her notebook. She took my left hand in hers and opened it up to expose my palm and her sweet smile returned. With her pen she wrote, in blue ink, inside of it. It tickled and she seemed to enjoy that as my hand squirmed inside her grasp. When she finished she closed my fingers in my palm and pushed my fist back to me. I looked at her curiously and she nodded toward my hand and I slowly opened it. She had written the number 99 and I looked up at her questioning the message.

"You owe me one more," she said with a warm and inviting smile. My goodness she was beautiful. I slid my hand through my hair and leaned into her.

"Sorry," I smiled. At that moment, we were fixed. Good as new. Maybe even better than new. It was so weird to be so absolutely calm and real with someone. A good weird though.

The rest of the day went much the same. Sam and I found our groove again, two peas in a pod. We were inseparable. Kai, on the other hand, seemed too engrossed with the upcoming beach party this weekend. He wouldn't stop talking about it and I found my nerves beginning to cringe with the mention of it. Devon kept his distance from us but never let Sam totally out of his sight. Marcus, Kai, and I jammed at lunch and after school again. First, with a couple dozen eyes at lunch admiring our sound and then only one pair of eyes at Kai's garage. But they were big and jade green and happy to watch me scream out my frustrations into the microphone. Sam's stare seemed to make me stand a little taller and sing a little stronger.

Asia was nowhere to be found and that was starting to affect me. At least in my dreams it was. I would find myself chasing after her, through the pouring rain and when I would finally catch her in my arms she would disappear with a flash of lightning. She was haunting me. That kiss was haunting me.

Thursday – 10:39 a.m. – August 17th.

Third period English had quickly become one of my favorite classes. I had Sam to mostly thank for that. We spent most of this class passing notes instead of talking and I discovered you could learn so much about someone from just their words. I discovered just how smart she was and that her heart knew no bounds. I also was becoming more aware of how she was beginning to affect me. It would be so simple to fall for her. To completely and totally give my every waking dream and bit of myself to her. It just seemed to feel natural, like it was meant to be.

I was still counting the minutes when I might see Asia again but with each passing day, Sam was making things more and more complicated. No matter how hard I would try and fight it, she was getting under my skin. But was that a bad thing? Maybe I wasn't fighting it as hard as I'd been telling myself.

"Max...can I ask you something?" her voice was sweet.

"Uh oh...you're asking me if it's okay to ask me something. This should be good," I teased, but she didn't seem to share the joke.

"Max," she said with a nervous shuffle in her seat.

"Anything Sam." I leaned in. "What is it?"

"Have you been to the beach yet?" she asked coyly. My mind flashed to that rainy afternoon when I met Asia for the first time.

"Why?" I asked. I was hoping to avoid lying to her again. She would not want to hear about my first time, I was sure of that.

"The annual beach party is tomorrow...I know you've heard about it..." she sounded so nervous. I liked the fact that I could have that effect on her. She continued. "I was wondering if maybe, you'd like to go." She paused and swallowed softly.

"You mean like friends?" I knew exactly what she meant but I wanted to hear her say it. I was feeling very cocky all of a sudden.

"No...I mean like..." she stopped herself to choose her words carefully. "Well, I'm kind of a heavy drinker and I need a designated driver...you know, for safety reasons," she said dryly.

"What the...?" I was stunned as I fell from my high horse. As my ego broke into a thousand pieces, she broke out in a fit of laughter.

"You're so easy Max!" she exploded.

"That's not funny," I pouted.

"Ahh...you're so cute when you pout." She was so proud of herself. Secretly I was proud of how well she had tricked me but I would never admit it to her. Kai leaned over me from behind us.

"Surprisingly he's quite cute when he's not pouting too," he laughed and my elbow found his chest and Sam laughed even harder.

Friday – 8:31 a.m. – August 18th.

The morning began unusually at school. Before my first class I felt like I was being followed. I was. Lucy was my shadow again this morning. A very curious and unhappy shadow by her posture.

"Good morning Lucy," I said without even turning around to see her standing a few feet behind me. I sensed that it startled her a little when I spoke but she tried her best to not let it bother her too much. I turned and found her about ten feet from me.

"Everything all right?" I asked with a smile. I had been wondering how she was doing after the incident with Devon and me, but mostly I wanted news on Asia.

"Yes," she barely spoke.

"Do you need something?" I asked politely. She only stared at me quietly. It was starting to creep me out a bit, so I decided to push her a little.

Ember

"Have you seen Asia lately?" I asked and like a vampire exposed to the burning sun, she retreated down the hallway and disappeared around the corner. I laughed to myself and walked into first period. My question would be answered soon enough.

Computers – 11:53 a.m.

Fourth period was dragging on and I had become easily agitated with the constant talk of the party tonight. All morning that was the topic on everyone's mouths. I even caught a couple of teachers talking about it, in between my morning classes. Personally...I was getting sick of hearing about the event. I guess I woke up on the wrong side of the bed this morning.

Now, as I fidgeted nervously in my chair, I was surrounded by the thoughts and comments of Devon and his crew on the party. As a matter of fact, they were so involved in their conversation that it would take a meteor strike to shut them up. You know, the type of male bonding that included words such as "laid" or "wasted" or my personal favorite "tap that ass".

Sam noticed my anxiousness and put her hand on mine.

"What's wrong Max?" she asked sweetly, trying her best to ignore Devon's stupid comments. The question caught Kai's attention and he leaned in closer to us.

"I just didn't sleep very well last night," I said avoiding what was really bothering me. Kai tapped the front of my desk with his drum sticks.

"Nothing a good night out won't fix!" he said proudly. I shot him a dirty look.

"If I hear about this party one more time...I'm gonna shove this pencil in my right eye!" my sarcasm was thick. Sam and Kai looked at each other surprised by my anger. Now I have nothing against blowing off some steam and having a good time, in fact I embrace it. But that's not what this party was about...it's about drinking and acting stupid and that is something I couldn't condone.

"I'm just not a big fan of drinking...too many demons I guess," I said. I can't afford to drink, not with my abilities. I have a hard enough time keeping them in check as it is, without alcohol in my system. But they didn't know that, so I let myself calm down a little.

"So whatcha saying bro? You're not gonna come tonight?" His voice filled with disappointment. Sam glanced down at my tattoo on my wrist as if she knew more than she was letting on about my defiance towards drinking. It made sense though, she's known my uncle most of her life and maybe he had mentioned something about the accident to her or her father at some point. Her eyes quickly found mine again.

"Yeah, I'm definitely going to pass this time. Besides, my uncle hasn't seen me in the last couple days. I think I owe him a night of catching up." I managed a small smile at the thought of it.

"Well, that sucks," Kai whined.

"Are you sure Max?" Sam asked restlessly.

"I was hoping we could go..." she hesitated. "Together." Her eyes looked deep into mine, searching. Kai took the hint and eased himself out of our conversation. From across the room, a pair of disapproving eyes caught my attention at the same moment.

Ember

"I'm not sure if that's such a wise idea," I spoke easy and nodded toward Devon's accusing stare. His beady eyes alive with spite.

"This could get messy," I said very serious. She turned to her ex's glare and looked at him, directly in his hazel eyes, and spoke calmly and clearly.

"I'm a big girl...I don't mind messy," she said loud enough for him and anyone else listening to hear easily. Her confidence was so sexy. I found my temples heating up with the thought of her strength. So I ran my hands inside my hair and took a deep breath. Devon on the other hand found her independence infuriating. His big arrogant face turned bright red with anger as he slowly walked over to our desks.

"Devon...not now...not today," she warned, but it was obvious in his state there was no talking to him. He gathered his anger and tried again.

"Sam, we need to talk," he demanded. His angry glare seemed to fall towards my face. I'm not sure why though. Maybe it was the mocking grin I was wearing that drew it towards me. Or maybe I had the biggest brown eyes he had ever seen too. A laugh rattled inside my head as I kept his stone gaze locked.

"Not right now," she snapped. She was fuming now and I found it strange that she would lose her cool that quickly with him.

"At lunch then...I really need to talk to you," he sounded more desperate with each passing second. I reached over and took Sam's hand and squeezed it gently. Her eyes pulled to mine and she looked confused.

"I don't know," she said more calmly. Devon watched as my hand caressed hers and he stormed off, back to his side of the room. At first I found that funny but when I saw the expression covering Sam's face, it was obvious that he could still get under her skin. Even though they were supposedly over and done. That scared me and when I caught him watching us from the corner of his eyes again; he could see that doubt in my face too. He smiled and winked at me and I let go of her hand. She didn't even seem to notice when I did. We spent the rest of the class not saying a word to each other.

At lunch Sam and Devon had begun a heated conversation. They argued almost the whole lunch hour and I couldn't take my eyes off of them. Finally their conversation stopped with a loud slap across Devon's cheek. The sound popped and echoed throughout the yard and some of the kids cheered. Devon shot me a dirty look and stomped away with his crew not far behind. Kai and Marcus used this noisy interlude to capitalize on his embarrassment and started a chant that the whole crowd seemed to embrace.

"Na, na, na, na...hey, hey, hey...goodbye..." they all sang. I found it extremely funny but was too worried about Sam's state of mind to join in. As I watched Devon's gorilla like walk, he passed by Lucy at the edge of the lunch yard. She had been watching us too. I waved to her and she ran around the nearest corner.

Sam made her way through the singing crowd, massaging her wrist. She really must have let him have it. She settled herself next to me and leaned into me gently and a faint smile graced her face.

"Things are a little less messy now," she winced. She didn't seem too upset but her confidence had been shaken. I slowly took her hurt wrist into my hands.

"I don't mind messy," I said dryly. Her eyes rolled as I softly checked her hand and she winced with a sharp pain, as I rolled it inside my grip. I think she might have sprained it. She tried to pull her hand back but I didn't give it up.

110

Ember

"It'll be fine."

"I know," I agreed but my tone came off much too arrogant. I let my hands fill with the slightest heat and began rubbing softly. Within seconds her pain faded and she turned her wrist with no soreness at all. Her face filled with a puzzled glance and I pulled away nervously. She paused for a moment and then slid closer to me and her hands found my bangs again. She brushed them behind my ears, and stared at me quietly. Kai and Marcus exchanged smiles and turned away from us.

"Will you come to the party with me tonight?" she asked. One of her hands had come to a rest on the side of my neck and her eyes were like laser beams. They cut through every defense I had. Every wall I had built during the last couple years. My defenses were crumbling and I became terrified. So I did the only thing I could think of...run.

"Sam I think you're better off if I didn't." Be easy Max...let her down easy. Then run like hell.

"Why?"

"I think I've already caused you enough pain," I said trying to think of anything to tell her. Anything but the truth. I didn't give her a chance to respond. I just grabbed my things and ran with my tail between my legs. As I rushed for my next class, I couldn't help but turn around to see how upset I had surely made her. To my surprise I found her smiling as she held her wrist that I secretly healed. I was in trouble. I was getting too close, too fast. I shook the thought from my head and walked to my next class.

I fought my emotions the rest of the day. I kept telling myself to just go and find Sam. Find her and tell her yes. Yes, with a capital Y. Say yes and don't look back. But then my fear stood up and pushed those crazy thoughts to the back of my brain to wither and die. Bury the truth. The unthinkable truth. I was falling for her.

The day ended and I found myself walking to the parking lot alone. I was a zombie walking around, struggling against the urge to find Sam and give in. Even if I did cave and let those feelings grow, there was still one major complication to deal with. Unbelievably, that complication was waiting for me in the school parking lot.

She looked amazing and I rubbed my eyes to be sure I wasn't just imagining her. She was waiting for me with her hip leaning against the side of her Jeep. She was slowly pulling her hair up into a ponytail, behind sunglasses and cherry red lipstick. Wearing a small black tank top and designer shorts, her long legs seemed to go on endlessly. My heart pounded quicker in my throat and my body just seemed to gravitate toward her on its own.

As I found myself in front of her, she shifted her hips and pouted slightly.

"Miss me?" she asked but it sounded more like a fact than a question. I took a second and thought of a million witty comebacks but settled on the simplest.

"Yes."

"Get in," she sounded sweet this time. I threw my guitar and school bag in the back and jumped in. She walked around the front of the truck and gave Kai and Marcus a quick wave before she climbed in. They could only look on in amazement. I shot them a glance and shrugged my shoulders with a smile.

She revved the engine to life as I felt my confidence build. The skies filled with gray streaks that stretched themselves above us.

"So…did you miss me?" It came out way too arrogant but it was the best I could manage with my heart racing. She slowly lowered her dark glasses to the tip of

Ember

her nose. She bit her bottom lip subtly and her eyes were like liquid sapphire from behind those shaded lenses. A smile grew across her face...the biggest I had seen on her yet. She whispered.

"Yes."

MADISON DANIEL

Rainmaker_11

~Caught In The Rain: Revis~

Friday afternoon – 3:34 p.m.

The sun was warm on our skin as the wind raced through the open top of her Jeep. She drove as if we were being chased and the thunder crashed behind us. I peeked at the side mirror to see a wall of purple and black storm clouds growing, almost as if they were following us. But that wasn't possible...was it?

"Where are we going Asia?" I asked with a curious tone but I really didn't care. I was enjoying the ride too much.

"It's a secret," she teased. "But I think you're going to like it." Her eyes twinkled when she spoke and the thunder snapped at the back of the truck. Her foot fell harder on the gas pedal and we were flying. After a moment I noticed her face and a determined squint in her eyes, like she was chasing something. I looked above us at the sun busting through the staggered clouds and realized...she WAS chasing something. The sunlight.

I closed my eyes with a small smile, and put my head back against the soft leather seat. The smell of rain was growing and it tickled my nose as I inhaled every inch of it.

"We're almost there," she said. I opened my eyes and found us rounding a corner at the top of a hill and that's when I saw it. Her home...Michaels Estate. It sat at the top of the hill and was absolutely huge in size. Kai had mentioned she was rich but this was bordering on royalty. It had to be at least four stories tall and was an off white color with giant dark windows. They seemed to surround the whole building. There was at least one noticeable balcony and from my vantage, the roof looked flat. Probably for her helicopter pad, I laughed to myself. It gave me the impression of being very inviting yet...distant. I know that sounded crazy but that's the feeling it made me feel.

The grounds were covered in the greenest vegetation I'd ever seen with my own eyes. Thick deep green grass, thick full trees, and a dozen different kinds of flowers. They were everywhere and they gave off a scent that was dizzying. It was all almost overgrown but that only gave the appearance a natural feeling, like some beautiful jungle.

As the Jeep rolled to a stop at the end of her ridiculously long drive way, and I do mean long. It was easily as long as the street my house was located on. A thought found its way into my head and it made me a little sad. Kai had also told me that she lived here alone. How could anyone live in a place this big all by herself and not go insane?

"What do you think?" she asked softly.

"It's cozy," I said and hopped out the side. Asia slid out her side as the softest of raindrops fell on us. She made her way to her front door and patiently watched me as I took my time to join her. She smiled and the rain fell harder.

"Are you coming?" she asked impatiently. I shook my hair from my face and walked in slowly. The second I stepped away from the rain and inside the door her smell hit me. I wondered how she could smell like cherry blossoms when that was one of the few flowers that weren't on her property.

She waited for me to notice the stunning foyer that was all around us, I think she was showing off. I kept my eyes focused on hers, even when her eyes filled with worry. I had something else on my mind and I moved in closer to her. Face to face. I put my left hand on the back of her neck. I was already generating a wave of heat from my hands and she flinched as my palm fell around her neck. My right hand found its way down the bottom of her back and stopped at the edge of her shorts. I pulled her in firmly and her body tightened. I was sure she would pull away at that moment but she didn't.

I leaned in and slowly kissed her, softly at first but then with more force. The rain pounded on the door behind us and I felt her body fill with goose bumps. My hands heated up more and the walls shook with the crash of thunder outside.

"I was right..."

"What do you mean Max?" she asked catching her breath.

"You taste like rain." I wanted to smile but forced myself not to. Her stare turned nervous.

"Why would you say that?"

"Because it's true," I smiled.

"Max...I think this was a mistake." She pulled away but didn't let go of my hand. Her face grew sad. "You shouldn't speak of such things."

"Why not?" I pushed. "You know my secret. You've seen my past...even felt them." I stepped back toward her.

"You've seen the real me Asia," I said softly and she looked away from me but I pulled her face back to mine.

"And I can see the real you." Thunder rumbled loudly and I glanced upward toward her ceiling and laughed lightly. It rumbled with a force that seemed to push the ceiling down toward us.

"It's crazy, your secret should be my kryptonite but it's not. It seems to be the opposite." I found her worried eyes again. "It draws me closer...it calls to me. You call to me." My voice was without any doubt.

"Maybe..." she half whispered.

"And I think you know it. I think you feel it too," I said convinced.

"I don't know anything..." she stuttered. Her words were far from convincing. My words seemed to be hurting her, so I decided to let the subject go. For the moment at least.

"I won't push. I'm sorry." I let her go and walked past her to the living room, which was gigantic. It was so big that I had to take a minute to take it all in.

A massive skylight, the size of a swimming pool took up most of the ceiling. The emotional thunderstorm above it, washed across the glass like a living piece of art. The furniture was placed in a strategic position and seemed to point your attention to one single painting on the far wall. A large black frame outlined an explosion of dull colors, scattered along its canvas. It was beautiful in a depressing way. The colors were so vivid but left you wanting more, almost like it wasn't finished. It made me think of my childhood and that made me instantly uncomfortable. So I turned my eyes from it and concentrated on the rest of the room.

The lightning flashed above and lit the giant room up but there wasn't much more to see. A TV and stereo in one corner, that didn't look like it ever got used. There were no pictures of family or friends anywhere. The rest of the walls were empty and the light almond paint gave it an open feeling. From behind, Asia walked up to me upset.

"My secret has done nothing but cause me pain…" she was angry. "You've spent your life in the light with your powers. Mine have kept me in the dark." She paused and took a deep breath.

"You are the good, Max. And if I am truly your opposite…than I guess that makes me the bad." She was direct and growing angrier. I reached out with my hand and gently caressed her cool cheek with my fingers.

"Asia…I find the real you, the darkness as you call it…" I paused and debated on how much I really wanted to tell her. "I find it simply beautiful."

"Why?" she snapped.

"You know exactly why," I said with sweetness. "The night I healed you, I think I passed something on to you. That's why you dreamt what you did."

She pretended to be confused but I knew better.

"You saw who I was. You saw how I see you. You felt our connection. Maybe all the pain we've experienced in our lives is what brought us together." I could tell that I had gotten through her stubborn fears but she was far from admitting it. A small smile crept back on her face.

"Maybe," she said. She let out a long breath and quickly changed the subject.

"Would you like a tour of the house?" she asked and her voice felt calm again.

"Sure." I really wanted to keep talking about the force that seemed to keep pulling us together but I guess that would have to wait.

On the second floor she pointed out the special architecture that made up most of the guest bedrooms and bathrooms. I found it quite boring and self- involving.

I've never been the type to care about how much something cost or whose fancy designer name was all over it. I could tell by Asia's tone that she found it quite boring also. So why was she putting up this facade? Maybe it's what she expected from me...to be impressed by material things. Maybe it was how she was raised. Either way I was ready for some real conversation and I was determined to find it. On the way to the third floor I changed the subject.

"Why aren't you in school?" I asked out of the blue. Her eyes grew suspicious.

"Why?"

"Because, as breathtaking as this house is, it's still not as interesting as its owner," I smiled and took her hand in mine. "So spill it?"

"I graduated." She smiled and pulled me into what was obviously her bedroom. It was soft and simple and spotless. "Most of the school thinks I'm a drop out."

"Well...are you?"

"Yes and no. I quit last year but continued my education from home," she said proudly. She quickly left her room and I followed right behind.

"Have you thought about college?" I continued. She walked us out on a large terrace that was covered by a giant glass awning. The rain slid along it and over the side. The wind from the soft storm filled our clothes and hair and I found my mind wandering to more intimate questions but her answer to my last one pulled me back to attention.

"Not really. I think I'd rather see the world instead." We walked to the railing and stood shoulder to shoulder as the rain drops tickled our faces.

Ember

"Like where?" I asked. I barely said it out loud because all I could think about was the need to kiss her again.

"Anywhere sunny." Her body leaned closer to me and a tiny lightning bolt flashed in front of us. "And you...what are you planning after school?" she asked softly.

"I haven't got a clue. Maybe a cruise down to Mexico or sky diving in the desert." I laughed at how silly I sounded, but she didn't laugh at all.

"We could take my boat," she whispered.

"You've got a boat?" I gasped.

"It's more like a yacht but it should get the job done." She turned and leaned herself backwards over the railing and let the rain sprinkle her hair. My eyes followed the lines of her neck and the curve of her jaw.

"I'll keep that in mind," I said. She brought her face back into view and stared at me and I tried to shove my eyes back in my head. She seemed to enjoy my awkwardness toward her beauty.

We made our way back inside and she started to head back down her staircase.

"Wait...what's on the fourth floor?" I was curious.

"Oh...my helicopter pad," she said and walked down the stairs. My mind flipped inside. She had to be joking. From the bottom of the stairs she called to me. "You thirsty?"

"Umm...yeah," I said dazed. Kai was right, she was loaded. I headed down stairs and found her in the kitchen. At her marble kitchen counter she slid me a glass of ice water. As my right hand gripped the cold glass I found her eyes inspecting my tattoos. I could tell she had something on her mind. Her eyes searched mine and the rain sounded stronger against the windows. My thoughts focused on the building storm.

"How long have you been able to do that?" I pointed to the rain pouring down the window glass. She hesitated and then answered cautiously.

"Since I was born," her smile faded. I felt bad for bringing it up. "And you Max...how long have you been able to do the things you do?" She sounded soft and caring. If I expected her to open up all the way then I guess I needed to also.

"I was five the first time I caught fire and it's been nothing but trouble ever since," I teased and her smile returned.

"The healing thing is new. I've only been able to do it for a couple years now. All I know for sure is the more I push myself, the stronger they seem to become." My lips found my glass and I quickly finished my drink. "I wasn't sure I could heal you that afternoon," I said slowly. Her eyes focused hard on me.

"I'd never attempted something so...advanced," she smiled at my choice of words. "I was afraid it might kill me."

"But still you did it anyways?" her tone felt playful.

"Well, the accident was my fault," I said embarrassed.

"No it wasn't. The accident was my fault."

"What?" I was confused.

"I caused that wave Max." She smiled and stepped closer to me. I was speechless.

"My emotions seem to have a certain effect on my abilities." She scrunched her nose playfully.

Ember

"And when you saw me flaming up in the rain...you kinda lost it. Is that what you're saying?" I was flattered.

"Yes and no." She was embarrassed now. "I lost it all right but not because of your powers." Her head tilted slightly. I held my breath.

"It was because of you." She blushed and my head felt dizzy with excitement. My ego felt like it was about to explode.

Minutes passed as we both stood nervously silent, not sure what to say next. I didn't want to ruin the moment but I found the need to bring our conversation back to something more serious.

"Can I ask you something Asia?" I took it slow. I knew this subject would be a touchy one.

"Okay," she said hesitant but sure of herself.

"Is what they say about your family true?" I tried to be sensitive but I could see her walls going back up.

"And what exactly did 'they' say...Max?" She was mad.

"About the curse...about Lucy..." Her face turned cold at the mention of her name.

"And that your parents are dead and that's how you received this house and the mountains of money that came along with it." I was direct but respectful but she looked livid with my words. She turned away from me and spoke very softly.

"What does Lucy have to do with my parents?" she hissed.

"Relax...I'll explain myself."

"Okay," She had begun to face me again but stopped herself halfway and looked at me from the side of her eye. I took a deep breath and continued.

"If your power over the elements is some kind of curse...then so be it. Cause personally I find it amazing." I was oozing confidence again. I took a step closer.

"As for Lucy, I like her. Most red blooded American males would find your "friendship" extremely exciting. But I could care less about your personal preference." I took a second to see how angry my words were making her and she was looking completely away from me again. Not a good sign.

"Look Asia, all I want to know is about you," I said as the rain picked up outside.

"And if Lucy is part of that in some way, then I can accept that." My words were getting through her defenses and she slowly turned back toward me.

"You mean that?" She was suspicious.

"Completely," I nodded. "So that just leaves your parents. You don't have to talk to me about them if you don't want to...I was just..." She cut me off and the thunder groaned louder.

"Lucy is...well...complicated. And I'd like to leave it at that, for now." She glanced into my eyes for some kind of reaction but I just held her gaze.

"My parents are very much alive and as far away as they can possibly get from their cursed little girl." She was filled with pain and anger.

"I'm sorry," I whispered.

"It's all right. I get a card around the holidays every year that lets me know where they've moved to now," her voice sounded drained. "And that's about it."

Ember

"And all of this?" I asked as I pointed to the surroundings.

"They built this place for me in hope that it would make me feel at home, even if there was no family to fill it. Just me and the full time staff." She couldn't hide how much that hurt her and I thought she was going to put her walls back up but she continued. "But when I turned eighteen I fired everyone."

"And this inheritance I keep hearing about?" I asked nervously.

"My grandparents left me a chunk of money but I won't receive any of it until I'm officially nineteen." She shrugged and took a sip of her water. "My parents always make sure that's there plenty for me to live on, in the bank account."

"Nineteen?"

"Some stupid stipulation that states I won't receive any of my grandparent's inheritance for up to a year after I am of legal age." Her eyes rolled and the lightning lit the whole house up.

"So you're alone?" I asked softly. Her eyes waited for me to judge her but the disappointing stare she was waiting for never came.

"When my little sister died my parents left me too. First my mother and then last year my father." My mouth felt dry but I continued. "They both blamed me for her passing. I haven't seen my mother since." Her eyes seemed to wince when I said that.

"My father didn't leave physically but mentally and emotionally he was a ghost," I spoke slowly and her right hand found the top of mine. "He hated me for Mia leaving and secretly blamed me for his wife leaving too," I finished. We stared at each other's eyes, examining both of our haunted pasts. She stepped toward me and slid her body next to my side.

"So you understand," she said calmly.

"That a gift can feel like a curse? All too well," I said.

We were so exposed right now, so raw. We were so different, yet exactly the same. I wanted to hold her and I wanted to run. Maybe she was right after all. This wasn't such a great idea. She was feeling vulnerable too and quickly lightened the mood.

"Do you like to dance Max?" She seemed scared, but a gleam was back in her eyes and a hint of a smile was growing.

The rain was barely falling now and the moon had peeked its white face out from behind the swollen black clouds. She threw her arms around me as I started up the truck.

"We'll have fun...I promise." The determination in her face was unwavering.

"Too late," I teased and pulled out of her driveway quickly.

As I drove faster and faster the cooling evening air was making my eyes water lightly. The smell of new rain was still fresh in my head but my thoughts were becoming tiresome. This party had me worried. Devon and his Neanderthals would most definitely be there. So would Kai and Marcus. But the big question was would Sam be there? And if so...would she hate me for showing up with Asia?

Yup, I was most definitely not going to have a good time tonight. I could feel it in my bones. I watched Asia as she threw her arms in the air and arched her back, as if she were trying to touch the moon. The growing moonlight cascaded down her face as the wind messed her dancing curls behind her. Lightning flashed as her hand found my hair which slid through it slowly. Another flash of lightning above us revealed the whole island in its bright light and my chest filled with fire. I was caught in her storm.

My beautiful rainmaker.

Bad Moon_12

~Paralyzer: Finger Eleven~

Friday night – 7:47 p.m.

About a half mile out from the beach it became quite clear just how big of an event this annual beach party had become. Even from this distance I could hear the pounding music fill the air. Three giant bonfires danced in the dark, reaching up for the starry sky. They swayed and twirled in the wind feverishly, lighting up Kanaha beach in all its glory. The fires were so big that I wondered just how legal those dancing flames were. In the night, with the growing pulse of music, I found my senses being pulled toward the bright flames. They felt comfortable, as strange as that sounded.

Thunderclouds began to circle the beach as we found a place to park. It was taking longer than I was expecting to find a parking spot, but I didn't mind though. I was enjoying the last few moments alone together. I knew the second that we stepped onto that beach, with all those wanting eyes; it would never be the same. For either of us.

"So...I guess its official..." I hinted as I turned the Jeep off and got out. Asia raced to my side and I gently took her hand in mine.

"What is?" she asked.

"This is a date," I said calmly even though my stomach was in my throat. She stopped moving for a second and glanced quickly at our hands locked together. I could see her thinking deeply about what I had just said and I waited patiently for her to pull her hand away from mine. Instead her grip tightened around my fingers slightly and she turned and began walking us out of the parking lot and onto the beach.

As our feet first met the cool sand my hand quickly squeezed hers and filled with heat. I hadn't even realized that I was doing it. I was so nervous to be by her side.

"Easy tiger," she said sarcastically and flashed her big blue eyes. "I won't let anyone hurt you," she whispered and her smile seemed devious. The ocean air and burning timber filled my nose as we walked up to the large crowd. From the edge of the crowd I heard a familiar voice.

"No way! You made it!" Kai screamed ecstatically. He had a drink in one hand and a thumbs-up in the other. Marcus was right behind him with a smile. His wanna be Mohawk flickered in the breeze.

"Mad Max in the house!" he cheered and grabbed my free hand and shook it fiercely.

"Hey my brothers," I said with nerves growing. Their beach bum bodies stopped as if they both had walked into an invisible wall. Their eyes filled with wonder as Asia's stare found them. She squeezed my hand harder; giving me the first indication that maybe she was not as confident as she was letting on.

"Asia this is the rest of the band. Kai and Marcus," I said politely. Her grip loosened and her other hand extended out and shook both of theirs. First Kai's and then Marcus'.

"Hello Kai...Marcus. It is a pleasure." She was sweet but protective. They could only offer her an approving nod as they shook her hand. She must have found their awkwardness funny because her posture softened and a tiny smile broke the corner of her mouth. We all stood in an eerie silence for a moment. I wish the moment had lasted a little longer but it vanished when she noticed the something or someone that had caught my eye.

Sam's face glowed pale in the dark with only the reflection of the burning fires lighting it. But I could still see the disappointment on her face and that made me feel a little smaller inside. Her eyes reached out and let a little air out of me and the sky filled with clouds. Asia stiffened and a single bolt of lightning slithered through the clouds.

"I can't believe you talked her into coming Max," Kai's voice was still full of wonder.

"Sorry fellas, she brought me," I sounded annoyed but Asia hadn't even noticed. Her eyes were locked on Sam carefully. I tried to break that concentration.

"I hate these things." I let the anger slide through my teeth and Asia's attention focused back to me again. The thunder cracked above the sea of dancing bodies along the beach. Most of the party goers were taken by surprise, some screamed with fear, some with joy. I glared at Asia with caution.

"You play nice," I warned.

"No promises," she almost growled and let go of my hand quickly. I started to boil inside. I knew this was a bad idea to come here. Kai and Marcus looked on nervously until Kai decided to ease some of the building tension. Well, at least he tried.

"Don't worry you two..." He put his hand on one of her shoulders. She did not approve of his gesture. "We're gonna have one hell of a night!" he cheered and clicked his bottle with the drink in Marcus' hand. I tried to smile but couldn't and then, almost on cue; Lucy appeared from nowhere. She rushed toward our small circle with her eyes on fire. She shoved her way through Kai and Marcus and proceeded to wedge her tiny frame between Asia and I.

"What the hell are you doing?" she screamed shaking. Her voice was filled with hurt and her speech sounded slurred. She had obviously been drinking already. I took a small step back, as did Kai and Marcus. Lucy started screaming in her native tongue Chinese and without missing a beat, Asia returned the anger. As their words grew louder and more confusing I began to feel completely out of my element and wanted to leave.

Seconds before I could turn and leave the girls beat me to the punch and stormed off toward the parking lot. Their words grew more passionate as more lightning flashed over us so brightly that the light from the giant bonfires seemed non-existent.

"Should I go talk to them?" I asked and started to walk toward them. Kai's hand stopped me and tugged at my tee shirt.

"Leave'em be. Trust me," he said.

"But..." I tried to say.

"They're known for this Max," he smiled.

"What?" I was growing angrier.

"Come on big guy, lets get you a drink," Marcus added.

"Max, trust me...you're better off," Kai tried to reason with me. "They do this all the time."

And with that, my head began to pound while a sobering thought scratched itself into my mind. Is that what I was to her; a catalyst to fight with her precious Lucy? Was I just a test of some kind? My eyes whipped around to find Asia and Lucy still fighting and then back to Sam's face again. Her face filled with concern as she watched us from a safe distance.

"I think I should go." I was no longer in the mood for any of this. The sand, the music, the girls. None of it.

Ember

"The night's still young brother..." Kai pleaded. "Don't go."

"Kai I need to leave," I said determined. From the corner of my eye I saw Sam still watching me patiently and I felt a calmness fill me slightly.

"Max I want you to meet some people," he continued and draped his arm around my shoulder. "They could be a huge help to a struggling band, such as ourselves," he winked.

"Come on," he said with a calmness that impressed me. He seemed to see the bigger picture. At least when it came to our music.

"Okay." I gave in and Marcus patted me on the back.

"Follow us," Marcus quipped. I hesitated at first but folded and let them lead the way into the pulsating crowd of bodies. The thunder rolled and the first few drops fell from the sky as we made our way into the crowd. Sam was no longer around. That was probably for the better, I was in no mood to talk.

After bumping into a half dozen people, and saying hello to another dozen, I became very intolerant of this supposed meeting.

"Where are these guys you wanted me to meet?" I asked Kai impatiently. I had to yell over the thumping music.

"They were right here just a minute ago," he yelled as his eyes scanned the jumping crowd. "Wait here bro. I'll see if I can round them up." With a whip of his dreads he was gone, surfing through the sea of bodies.

"Is this really that important?" I asked Marcus but his attention was on a lovely little island girl, in a pink bikini. Her eyes followed his and without a word he disappeared into the crowd too. I was now surrounded by a hundred strangers but I felt totally alone.

I stood on the tips of my toes and tried to see over the crowd, if Asia and Lucy were still going at it. But it was no use; I was too far from the parking lot now. Then the thunder shook above me and I was sure that things were still pretty ugly between them. So I stood and waited, as people bumped into me over and over again. The music would change but the beat would stay the same.

"What am I still doing here?" I said to myself. My anger was growing again. I couldn't take it anymore. I shook my head in defeat and started pushing myself through the dancing bodies. I pushed harder and faster with each passing kid but I did not get very far. My charge was stopped as I slammed into Sam blindly.

"Sorry," I said disgusted before I realized who had stopped my retreat.

"Sam...uh...aloha." I felt embarrassed. She looked happy to see me and that confused me. She was holding two drinks in her hands and handed one to me.

"I don't drink," I reminded her and my throat cracked with nervousness.

"Neither do I," she smiled and took a quick sip. I did the same with complete trust and found my cup was filled with ice water and a twist of lime.

"Thanks," I said. I waited for her to explode with anger too. Surely she would call me out on all my excuses I had to not come with her.

"I'm glad you made it Max." Her smile grew naturally bigger. Why was she being so nice to me? I certainly didn't deserve it.

"About that Sam..." I began to explain myself when she cut me off.

Ember

"It's fine. I'm just glad that you are here." She leaned into me. "I don't care how you got here...just that you're here." Her eyes were filled with the confidence that I had grown so fond of. That instantly put me at ease and for the first time that night I let the pounding beat of the music in. Finally I let a big smile escape.

"How do you do that?" I asked sweetly.

"Do what?" her smile widened.

"Make me smile."

"Just returning the favor," she said. I laughed and took another drink quickly hiding behind my giant red plastic cup. Her eyes followed mine and her hair trickled down her shoulders. Her body was wrapped in a light green top, with long sleeves and a hood. Her shorts were white and exposed most of her little legs. The sprinkles of rain seemed to stick off her hair like colorful crystals.

"You look...nice," I spit out and it sounded as stuttered as I had feared. She just laughed and nodded.

"Thanks." She softly took a drink and stared at me as the music raced around us. Without even realizing it we were both gently rocking back and forth to the rhythm of the music and we were much closer to each other than when we started talking. I was close enough to smell her strawberry conditioner that she loved. One of her hands caressed the top of my arm lightly and time seemed to fall away. I could barely hear the pounding music anymore. I took that as a chance to apologize and I leaned in slowly to whisper in her ear.

"I'm sorry," That was all I could get out before Asia was standing right behind her. She didn't look upset at the closeness Sam and I were sharing but she did look dangerous...almost primal. My heart started to pound. This was going to be awkward.

135

"What's wrong?" Sam asked. Asia strutted past her, watching her closely as she walked. She cuddled up behind me with her head on my shoulder and her right arm extended itself across my chest and rested on the opposite shoulder. Her soft curls rustled along my neck and my body tightened up.

"Samantha Summers," Asia said with the venom of a snake. Her left arm slowly crawled up my left side.

"Great...you've met..." I winced.

"Thanks for keeping my place warm for me." Her left hand came to rest on my chest and an evil smile filled her face. My heart pounded and she stared into Sam with daggers in her eyes.

"I finally got him to smile again. Try not to chase this one off this time," Sam said as calm as I have ever heard her and walked off slowly. She faded into the crowd and I found my emotions spinning. I was so proud of Sam for not letting Asia get to her. I was flattered by the jealousy in Asia's tone. But most of all, I was mad again.

"I thought you left," I said coldly.

"Not yet," she said and turned to face me. "She's a little short for you, don't you think?" she asked cocky.

"Funny...I could say the same about sister psycho!" my anger boiled over. Her face fell cold like ice. The storm overhead gurgled to life.

"Is that supposed to be a joke?" she demanded.

"It seems that's all I am to you." I was beginning to burn up inside and I wasn't sure how long I could keep it under control. Her eyes filled with hurt and the rain started to fall thicker. She stepped into me ready to do more damage as Kai flew from the crowd and in between us.

Ember

"Max...there's trouble. I need your help," he said urgently. He shot Asia a worried look and grabbed my arm.

"What's going on Kai?" I asked as he began pulling me through the crowd.

"Just hurry," he called from in front of me. Asia was not happy and followed closely behind us.

"Wait!" Asia huffed. I glanced back toward her as my feet stumbled away. I was so angry with her but my over-heating hands wanted to reach for her.

We were bobbing and weaving within the wall of bodies and my temper was at its limit. I was just about to stop Kai and demand to know what was going on when my eyes finally focused on the trouble. My heart sank and my hands began to steam. I was hoping my eyes were playing tricks on me. For Asia's sake. But they weren't, and the awful truth hit me like a locomotive.

"Oh no..." I mumbled.

This was going to be ugly.

High Tide 13

~Break The Ice: Britney Spears~

Devon and his friends had decided to pick on a fellow classmate at the end of the beach. My first impression was that they were all very drunk or on the path towards it. They stumbled around laughing and mocking their fellow classmate. Anyone who was in sight of the situation kept his distance and watched with nervous eyes. That angered me immensely. I wondered why no one would stand up to these five guys. I didn't care how rich or important a person's family was, there had got to be a line drawn.

"No more!" I growled through the new falling rain. It was time to draw that line.

Quickly I made my way past the last few kids in the crowd. Instantly I realized who the young girl was that they were harassing, I didn't even need to see her face. My heartbeat doubled as my eyes focused on the blue streaks hanging in her hair.

"Lucy..."

At first I thought by her position, that she had been getting sick. She had drunk her share of the party favors after all. She was on her knees; face down in the sand with the waves from the increasing tide closing in.

"Max...she's hurt," Kai warned. His eyes filled with worry.

"What happened?" I asked without stopping my advance. His hand caught my chest and he froze when he felt the heat I was generating.

"Someone said that one of them hit her..." his voice sounded distant. His eyes were locked on my warming torso and then Asia's approach. I knew Asia was close behind me, but I wasn't sure just how far back and I hoped that she hadn't heard the gruesome detail. Even if she hadn't...I had and my ears popped from the building pressure in my head.

Jason, the biggest of the four horsemen, was standing behind her and simulating a sex act. His big hips thrusting back and forth as the others cheered him on. Their beer bottles in hand, waving in the air like spears and drunken smiles plastered across their faces. My hands felt like fire and my vision began to blur as I locked onto Jason's face. His little ponytail was flipping from side to side, making my muscles tense and crack with heat. The word had spread that Mad Max was on the warpath again and the beach filled in behind me with excited fans.

"Max!" Asia screamed and lightning split the sky with an ear deafening crack and the waves grew larger. I ignored her warning and embraced my rage. Steam billowed from my shoulders and hands as I raced for Jason. My hand found the back of his head and I threw him backwards in one quick motion. His shocked body flew behind me, sliding like a rag doll and coming to a rest at Devon's feet. Devon looked up at me surprised.

"My hair!" Jason bellowed but the sound from the rising tide smothered his cries. The smell of burning hair filled the air as I looked down at my fist and found his scruffy ponytail still in my hand. The tiny hairs were still burning on the ends. They quickly faded to black in the cooling air. The rain pounded the beach much more severely now and I tossed the chunk of hair into the water.

Devon's eyes filled with disgust as he threw his bottle to the ground, shattering it into a thousand pieces. Brian and the twins just stared at Jason as he flailed wildly, cursing about his new haircut. Lucy groaned from below me and I could tell she was in pain.

Ember

"Lucy, can you get up?" I asked, never taking my eyes off of the boys. She coughed and Asia stepped toward us. I quickly shot her a look not to come any closer. She watched me hard but stopped and glanced down at Lucy. Devon motioned for the horsemen to surround me and I stepped in front of Lucy, completely blocking her from the oncoming attack.

The waves crashed on my left side and the rain was falling thick now. Asia stood about fifteen feet from us and Sam was directly behind her. Her eyes were filled with shock and terror, but Kai and Marcus were right beside her too. It seemed to ease her slightly as she used Kai's broad shoulder as her guard.

Devon and Brian approached slowly, staggering a little as they did and the twins mirrored their every move until all four of them were fanned out in front of Lucy and I. As they slowly circled us, I turned along with their movements, to shield Lucy as best I could. But now we were cut off from the beach, with our backs to the ocean. The air rushed off the waves quickly cooling my back and bringing Lucy to shivers. Her teeth chattered from below me.

The rain was falling thicker and thicker, making it harder to keep my heat up. That's when I noticed just how much steam was coming from my shoulders but in this thick downpour, the only one who could really see anything was Lucy. She stared up at me with tears running down her face, and confusion setting in. I doubted that any of the crowd could see me as clearly as she did and that's when it dawned on me...

"Very clever Asia," I whispered. She may be completely upset with me and this situation but she still did what she could to protect me. My chest filled with proud fire.

"You're going to play the hero?" Devon taunted. "Or is the new kid just trying to make a name for himself?"

"I already have a name," I said as calmly as I could, which wasn't very calm at all. My eyes were locked again with his and I couldn't believe how much I wanted this to happen. Not the suffering that Lucy had been through, just the aftermath. This moment was calling to me on an instinctive level. My body grew impatient with all this talking and filled with more heat. The rain dripped from my bangs blurring my vision for a moment.

"No. What you have is a big problem," he screamed through the drenching rain. A small smile slipped onto my face.

"Eddie...Alex...grab him," he ordered. They looked at each other and back toward him with hesitation and his face twisted in anger. I stepped forward growing even hotter.

"Bring it!" I demanded. Water flew from my mouth as I screamed and waved for them to do like they were told.

"Max stop!" Asia called out and the power cut off with another streak of lightning. Sam jumped and watched Asia closely. Thunder replaced the pounding music and the crowd began to panic in the dark. Many kids retreated back to the parking lot as the wall of falling water doused the bonfires. They all burned out at almost the same moment, leaving only fading embers.

"Just take care of Lucy," I yelled back at her. My eyes stole a quick glance at Lucy who was trying to stand now but not having much success. Her hands and knees were covered in muddy sand.

"Let's do this!" Devon yelled at me. He motioned for his buddies to attack again but they were in no mood to be wrestling around this close to an angry ocean and beaching storm.

"Come on Devon...let's get out of here," Brian pleaded with him.

"Yeah, there's a hurricane coming," Jason said from behind the other four with his hand along the back of his neck. I guess he had found the courage to stop crying about his hair and join the party. The twins watched the sky nervously and started to back up. Jason shook his head in annoyance and followed. Brian held his ground but positioned himself away from the blowing wind and away from my view. They were giving up. All except their precious leader. That infuriated Devon.

"No!" Devon screamed and his voice cracked with the strain. Lightning flickered all around us, lighting every inch of the beach, but only for a second. But that was long enough for me to see the red and swollen eye on Lucy's face. It had already begun to turn purple along her left temple. Time slowed as my hands balled into fists at my sides and I focused my wrath toward Devon's spiteful face. His eyes returned the rage and he brought his arms up ready to strike.

"Lucy! Get out of here! Now!" I yelled out. She stumbled to her feet and made her way to Asia who caught her in her arms. She was safe now but it was too late for me, I was past the point of return. I felt a burning from deep within me, calling to be free. An evil grin grew larger on my face and I let it out. Devon lunged forward with rain splashing off his charging body and I let go.

"No!" Asia screamed out.

Just a few feet from me he attacked like a bullet with his fists ready to swing and my hands ignited in a flash as I burst forward. In the same split second, a five foot wave slammed into my back, washing itself over the top of me. Its weight was undeniable. My flames disappeared as quickly as they came to life as my body was slammed into the sand. With my arms at my sides to brace the crushing force, I barely stopped my head from bouncing off the beach. Devon was thrown backward but managed to stay on his feet.

"Nice try hero," Devon said pointing at me. Thunder rumbled over me and the sound was joined by the growing laughter coming from Devon and his boys. The other kids left along the beach joined in making my face burn from embarrassment. Everyone quickly collected themselves and stumbled off into the darkness. Devon saved me a final 'I told you so' look as he stumbled away with his friends.

"Hero," I spit out as the ocean water receded and the rain started to fade. Asia and Lucy glared at me and I found my head spinning again. I was so embarrassed and angry.

"Let's get you home," Asia said to Lucy. The rain came to a complete halt and the last few party goers left on the beach looked around in amazement before loading into their cars. Asia disappeared in the darkness and the clouds pulled back revealing the full moon.

"Well, that was fun," I coughed out and pulled myself up. I was still unnaturally hot but gaining control again. Kai and Sam ran up to me and tried to help me to my feet but I wanted nobody's help. Not now, not ever.

"That was quite a show," Sam said sarcastically. I only looked at her annoyed and started ringing out my drenched clothes.

"That was friggin intense brother," Kai sounded excited but relieved.

"Where's Marcus?" I asked not really worried about it.

144

Ember

"He headed back to the car when the power popped off."

"Why?" I asked.

"He figured if things were to get much worse, we'd probably need a quick get away," Kai smiled.

"Funny," Sam nodded. "I take it you need a ride home?"

"No thanks," I said pouting. How could she just leave? Especially after helping her precious Lucy. My head was officially throbbing now.

"I'm not asking Max," Sam said boldly. Her confident tone only made me angrier.

"I'll walk," I grumbled. I wasn't even really mad at her, just at my stupid illusions of this doomed night. She walked up to me and slowly caressed my cheek with her hand. It was still very hot and she noticed immediately but said nothing of it. Her touch was cool and calming and soothed me easily.

"Come on...let's go home," she sounded sweet and safe. But I didn't want to let go of this anger yet and if she stayed, that's exactly what she would make me do.

"Just leave!" I snapped. Her smile disappeared and she leaned into me, looking up in my eyes.

"Hey! Don't be that guy!" she spoke forceful and direct. This hit my already raw nerves hard and I wanted to get even angrier. Her hands found my wet bangs and she gently brushed them to the side and smiled.

"Okay." I gave in.

"Okay," she agreed.

Kai watched us closely before finding a nervous Marcus back at his old car. Kai slid into the driver's seat.

Marcus anxiously watched Sam and I from the side mirror.

"Well?" Marcus asked impatiently. Kai smiled and turned on the stereo.

"Round one goes to Sam!" he announced. Marcus shook his head and laughed.

I collected myself and walked back to the parking lot. Sam walked by my side the entire way, not saying a word. Slowly I felt peace settling back into my mind. She even held my hand the last thirty yards or so. My fires cooled inside me as the simplest of thoughts comforted me…Sam was there for me when I fell. She picked me back up. She healed me.

Ember

Sunburn_14

~Sunburn: Fuel~

Monday morning – 8:01 a.m. – August 21ˢᵗ.

"Two weeks," Kai said with the biggest smile.

"What happens in two weeks?" I asked still tired from the long weekend.

He removed a piece of paper from his pocket and handed it to me while he turned down the volume of his car stereo. He drove faster as his nervous excitement took over.

"Two weeks from now we will be performing in all our glory. It's the beginning of the world dominance known as KID EGO." His arms rose above his head like some silly wrestler on a pay per view event.

"A night with KID EGO," I read the flyer aloud. "Music and dancing at Club Tsunami."

"Yup!" he smiled even bigger.

"And we're KID EGO?" I asked looking down at the same two words tattooed along my left forearm. It was a tattoo I had gotten a few years back, just before I started healing myself. My former band members said it fit me perfectly. They were probably right about that at the time but now I wasn't too proud of it.

"This is it my friend," he sighed as he leaned back in his chair.

"You think we'll be ready in two weeks?" I asked.

"Silly rabbit, tricks are for kids," he laughed. "You know we're ready."

"It's been over a year since I have been on a real stage," my voice sank with nervousness. Kai slowly leaned over to me, placing his hand on my shoulder.

"Don't worry your pretty little head about that. You have got much bigger things to worry about that night." He looked at me serious and pointed out the front of the windshield as the car pulled into the school parking lot.

"Uh oh," Marcus whined from the back seat. The cool familiar scent of rain rushed through the cars open windows just as I realized what my new best friend was pointing at. Asia's Jeep was parked right next to us in the parking lot. My stomach turned over on itself.

"Uh oh," I mimicked Marcus' tone.

I stepped from the car crumbling under the weight of my nerves as Asia's scent found me. She stood tall and beautiful under a giant tree on the campus lawn. Her arms were folded tight with her heavy blue eyes on fire. She was anything but happy to see me.

"Uh oh," Kai whispered to himself and walked up to me.

"My head hurts," I calmly said as he approached. He smiled and nodded, knowing that I had already decided to try and talk to her, even if I hadn't admitted it to myself yet.

"Good luck brother," he encouraged. I swallowed a dry lump down my throat and started walking towards her angry face. My energy had already started to build, even before the sun completely disappeared.

"Is Lucy all right?" I asked softly but with confidence. Her eyes filled with even more cold blue contempt.

"She's fine," she said cold. The wind blew around us, blowing her hair across her face.

Ember

"Good..." I started to say.

"I told you that she was off limits Max!" She sounded mad but her voice seemed to be calm. I was getting the impression that she wasn't really mad at me, but forcing the anger on herself. But I couldn't figure out why.

"Asia I didn't mean to hurt your feelings," I apologized. The thunder began to rumble over our heads. "I thought I was doing the right thing." I was growing defensive.

"By throwing your testosterone all over the beach?" she accused and stepped toward me. When she did her smell dazed me for a second.

"Or were you just showing off for your blonde friend?" her voice sounded hurt now.

"She has nothing to do with the other night! My actions were completely noble. I only wanted Lucy to be safe...nothing more." It came out a little angrier than I was expecting and her eyes flashed with nervousness.

"Is that so?" she bit back and the thunder shook again. The crowd that had gathered behind us squealed with delight at the approaching water works. Lightning flashed and I looked to the sky and then back to her fiery eyes.

"Calm down please," I threatened. That only made her angrier.

"I saw the look in your eyes Max. That fight had nothing to do with being noble and everything to do with putting Samantha's ex in his place." She was so hurt but using the pain to fuel her anger. This wasn't about Lucy; this was about her being jealous. I was lost in my own thoughts when she grabbed my collar and forced me to look in her devastating eyes again.

"You did what you did for you...admit it," she roared. Now I was mad and my hands filled with heat. But I wasn't just mad with her, I was mad at myself because she was partially right. I wanted to get into it with Devon for my own selfish reasons.

"Maybe your right." I conceded. "But why does that bother you so much?" I quickly threw back at her pout. Her face tightened and she bit her lower lip.

"It doesn't," she insisted but I could see through the hole I had just punched in her armor.

"Yes it does. And I think that scares you Asia." I was firm in my claim.

"You're wrong!" her voice wavered and she turned her face away from mine. So I made her look at me again. My hand found her chin and gently pulled it back toward my eyes. Her skin was chilly and the heat I was generating made tiny goose bumps pop up all over her body instantly. Thunder cracked again and she began to shiver slightly.

"Why are you so afraid to admit to yourself that this isn't about Samantha or Lucy?" My hands fell to her sides.

"You're scared of the way I make you feel," I scolded. My temper was almost totally out of control now and so was hers. My head started to pound with how beautiful her doubts were to me and my emotions took over.

I pulled her against me and kissed her passionately. Rain fell like a tidal wave and all the surrounding students ran for dryer accommodations. The morning bell rang but I barely heard it over our pounding hearts. At first her lips embraced mine, sending my head spinning as the fresh rain cooled my heating face. But her anger took over again and she slowly pulled away, and shoved me with a strength that surprised me.

"Don't Max!" she warned with tears in her eyes. They were hard to see in the falling rain but they were there.

"Don't make me feel this..." She stopped herself as Lucy walked up from behind her. Her eye was still swollen and red but it looked better. Asia's words hurt more than I thought they should have and I wasn't sure if I could keep my temper under control any longer. As the steam started pouring off my face...I snapped.

"Fine..." I roared from behind my clenching teeth. The rain slid down my bangs and past my face. "Go and hide Asia!" I snapped. Her eyes searched mine for a moment and my panic button went off. I shook the rain from my hair and stormed past her and then past Lucy. The thunder rolled behind me as if it was speaking to me and I knew she was watching me walk away. The thought only made things worse.

"Just go!" I yelled without looking back. My hands found my ear buds and mp3 player, and I yanked it from my shirt and pocket violently. Flames covered it in my right hand with a white hot flash. Quickly I tossed them to the ground and stormed off. The rain quickly put the burning hardware out and Asia and Lucy walked off together. They didn't say one word to each other as they left. Shortly after, the rain left too.

I decided not to go to any classes that day and continued walking past the school buildings. I walked down the road until the school could no longer be seen and kept walking. I walked all day. Even when my cell phone flashed with Kai's number, I ignored it and kept walking. Eventually I found myself back at home, locked in my room. I came out for a quick dinner with Frank but returned to myself made prison afterwards. I didn't take any calls from anyone. Not even when Sam's number came up on the caller I.D.

I spent the rest of the night listening to the distant storm that seemed to circle my neighborhood and call to me.

"...Let the sun fall down over me..."

~Days Of The Week: Stone Temple Pilots~

Tuesday – Biology – 9:50 a.m. – August 22nd.

It took all my strength not to look at Sam's inviting smile as I sat with my neck all tensed up. She looked worried for me and scared to talk to me but I couldn't really blame her. I was giving off a very serious 'don't bother me' vibe but her silence did not last long.

"Morning hero, where have you been hiding?" she asked soft and sweet.

"Not this morning Sam. I'm in no mood." I sounded much grumpier than I really was, but she only took my attitude as a challenge.

"Let's get things straight Max, you may be able to avoid my phone calls at home but here I will not let you ignore me," she said serious yet her tone still felt very sweet.

"I'm sorry I haven't called you back." I tried not to look at her smile but failed miserably.

"That's all right. I was just worried about that smile of yours. If you don't use it, you just might lose it." Her smile was so warm and inviting.

Ember

"I've just had a hard couple of days," I sulked.

"Yeah...I heard about yesterday morning." Her smile started to fade.

"You did?" I asked embarrassed.

"It's a small school...everyone heard about it," she said and then fell quiet for a second. The tension in the room doubled. I wasn't sure what to say.

"She's very beautiful Max," she spoke softly but with that rigid confidence still there. I didn't know how to respond to her words and froze in my seat.

The teacher began the day's lesson and complete silence was the main rule she enforced during it. That was probably for the best anyway, I had no idea what to say to Sam, after her last observation. I watched as she nervously tapped her pen in her hand as the lesson continued. That gave me an idea and I flipped open my notebook, to an empty page, and began doodling.

I spent the rest of the class scratching away and I couldn't tell you a thing about the day's lesson. I was in my own little world. With only minutes left in class I slid the piece of paper to Sam and whispered in her ear.

"So are you."

I smiled as she unfolded the paper and saw herself. In the short amount of time, I'd drawn a sketch of her. It wasn't completely finished but enough that hopefully she would get the point. I concentrated on her big green eyes and the curls of her hair as it trailed along her neck and shoulders. She blushed instantly and her eyes filled with moisture. I guess she liked it.

"I love it," her voice cracked.

"Thank you again," I whispered. "For finding that ever elusive smile of mine."

"My pleasure," she said beaming.

153

We walked each other to our next class, where we spent the entire hour staring at each other, not saying a word. Kai watched us as if we were crazy. Samantha and Max sitting in a tree. We passed notes back and forth and my mind was racing. I thought about so many things that hour. What would it be like to kiss her? Should I ask her out tonight? Is that moving too fast? How the heck was she able to make me smile so easily? I thought about everything. Everything except Asia. The rest of the day flew by and it felt fantastic.

Wednesday - 3:33 p.m. - August 23rd.

Today was a turning point for me as I decided to forget all about my troubles and threw my attention into my school work. Well, that wasn't entirely true. My new found excitement about school work had everything to do with spending time with Sam. Our friendship was growing stronger and much faster than I had planned. Her brilliant smile and sensitive emerald eyes had me floating at school. Another day flew by and I found myself walking to the parking lot with a smile.

Sam was waiting for me on the hood of her car, with her legs crossed. She had a huge smile and a wave waiting for me.

"Would you like a ride home?" she asked. I smiled and quickly tossed my bag and guitar in the back.

"I thought you'd never ask." We drove off and thunder rumbled far away in the distance.

At my house, I found that Frank had made it home from work early. I thought he would get a kick to see Sam walk in with me. So in the driveway, I worked up enough courage to ask her inside.

154

"Do you want to come in for a few?" My mouth was dry and my voice sounded weird because of it.

"Sure," she said.

As we walked in Oz ran to her feet and sniffed her rambunctiously. His tail whipped back and forth like a helicopter. He liked her immediately.

"This is Oz. He kinda runs things around here," I teased and he barked at my comment.

"Pleased to meet you little sheriff," she scratched him behind his ears.

"Samantha...is that you?" Frank asked. He tried his best to sound uninterested but failed completely. She offered a hand shake but he insisted on a hug.

"It's been awhile Mr. Valentine, nice to see you again."

"Samantha please...call me Frank." His smile shined.

"Frank it is." A sigh of relief escaped her mouth. Frank winked at me and I gestured for him to calm down. I set my school stuff on the couch and we all sat in the kitchen.

"So, how long has it been? Two...three years maybe?" Frank asked as he poured us a couple drinks.

"At least three..." She glanced my way. "The company picnic I think."

"That's right." He smiled and I could sense he was up to something and I became very nervous. "I see you've taken to my nephew," he said coyly.

"Easy uncle," I warned as I almost choked on my drink. I couldn't believe he was asking her that and I blushed.

"It's fine Max," she comforted me. "He's right." She gently nudged me. "That is when you keep that temper of yours under wraps," she teased. I groaned knowing exactly what was coming next.

"Mad Max!" they both said in unison, sending my embarrassment into another level of pain. They both laughed uncontrollably as I stood up from the table.

"I'm going to go and freshen up," I pouted. They continued laughing as I headed for the bathroom.

"You know...I have to be careful with him," Sam said.

"Why is that?" Frank asked as he wiped tears from the corners of his eyes.

"As you can tell...he bruises easy." Her smile brightened and Frank filled with pride.

"I almost forgot how clever you were Samantha," he paused. "But in Max's defense, he really hates that name."

"But it's so cute. It's so him."

"I can't say I blame him, but with his temperament, he has earned it," Frank smiled.

"Has he always been this dramatic?" she asked sweetly.

"Yup...it's in his nature. He inherited that from his mom's side," he said and peered around the corner of the hallway. Sam watched with a smile.

"Did you know that Max isn't his real name?" Frank grinned widely and Sam stared at him speechless. "Max was a name that just sort of stuck with him. He hates his real name."

"What's his real name?"

"Madison," he winked. Her mouth dropped open.

156

"Madison Valentine," she said slowly.

"After the first few times he lost his temper, some kids from school saddled him with the name Mad Max. They took his first name and dropped the end of it and added the Max. It fit his personality so well but he hated it." He sipped his drink and continued.

"He embraced the name Max around 3rd or 4th grade I think."

"That's great," she said suspiciously.

"No one's ever been able to address him by his true name since. He won't even acknowledge it," he laughed.

"Drama queen," she whispered.

"Now promise me you will use this information for good and not evil, my dear."

"I promise." Her eyes were ablaze with so many thoughts.

Later as I walked from the bathroom I noticed Sam had found her way into my bedroom and was quietly looking at the pictures on my dresser. As she began to lift the one on the end, the one I had placed face down, I spoke up.

"Hey," I called out. She jumped a little and turned to face me quickly.

"I was just checking out your room. I hope you don't mind?" she asked politely. My eyes fell to the picture she had almost turned over and I found myself lost in thought.

"Max?" she asked.

"Oh...sorry about that. Yeah, it's fine." The cobwebs began to retreat. She could see I was hiding something though. "It's not much, but its home."

"It's perfect," she smiled.

Sam stayed for another hour before leaving. I felt excited about seeing her again and I fell asleep easily that night. No storm clouds to be seen...outside my window or in my dreams.

Thursday - 12:36 p.m. - August 24th.

It was lunch break and Sam was at my side, as the band practiced all hour. We were all tucked away in our usual spot at lunch, with a small crowd surrounding us. Devon kept a watchful eye but he did it from a distance. He did not look happy.

At the end of one particular slow song that the girls in the audience seemed to enjoy, Sam leaned into me. I could feel her breath on my neck as her hand found my leg. I turned my face into hers and watched her eyes for the okay to kiss her. I was swept up in her sea of green, ready to fall over, when a tap on my shoulder ruined the moment.

"Hey bro...that was pretty good. I think the girls were digging that one," Kai said oblivious. I looked at him annoyed and nodded.

"Thank you captain obvious." I was being overly irritated but I didn't care, I just wanted the moment back.

"Oh," he said finally understanding what he had done. Sam laughed but never let go of my hand.

Lunch ended and we all moved on to our other classes but I had noticed that I was being watched from across the school yard. Lucy watched closely as Sam and I left. That filled me with a nervous heat.

Ember

~Oxygen: Colbie Caillat~

4:02 p.m.

After school, outside my house, Sam and I sat in her car again, with her car stereo serenading us. She was acting very nervous and that made me uneasy.

"Is everything alright?" I asked. Her eyelids pulled together as she inhaled a deep breath and a smile curled around the edges of her mouth.

"Will you go out with me sometime?" She looked toward the dash of her car and continued. "No more teasing...no more flirting...just you and me." Her eyes fell upon me again.

"Together."

"Okay," I said softly.

"Tomorrow night."

"Tomorrow," I agreed. A few moments passed.

"I guess I should get home soon." Her posture became uncomfortable. "I'll pick you up in the morning, if you'd like?" Her voice felt unsure. That's when I decided to make a move.

I leaned my body toward her slowly and stopped with my face only inches from hers. My breath had become hot and my hands filled with heat. Her eyes watched me closely but she never pulled away. I let my lips graze past her right cheek and her amazing skin, intoxicated me. I slowly brushed her hair behind her left ear and she noticed the burning heat coming from my hand. I was scared that maybe it was too hot but she never moved or said a word. Her breath grew quicker and the windows slightly fogged with the growing heat. My lips slid past hers and stopped on her left cheek. I felt her hand pull at my shirt and I stared into her jade eyes and waited.

My eyes followed the lines of her neck and muscles until they collided with her collarbone. Her head tilted slightly as I brought my mouth to hers and inhaled her kiss. All of it. Every inch of her lips I tasted until we ran out of breath. As I pulled myself back I found her eyes still tightly closed and her hand was gripped around the collar of my shirt.

"I would like that very much," I said in the softest tone I could.

"Huh?" she stuttered as her eyes opened again and focused right through mine.

"A ride," I said and she blinked at my response. "In the morning," I continued. She was dazed and it was taking everything I had to control my smile. If I didn't keep it under control I was afraid that it would split my head completely open with the joy that was radiating inside of me. Not to mention my chest felt like it was filled with lava, from my excitement.

"Oh..." she finally said. "Okay...see you then." She smiled with flushed cheeks.

"Until then," I said and jumped out of the car and strolled to my front door. It was a perfect moment and my head was spinning from the heat I was generating. It felt like a thousand tiny fires wanted to explode from me but I managed to keep them subdued. I turned to wave goodbye before she drove away but found that she was right there in front of me.

"Is everything o..." I tried to spit out but her lips cut me off. Her body pushed forward as she pressed her mouth against mine and I had no time to catch my breath. Her hands found the back of my neck and her legs outstretched as far as they could, to reach my mouth comfortably. This kiss was much quicker but it was no less potent. My legs felt weak and my chest felt like it was about to be covered in flames any second.

"Goodbye Max," she whispered. I was speechless. She quickly ran back to her car, very proud of herself. Her long hair whipped through the air like a golden silk ribbon and my heart dropped into my stomach.

"I'm in trouble," I whispered as she drove away. I had given in...I had let her inside my walls. I had spent so many years crafting those walls and she tore through them as if they were made of paper. A steaming trail of nervous heat escaped my mouth and that's when it hit me...I couldn't keep doing this around Sam. She needed to know the truth. If I dragged my feet long enough, she would surely figure it out herself. She was as smart as they come, but that wasn't good enough. She deserved the truth and she deserved to hear it from me. I had to tell her the truth. All of it.

Friday afternoon – 4:32 p.m. – August 25th.

Sam pulled me from her car and dragged me up the driveway. Her house was modest but very beautiful...just like her. The front door was deep red with a rectangular window in the center. The crimson door was surrounded by yellow walls with big rose bushes running along each side of the home. She stopped me at the door and grabbed both of my hands. Her eyes found mine with a smile. Her touch was cool and calming against my warming skin. She was complete confidence and I was a shell of fear. She popped up on her toes and planted a sweet little kiss on my lips.

"Thanks for coming over," she whispered.

She opened the door and we entered her living room. Her home was quiet and peaceful. It felt like her, safe. Slowly I surveyed my surroundings and found my eyes pulled to a large picture frame above one of her living room couches. It was of her parents. They were locked in a close embrace on the beach with the sun cascading around them. It was personal and beautiful. A romantic movie frozen in time.

"Wow," I gushed. Sam let me have a moment to enjoy the picture.

"That's my parents," she spoke softly.

"They look so happy. I love it. I've always enjoyed photography like this...it's like a moment in time," I said. She walked up to me with a curious smile.

"Ahh...then you have chosen your company wisely," she boasted as she directed my eyes to the opposite wall. It was covered in about a dozen or so picture frames. All of the frames were black to bring out the features of the black and white photos they enclosed. My eyes grew wider.

"It's kind of my hobby," she said as she slid herself closer to me. I absorbed each image slowly, enjoying each one more and more as I did. They were pictures of all the local beaches at different times of day. One beach in particular was much too familiar as I recognized the crescent moon shaped cove, where I first met Asia. My eyes pushed themselves from it quickly and Sam noticed my reaction immediately.

"What do you think Max?" she asked with a hint of skepticism. I kept my eyes focused on the photos when I finally answered.

"They're amazing," I smiled. "Take this one for example." I pointed to one on the end. It was a simple shot of a couple palm trees reaching for the ocean with the sun setting in the background. In the middle of the beach was one lone body. Just a little girl with pigtails in her hair and a giant seashell in her hands. I said giant because it was the size of her head and she couldn't have been more than 4 or 5 years old, judging by her size. It was basically just an outline of a girl because the setting sun cast her as a shadow.

"The way the trees bring your focus to the lines of the water coming in is genius." Sam looked at me as if she would burst with excitement.

"That's my favorite too," she said. My eyes caught hers and they seemed to be searching mine for something. I tried to distract her curiosity quickly.

"Great minds think alike," I teased.

"The little girl was only there for about fifteen-seconds before her father ran up and took her away. It was a one in a million shot, but I caught it," she added.

I didn't mean to seem distant at that moment but all I could see was Mia with her arms in the air as she spun around in circles in slow motion.

"The girl is my favorite thing about the photo," I said distant and Sam leaned in and gently grabbed my hand.

"Why's that?" she asked.

"Just reminds me of someone," I forced a smile. She sensed my pain and slowly reached down taking my wrist into her hands and exposed my tattoo. She stared at the three letters for a second.

"Mia's your sister," she said as if she should have realized it sooner. I just looked at her patiently. "I can't believe I thought this was a former flames name. I feel so stupid."

"It's okay." I didn't want to talk about this now.

"I remember the day she passed away," she said and my chest felt heavy. "One afternoon my dad came home early and he was upset. I overheard him telling my mom that your uncle had gotten some terrible news." My arm stiffened as she spoke.

"He would have to cover for Frank's shift at work because he had to fly back to help with the funeral." She reached up and slid my bangs behind my ears and smiled softly.

"My dad came in to my room and gave me the biggest hug I had ever gotten from him. He told me how much he loved me and I didn't fully understand what had happened, until I was older. I think I was about nine." She finally stopped talking and I felt the tears behind my eyes.

"Mia used to wear her hair in pigtails everyday." I put my hands in my pockets. "She was six...I was ten." I had to stop talking before I wouldn't be able to stop and with a quick glance she understood.

"I'm sorry Max." She gently pulled my hands from my pockets and slid her tiny body up to mine. I had already begun to warm up. Her lips found mine again and we spent the next few minutes there in a perfect embrace. As great as the moment was, my mind could not shake the image of my little sister. I had to tell her about my secret. A rush of questions swallowed me. Will she understand my demons? Will she hate me? Will she be scared of me?

The pizza arrived shortly after and she convinced me to eat it in her room. What was going on here? Inviting a boy into her room with no parents around. She was supposed to be the good girl. Her room was very clean and very soft and warm. There were a few more of her photos neatly hung around her room. Her computer was on but asleep with a pair of 'The Rolling Stones' lips floating around the screen. There was a giant mirror in the corner and it had photos tucked inside the sides of the frame. Mostly friends and family, but one picture stood out and made my skin crawl. It was a picture of Devon with his arms around her and they both looked disgustingly happy. Hate welled up in my throat immediately. I turned from it to find Sam holding her camera in her hands.

"Smile big handsome," she smiled. It was hard to do with Devon's disapproving eyes watching me. She clicked a few shots and I started to become self-conscious. I walked up to her slowly and gently took the camera from her hands.

With a devilish grin I said, "My turn." Her face filled with uneasiness.

"Alright," she sounded anything but all right. Reluctantly she posed for a few shots at her window and a couple more sitting on her bed. I was enjoying myself when she suddenly stopped me. Her hands pulled the camera from me and she set it on her desk.

"What's up?" I asked.

"I was thinking about the first time we kissed." Her lips curved with a smile.

"What about it?"

"I know this is going to sound crazy but when you kissed me...I felt things." She was cautious.

"I felt things too," I teased with a wink but I knew exactly what she meant. She didn't find anything funny and continued.

"It felt like we were in a sauna...no, that's not exactly what I mean." She collected her thoughts. "I felt warm inside, like a fever breaking throughout my body." Her eyes were fixed on mine.

"And you were..."

"On fire," I interrupted. She nodded slowly.

"When I got home I found this." She pulled her hair from her shoulder and exposed the back of her neck and her left ear. Peaking from her hair was a faint but obvious burn scar from my fingertip. She stared at me with a longing to understand and I laid down my defenses. All right Max...this is it.

"Sam I need to show you something but I need you to promise me that you will not freak out," I sounded so scared.

"Show me what?" her voice began to tremble.

"Sam please," I was officially scared now. "Promise me."

"I promise," she whispered.

Truth_16

~Policy Of Truth: Depeche Mode~

With a long deep breath I turned and took a pair of scissors from Sam's desk. I slowly opened them up, until the plastic handles stuck against the cold metal. I stared at her one last time and realized that this was it, no turning back now. Things would never be the same after this moment. Her eyes followed my hand without breathing and she was obviously scared now. The blades of the scissors were cold against my burning touch and I took another deep breath.

"Just breathe," I said to myself and quickly sliced open my left palm. I dragged the blade along my wrist and down my forearm.

"Max..." she gasped.

"Trust me," I said as I pulled the bloody scissors from my arm and set them back down. The faintest line of smoke danced upward and Sam's face fell white as her blood drained from it. I thought that she might run away in horror but she held her ground. My blood poured from the fresh wound before the steam started to rise from the open slit. As more steam came off my arm the wound began to pull together and a red and white flame glowed along my arm. Her eyes intensified and her body leaned backwards against her bed. The flame grew to the top of my arm and with one final burst, engulfed my hand in a yellow and orange teardrop of fire. It twisted and swayed with the movement of my fingers and I could feel that the wound was totally healed now. I watched her reaction from behind the flame and then let it fade away. The fire disappeared as quickly as it had appeared and I turned my arm toward her to show her that I was okay.

"Surprise," I said nervously.

Sam only looked at me in disbelief. I brushed my hair from my eyes and crossed my arms impatiently. She leaned forward and stood up from her bed, stepping toward me. I took a slight step back.

"Please don't be scared of me. Sam, I would never hurt you," I swore. She said nothing and reached out for my arm. Her eyes inspected every inch closely. Her fingers felt freezing against my newly healed skin. I found that quite comforting.

"Does it hurt?" she asked in a whisper.

"The wound hurts like hell but only for a second. Then there is only the heat." I let a half smile creep from the side of my mouth.

"Could you do that to me too?" she asked as if she already knew the answer. My hand found her earlobe and I slowly caressed the scar behind it.

"Yes, I can fix that scar for you." My hand filled with heat again.

"No," she exclaimed as her hand pulled at mine. I froze with confusion.

"I think I want to keep it." Her smile returned.

"Why?" I didn't understand how she could possibly want to keep it.

"Because every time I see or feel it I will think of our first kiss." She moved her body into mine. "I don't ever want to lose that."

"I guess this means you're not too scared of me?" I asked.

"A little..." Her confidence was back. "But it doesn't change the way I feel for you."

Ember

"And how is that?" I swallowed and waited for the worst possible answer. Her arms wrapped themselves around me and she buried her head in my chest.

"I'm falling for you Max." Her words shook my very core but I felt safe at the same time.

"You are?"

"I can see the real you." She looked up at my scared expression.

"The real me?" I choked.

"I see the boy who hides behind his bangs when he's nervous. The boy who believes that if he's alone he won't be hurt again." She took my wrist in her hand and covered Mia's name with her other hand.

"And I see the big brother that you will forever be."

Her last words knocked the wind out of me and I pulled myself away from her grasp. Without any more stalling, I began to tell her about that day. That horrible afternoon I've dreamt of almost every night since.

"I told my mother once that I thought Mia looked cute in pigtails and she overheard me. From that day on she would only let our mom fix her hair in two little pigtails. She told mom that...'If my big brother says I look pretty like this...than that's good enough for me.' The thought still makes me smile." Sam settled in and watched me patiently.

"She was wearing those little pigtails the day of the accident. They were wrapped in two long red ribbons, because that was her big brothers favorite color," I laughed softly.

"It sounds like she was your biggest fan." She tried to sound light hearted but I ignored her and kept talking.

169

"We were both sitting in the back seat of the family car. She was fast asleep and I was busy staring out my window at the scenery. We had just spent a week up in the mountains, at some over- priced lodge that promised fun for the whole family. It was supposed to be covered in snow, ready to fill our week with hours of skiing and snow ball fights but it wasn't meant to be. There was hardly any snow and when we arrived, Mother Nature never supplied us with more. Except for the night that we left." I inhaled a deep breath to gather my bearings.

"So I watched the clumps of new snow that were spread along the landscape. We were driving on a stretch of road that hugged an edge of the mountain for a few miles. I found out later that it's one of the most dangerous stretches of road in northern California. It was known for patches of black ice during certain months of the year. It seems we were lucky enough to experience that first hand." My attempt at a joke just made me feel more alone.

"I remember looking over the edge of this mountain thinking that it was so far down. The thought made my head spin a little. My dad asked our mom to check on Mia because she hadn't made a sound in a while. I can still see my mom's smile as she turned around in the front seat to check on us. She was so happy," my voice cracked. Sam moved around to the side of me.

"About then was when we hit the first patch of ice. It spun our car sideways in an instant, sending my head into my window and jolting my sister awake. Her face filled with shock, which made me heat up instantly. The windows fogged quickly as my dad had almost brought the car back under control. That's when we hit the second patch of ice," I stopped talking long enough to look at Sam and she looked sad. That almost made me stop right then and there.

"The car spun the opposite way this time, toward the far side of the road, away from the cliffs edge. The tires clipped something and the next thing I knew, we were on our side. My mother was thrown from the car and she lied motionless in a near-by ditch, unconscious. She hardly had a mark on her but my dad wasn't as lucky. He wasn't moving and stuck against the air bags, bleeding from his head. Mia hung from her seatbelt, above me with her tiny arms reaching for me. She was crying and calling my name but all I could hear was the ringing in my head. My body had already started steaming. Back then I couldn't control it very well. I kept telling her it would be okay and not to worry. I was wrong." A single tear cut down my face and I wiped it away.

"The smell of gasoline was growing stronger and that filled me with a crippling fear. My little gift doesn't play well with gasoline. The thought freaked me out and I ignited, uncontrollably but only for a moment. In that moment I had burned through the seat belt and I was free. I reached up toward Mia to free her too but when my burning hands found hers she screamed in pain. I took a second to calm my racing fear and for a few minutes it seemed to be working. I reached up and undid her seatbelt. I had to fight it because it was jammed. Just as I figured it out and relief began to wash over Mia's face, I heard the worst possible noise." I stopped drained.

"Go on Max," Sam pushed gently.

"The sound of screeching tires from the other lane pierced the cab of the car. Mia screamed as the truck slammed into the front of the car, spinning us like a top across the icy road. The stranger's truck exploded on impact, sending a fire ball into the sky and our vehicle toward the cliff. The metal roof exploded with sparks as we twisted toward the railing out of control." Anger had seeped into my voice as my eyes filled with rage.

"We were already in bad shape. We didn't need that damn drunk driver to make things worse!" I shook the thought from my head quickly as Sam gasped with a stuttered breath. Now she really understood my hatred for alcohol.

"Everything was spinning and there was a buzzing in my ears as I bounced around the back of the car. Flames erupted from me as I tried to find my footing. I finally found that footing as the car came to a rest on its roof, at the edge of the road barrier. The cool mountain air rushed inside the car and my flames disappeared. Everything was quiet and I started to believe things could still be okay. I could finally get Mia out of this nightmare and get us some help. There was just one problem with that...I was the only one left in the car." I refreshed my dry throat with a sip of the soda we had been drinking with dinner. Sam leaned into me and noticed how much heat I was generating.

"My dad had been thrown from the car and was lying in the middle of the road. Mia was nowhere to be seen and I began to panic. My arms tensed and filled with burning orange flames as I focused my eyes all around the devastation. There was smoke and ash and burning gas but no little sister. I called for her but all I heard in response was the echo of my own voice. I climbed from the wreckage, my arms still full of flames, and called for her again. From the corner of my bloody eye I saw something flickering in the breeze, just on the other side of the bent barrier. It was red and sparkling like it was covered in tiny diamonds. It was Mia's ribbon from her hair and it was covered in glass." I stopped talking as Sam started to cry softly. Slowly I took a long deep breath and continued.

"She was covered in it and her body clung to the side of the cliff, not moving. I could hear her voice whimpering quietly and the sound filled me with hope. She was still alive! I wasn't too late! I stumbled forward, dizzy and crying with my arms still burning. I began to hop over the barrier railing when I realized just how bad things had become. The car couldn't have stopped at a worst spot. There was only a few feet of dirt past the metal railing and then it turned into a dead drop. Just a little over 300 feet...I think." Clearing my throat, I found it hard to continue; it hurt so much to be saying these words.

"Mia's body was hanging half way over the edge, so I tried once more to calm the rushing fire on my arms. I wouldn't be able to pull her to safety while I burned out of control. It was working until I heard the sound of clothes slowing ripping. In my dazed state I wasn't sure what the sound was until it was too late. It was the fabric of her white summer dress that was holding her entire weight from sliding over the edge. Her silhouette disappeared into the blackness and I lunged forward with everything I had left. My blazing arms singed the air hotter and hotter as I lost control. My right hand caught the back of her dress, filling it with flames instantly and waking her from her slumber." My eyes filled with tears and I was starting to feel sick to my stomach.

"As I pulled her up, her big brown eyes turned to me in pain and she called out to me, 'Max it hurts!' That's when her dress gave out and she started to fall again. I was in shock and instinctively I grabbed her hands. They were already bloody and broken when the flames began searing her flesh. She screamed louder and I screamed along with her, trying not to pass out. My head was spinning and the smell of everything made me sick to my stomach. Her tiny voice begged me to help her over and over again as I started to black out. I couldn't control any part of my gift now and the flames intensified with my anguish. Time slowed down and her hands couldn't take anymore. They crumbled away from me as she fell. The darkness over took me and I passed out with the image of my little sister falling away from me...on fire. She was calling my name." I couldn't look at Sam now. I felt disgusted with myself. She wiped her eyes and sat down on the floor next to me. I hadn't even noticed that I was on the floor of her bedroom.

"I woke up two days later in the hospital, remembering everything that happened vividly. My mom had already packed her things and left us without a word. My dad was pretty banged up...physically and emotionally. He didn't talk too much in those first few days. He was different now, like a ghost. He had lost the woman he loved most in this world and his beautiful baby girl. He healed quickly, all except his heart. There is no doctor in the world that can heal that. I healed even faster but things were never the same again between us." I tried to smile but I couldn't.

"My father didn't physically leave me until last year when he had a heart attack, but I think I was just as dead to him the moment I let her fall. The thing he didn't seem to understand though was that he had lost a wife and a daughter, but I had lost the same. Now I was losing a father too." I shrugged slightly with a massive headache pounding in my head. I was completely drained and wanted to leave.

"Max...I had no idea," her voice was weak and shaking. She looked as if her heart was broken too and in that moment all I wanted to do was hold her.

"It's okay, things are better now," I lied and let a fake smile appear.

"Don't lie to me...things are not okay," she scolded as she wiped more tears from her cheeks. She slid herself in front of me and ran her hands along my cheeks.

"But they will be," she spoke soft and soothing. Her lips pressed gently against my closed eyelids and my head felt better immediately. I kissed her back and could taste the fresh tears on her lips and my insides warmed just enough to make the headache go away completely.

Ember

"Sam...I think I need to go," I said as I stood up.

"I think you need to stay Max," she said determined.

"I think it would be best if I left." My heart was pounding now.

"It's barely 7:30...you don't have to go." Her eyes filled with worry.

"Yes, I do," I said looking at the tattoo of Mia's name. "I'll call you tomorrow. Promise."

"Let me at least give you a ride home." She was upset now and that made me feel guilty for sharing so much with her. It was not her burden...it was mine.

"I'll be fine. It's only a few miles to my house." I leaned in and kissed her lips gently.

"I'll call," I said again and left her with tears running down her face.

I needed this walk. I needed this time to clear my head again. It amazed me just how much my sister's loss still hurt. I saw Mia's face every step of the way home. I felt horrible. I felt guilty.

I felt alone.

MADISON DANIEL

Ember

~I Don't Trust Myself (With Loving You): John Mayer~

Friday night – 10:02 p.m.

I had been walking in the dark for a couple hours now when I finally made it to the end of the driveway to my house. It had been a long emotional night at Sam's and I was so relieved to see the glimmer of my porch light. There was no sign of my uncle who had planned a night out with some of the guys from work. He must have been having a good time because he was usually in bed by this time. I was glad that he wasn't home though; I was in no mood to talk to anyone right now.

The night air was becoming quite chilly as I walked to the front door. In the distance I could hear the faint sounds of a thunderstorm. That's when I first saw the gift that had been left on the door step. A brand new electric guitar, with all the trimmings, was leaned up against the door. Its paint finish was so shiny that the moon reflected brightly off of it and that made it hard to tell exactly what color it was. I leaned in for a closer look and it was love at first sight.

"Whoa."

It was jet black with a rosewood fret board and sapphire blue inlays. It had the shape of a long lean dancer and reminded me of Asia. This outrageous gift had all the signs that it was from her. The color and the shape of the instrument was enough of a clue but this particular brand of guitar was extremely expensive. I would be surprised if it could be bought anywhere on the island. That meant that it had to be imported.

The second clue was the giant blood red colored bow that was tied neatly to the neck of the guitar. I slowly ran my fingers along it and found that it was made of silk.

"Nice touch Asia," I teased.

A small tag dangled from one of the tuning keys. It gently wiggled in the cool breeze and I didn't even have to pull it up to read it. In big bold red letters it read...

"I'M SORRY... XOXO."

I stood there quietly for a few minutes, trying to make sense of the gift. Was this supposed to make things better?

"Did she really think I was this shallow?" I grunted to myself. All she had to do was throw some money at me and I would cave in? The nerve of her.

My anger overtook my hands and I almost knocked the guitar over as I shoved my way inside the front door. I even started to slam the door behind me when the musician in me gave in. I quickly turned around and scooped up the work of art in my greedy hands. It was much lighter than I was expecting and it felt wonderful in my grasp. I couldn't help myself. The sheer beauty and craftsmanship of it called to me. A haunting thought stopped me in my tracks. I felt the same way about Asia...and she knew it. This was her way of showing me that.

I wanted to hate her for that but I couldn't...not even a little bit. How can I possibly hate someone that felt like a part of me? Someone who seemed to call to every aspect of my body physically and emotionally.

Like a shadow in the dark I stood quietly holding my new prize when I realized that Oz hadn't greeted me

178

yet. He always came running when he knew I was home. At that moment my senses were hit with cherry blossoms and I almost fell over. Thunder rumbled outside as if teasing me and my blood filled with heat. I ran to my room and was stopped dead in my tracks by the sight before my tired eyes.

Asia was sitting in the middle of my bed, her long tone legs folded together in her lap. Her body was straight as an arrow and Oz was stretched across her legs with his paws folded in the air above him. I could barely hear him growling because it sounded more like he was purring. Traitor, I thought as I saw how happy and content he was.

She was slowly caressing his stomach with one hand and holding her other hand up to her ear. Her eyes were closed as she sat rocking back and forth, like she was dancing. Her hand concealed the ear buds to a shiny new mp3 player that settled in front of her on the bed. The chords swayed softly as she rocked from side to side. She was wearing a black sports bra that seemed to accentuate her natural curves and exposed her belly. A tiny diamond piercing winked at me from her belly button and I almost choked on my tongue. She was also wearing tiny black shorts. The kind a runner in a marathon might wear and they exposed most of her legs. Her feet were bare and tapping along to whatever music she was lost in at the moment. Another dozen diamonds stole my attention as they danced along the chain around her left ankle. I stood there silently gripping my new guitar and found it harder and harder to breathe.

"Well, do you like it?" she asked without opening her eyes. I was afraid to say anything for fear of what angry tirade might escape my lips. Also, I didn't exactly want the view to go away yet. I tightened my lips and said nothing, only watching her shape in the dark.

"Well?" Her eyes opened and her tone became impatient. That woke the beast in me and I slid the guitar

179

onto the bed, next to her leg. Oz rolled over with a smile and a tail wag and I gave him a disapproving look. His head fell down and his ears tucked behind him.

"I can't accept this Asia." I was mad. She quickly stood up, pulling the ear buds from her ears. Her movements were so swift and graceful I found my anger getting lost in her web. She stepped up to me and stopped only inches from my face.

"Why not?" her voice filled with hurt. She smelled amazing and I wanted to taste her lips with every fiber that made me human. It was painfully obvious that I couldn't trust my judgment when it came to her. I felt powerless to the force that seemed to pull me so easily to her like a magnet. It took every bit of concentration to focus myself and let the anger grow again.

"You think you can buy my forgiveness?" I said under my breath.

"Not at all...that's not what this is."

"Than what is this Asia?" I had a hold of my anger again. Her eyelids squinted together and it seemed to upset her that I was being so stubborn.

"A sorry," she smiled.

"That is not a sorry...that is a bribe." I felt my hands heat up with my anger but I couldn't be completely sure that my desire to reach out and hold her wasn't the cause of it.

"You say sorry, you don't spend thousands of dollars!" I snapped. The thunder grew outside my window to warn me but I didn't even give it a second glance.

"Why are you acting so ungrateful?" she snapped back and her smell hit me again.

Ember

"Because I don't want your money and fancy things! I want the truth! I want you truly sorry." It felt good to stand up to her.

"That's just a gift. For you because I saw it and thought of you," she said with confidence. Her hands slowly slid around my neck.

"And this is for my stupidity." She kissed me slow and deep and an inferno exploded behind my eyes. Her lips destroyed me and she knew it as soon as she pulled away from my mouth.

"I am sorry Max," she whispered with her hands still on my chest.

"Really?" I asked blankly. I was still reeling from her touch.

"I want to earn your forgiveness," she said as tears welled up in her eyes. "I'm so sorry."

I was speechless. This night had gone on way too long and I was feeling emotionally weak. Maybe that's why I was going to forgive her so easily. Or maybe it was much more serious than that. Maybe there was no defense against her with me. Maybe she was my kryptonite.

"Can we start over?" she asked as her blue eyes swirled in front of me. "I promise to give you everything I have. Everything you need." She sounded heartfelt but something kept me from completely believing her words. I pulled away from her and turned my back to her.

"Yes," I said quietly giving in to her. It felt good to forgive her but I was being overcome with confusion now. How can two girls have such a pull on my soul? I was beginning to drown in my guilt but I was too tired to care anymore.

Asia's arms came around my chest from behind me like a warm blanket and the thunder called my name again. I could hear the first drops of rain tap the roof now.

She pressed her body into my back and snuggled her lips behind my right ear.

"I've missed you," she whispered. My heart pounded like a drum.

"Me too."

She spun me around and settled her body against mine and pulled my hands to her face. The warmth filled her skin with goose bumps and her cool skin soothed my fears.

"So...do you like her or not?" She nodded toward the guitar.

"I love it. She's beautiful." I paused and ran my finger along her arm, teasing the goose bumps as I went.

"She's you," I whispered. We embraced each other again and the rain washed along my window. Our embrace felt like it lasted for an eternity and when we were done I felt winded. She grabbed the guitar from the bed and turned to me.

"Will you play for me?" Her eyes seemed to taunt me a little.

"I would but I don't have an amp to play through at the moment." I was just making excuses. I didn't want to stop holding her yet. Asia shook her head and pointed to the shaded corner of my room.

"No more excuses," she giggled devilishly.

In the corner of my bedroom was a brand new guitar amp with another blood red silk bow stuck to it. The amp was black and square with four speakers housed inside it. I felt extremely silly that I hadn't seen it before that moment but I did have an excuse. I was distracted by the lips and eyes of my angel.

"I can't take..." I started to say and her arm shoved the guitar into my face.

Ember

"Don't even finish that sentence," she warned with a smile.

"All right," I smiled and took the guitar from her hand. I plugged it in and flipped the power switch to on and it hummed to life. I smiled with delight and the air filled with electricity. My eyes found hers and she nodded in approval as if to say...'go ahead.'

I set my guitar on the floor, leaning it against the humming speakers. I flipped the power switch off to the amp, letting the power fade away. My face filled with uneasiness and she slid up to me and propped herself on top of the amp. Her feet dangled a few inches from the ground.

"What's wrong?" she asked sweetly.

"Asia I have to tell you something." I don't know why but I felt it necessary to tell her about my earlier date with Sam. I thought for sure she would be furious with me.

"Anything," she said as a smile appeared.

"If we're going to make any of this work than I need to be honest with you...about everything." I was scared and my words sounded desperate.

"Just say it. I'm a big girl. I can handle it," she teased without the slightest hint of insecurity.

"I went out with Samantha tonight." I waited for the daggers to appear in her eyes. "On a date," I added. She said nothing. She slipped a hair tie from around her wrist and gathered her hair in her hands and tucked it into a loose ponytail. A hand full of her bangs slid from the tie and fell down her face.

"It's fine," she whispered from behind her bangs. The moonlight was reflecting through the streaking rain on my window and filling her eyes with a silvery glimmer.

"I don't understand," I said.

"I don't own you." An aggressive smile filled her lips. Standing in my darkened room I fidgeted nervously. Why wasn't she upset with this news? Was this still some kind of game to her? My ego began to crack and that hurt a little. Her bare feet fell to the floor and she walked up to me with that wicked smile.

"Asia..." she stopped my voice with a single finger to my lips.

"Relax...you don't belong to me," she said brutally honest and then kissed me soft and slow. With her sapphire eyes locked on mine only inches away from each other, she whispered.

"Yet."

Her smile grew even bigger as she walked past me and out my door. My heart was racing and my veins burned with fire. I didn't want her to leave but like a stone I was frozen again. Thunder shook my room intensely and as if she could read my mind, she popped back into my room and the rain pounded against my window with big fat drops.

"Is everything okay?" I asked surprised but I really didn't care, I was just glad she came back. She ran up to me and kissed me quickly.

"I left you something on your new mp3 player." She playfully tossed her ponytail. My hands found hers as she began to pull away again.

"Don't go," I begged. Her eyes filled with joy and the storm rattled the house once more.

"Am I supposed to believe that my date doesn't bother you at all?" I asked firmly.

"I didn't say that," she said cryptically.

Ember

"Then why so mysterious?" I felt stupid for begging but I was powerless to this spell she was weaving around me. Her eyes looked through mine and she said nothing. I felt my confidence falling away again as my stare turned to a worried glance. She inhaled a deep breath and walked away from me once again. When she reached my doorway she slyly looked at me over her shoulder. The thunder crashed loudly behind me as her face filled with a smile.

"May the best girl win!" her voice was soft but you could feel the intensity in her tone. Time slowed and we stared at each other just like the first time we saw each other on the beach. My room filled with electricity, mentally pulling me toward her. Her body was covered in goose bumps.

"Miss you much!" she giggled. That made me smile and she disappeared around my door for a second time. The rain fell even harder, making Oz more nervous by the second.

I walked to my bedroom window and opened it slowly, letting the rain wash over my face and chest. The breeze blew wildly throughout my room as her smell filled my head. The rain slowly faded as she jogged away down my street. I followed her bouncing shadow until the darkness over took her but I could still smell her signature scent. Oz bounced up to the window and shoved his nose upwards in the air. He sniffed twice and his tail wagged furiously as a tiny growl escaped his muzzle.

Looking down at him, I scratched the top of his head and he let out a single bark. "Yeah...I agree big guy."

Leaning back on my bed, I let a long stress relieving sigh out of my chest. Steam billowed from my mouth as if I took a long drag from a cigarette. Oz watched carefully and then snuggled under my arm. As we both lay, there the rain faded back to nothing. My eyes closed as I relived the nights better moments. Sleep almost gripped me but my hand slid over something cold and smooth.

I pulled the new mp3 player to my face and clicked it on. As I scrolled through the music playlists I found the one Asia had mentioned. It was titled "FOR MAX..." I placed the ear buds in my ears and clicked play. The music filled my head and instantly soothed my tired eyes. The playlist was filled with slow, mid tempo songs about sexy encounters and different kinds of environments. Beaches, sunsets, rainstorms and other exotic locales.

I slowly fell asleep and my dreams filled my head instantly. I spent half the night chasing Asia along an endless beach with the waves crashing all around us. I spent the other half watching my sister fall away from my hands over and over again. But instead of falling into the blackness, she fell into Sam's arms.

They say your dreams are a mirror image of your soul. If that were true, than I was in big trouble. I was falling in love with two women and I could not stop it, no matter how hard I fought it.

"...Who do you love?...Girl, I see through your love...Who do you love?...Me or the thought of me..."

Ember

~Beast Of Burden: The Rolling Stones~

Saturday morning – 10:39 a.m. – August 26th.

I was so angry that I thought I could send a fireball screaming down from the heavens on top of my uncle's house and crack a smile while I did it. At least that's how I felt when he first mentioned 'the barbecue.' An early dinner party he had decided to throw for me and my newest friends. And which two friends had he put at the top of the invitation list? Two lovely individuals who have made my life extra complicated lately.

"Max you're acting like a two year old," Frank scolded as he began scraping the grill.

"I just don't like surprises uncle and this one's a doozy." I did sound like a two year old.

"It's just my buddy Tim and his family..." he shrugged. "And your buddies from the band." He knew I would lose this battle.

"And Sam!" I pouted.

"Well, she is Tim's daughter. Besides, I thought you two were hitting it off quite nicely?" he asked with a wink.

"Too nicely," I said under my breath. He looked at me with a puzzled face.

"So if you understand that Sam will be here, then why would you invite Asia?" I asked way too dramatic.

"Because she's important to you," he said point blank and I was stunned. "And if she's important to you, then I need to know why that is."

"Oh." I still felt blindsided.

"Max, you are one of the smartest kids I have ever known but you can't have your cake and eat it too," he offered wisely. So there it was...the truth. This dinner was about making a choice.

"That's not what I'm doing uncle." I sounded calmer now. "I'm just so confused. I feel like I'm being torn in two different directions."

He nodded as if he completely understood, "I see."

"And I think I'm enjoying it on some demented level." My hands filled with sweat.

"There are worst problems to have in this crazy world than having two beautiful women chasing you," he laughed. "But you know that already."

"You're right." He always was.

"Here's what I purpose. We have some laughs, some good food and let things be." His hand fell onto my shoulder.

"You never know, you just might have a good time son." He was so sure of himself but all I could imagine was the two girls...my two girls; at each other's throats and hating me by the end of the night.

"Promise me you will give Asia a fair shot," I said. He hugged me lightly and walked to the living room. Music began to pour from the opened windows of the house. Frank strutted back outside to the beat of the music. More golden oldies classic rock.

"And promise me I can pick out the music for the party. Please," I begged over the music.

Ember

"Deal. But you can only pick from my collection," he teased as he danced behind me singing along. I groaned and started cleaning off the patio.

"Collection? You only have three albums!" I yelled over his broken singing. "And you've had them since you were my age."

"That's right...and one day, that collection will be yours." His chest filled with a hearty laugh. I couldn't help but laugh too.

The morning blurred into lunch and the afternoon barbecue was approaching much too fast. I was starting to become scatter brained as the tension filled my body and mind. Frank noticed my building stress with a smile.

"You don't look so hot," Frank said with a wink.

"Funny." Man did he need some new jokes. Secretly though, I loved his sense of humor, even when it was at my expense.

"Here." He tossed me the keys to the truck. "Get out of here for a few. I need some more ice for the drinks anyways." Driving to the market was the last thing I wanted to do at the moment but he was right, I needed to clear my head.

"Okay...I'll be back." As I walked out the front door to the truck, his singing grew louder. I just shook my head with a smile and climbed in the truck.

2:03 p.m.

Sam and her parents arrived early with giant smiles and handfuls of food. Sam's mother was small like her with the same golden blonde hair. Her father was much taller with the familiar green eyes Sam was known for. Frank greeted them with open arms and his best smile.

189

"Tim, Rebecca, I am so happy you made it," he said offering them hugs before he turned his attention to Sam.

"Good to see you again Samantha." His smile almost jumped off his face.

"You too Frank," she smiled as she quickly surveyed the house.

"Max will be here shortly." That calmed her curiosity. "I sent him for some more ice. He should be back any minute." He winked at Sam. He then pulled a white and pink hibiscus from behind his back.

"Max wanted you to have this." He slid it into her hair, just above her left ear. Sam looked at her parents and blushed a little.

"Thank you," she said shyly.

"Oh, I almost forgot the pies. Samantha will you grab them for us sweetheart?" her dad asked.

"I'm on it," she chirped and walked outside. Frank invited them to have a seat in the living room. She enjoyed watching her parents around Frank. He always seemed to bring the best out of them. But her smile faded quickly as she walked up to her parent's car. Asia's Jeep bounced around the corner and into the driveway.

Asia stepped from the truck dressed in a designer black dress. She tilted her tall frame on matching black heels that slithered around her ankles. She looked as if she were dressed for a night out on the town and not a simple family barbecue. Sam glanced down at herself and questioned whether her little green and white summer dress could possibly be enough to capture my attention now. But she was perfectly confident in her attire and squashed any doubts right then and there. Quickly she popped open the car door and leaned in, grabbing two warm pies. As she set them on the roof of the sedan, she was annoyed to discover Asia standing over her. They stared at each other intensely.

"Tonight's going to be fun," Asia spoke with arrogance. Sam tried her best to keep her cool.

"Hello Asia...that's quite a dress." She bit her tongue and continued cautiously. Asia only looked down at her oddly.

"You look...sweet," she mocked her. Sam let the comment roll off her shoulders.

"Max isn't here yet but he'll be back soon," she smiled confidently. Asia returned the same smile and Sam found her tolerance breaking a little.

"Good," Asia said.

"I just thought you'd want to know," Sam said as she grabbed a pie in each hand.

"Dessert?" Asia asked. Sam laughed a little.

"You mean you didn't bring anything?" She was trying to get a rise out of Asia and it was working.

"That's kind of rude," Sam continued. Her nose scrunched up as if something smelled bad. "Oh well..." she finished. Asia looked at the pies and back at her expensive dress and then back to Sam.

"I guess I was too worried about looking nice for Max and his uncle. I should have put more thought into the little stuff." Asia sounded sincere and Sam found that very awkward.

"Look Asia, I'm not here to be a thorn in your side." She didn't want to be this open with her but it was just the way she was raised.

"I care for Max...a lot." She waited for a reaction from Asia. Thunder shook from behind them as Asia shifted uncomfortably in her expensive shoes.

191

"I suppose we are not that different," Asia sighed as she crossed her arms. "Truce?" She asked Sam politely. Sam took a moment and thought about it. She searched Asia's eyes for any sign of deceit but found none.

"Truce. For Max," she managed a small smile.

"For Max," Asia nodded in agreement. They both walked to the front door unsure of the other. Asia began to open the door and Sam stopped her and handed her one of the pies. Asia looked at her confused but appreciative. Slow and steady they both made their way through the door.

A few minutes later I found myself frozen with fear. I sat in the front seat of the truck with my hands tightly gripping the wheel. I could feel my hands burning already. I couldn't even move when the front windshield fogged over from my steam.

"Get a grip Max," I told myself. What's the worst that might go wrong tonight? Like an enema to the brain, a thousand images raced through my skull. Not a single one of them good.

"Enough of this," I scolded. It was time to pull it together. Just breathe. I inhaled deeply and stepped from the truck. Storm clouds were rolling closer toward the house but they felt calm. I grabbed the four bags of ice, two in each fist. This was probably my last chance to run but my feet kept pushing me forward. I felt as if a fever had broken all over my body. Even the cool breeze from the nearby storm wasn't helping.

"Just breathe," I whispered. From behind the door I could hear people laughing. My confidence fell away and I turned to run when Oz came running from around the corner of the house. He was barking with vigor and his little tail spun as if he might take flight.

Ember

"Shhh little man!" I gritted my teeth. To which he proceeded to bark louder and run around me in a happy little dance. With a hearty laugh my uncle opened the door and waved me in.

"There he is. Come on in son." He tugged me through the door by my shoulders. I didn't think my feet would work but I managed to stumble in somehow.

"You're just in time! Asia has us all in stitches with stories from her many family vacations around the world," Frank cheered. Family vacations? In what parallel universe did I walk into? I was floored by the sight before me. Asia and Sam were sitting next to each other on the couch, with drinks in hand. Both girls were wearing a single white flower behind their left ear and the craziest thing was that they both looked...happy. Sam's parents sat enjoying themselves and offered me a kind glance. I found myself speechless yet again.

"Aloha Max," Sam said smiling nervously. I returned a crooked half smile. Asia tilted her head with a seductive glance and my hands warmed aggressively. Say something Max; just don't stand here like a mannequin. I raised my hands up in front of me with my eyes half closed.

"I got ice." That was all I could spit out. Unexpectedly the entire room erupted in laughter.

"Where's the ice Max?" Tim asked with a grin. I focused my eyes on the four bags in front of me and a wave of embarrassment washed over me. I was standing like a scarecrow with four fresh bags of water. They had been fresh bags of ice only moments ago. Frank shot me a silly look, as if he knew exactly what had happened. He mouthed the words "it's okay" but I still felt humiliated. The girls looked at each other, both realizing the other knew my secret. This angered Asia slightly but Sam didn't seem bothered at all. I on the other hand wanted to climb back under my covers and start this magical day over.

Frank came to my rescue and guided me to the kitchen, trying his hardest not to laugh.

"That was fun," he said grabbing the bags of water from my still warm hands. The room felt sticky with heat.

"Those two have really got you turned inside out, don't they?" he asked quietly. I shrugged and threw my head back, signaling that I had given up.

"I guess." I tried not to sound like he was 100% right, but it was obvious that he knew better.

"Now this afternoon is going to be fun," he promised.

"What do I do uncle?" I was desperate. He enjoyed how much I was squirming and quickly tossed me a stack of raw meat.

"Nothing...make them come to you."

Staring at the pile of meat in my hands, "What?"

"You start those up for me." He pointed to the grill. "I won't be able to get that one burner lit without you." I stared at him with wide eyes. "Trust me. You just be yourself and let the girls make the first move. You'll know where to go from there."

"And what if they don't make the first move?" I felt silly even asking.

"Well then...I guess you are not as irresistible as you think you are my boy." A giant laugh exploded from his gut as he spun me around and with a hefty shove, he sent me toward the side patio.

I quickly lit the defective burner, making sure no one was watching and started tossing slabs of meat on the sizzling grill. I almost had all of them on when Kai and Marcus slipped through the back gate.

"Hey guys!" I waved the spatula at them furiously.

"Aloha!" Marcus called out.

"Aloha my brother," Kai added.

"Thank god you guys are here, I need some back up." They looked at each other and then back to me.

"Back up?" Kai asked.

"I got your back. What's the situation?" Marcus asked. At that precise moment, Asia and Sam strolled out on the patio. A resounding gulp could be heard from both of their throats as they fell still.

"Exactly," I whispered and they both shot me a nervous grin. In a matter of seconds they had found the situation just as funny as Frank had. What were friends for I thought sarcastically?

Then from Sam's hands I heard a familiar clicking noise. I recognized the sound of her camera immediately as she quickly snapped a few shots of us silly boys. Asia found this annoying and set her drink down and pushed her frame past Sam, slithering up next to me. Kai and Marcus offered her a polite hello before retreating to the kitchen. As they passed Sam, Kai extended a sweet hello and a hug.

"I hope you caught my good side?" he joked as he continued past her. She smiled but never took her eyes off of Asia and I.

"You don't have a good side!" Marcus called from the kitchen door. They disappeared in the kitchen and my nerves filled my stomach. So much for my backup.

"It's all right Max," Asia said caressing my heated cheek. "We've decided to play nice this afternoon." Sincerity poured from her voice as her eyes met Sam's.

Sam only nodded in agreement and lifted her camera toward her eye.

"Say cheeseburger!" she sounded soft but it was painfully clear that she didn't enjoy Asia that close to me. Asia leaned into me as if we were two long lost puzzle pieces finally pushed back together. And I'd be lying if I said it didn't feel absolutely amazing. Her smell washed over me and my chest began to heat up. I needed to concentrate to keep my mind off the desire to taste her lips again. The thunderclouds rumbled in agreement with my thoughts as Sam snapped a couple more shots.

"All right," I said nervously pulling away from Asia and focusing my attention back to the grill. A glimmer of light flickered in Sam's eyes when I did and she walked up and kissed me gently on the cheek. Asia ran her fingers through her dark curls and rain started to fall from the sky. Sam quickly covered her camera and I gave Asia a disapproving stare.

"I better get this out of the rain. I'll be right back." Sam slipped away into the kitchen and the rain stopped.

"That's not fair Asia," I said pointing to the darkening sky. She smiled and shrugged.

"Can you try and ease up on the waterworks? At least for my uncle's sake, he's got big hopes for this dinner," I pleaded.

"I'll try, for you," her eyes smiled.

"Thank you," I smiled back. She slowly walked toward the kitchen door and glanced over her shoulder to make sure I was watching. I was.

After a few precious minutes alone the kitchen door flew open and Frank led the guests outside. Everyone found themselves a seat around the patio table. Everyone except Asia. She walked over to the shade of the corner trees, fumbling her cell phone in her hands.

196

Ember

The wind blew through her hair and her smell overpowered the smell of the grill. It smacked Frank across his face.

"Wow," he chuckled as he strolled up to me.

"I know," I said.

Sam sat with her parents and watched me, snapping a picture every once in a while. Her parents were more interested in Kai and Marcus though.

"You boys are all in some kind of band together, right?" Sam's mother, Rebecca asked.

"Yes, we are," Kai said with a grin.

"Things have been pretty nice since Max came along and joined the band. Our songs have grown so much," Marcus said excited. "He is so talented."

"Well, so I have been told," Rebecca agreed and found me watching the table cautiously. She smiled at me and Sam turned her head embarrassed.

"Maybe we could hear you gentlemen play sometime?" Tim suggested. Rebecca nodded politely in agreement, even though I didn't think we were exactly their cup of tea.

"We have our first show next weekend. You should come and shake what the good lord gave you," Kai said as Sam's big green eyes rolled in her head. Her mother laughed and blushed at his words. She seemed to like Kai. Sam's father on the other hand, just looked at him with a false smile.

The thunder rumbled, pulling my attention back to Asia who was now pacing back and forth, with her cell phone pressed to her ear. Funny, I hadn't heard it ring. Back at the table things turned awkward.

"Well, we will see if we can juggle our schedule around next weekend and pop in," Tim said kindly but you could tell that he had no intention of doing so. Sam's face filled with relief.

"That would be phenomenal!" Kai exclaimed. "I'll get my secretary Marcus, to juggle up you three some tickets."

"Wrong," Marcus announced. "We leave the juggling up to Max. You know...Sam, Asia, Sam, Asia." He made a juggling motion with his arms. Kai choked on his soda as Sam's parents stared blankly with eyes as wide as saucers. She smacked Marcus on the arm and covered her face.

"Marcus!" Kai choked.

"What did I say?" Marcus hadn't tasted enough of his foot apparently and began to open his mouth again. Without even looking toward the grill, I reached behind me and grabbed the first piece of meat I touched and whipped it like a baseball at the back of his head. My uncle watched with his mouth open in disbelief as the beef slapped Marcus on the back of his neck with a loud thwack. It slipped down to the ground and left a nasty welt in its place.

"Ouch! What the...?" he screeched. Marcus whipped around and found my angry glare.

"Max...I was going to eat that piece," Frank scolded. "I had been saving that particular piece for this very barbecue." He was mad but was having the hardest time not laughing at the same time. At the table Kai had laughed hard enough for his drink to fly out of his nose. Sam sat blushing; doing everything she could to not lose her mind. She smiled at me and that filled me with calm. Oz had already made his way off with the chunk of beef and was quite content for the rest of the evening.

Things settled down from there Frank and I served everyone their food. I apologized to Marcus as I slid him his plate and he sulked while he ate. Everyone began to eat except Asia. She was still on the phone and Frank nudged me. As I started to gather her some food on a plate, Sam stopped me.

"Let me," she said walking over to the shaded trees where Asia stood. I stood mortified watching her cross the yard. My hands sizzled as the storm called out a warning.

"Oh no," I whispered.

MADISON DANIEL

~Underneath It All: No Doubt~

Sam approached Asia slowly as Asia hung up her cell phone angrily. She was very upset by the call and the sky darkened.

"Bad news?" Sam asked. Asia looked directly at me and then back to Sam, but said nothing.

"Dinners ready," Sam added as she extended her arms with the plate of food. A small crack of lightning flashed behind the house, sending the hairs on my neck to attention. This was about to get ugly.

"Why are you doing this?" Asia demanded. Sam stepped back cautiously.

"Why are you acting like this?" Sam demanded right back.

"Ugh! I do not have time for these childish high school games Sam. If you want to spend the rest of the night pretending to be best buddies, then fine. But I'm not going to embarrass myself any further." Her voice was so angry and I wondered who was on the other end of that phone call. The list was a short one.

"First off, we will never be buddies. Second, Max and his family have gone to a lot of trouble for us tonight." Sam's eyes blazed over with anger. I took a step closer but Frank held me back by my arm.

"I don't belong here," Asia gritted through her teeth. "And you know that," she called out over Sam's shoulder, making sure I heard every word.

"Let's not pretend anymore!" Asia stomped forward, knocking the plate from Sam's hands. It started to pour rain over everything as she walked past me with her head down. Sam's scared eyes found mine and I lost my temper and chased after Asia. I followed her through the house and out my front door, finally catching up with her at the side of her Jeep.

"Asia...wait...please," I called through the falling rain.

"Max this was a bad idea. I should never have come," she cried.

"Why?"

"Look at me Max...I look like a high class call girl, not someone you bring home to the family. I don't fit here!" Her tears only seemed to upset her more.

"This doesn't make any sense Asia. You were fine until that phone call." I had touched a nerve and she turned defensive.

"Max...don't!"

"What did she say to you?" I demanded. "What does Lucy have over you? Tell me!"

The thunder cracked over me as if to warn me that I was pushing too hard but I didn't care about her warnings anymore. If I was to make any kind of decision, any sort of choice between her and Sam, then I needed honesty and I needed it now.

"Max, don't push me. You have no idea what you're talking about," her voice cracked. I stepped closer to her and she stepped back.

"Damn it Asia! Don't be scared of me!" I screamed as the rain poured down my face.

"She fits Max...not me!" She stumbled into her Jeep and started revving the engine loudly.

"Sam fits," she said again but I could barely hear it. She threw the flower from her hair to the wet ground. It spun in the air, twisting down like a paper top. Her heavy foot smashed the gas pedal, spinning her tires in the building mud and drove off. I stood in the rain with my head down and my hands steaming. My mind felt numb. What was I doing? I was begging one girl for her acceptance, her heart. That scared me. I was running from the other girl who made that acceptance easy to have and easy to give. Almost like it was natural to do so and that was even more terrifying.

The rain faded quickly as I stood out front, letting the sun warm my drenched and wet body. I sped the process along a little with a puff of heat. The storm rolled away down the road behind Asia's Jeep as I collected myself and slowly walked back to the house. Inside everyone had gathered back in the living room quietly, making small talk. Everyone but Sam, she was cleaning up the kitchen. Dishes clanked softly from the other room. I felt drained. I felt embarrassed. Everyone looked at me with quiet smiles. Frank motioned for me to go into the kitchen and help, so I did.

"Sam...I'm so sorry for..." I choked as I walked up to her small frame.

"Max, you don't ever have to apologize for her."

"But..."

"But nothing," she had quickly ended the subject, point blank. I stood there for a moment while I listened to the conversations in the next room. She turned the faucet off and dried her hands. Gently she pulled her bangs behind her ear, exposing the lines of her neck and I followed them down to her lightly freckled chest. She was so beautiful.

"I like your dress Sam," I said softly and she stopped what she was doing and looked up at me slyly. "You look beautiful tonight."

"You've got kind of a sexy, wet dog thing going on," she teased watching my still wet bangs and just like that I was happy again.

"Thank you for coming today," a smile broke across my lips again. She gently spun me around, pushing my back against the counter and leaned her soft frame into me. Her hips pressed against mine and her fingers slid into my front pockets of my jeans. With a slight tug she whispered.

"Thank you."

I leaned down to give her a kiss when the clicking from her camera startled us both. Kai had snuck in and decided to capture the moment on film.

"Nice," he exclaimed. I rolled my eyes and looked down at her to see what she thought.

"Say cheeseburger!" she smiled and turned toward Kai and he took a picture.

7:31 p.m.

The evening ended a little earlier then Frank had hoped for but he was content. He gave out hugs and handshakes to Sam and her family. They all thanked him again for his hospitality and began walking to their car.

"A gentleman never lets a lady walk alone," Frank said to me quietly. I took the hint and ran outside to catch up with Sam. She watched me with a smile as I bounced toward her family car.

Ember

"Be safe." I smiled and leaned in to kiss her goodnight. Her father honked the car horn, his disapproving smile shined through the windshield, with his palm against the steering wheel. One finger waved in the air, back and forth, signaling no, no, no. I blushed a little. She stood up on her toes, letting her fingers grasp my forearms and whispered in my ear.

"Raincheck..."

"Definitely," I said.

Kai and Marcus had already started to make their escape as well, arms full with bags of left overs. Both of them piled into Kai's car.

"Catch you later Max," Kai called out.

"I owe you one brother!" Marcus grunted with a mouth full of food.

"Get out of here you two fools!" I yelled and they laughed as they drove off. I could hear them continue laughing the whole way down the road.

As I strolled back to the front door, a quick flash of lightning in the distance caught my eye. Asia's brilliant blue eyes flashed inside my head.

"Maybe you're right Asia..." I said out loud to no one. Maybe you don't fit. Maybe I have been kidding myself the whole time? Maybe it was time to make things a little less complicated. I shook my head until her icy glare was no longer there. I walked in and helped Frank finish cleaning up. He didn't press me for information and let me retire to my room.

"See you in the morning son. Sleep tight," he winked with a calm look on his face that I hadn't seen before.

"Okay," I called from my room. What was he up to, I wondered? In my room the moon shined through the window, making me think of Sam and how calm she was when everything went crazy this afternoon. No more fighting it big guy…it was time to let her in.

11:03 p.m.

As peaceful as I felt after tonight's fireworks at dinner, I was having the worst time falling asleep. I sat and stared at my clock, watching the minutes flicker by slowly. My body had no intention of falling asleep anytime soon. So I jumped from my bed, trying not to disturb King Oz as he lied snoring away at the end of the mattress. I had to admit it, I was jealous of how easily he could fall asleep and how grumpy he could become when you did actually wake him up.

I stretched my limbs as I stood up letting various joints and bones crack, before I heard a faint tapping at my window. I couldn't see anyone outside in the dark so I went to the window and opened it quietly. With a playful little growl, Sam jumped from under my window. Her eyes were spinning around in her head and she stuck out her tongue and giggled. I wanted to pretend that she had startled me but I was enjoying her cheerful spirit too much.

"Hi Max," she chirped.

"Greetings Sam. And what do I owe this terribly late surprise to?" I asked. She smiled holding up my uncle's truck keys.

"Put a shirt on handsome, we've got ourselves a date." She sounded as if she was buzzing; too much caffeine or something. She flipped her golden hair and walked away, leaving me stunned.

"Have you been drinking?" I called to her half kidding. She stopped and caught my eyes over her shoulder.

"Then again...forget the shirt." A giggle followed. Her eyes were as green as emeralds, with the moons reflection spinning inside of them. That's when I realized that she was wearing her bikini. It was covered by her over-sized tank top, which had begun to fall down one of her shoulders. The white strap from her bikini top peaked from behind the black and white stripes painted across the tank top.

"Come on, the nights still young," she said a little breathy. My mind stalled out with excitement as my eyes traced the outline of her exposed shoulder in the moonlight. I glanced down at the dark board shorts I was wearing and grabbed the closest tee shirt I could find. With it dangling in my hand I jumped through the window opening and ran after her. She was almost to Frank's truck before I caught up with her.

"What are you doing with my uncle's keys?" I asked as I slid my arms through my shirt. Sand squished through my toes of my bare feet. Sam whirled around, glancing back and forth.

"Kidnapping you," she laughed.

"What?" I felt confused. That only seemed to excite her more. Her little body fell into mine and she kissed me. Softly at first, but the passion simmered quickly, making my hands fill with heat.

"I thought it was the perfect night for a swim." She climbed up into the cab of the truck. I stood there with my left eyebrow cocked, staring at this crazy girl, as the engine clunked to life.

"Sam, are you insane? Frank is going to freak out," I yelled in my loudest whisper I could manage. Her hair fell in front of her glistening eyes as she smiled and revved the engine.

"You're out of your crazy little mind!" I snapped as I climbed in the truck.

"Only when it comes to you." The truck clanked into gear and she started down the road. I watched from behind us to make sure Frank didn't come running from the house with a shot gun. He was surely going to kill me over this one.

We were far enough from the house now that it didn't matter if we turned back or not so I let the stress fade and enjoyed the ride.

"Kidnapping huh?" I asked with my arm sticking out the window. I let my hand surf the midnight air. "Haven't you tried this one already?"

"It's okay," she winked. "Frank is the one who gave me the keys." I was speechless. My jaw hit the floor and she found my expression...cute. I guess that simple barbecue was not merely to get acquainted with my friends at all. Frank had this planned from the beginning. Size up the girls and pick his favorite. Classy.

"My uncle is very fond of you," I said with caution. Her eyes fell still on my face.

"And what about you?" she asked.

"You're growing on me," I said trying not to look at her. "Kind of like mold," I laughed.

"Funny," she scoffed as her smile returned. The gears of the truck ground together lightly as she shifted its gears.

"I've been dying to take you to the beach." Her tone was cool and calm now.

"Sounds..." I caught her glance at me again and calmness blanketed me. Maybe my uncle was right.

Ember

Maybe I knew it all along too. I scooted my body next to hers and slid my hand on her leg.

"...Perfect."

MADISON DANIEL

Destiny_20

~Destiny: Zero 7~

It took just over an hour to reach the secluded beach. Sam drove the truck onto the sand and backed it up against the incoming tide. Now I understood why she needed the truck, her tiny car would have never been able to manage this thick sand. I recognized the beach from one of her pictures she had taken; my favorite one with the palm trees and the little girl with her sea shell. She watched my expression closely as the thought filled my head.

"It's beautiful, isn't it?" she asked. It truly was. In the dark of night with only the full moon for light, it resembled her black and white photograph.

"Yes," I spoke soft and slow. She watched me with intense eyes that scared me for some reason. There was something behind those wonderful eyes. There was more to this night than just some swimming I thought.

"So what did you have planned for tonight?" my voice cracked.

"Definitely swimming," her eyes flickered again. "Probably some making out." Her smile grew to match her wild eyes.

"Maybe more."

As I sat there choking on my own nervousness she darted from the truck. Her feet fell quickly, pushing her tiny frame for the moonlit water and she threw her tank top into the air. I watched it fall to the shaded sand as she reached the first wave.

"My Samantha," I said to the empty cab of the truck. Quickly I removed my shirt and ran after her.

The water was cold but bearable and seemed to make every inch of my skin heat up instantly. Steam billowed up into the sky and I could feel her eyes watching heavily. She slowly waded up to me as the steam faded and my temperature leveled off to almost normal. I pulled her closer to me and the waves gently helped by sending her into my arms. I smiled and held her tightly. Her body felt like ice which soothed me immensely. We stood together for a moment letting the water rock us back and forth.

"Sam," I finally said.

"Yes Max."

"I really do think I owe you an apology for earlier this evening." A little mist of steam danced off my words as I spoke.

"We've already discussed this. No, you don't," she said proud.

"Asia should have never..." I continued but she cut me off with a glare. Her fingers dug into my stomach with a gentle force. She shook her head in disapproval.

"She has nothing to do with you and I. She has nothing to do with this night." Her eyes held me hostage as her cool hands searched my chest.

"I understand." At least I understood a little.

"Tonight is about the truth Max. Our truth." She paused long enough for me to heat up again.

"Our truth?" Okay...I didn't understand.

"I already told you that I was falling for you and I think that scared you a little." More like a lot.

"It scares me too." She slowly pulled away from me but made sure our hands stayed locked together.

Ember

"The way I feel about you is stronger than anything I have ever felt before but I am not going to lie to you." She stopped and took a deep breath. "Your abilities terrify me."

"Oh," I said sheepishly. Terrify is a pretty bold word. I looked out over the water and felt trapped. I wanted to run but I couldn't now. I wanted Sam's acceptance but now I felt like a monster.

"Part of me wants to run from you," she continued. Great...here come the torches and pitch forks. My chest pounded like a drum signaling an over load, as it filled with more heat. She pretended not to notice.

"And part of me wants to embrace you and never let go, no matter how much you burn," she whimpered.

"I would never hurt you Sam. Not like that. You have to know that."

"And that's why this night is so important." Her hands trembled. "I want to show you just how important."

Her words were direct. I on the other hand stood clueless, with the water gently swishing around my waist. Her body pushed up against mine and she pulled my head down and kissed me softly. When she was finished she grabbed my left hand and led me back to the beach.

We both stood together so closely as our wet bodies filled with goose bumps from the chilling breeze. This time I kissed her and she shivered in my arms. I let my body heat up enough to gently warm us both. The water on our skin disappeared and our hair started to dry slowly. Our bodies were warm again when she locked her arms around me. She kissed me with everything she had and when I finally thought we would need to take a breath, she kissed me even harder. My core temperature was off the charts now but she only increased her assault. My walls were crumbling fast.

"Sam…" It took all of my might to pull my lips away from her. "This is a mistake."

I knew it was crazy to want to stop this heaven but things were moving fast now. As much as my young hormone driven body wanted this, I had to be smart about the next step. With my abilities she could get hurt. Her face went still as her arms dropped to her sides. Her soft skin pulled away from mine and I swear my body actually ached when she did.

"You're right," she said coldly. The waves grew behind us with a fizzling crash. Her hair danced around her shoulders as if it was taunting me to touch it. Her reddish highlights flared under the glow of the moon. She looked stunning.

She ran back to the truck and climbed into its bed. She moved quickly, sliding a large, dark green duffle bag from the front of the bed to the opened tailgate. I slowly walked back to the truck, letting my toes dig into the cool sand as I did. With a long zipping sound she poured the contents of the bag on the floor of the bed. Two pillows and two blankets quickly found themselves tucked into the form of a bed.

"Sam, that's not what I meant." It was no use; she was no longer paying any attention to my voice. She then pulled one final blanket out and snapped it in the crisp air while she shot me a wanting glare. This blanket was blue and much thinner than the others. She swiftly wrapped it around her barely five foot frame. She straightened her back and cocked her hips to the side as she removed her bikini top from underneath the blanket. She let the top drop to her side and she motioned with her finger for me to come join her.

Steam flickered from my shoulders and I closed my mouth with my hand. I hadn't even realized it was wide open until I could literally taste the beach air. She laughed sweetly at me and took a step forward.

"Sam...are you crazy?" I asked bluntly with my mind racing.

"I thought you were a bad boy?" she teased back.

"And I thought you were a good girl..." I stuttered out. She kneeled down slowly sliding her legs to her left and propped her curvy frame up with one hand. Her other arm draped along her breasts, holding the blanket in place.

"Sometimes," she whispered and let a long seductive breath escape her lips.

"Come here Max it's getting chilly." I looked around us for any signs of other beach combers and realized I was stalling. Against my better judgment I climbed in the back of the truck. She silently pulled me down on top of her and ran her hand up the back of my neck, twisting her fingers in my hair.

"I thought you were scared of me?" I sounded anxious.

"Not tonight Max...not right now." Her cooling breath cut along my chin and down my neck as the fire filled my pores.

"Then why are you shaking?" I asked as I watched her eyes fill with the stars from above us.

"Because I want you."

We spent the rest of the night in the back of the truck until the sunrise scolded us the next morning. We never fell asleep or spoke a word until that morning. We were one, slow and cautious for hours and when the moment was finally over, it seemed not nearly long enough. I didn't want that sun to rise, no matter how amazing the colors were. I didn't want to start another day buried in possible regrets. I only wanted Sam. I wanted

215

her comforting embrace. I wanted her kisses. I wanted her love. And for the first time in a long while, I didn't want to be alone.

As the fluid purple skies filled with shining orange rays of light and soft burgundy clouds, I kissed her freckles along her stomach.

"So how much trouble do you think we're in for staying out all night?" I asked, breaking the silence. She sighed and stretched her arms and legs and wrinkled her nose.

"A lot." She started to laugh. "But I don't care." Honestly, neither did I.

We slowly gathered our things, stopping only long enough to enjoy each other's bodies as we dressed. I made it a point not to kiss her too much this morning in fear that I wouldn't be able to stop. We finished up and hit the road not knowing what kind of punishment we had waiting for us. We both were very quiet on the drive home. There was however a ton of goofy smiles and major hand holding.

However, in the back of my mind a thought kept raising its dirty little hand, disturbing the rest of the class. Sam was scared of me. Well, not me exactly but what I was capable of. I can't say I blamed her but I still didn't enjoy that thought. Could she still possibly feel that way now? After the last few hours we spent so close, was I still a monster? Part of me wanted to ask her but I was afraid of ruining this perfect moment. So I stuffed the little thought and his dirty hand to the back of the class, and the back of my mind.

Our drive home ended with me stopping a few houses down from her house. We didn't want to wake her parents; it was still a little early. With any luck they were still asleep. As she stepped from the truck and walked around to my open window, I realized something. I loved Sam. All five foot two of her. That thought should have made me so uncontrollably happy that I wouldn't be able to sleep for a week but it didn't. It scared me mostly. Not because I was afraid of committing to her or all the issues of letting someone totally inside your soul. No, I was scared that in my head I could still hear the thunder rolling somewhere. It was barely there, but it was still there. Asia was still there.

"Good night Max." She leaned inside the open window and kissed me passionately.

"I mean good morning." Her face blushed in a soft strawberry tone.

"Good morning Sam." I smiled big but it hid the ugly truth. I loved Samantha Summers but I think I loved Asia as well.

"Something wrong?" she asked still smiling.

"Nothing. I just don't want you to go yet." My smile faltered.

"You're sweet." She kissed me again. "I'll call you later," she said and then bounced off toward her house.

"Okay," I said with my own doubt choking me. I started the truck up and drove off for home with one single thought filling my head.

I was a horrible person.

<u>Sparks_21</u>

~Are You Happy Now? : Michelle Branch~

Monday morning – 8:13 a.m. – August 28th.

The worst thing about gossip is that it spreads like wildfire. A giant ball of half-truths that burn up everyone and everything in its path. Lies become truth and truth become vicious lies. I was learning this lesson the hard way.

The day started sane enough with a quick breakfast and a ride to school courtesy of Samantha Summers, my newest muse.

"Good morning," Sam smiled as I slid into her car. I kissed her softly.

"Morning. You get in trouble for being out all night?" I asked shyly.

"Nope. My parents were still sound asleep." Her smile faded as she spoke. Something was wrong.

"Everything all right?"

"I dreamt about you Max," her voice was gentle and shy.

"Am I already giving you nightmares?" I joked. Her eyes fell silent. I at least expected a smile at my dumb joke.

"I dreamt of you leaving," she said cold.

"That's weird." I shuffled anxiously in my seat. "You trying to get rid of me already?"

"No," she said and then forced a half-hearted smile on her face. I thought about digging a little more but stopped myself at the last second. Besides, if I dug too deep, I may not like the answer I found.

The ride to school was spent quietly side by side. Her face looked genuinely happy to be with me but there was something missing. A certain sparkle behind her eyes was gone. I wondered if I had anything to do with it. Her car came to a stop in the school parking lot and I was so lost in my thoughts that I almost didn't notice when she started to exit the car.

"Sam...wait," I shouted. She sat back down quickly.

"What is it?" her tone was unsure.

"Don't worry..." My hands brushed the sides of her face. "It was just a dream." I looked at her determined and watched as her eyes filled with her special confidence. She nodded in agreement and kissed me slowly. As we stepped from her car, Marcus and Kai were waiting for us on the grass of the school lawn. They greeted us with smiles and playful teasing.

"Howdy lovebirds!" Marcus shouted loud enough to embarrass Sam and she let go of my hand. I found it unusual that she let go so quickly.

"They know already?" she asked annoyed.

"Yeah, I talked to them late last night. Is there a problem?" I asked worried.

"No problem," she was lying. I tried to let it go. Kai shook my hand with a large goofy smile.

"It's going to be a great week brother." He was obviously excited about the looming gig we had planned.

"Sure is," I agreed. My eyes spied Sam as she stood nervously looking around.

"See you in biology," she said just before she turned to run to her class.

"Okay," I said a little hurt. I watched her until my attention was torn back to Kai and Marcus.

"You two looked awful cozy!" Kai teased.

"Something's wrong Kai."

"What do you mean?" he asked. We didn't have time to get into it; we were going to be late for class.

"I'll tell you in class." We started walking to first period when we were stopped by a couple over anxious girls.

"Max, is it true?" one of them asked.

"Is what true?" I was lost.

"That you stole Devon Wahlberg's girlfriend," she said with a sick gossipy grin.

"What?" I instantly was mad.

"Yup, it's all over school that he told you to stay away but you decided to sleep with her anyways." The girl giggled and my hands almost reached out for her neck. Kai saw the murder in my eyes and jumped in just in time.

"Alexis...you know that none of that is true," he smiled.

"But Toni said that she saw Max dropping Samantha off at her house first thing in the morning on Sunday..." she clung to her desperate half-truth. Kai looked at me and I shook my head like I had no idea what anyone was talking about.

"Look, it's not true, but if you come to our show on Friday night, maybe we'll have some answers for you then," he sounded like a used car salesman again.

"Bring Toni too," he winked. My stomach rolled and I stomped off to my classroom.

"Wait up brother," he called to me as he pushed through the couple girls.

"What the hell is wrong with everybody this morning?" I snapped.

"It's a small school Max. You can't hide things for very long around here," he said with a sad smile.

"And that crap you were spewing back there?" I said angry.

"There is no such thing as bad press," he joked. I didn't find it funny.

"There is when it comes to Sam's reputation Kai," I shouted. Maybe this was what she was upset about? Had this nonsense gotten back to her already? Kai and I were almost through the door of our class when his latest comment stopped me.

"Uh oh," he said under his breath. His eyes were focused down the hallway, so I pushed past him to see what was so wrong.

"Uh oh." It was all I could think of to say. Down the hall Devon had stopped Sam in front of her class and they were talking. I pushed forward but Kai's long fingers wrapped around my arm and stopped me as the second bell rang.

"Max, let her handle it."

"She needs..." My mouth froze by the next thing I saw. Sam slowly pulled a note from her notebook and handed it to him. This was followed by a quick hug and a kiss on his cheek. She then ran into her classroom. My blood literally boiled and Kai noticed the change in my temperature but ignored it.

Ember

"Come on Max. I'm sure there's a logical explanation for the note." He didn't sound convincing.

"And the kiss?" I yelled back.

"Umm..." he froze. We sat down in the classroom and I quickly pulled my cell phone out. My hands were shaking with heat and I was afraid I might damage my phone. I typed a text message as fast as I could and sent it to Sam.

"WE NEED 2 TALK ..." – Max

"WHATS UP?" – Sam

"I SAW THE NOTE..." – Max

Nothing. She didn't write back, so I waited...and waited. Kai watched as I sat nervously tapping my phone on the desk waiting. Finally I couldn't wait any longer.

"I NEED THE TRUTH!" – Max

"NOT NOW MAX..." – Sam

"Y NOT?" – Max

"PLEASE DON'T STRESS...L8R." – Sam

She was gone and I was furious. Why was she shutting me out? What had I done wrong? Maybe I was over reacting? The hour crawled by slowly and Kai did his best to wrestle my stress with jokes but I was having none of it. My mind raced with the worst possible scenarios and I felt alone...again.

Biology – 9:47 a.m.

Sam was already at her desk when I entered the classroom. She watched me carefully as I sat down next to her. She leaned in to kiss me on my lips but I turned my head at the last moment and she barely caught the side of my cheek. It was flushed with heat as her soft lips cooled it for a split second. My mouth watered for hers and I felt embarrassed that I didn't have the strength to stay focused on my anger.

"So that's how it's going to be?" she said hard.

"I need an explanation Sam," I demanded as I sat there pouting.

"And you'll get one when you pull your head out of your ass." She crossed her arms and her lips stretched into a thin line. I was stunned. I couldn't believe she was upset with me. How dare her!

"Please explain what you were talking to Devon about," I said as calm as I could.

"Max, you're overreacting," she snapped.

"It's our first day as a couple and you're hiding things from me," I snapped back.

"I am not hiding anything from you," she sounded sweet again. It was the first sign that she knew that I was hurt by her actions.

"This is a small school. I knew it would only be a matter of minutes before it got around that we were together now." She seemed calmer.

"Devon's a big boy, he can handle it." My words brimmed with anger again.

"Yes, he is," she paused. "But we have a history together." Her words cut me like a knife.

Ember

"Even though he hasn't earned it lately, I thought he deserved a proper explanation about you and I." She watched me closely as my hand burned hot. The pen I was holding began to heat up. Her hand slid gently over mine to settle the fire.

"And?" I pouted.

"And the word had already reached him this morning and I was prepared for that. I wrote him a letter explaining just how over he and I are." I let my stubborn eyes find hers again.

"That was me telling him it's over. Done. For good Max," she whispered.

"Really?" I asked unsure.

"Um-hmm." Her big green eyes twinkled at me and I knew it was no use to try and hold onto my anger. I was crumbling now with guilt.

"I'm sorry." I leaned into her. "I'm still a little high from our weekend together and seeing you two like that brought me back down to earth a little."

"It's fine. Tonight will be even better." Her breathing increased as her hand ran along my leg.

"Naughty," I whispered. Then I kissed her quickly before the teacher caught us. Sam made a tiny growling noise which made me laugh.

"I wrote you a song last night," I bragged. She turned red instantly.

"For me?"

"Yup," I smiled.

"Can I hear it?"

"Nope," I teased. She gently hit me as I stared at her through my bangs. "Okay."

MADISON DANIEL

Computers – 11:50 a.m.

Devon and the four horsemen spent the first half of the class talking amongst themselves. But they made it quite obvious who they were discussing. My name came up frequently. So much that I had to stop Sam from going over and saying something to them. She was so angry.

"Max I don't like this, he's up to something," Kai whispered in my ear so Sam wouldn't hear. He wasn't doing a very good job though.

"Let him talk Kai, that's all he's got anyways." I spoke the last part loud enough for the entire room to hear. Sam glared at me and I didn't like it one bit. Neither did Devon. He quickly rose to his feet and walked over to us. He was cool and calm for once.

"Devon, I have nothing else to say to you," Sam said. He smiled like a wild predator.

"Sorry princess, I'm not here to talk to you." His steel eyes fell on me. I twitched in my chair with the image of me shoving a ball of flame down his throat.

"What's up Dev?" I said with a mocking tone. He didn't like being called that and I smiled at the thought of irritating him. The four horsemen walked up behind him slowly.

"You and I got off on the wrong foot," he smirked. I laughed out loud.

"Really...you think?" I was pushing it. Sam's body language disapproved. Kai on the other hand couldn't stop smiling.

"Maybe we could start over. Have you ever been to the Lookout?" his grin widened.

226

"Devon, no!" Sam shouted. She was scared but I couldn't tell if she was afraid for me or him. That made my judgment cloud easily.

"Never been Dev," I taunted. He snorted like a bull and gripped his hands around the edges of my desk and leaned down inches from my face.

"Maybe you'd enjoy a quick tour. It's only a quick two minute ride up the mountain on our bikes. We could go at lunch." His friends leaned in too and Sam's nails dug into my leg.

"It has the best view," Jason added. They all laughed as Sam jumped up.

"We need to talk!" she grabbed Devon by the shirt and dragged him to the back of the classroom. The four horsemen stared Kai and I down for a few seconds and then returned to their desks. Jason had a ball cap on to cover the special haircut I had given him at the party.

"Those curls are coming in nicely J. You should be able to ditch the Mickey Mouse hat next week." I was pushing it again. He whipped around furious. Kai almost fell out of his chair in a fit of laughter.

"Priceless bro," he chortled. Jason turned back to his friends stewing.

"Alright, tell me what's so special about this lookout," I demanded with a serious tone.

"It's a challenge my friend." His smile faded. "The Lookout is where everyone goes to fight."

"Of course..." I said rolling my eyes.

"Devon likes to throw a twist in there though. He wants you to race him up there," Kai sounded nervous.

"He wants to race me?" I was dumb founded.

"The last kid that took him up on his offer ended up in the hospital for a month." He looked me in the eyes. "And when the kid was released Devon sued him…and won."

"Sued him? For what?" I asked amazed.

"For scratching his bike." Kai shrunk back in his seat. I sat there confused. "That's how powerful his family is now bro."

"Well, I haven't been on a bike in years but I do love the feeling of wind rushing through my hair," I joked.

"You're not thinking about it, are you?" Kai was scared.

"Maybe," I smiled.

"Not funny Max," Sam scolded me as she sat down.

"I was just having some fun Sam."

"Fun for you, but he is dead serious," she said. I looked over and Devon's eyes watched me devilishly.

"Maybe he should learn a lesson."

"Damn it Max! The last thing I want is for either one of you to get hurt," she cried out. I didn't like how she included both of us in that sentence.

"I can take care of myself," I argued and her face filled with pain. My temperature was rising and she let go of my hand quickly.

"I know," she said under her breath.

Wildfire_22

~I Don't Care Anymore: Phil Collins~

The class ended with hardly anyone talking to each other. We gathered our things and headed for the food court. Sam stopped me in the hall as Kai continued by himself.

"Max, promise me you won't race him."

"Why are you so worried about it?" I was annoyed now.

"Devon doesn't understand what you're capable of and he really isn't in the best frame of mind right now," she pleaded.

"Wait a second..." Now I was fuming. "Are you worried about me?" my voice carried down the hall. "Or are you worried about him?"

"Max, the whole idea is stupid! That's what I am upset about." I didn't believe her and that killed me to feel that way. Especially after our intimate weekend.

"I'm not going to do anything," I said as she calmed down but I don't think she believed me fully.

"Thank you," she kissed my lips. Her hand slid into mine again and she playfully pulled me along behind her. I smiled and followed even though I felt that this was far from over.

We continued to our familiar spot across the court yard but when we arrived there, someone was waiting nervously for us.

"Aloha Lucy," I said quietly. Sam squeezed my hand tighter and Kai and Marcus stared at each other and shrugged.

"I need to talk to you Max. Alone," her voice trembled. Sam leaned into me making it obvious she did not want to leave me alone with her. Kai and Marcus nodded at each other, without a word and walked over to the snack counter. Sam on the other hand took a little more convincing.

"Sam, just give us a minute...okay?" I asked politely but I was not comfortable talking to Lucy alone. The day had already been more stressful than usual. Sam thought about it for a moment, and then kissed me gently.

"I'll grab us something to drink." Her eyes watched Lucy closely. "Be right back."

From across the yard I noticed Devon watching me again and he smiled when Sam left. My teeth ground together tightly as he walked over to Sam. I didn't trust him at all. I hoped Lucy would make this quick.

"What's going on Lucy?"

"I needed to tell you something," she said as she fumbled through her bag and pulled out a cigarette.

"Do you mind?" she asked as she lit it up.

"Knock yourself out," I said impatiently.

"I think I owe you an apology," she spoke softly. I glanced at her shocked but I don't think she even noticed. She was lost in thought.

"You're a good guy Max," her eyes looked up at me. "You're good for Asia."

"I don't understand..." I was scared.

"I've known her since we were kids and I have never seen her this happy before." Her eyes filled with pain as she spoke those words.

"Or now...this miserable." My mind started racing. Just get up and leave Max. You do not need to hear anymore. Walk away you big dummy. But I didn't take my own advice. I couldn't, I was locked in place like a stone.

"Lucy I think you're exaggerating." I tried to stay calm but I was burning inside.

"I know this must be crazy to hear from me but it's the truth. I know her better than anyone." Her eyes filled with tears as mine began to blur from the heat coming from my cheeks.

"She would probably kill me for telling you this but I can't take her pain anymore."

"Her pain?" I was now terrified.

"Max…Asia loves you." At that moment the Earth cracked and my head split open with a blinding headache.

"What?" I gasped.

"Listen to me Max, she needs you," her tone grew cold. "I hate it but it's true." She took a drag from her cigarette and wiped a fresh tear from her face.

"Lucy…" I said with my head spinning.

"That's why I wanted to apologize to you. You are a good person. I knew it the day you came to my defense, even after I said those horrible things to you." Her jewelry jingled as she messed the back of her hair.

"I'm sorry Max."

"I don't know what to say Lucy," I gasped. She stood up and looked down at me tensely.

"Just don't hurt her," she warned. My eyes caught Sam and Devon talking in the corner of the yard. They were both very upset. Lucy started to run off but then whipped back around.

"Oh yeah, that call the other night. The one Asia received during your dinner…that wasn't me." She started to smile. Now I was completely confused.

"It was her parents."

"And?" I asked losing the last bit of patience I had left.

"They told her that if she cared about you, that she should let you go." Lucy fidgeted her feet.

"I don't understand," I said with my head throbbing.

"Think about it Max, the ones she loves the most leave. Or worse." Lucy sprinted toward the parking lot. Or worse. Those two words kept rolling around my head like a lotto machine. In the back of my brain I could hear Kai's voice…

"THEY SAY SHE'S CURSED." And before I could get my bearings, my day became a whole lot worse.

"Hey newbie!" Jason screeched as he walked up to me. "You have enough time to think about that ride?" I could tell he was still pissed about the comment from earlier but I was in no mood to play now.

"Go away Jason," I said from the back of my throat. Brian took that as a signal to get involved and the twins followed. My hands filled with steam as they surrounded my table.

"I'll tell you what…you can even use my bike," he smiled and placed his hat backwards on his head. The crowd had noticed the testosterone in the air and quickly began to gather. Sam and Devon followed too.

"Knock it off guys!" Sam yelled as she shoved her way through the crowd to me.

"Come on Max…walk me to my next class," she demanded.

Ember

"Just one race newbie," Devon teased. I turned to look away.

"Come on, I've heard you have plenty of experience with...cliffs." He blew me a kiss. Sam watched as my eyes filled with red hot hate and my mind snapped. Had she mentioned my past to him? Had he been checking up on me?

"Keys!" I growled and the crowd cheered. Jason and Brian quickly high-fived each other and tossed me the keys. They flew through the crisp air jingling lightly. Sam grabbed me by my shirt as I stood up.

"Max, think about what you're doing." She looked so disappointed in me, making my anger consume me more. Why didn't her ex get any of that disappointment?

"You heard what he said Sam...my experience. I'm going to show him exactly what I know." I ripped myself from her grasp. "This will only take a minute."

As I stormed off toward the parking lot, with the excited crowd rushing behind me, I waited for her to try and stop me again but she didn't. Instead she pulled Devon aside and began pleading with him.

"Fine then!" I cursed. My walking sped up as I pouted even harder. I was acting like an ill-tempered two year old again but I no longer cared. I cared about only one thing now. I wanted this to happen.

All the kids piled into car after car and drove off in the direction I assumed the Lookout was at. Lucy caught my eye as I walked past her in a fit of rage. She was on her cell phone and by the look on her face; she knew exactly what was happening. I ignored her and the haunting words she had delivered to me the best I could and hopped onto Jason's motorbike.

It was exactly the same make and model as Devon's, just different colors. It was shiny silver with black stripes running along its sides. The tires were brand new and it looked as if it had just been detailed. Devon happily mounted his bike beside me and offered me an extra helmet.

"Last chance to back out of this Valentine," he said with a cocky laugh. I turned and found Sam standing with Kai and Marcus. She was irate with us or just me. I was too pissed to care at that point. I smacked the helmet from his meaty hand and turned the key to my bike. As I winded the engine into a scream a giant lightning bolt split the sky in the distance and thunder shook the parking lot. At that moment I knew exactly who was on the other end of Lucy's cell phone.

"Not a chance," my voice was venom.

~Out Of Control: Hoobastank~

My temper flared and my bike responded to that hot blooded will like it was an extension of me. I wasn't even sure where we were headed, only that I would get there first. Faster and faster our bikes went, blurring the scenery as we did. The black pavement had become a shaky dark blur with a yellow streak slithering along the middle of it like a wicked serpent.

Devon weaved his machine along my right side. Damn he was fast. I pushed my bike harder and it responded with a high pitch squeal, making me smile. The wind was a cooling feeling of being alive as it whipped through my hair. Back and forth we shuffled our positions. He would push himself in front of me and then I would will myself back in front of his bike. Or maybe he was just toying with me? I knew that these motorcycles could go even faster but as the elevation increased, it became harder on them to do so.

Ember

That only seemed to focus me and my responses more. As we rushed up the side of the mountain, we had an audience far behind us. A dozen or so vehicles were in hot pursuit of these two stupid dare devils. They were hard to see in my mirror because of the vibrations of the speeding bike. Making it even harder was a tiny film of fog that had built up on them as my body had heated itself up. The one vehicle I could make out was Sam's and it looked like Kai was behind the wheel.

The winding road started to whip past us at dangerous speeds now but the tiny machines handled the curves with the ferociousness of two leopards stalking their prey. The green of the mountain side washed past my eyes as my inner core heated to extreme levels. I was officially out of control now and I did nothing to cool it. Faint steam trailed off of me leaving a ghostly trail that I hoped no one could see too well at this speed.

But Devon saw it with wide open eyes from his visor helmet. That forced him to hesitate long enough for me to push my smoking body in front of him. I had now taken the lead by a car length, sending my ego into a fit of joy. I was blissfully losing my concentration and my body kept heating up. That was a mistake.

As my body ignited into a faint orange flame the first raindrops hit me. At this speed they felt like bullets to my burning skin. Asia must be close but I didn't have time to think about that now. I was sacrificing agility for speed. I wasn't going to be able to keep that up in this rain. I noticed that even though I was easing my grip on the accelerator, little by little, Devon was still falling farther behind me. He was almost as far back now as the parade of cars following us. I chalked that up to him freaking out by the burning water drops flickering off of my body but I couldn't have been more wrong.

My flames disappeared, filling my eyes with the burning rush of cold air as they focused on the devastation that lied directly ahead. That is when my mind cleared and my heart dropped. This was never just about a race...this was a trap. It was about to work brilliantly.

The road broke off into a hard left turn that was physically impossible to make on a motorbike traveling over 35 miles per hour. I was easily going three times that speed. A couple of vehicles were already parked along the side of the curve of the look out. One was a giant red pick-up truck with two motorcycles, just like the ones we were wrestling. The twins, Eddie and Alex were smiling from the front of it. Brian and Jason were pacing next to them angrily. They must have used a short cut to beat us to the Lookout.

The Lookout itself was just an empty clearing of dirt and gravel, with a chunk of heavy vegetation on the left side. That was good news because that's exactly where I was headed. But there was bad news too; the railing along the Lookout was thick and strong. This meant that it was probably a hell of a drop down the other side of it and at 100 miles per hour. I was about to find that out first hand.

Slow motion slammed into me forcing my sight to fall into blackness. In the dark all I could see was Mia falling away from me. Her eyes filled with tears and her mouth stretched wide open in a silent scream. Her tiny voice called out to me but I couldn't make out her warning until it was too late.

"Burn Max! Let go!" she pleaded in the dark.

My eyes refocused as a lightning bolt stabbed directly beside me, searing my ear. I had never witnessed a strike so close before and it shredded the rain like a dragon on fire. And then there she was...Asia with her brilliant eyes on fire. She screeched the tires of her Jeep to a violent stop as she crossed my path.

Ember

"Max!" she yelled. That was the last thing I saw when I threw my bike sideways and let my body catch flames. I was a giant spinning ball of fire when I slightly clipped the edge of the twin's truck. Smoke and raindrops twirled from my death spin just before I smashed directly into the middle of the brush, igniting it in a furious explosion. The motorbike continued its death roll as I flew from it and it cut through the railing like a hot knife through butter.

This was lucky for me because the twisting hot piece of steel that ripped from the railing into the air, like a jagged sword, stopped my flaming body from flying over the edge. Of course it impaled me and I went numb instantly as blood flew everywhere. The screech of tires and screams from our audience could barely be heard over the crackling of fire and pounding rain.

Devon slid his bike to a stop next to his buddies and quickly removed his helmet. Sam ran from her car screaming, even before Kai had gotten it to a complete stop.

"Call 911!" She screamed.

Most of the crowd turned around and raced back down the hill. I guess this was not what they expected. As my eyes peered through the wall of flames in between Devon and I, my throbbing body began to burn uncontrollably. I could barely make out his face but it quickly turned from shock to content. He was happy.

"Mad Max," I growled. My mind folded in on itself with rage and my body took over. The world washed over in a crimson hue as the inferno exploded all over me.

MADISON DANIEL

Inferno_23

~24: Jem~

The falling rain saturated the ground in huge fat drops, which made the Lookout fill with puddles in seconds. The sounds of screams were drowned out by the closing thunder. It shook so strongly that the piece of shredded steel stuck through my chest, began to vibrate with a low hum. Slowly I pulled my bloodied torso from it, which should have been excruciating, had the devil inside me not rose up and taken over every waking sense and instinct I had. Fire fueled by hate escaped from every pore I had and the most terrifying thing was...I think I liked it. A lot.

I wasn't even free of the steel shish kabob when my body started to heal itself. The flames from the burning brush were still big enough to hide this holy sight from everyone. Everyone except Asia. She was the one closest to me and the only one who knew I was still alive. Her face danced behind the flickering flames as the rain pushed its weight onto the burning brush. She looked like an angel. That calmed me enough to regain control over my actions. Slowly I rose to my feet stretching my face to the drenching rain, filling my mouth with the falling water and I felt reborn. My body absorbed the rain drops as if it were the first time it had ever felt such a creation. My shirt fell at my sides, shredded and soaked, exposing my newly healed chest. It beat heavy with life as the water washed over it. I was revitalized. I felt new. I felt strong. But mostly I felt...mad.

The rain let up slightly as the brush surrendered its crackling wall of fire, exposing me to the last few onlookers. Sam stared in disbelief. Kai and Marcus were frozen in awe with their mouths wide open. I wanted so badly to run to Sam and take her in my arms. Kiss her hard and show her that I was all right. I wanted to high-five Kai and Marcus as we laughed about how ridiculous I must have looked spinning through the air. Finally, my eyes fell upon Devon's spiteful glare. I wanted to end him right where he stood.

Rain dripped from my bangs and the lightning flashed above me, scaring the sun behind the clouds. Fists tightened at my sides. The muscles in my arms flexed. My chest rose to attention with the fire of a thousand suns coursing through its veins. This was my truth. This was me, in all my glory. I exhaled a stream of smoke from my mouth as I marched forward. I was focused only on Devon's face, with my lips pulled back in a devil's smile.

"Max no! Don't do this!" Sam pleaded as loud as she could but the crumbling thunder muffled her plea. Her hands fell against my exposed chest as she pushed herself in front of me to stop my progress but it was no use now. Devon and his gang had positioned themselves and walked nervously toward me. Not even the terrified anguish in Sam's green eyes could stop me now. She tried again but Asia stopped her this time and wrapped her arms around her. This infuriated Sam but Asia did not bend in the slightest.

"He'll never calm down if either one of us pushes him!" Asia scolded her. Sam only fought her harder.

"They don't know how much danger they're in!" Sam spit out. Asia lost what little patience she had and whipped Sam around and stared directly in her eyes.

"They will," Asia said coldly and let Sam go.

"Whose side are you on anyways?" Asia dared her. Sam retreated to Kai and Marcus. They were both still frozen and trying to see through the blanket of falling rain.

Devon and I met about ten feet from each other. We paused for only a second before we began to circle each other. Jason and Brian followed his lead as if they were his shadow and the twins circled the opposite way. They cracked their knuckles at the same time and made cackling noises at me. I continued my cautious dance, never taking my eyes from Devon.

"I guess you lost the race," I laughed.

"This was never about a race Valentine. This was about you knowing your place," Devon spit back.

"You owe me a bike Valentine!" Jason screeched from behind Devon's shoulder.

"Yeah! Do you have any idea what that bike cost?" Brian added. I only smiled bigger at the two henchmen.

"Damn! I'm going to smash your teeth in!" Jason bellowed. He quickly ripped his ball cap from his messy, wet head. Slowly our dance continued. Our vicious circle became smaller with each rotation.

"Now's your chance to back out of this," Devon warned slowly. Steam rose from my shoulders and my fingernails glowed white with heat.

"Enough talking," I growled.

"Somebody help him!" Sam screamed at Kai and Marcus. Kai took a shaky step forward and I shot him a grave look. I shook my head no, water dripped from my dangling bangs. Kai slowly stepped back with Sam, placing his arm around her. She cried harder in his arms.

"This is going to be bad," Marcus said with a chill running down his spine.

Their attack happened quicker than I was anticipating. The twins, Alex and Eddie, came at my sides first. Their skinny bodies whipping through the downpour.

Jason grabbed me from behind as Devon's head and shoulders slammed into my chest, crushing me between the two. I gasped for air as Brian went for my legs like a starting tackle football player. His solid shoulders plowed into my legs with a force that should have sent me crashing into the mud but the twins had a hold of my arms too tightly. Big mistake.

My arms blazed over in a thin white hot flame, scolding their hands seriously. I grinned at the smell of burning flesh and then threw my head back, smashing it into Jason's nose. The dull thud of wetness smacking bone, echoed in my ears as his face split open. He screamed with a choking gag from the gushing blood but was drowned out by the thumping raindrops on the ground. Devon saw this but never stopped throwing his fists into my stomach. Jason fell to the ground gripping his broken face and moaning. Blood washed down his hands in front of his face.

Brian shook off the sight and stepped back, readying another assault on my body. He fell to one knee readying another tackle. I clenched my teeth together so hard I thought that they might shatter in my mouth and pushed the inferno down my spine. The heat and flames seared what was left of Alex and Eddie's exposed arms and they jerked their hands from me. Their pain was massive. Eddie ran screaming back towards his truck and Alex fell to his knees, slamming his hands in the nearest puddle. He was crying feverishly and that made me pause long enough to find my footing again.

Devon paused as well as he realized the odds had drastically changed in a matter of seconds. But he did not retreat, he only grew angrier. His giant paw of a fist swung towards my head but missed as I shifted my weight and shoved a glowing hot fist into his gut. His breath stuttered as the flames hit him. Devon fell backwards and Brian lunged again but missed me this time and slammed all of his body into Alex, who was still on the ground crying. The two tumbled over one another into the mud. Devon could not believe his eyes as he screamed holding his charred stomach.

"I'll kill you!" he spat through the rain. "I'll freakin kill you!"

"Me first!" I cursed back. My throat was caked with blood and the rain streamed from our grimaced faces like gargoyles. I inhaled a quick breath and with the swiftness of a sword, I cut through the rain and stabbed my hands into his chest and neck. He grabbed at them and gasped as they began to burn. The unleashed rage within me was now a monster. I watched as his eyes filled with fear. My face was only inches from his as my breath burned his eyes and the falling rain hid his tears. He started to lose his footing from the lack of oxygen, shrinking toward the mud. Lightning slapped the clouds around us and the wind swirled like a vortex.

"Max...look out!" Asia warned but it was too late. I barely caught Brian with the corner of my eye before he ran up with something in his hands. I started to turn toward him when the long cold metal of the softball bat collided with my ribs and chest. My equilibrium went spinning and my flaming hands snapped back to normal.

"How's that feel freak?" Brian shrieked with fear. I winced as my breath left me and my grip loosened from Devon's neck. Before I could get my sense of direction again the bat connected a second time, sending a shooting pain down my spine. My left arm managed to close itself around the bat and I heated it instantly, burning Brian's slippery hands. Amazement flashed over his face as he ran back toward the truck in agony. He had easily broken almost half my ribs and the pain was crippling. Devon choked as the oxygen returned to his lungs. Jason slowly pulled himself to his feet, clutching his bleeding face with one hand and dragged Alex back to the truck with his

243

other. His twin brother Eddie was still cowering and shaking uncontrollably.

"Samantha belongs to me!" Devon howled with his last breath. A shooting pain blasted inside my chest and Asia screamed. The rain fell black as night, blinding everyone for a moment. My eyes fell to my chest. In slow motion, Devon's hand pulled a 5 inch blade from a new gaping hole. The wound was horrific and spewed blood like a waterfall. He smiled at me with blood in his teeth and my survival mode kicked in again.

My hands reached out for him and caught him by his collarbone. He cursed like a banshee as I spun him around and slid behind his back. My hands burned white hot again and fell through the skin on the back of his neck as I shoved forward with all my might. He thrust forward, with his legs flailing from behind him. He crashed into the muddy puddle below us with a thick splash. I fell to one knee and shoved even harder.

"Stop! You're going to kill him!" Sam screamed at me but I couldn't hear her very well over the pulsating waves of rain and ringing in my head. When I managed to open my mouth to answer her I was cut short.

Eddie had found his second wind and was running toward me at full speed. His face looked terrified but he moved like he was in complete control.

"Ahhh!!!" he groaned as the tire iron connected with my face. It tore open my left cheek, slicing all the way to my ear. With one blow he had leveled the playing field and my grip fell from Devon's shoulders as I collapsed into the mud. Rain poured over me, blurring everything around me. He stood above me screaming and laughing in hysterics when the first hint of emergency sirens penetrated the torrent of rain. I lied dizzy and choking on the falling rain.

Ember

Sam ran up to Devon and me crying uncontrollably. As I let my eyes focus on her, her gentle hands began to help Devon up from the puddle and I snapped...again.

"No!!!" I screamed with mud in my throat.

Like a bullet I was on my feet again and barreling into Eddie's skinny, trembling body. I shoved him all the way back to his truck and we crashed into the side of it with a solid thud. He squealed in pain as I realized my hands had dug themselves into his chest and were scorching his flesh. Asia ran up behind me quickly, placed her hand on my shoulder and her electricity zoomed through me like a drug.

"Enough," she said confidently. I broke my grip on him only to feel my rage over take me again. My hands slammed into the truck on both sides of Eddie's shoulders. He slid down through my arms weeping like a child as I shook the bed with every bit of strength I had left. The metal surrendered to my rage, bending and vibrating.

The sirens were almost upon us now and I felt my control slowly coming back. Asia turned me around as the rain fell away. The sun rolled from behind the clouds again, bringing much needed light again.

"Easy Max. I'm here now," she said as she caressed my face and her cool hands felt so soothing. Her voice was also comforting and calming.

"It's going to be okay," she promised and shifted her body so no one could see my face heal itself. The skin along my face slid together in a white hot seam of fire. The last of her storm washed away the excess blood quickly.

"We have to go Max...now," she scolded. She led me to her Jeep with one hand. Sam had already begun walking Devon to the approaching ambulance and my heart sank. She warned me not to do this but I didn't listen. She only glared at me through her wet blonde locks as Asia and I drove off in the opposite direction.

"Take me home Asia," I said exhausted. "I don't know how I'm going to explain this to anyone."

"Don't worry, you were only protecting yourself," she sounded confident enough. I didn't believe her.

"Most of the witnesses couldn't see what was really happening during the fight. The rain was too thick," she winked. I was too exhausted to think about it.

"Thanks," I tried to smile.

"Besides, if anything comes of this, I have the best lawyers on the island." She floored it and we raced away.

Back at the Lookout the police looked for anyone to question but everyone had already left. Devon and what was left of the four horsemen were placed in the ambulance. Not a single person said a word about what had just occurred. Sam held Devon's bloody hand all the way to the hospital. Kai and Marcus drove Sam's car back to the school parking lot to get Kai's vehicle.

"I've never seen anything like that Kai," Marcus said coldly.

"Me either brother," Kai tried to smile but couldn't. They said nothing else and drove home in silence.

2:07 p.m.

As Asia and I pulled up to my house, the weight of my actions had begun to fall on me. She leaned over and checked my chest and left cheek, then ran her slender fingers through my messed hair.

Ember

"We make a good team," she said coyly. I was way too tired to play any of her games. Not today...not now.

"I guess," I shrugged with guilt in my words.

"Max I know I walked away but you don't have all the facts."

"Lucy told me all about the phone call," I said cold. She stared at me searching for the right words.

"Oh," she was soft.

"I don't care what your parents think about me Asia," I spit out. She slid closer to me.

"I don't care either," she whispered. Her lips pressed softly against mine. I tried to pull away but I no longer had the strength to fight the urge. As I opened the door and stepped from the truck her eyes flashed with confidence.

"I can fix this Max," she smiled and flipped her hair a little.

"I can fix us." Then she drove off.

MADISON DANIEL

Crave_24

~Crave: Nuno Bettencourt~

Tuesday morning – 9:27 a.m. – August 29th.

The smell of cherry blossoms filled the air as my eyes pulled apart to the morning rays of sunlight dancing across my face. At first I thought I might still be dreaming when her dark curls tickled my cheeks and her breath swept across my lips. Finally, when her cool hand traced my stomach, I realized that Asia was here in the flesh and starting my morning off as if I were royalty.

She was wearing a thin white top with spaghetti straps and the word 'DAMSEL' in bold red letters, stretched across the front of it. Her little denim shorts exposed the arch of her lower back. A much better ensemble then I was waking up in, an Aerosmith concert tee shirt and faded boxers. As my brain tried to make sense of this morning delight, a horrible thought crashed the party and I turned my head quickly. Morning breath.

"Wake up sleeping beauty," she whispered. She then tossed herself on the bed, only inches from me.

"I have a surprise for you."

"What time is it?" I sounded grumpy. My fingers pealed the gunk from the corner of my eyes, while they tried to accept how bright my room was from the blasts of daylight peppering my window.

"It's time to get up. You are officially ditching school today...lets go," her voice was cheery and light. School was the last thing I wanted to deal with today and I was sure Frank would not approve of another day off. My eyes caught the flashing green digits of my clock and it read 9:30 a.m. Crap, I was already late; I might as well take Asia up on her offer. I did find it weird that no one had swung by to pick me up for school.

"Okay...you win."

I sat up slowly in my bed wondering why Asia sounded so cheery, especially after the drama of yesterday afternoon. Suddenly, I realized the sun was shining brightly and there wasn't even a hint of a cloud in the sky. She noticed my face fill with doubt at this realization. Her face filled with a soft smile.

"Weird huh," she joked as she ran her arms through the warm sunlight. It washed over her skin, warming her gently. I hadn't seen her in direct sunlight too often, at least not like this. She was stunning. She moved like a poem. Her healthy almond skin complimented her rich dark hair, which had the faintest hint of blue scattered throughout it. We settled into a sweet, peaceful moment where I wished time would stop.

"No...not weird at all," I said as I rolled over the top of her and swept her hair off of her shoulders, making it fan out on the bed above her.

"So what's different?" I asked.

"Hmmm..." She softly bit her lower lip and shrugged her shoulders. "Just really happy I guess," she finished with a whisper. I could have spent the rest of my life in that moment, soaking in every ounce of her being, but I was becoming more aware of how much I needed a shower. As I rose from the bed I stretched my arms out, cracking a few bones in my back. Stumbling across my room I glanced back at her.

"Be back in a few." I shuffled toward my door, removing my shirt and tossing it into the dirty laundry basket by my closet. A low rumbling came from outside my window and the sun's rays fell behind a cloud, changing the color of my room. I turned back to Asia who was now on her stomach with her legs folded up in the air behind her. They were slowly swaying from side to side and she was staring at me with her hand under her chin, looking as if she were hungry. Her eyes scanned my body and the thunder rumbled again, which made me heat up in embarrassment. I think my entire body blushed.

"I'll be here," she purred.

I climbed in the shower and cleaned my ins and outs as fast as I could, in fear that she would be gone before I was done. To my surprise, I was pleasantly proven wrong. She lied along my bed in the same position that I had left her in and she hadn't moved an inch. Her smile greeted me as she tossed me one of my old tank tops.

"You'll need this," she said sitting up slowly. I wasn't sure what she meant but I slid it over my frame, pulling it tightly down over the waist of my black and grey board shorts.

"How's that?" I asked.

"Perfect," she glowed. She met me in the middle of my room and kissed me softly, while her hands teased my still wet hair.

"Do I at least get a hint of where we're going?"

"Nope."

She grabbed my hand and led me to her truck. The skies had filled in with off white clouds but the sun managed to find an opening every now and again. I took a deep breath as I climbed into her Jeep. The merry-go-round of emotions I had been on lately seemed to weaken my better judgment more than once. I was going to keep my guard up today...no matter what. She leaned over and kissed me long and passionately. A faint shower of sprinkles fell upon us like a mist and the sky shook with excitement.

"What was that for?" I asked winded. The tiny raindrops glistened in her hair like slivers of diamonds. My guard fell too easily when she smiled and said.

"It's my turn." She bit her lip nervously and drove off.

After about twenty minutes the Jeep came to rest in front of a small building that was home to four different businesses. The farthest one from us being a tattoo parlor called Island Ink.

"So who's getting inked today? You or me?" I asked already sure of the answer.

"Both," she was filled with optimism. I was anything but.

Inside there were hundreds of designs plastered over every inch of the walls. A thousand colors and shapes filled my head. As I soaked up the different styles of art my body broke out in goose bumps. The shops air conditioner was blowing at full force and the room felt freezing. It couldn't have been much more then forty degrees in the place. Asia called to the owner who popped from behind a purple curtain in the back of the shop and waved at us to come back and join her. She looked to be about 40 or so, with medium length, brown hair. Red streaks cut down the sides highlighting her natural color and her arms were covered in colorful sleeves of tattoos. She was dressed in brown leather pants and a black tee shirt with the shops logo printed on it in white. A matching long sleeved shirt dangled from her hand.

"Asia doll...how are you?" the woman shouted and tossed it to Asia.

Ember

"Better than usual Rose," Asia said smiling at me. She leaned in and offered her a big hug. "Is everything ready?"

"Don't be silly!" Rose said almost offended. Asia slid the shirt over hers and winked at me.

"Max is it?" Rose asked turning her attention to me. She grabbed my hand, pulling me through the doorway to an even colder room.

"Yes. Pleased to meet you Rose," I said unsure.

"So you're the one that's had my girls head filled with hearts and rainbows," she teased heartily. Asia groaned and I laughed.

"Rainbows?" I asked with a smile. She blushed and turned from me quickly.

"See!" Rose shouted. "She's a mess because of you."

"A beautiful mess," I added. Asia turned back to me and Rose rolled her eyes.

"Easy Romeo..." she warned. "Are we still going with the designs we had talked about before?" Rose asked.

"Yes." Asia smiled at me.

"And what designs are those?" I was nervous now. Not to mention, officially cold. Asia laughed softly and shoved me down in a chair next to a table full of tattooing equipment. Rose pulled up a stool next to me and started preparing her tools. Asia stood in front of me, rocking softly on her feet with a large bag of ice in her hands.

"Asia I can already see my breath in here. What's with the ice?" My teeth chattered and she giggled.

"I have a theory...so bear with me." She met my eyes and handed the bag to Rose.

"Shirt off son," Rose demanded. Asia reached out and pulled my tank top over my head, messing my hair up in the process. Worry filled my face and my core jump started itself, heating up my skin instantly. This annoyed Asia.

"Max I need you to focus."

"I will just as soon as you explain what the hell you two are doing," I spit out growing a little annoyed myself. Just then a long cold needle penetrated the skin of my right shoulder blade, causing me to flinch.

"Hold still son," Rose warned. I looked at Asia for answers.

"It's Novocain Max." Her eyes filled with worry.

"Novocain!" I panicked.

"Rose has made her shop as cold as possible, at my request. The ice pack is back up, in case we need it colder." She paused as the first effects of the Novocain kicked in.

"And the drugs?" I said angrily. Asia only smiled bigger.

"If your abilities are truly instinctual, then maybe this will give us enough time to let the ink take." I rolled my eyes at her.

"And that's where you come in. I need you to concentrate. Don't let yourself heat up at all."

I looked up at her with surprise. "And how do I do that?" I was already heating up.

"Just breathe and concentrate," she said confidently. I wasn't convinced but I was also too far along now to stop.

"Alright, let's get this party started," Rose announced and Asia ran behind me.

"Wait a sec, I almost forgot," she said and pulled a fresh tube of bright red lipstick and painted her full lips deeply. With a pout she leaned down and kissed my back.

"There. What do you think Rose?" she asked proud of herself.

"Perfect honey. Now stand back, we need to get this show on the road before I lose all the feeling in my hands." A hearty laugh jumped from her throat. I didn't find it particularly funny and a shiver ran down my spine. Asia walked back into my view...she was so beautiful. Her candy apple, red lips made me burn for her inside. So I quickly closed my eyes and took a long deep breath.

An hour in a half later my eyes snapped open with a slap from Rose's hand on my opposite shoulder...THWACK!

"All done son, go and have a look." Rose pointed to a mirror on the other side of the room and Asia watched me nervously as I stood up. I walked to the mirror half expecting the new artwork to already be fading but was shocked to find the exact opposite. The new tattoo glowed as if it were three dimensional. The color was twice as rich and bright than any other tattoo I had ever seen before.

The image finally hit me like a ton of bricks. In dark bold capital letters were two words...'CRAVE YOU.' They were outlined in sapphire blue with dozens of cherry blossoms intertwined throughout them. At the bottom corner of the U was Asia's lips, as full and luscious as they were on her face. My pulse began to race and her arms wrapped around me.

"I take it you like it," she said softly.

"It's amazing," I said. She noticed how hard my heart was beating and slid her warm hand over it.

"Good," she smiled. I froze for a second in her arms, worried that my blood pressure was increasing and might ruin this wonderful piece of art. Inhaling a long slow breath I closed my eyes and slowed my heart rate a little.

"Great!" Rose announced. "I'm turning the heater on before I die of hypothermia." She stormed past us, handing the bag of ice to me as she did.

"Just in case," she said with a gleam in her eyes.

"Great," I whined. She then pulled Asia off of me and gave us a quick glance, up and down.

"Hmph...kids and their hormones." She disappeared behind the purple curtain, back to the front of the shop.

"Asia, how much did you tell her about us? About me?"

"Relax, I've known her for years. She knows everything about my special abilities," she said as she removed the long sleeved shirt she had been given earlier. "And when it came to you, she didn't even bat an eyelash. She did what I asked."

"So how much does she know?" I was still nervous.

"Enough," she smiled and walked through the curtain. I left it at that and slowly put my shirt back on, giving my newest tat one last glance in the mirror. I truly did love it.

A few minutes passed as Rose fit her stencil to Asia's bare right shoulder. The tattoo gun began its tiny hum shortly after and the shops temperature seemed to heat back to normal. Thunder rolled outside as Rose's gun inked over a sensitive spot on Asia's shoulder blade.

Ember

"Stop being a sissy!" Rose scolded her. We all laughed and the hour passed quickly. The rain had started to lightly pepper the windows and I watched Asia closely. A few minutes later Rose was slapping her on the shoulder too, announcing she was finished.

"Not too shabby, if I do say so myself," Rose said smiling. Asia ran to the mirror I happened to be standing next to and turned her shoulder into the shiny reflection. Puffing up from her flawless skin was one symbol. It was jet black with orange shading around it and looked to be Asian. It was surrounded by light and dark blue waves swirling around in a circle. The waves were so perfectly drawn I would swear that they were moving. At the bottom was two numbers written in bold black ink. '8/13.'

"What does the symbol mean?" I asked quietly but Asia only looked in my eyes through the reflection of the mirror. Rose chimed in from behind us.

"It means 'FIRE' in Chinese," she smirked at me. Of course it does, I thought to myself.

"And the numbers?" I asked while Asia's eyes filled with tears, making them liquid pools of blue diamonds.

"The day we first met," she wiped her eyes gently. "August 13th."

"The day on the beach." I pulled her face to mine and kissed her deeply. Rose grunted disgusted and gathered her things and walked toward the front door.

"Well, I think I'm done for the day," she announced loudly.

"What?" My question stopped her momentum. "It's barely lunch time and you're done for the day?"

"With what she pays me, I'm done for the week!" she bellowed with a wink. "Asia, be a doll and lock up for me when you are done."

With a wave she was gone. We were alone with only the gentle rain against the shop windows.

The rest of the afternoon was a blur. We ate lunch at a local diner which catered to mostly seafood and she found out how much I hated it. Ice cream followed as we walked and talked all afternoon. We raced the sunset home and I felt renewed. The rain followed us closely the whole day.

"Thank you for a great day. I needed it," I said as the rain picked up a little.

"Good..."

"I needed you," I added and her eyes flashed with comfort.

"Max...I...I..." She stopped and looked toward the horizon. I knew what she was thinking at that moment, what she couldn't let herself say. She loved me.

"Will you come in and say hello?" I asked changing the subject quickly. We had come too far emotionally today; I didn't want to ruin it by pushing her. She thought about my invitation for a few quiet seconds and finally nodded her head no. I knew she wouldn't want to come in and go a couple rounds with my uncle, but I tried.

"I better not," she said in a whisper. I wilted a little when she said no but I was still on cloud nine. She kissed me one last time before she ran back to her Jeep and drove away. I waved goodbye in the rain and wondered how soon before I would see her again. I shook off the rain and walked in my house, expecting the third degree from Frank, but it never came.

"There's my boy," he sounded almost jolly. "Is it raining again? I can't remember a summer this wet before." He let the thought go and focused on me. Oh boy, here it comes.

"Good day at school Max?" he asked kindly. What? He hadn't heard that I ditched today? Or about the big fight yesterday? My brain started to lock itself up with question after question.

"Uh...yeah. Great day uncle." I decided to go with the flow and not push my luck.

"Was that Asia I heard driving off?" he was stern.

"Um...yeah. She picked me up today." Now I was nervous.

"I guess that makes sense with Samantha being stuck at the hospital all day with her friend," he said the words so calmly, never noticing the miserable expression that washed over my face.

"Her friend?" I played dumb.

"Yeah, her father told me that Devon Wahlberg and his friends got in a wreck out on Highway 36. That's always been such a dangerous pass. I guess they're pretty banged up." I was frozen and confused. "Sam didn't mention any of this to you?"

"She doesn't appear to be talking to me at the moment. And he's more than just her friend." I felt the anger welling just beneath the surface and walked to my room.

"Oh," Frank said as if he would continue his questioning but he never did.

I went into my room trying not to think the things I was thinking. Sam was with him. That killed me inside. They weren't pressing charges. That confused me. I still hadn't heard a peep from Kai or Marcus. What the hell was going on? I could have gone on like that for hours but

I stopped myself and ran to the mirror and looked at my tattoo. Why wouldn't Asia admit to me how she feels? Why couldn't she say those three little words? Quickly a sobering thought hit me. Could I say them?

I wanted to...but could I? Should I?

Numb_25

~Straitjacket: Alanis Morissette~

Wednesday morning – 8:05 a.m. – August 30th.

I hadn't heard a peep from Kai or Marcus in two days, since my very public unveiling of my temper. My real temper. I still wasn't sure how much they had witnessed during the fight. The wall of rain that Asia provided was dark and thick and they may not have seen anything supernatural at all. But here I was, strolling up to Kai's car like normal.

Kai offered a welcoming smile as I climbed in the passenger's side. From the back seat, Marcus seemed to have trouble making eye contact with me. Almost as if he was scared of me. That hurt my feelings a little but I couldn't really blame him.

"So where have you been hiding stranger?" Kai joked. I was relieved to hear his relaxed and playful tone but at the same time, I found myself mildly angry. Why hadn't he returned any of my calls? I had called him at least a dozen times.

"Asia kidnapped me yesterday," I said calmly. His eyes widened with excitement.

"Nice!" He slapped the steering wheel. "I knew you were in good hands."

"Kai, I've been trying to get a hold of you for the last two days." I turned to Marcus and he smiled nervously. "Both of you."

"My bad Max," Kai laughed. "I left my phone in Sam's car after the fight and since she's been missing in action too, I haven't had a chance to get it back." He saw how I winced when he said her name.

"She hasn't left Devon's side," he spoke carefully. I paused for a second.

"Yeah...that's what I heard," I said a little sadder than I was expecting. Marcus fidgeted in his seat and I figured I needed a little damage control.

"Sorry Max," Kai added.

"No, it's okay. I'm the one who should be apologizing to you two," I said. Marcus leaned forward a little.

"Things got a little crazy Monday and I should have warned you about my temper."

"Temper? That was more like a reckoning!" Kai laughed. "Devon and his friends had it coming Max."

"Yeah...but..." I tried to say but was cut off.

"But nothing brother," he smiled. "I'm just glad we had front row seats," Kai cheered.

"You two didn't see anything...well...a little hard to explain?" I stuttered out the question. They both looked at each other quietly and I filled with a nervous fire.

School was weird now. Either the kids would ask me the most ridiculous questions about the fight or they would just point and stare. Sam wasn't here and that made our classes together drag on and on. I did see Brian walking through the halls but he avoided me completely. It made sense that he was back at school; he was the one who had only suffered a few bumps and bruises from the fight. He stumbled off pitifully with his taped up hands crossed under his arms.

At lunch I took a few moments from jamming with the guys to call Sam. It was the fifth time today and Kai just shook his head at my desperation. It rang and rang before someone answered.

"Hello." It sounded like Sam's mom, Rebecca.

"Is Samantha there?" my voice cracked.

"Max? Is that you?" she asked worried. "How are you? I heard you were involved in the accident too."

"You did?" I was confused.

"Yes...Samantha told us you refused medical treatment. Are you all right?" her voice was kind.

"I'll live." I felt guilty using those words with where she was at the moment. "Can I talk to Sam please?"

"Hang on, she just walked in," she spoke softly with her hand covering the phone so that I couldn't hear anything. I could still hear Sam's muffled voice on the other end though. She was upset and then the line went dead.

"Damn it."

Thursday lunch – 12:27 p.m. – August 31st.

My morning went the same way as the day before. The rumors increased and so had my celebrity. There was still no sign of Sam, which made my morning classes unbearable again. Brian was joined by Jason and one of the twins, Alex. Brian was wearing smaller bandages on his hands now. He looked almost back to normal. Jason on the other hand looked the opposite. Both of his eyes were black and almost entirely hidden by the large bandage across the middle of his face. He had bruising and some scrapes along his neck and he blushed when we made eye contact. Either from embarrassment or anger, I wasn't sure which. Probably a little of both. Alex wouldn't even look my way. Both of his arms and hands were covered in bandages and they couldn't move very well. His face was scratched up with one of his cheeks bruised. It was obvious he didn't know how to act without his twin brother around.

No one talked to them much, at least not while I was around but they did get their fair share of stares and glares. Those stares and glares were taking their toll on me also. My sanity was at a breaking point when we had finally sat down at lunch and started jamming. Half way through our first song Kai stopped playing and asked me if I was okay.

"I guess," I said.

"You shouldn't be stressing yourself out like this Max," he smiled. I just ignored him and found Lucy walking on the other side of the yard.

"I'll be right back guys," I said standing up. The two kept playing as I walked off in the direction of Lucy.

Now I had no idea why I was seeking her out, I just did it. Even as I approached her I hadn't the slightest idea what I was going to say.

"Hi Lucy." I was nervous and she watched my hands as I spoke. That made me nervous so I slid my hands into my back pockets and continued. "I wanted to say thank you."

"Why?" She was surprised.

"For the other day, when you called Asia." I chose my words carefully. "If she hadn't shown up..." I traveled off. I wasn't sure how much she knew about my abilities.

"She calms you doesn't she?" she said point blank. I was shocked and had to remove my chin from the floor. "You two balance each other out."

Ember

"What has she told you Lucy?" I asked with my fingers crossed.

"Everything." My stomach sank. She smiled at my obvious discomfort.

"We've always been as close as sisters. Most people took that as something else but we really never cared what other people thought," her voice was sharp. "We love each other. That's all that ever mattered to me," she searched my eyes.

"Oh." I couldn't find any more words.

"I won't say anything about what I know Max. Only because she made me promise not to," she chose her next words carefully.

"But that doesn't make us friends." Her face fell hard on mine.

"I wasn't trying to..." I started to say before she stepped forward.

"She may present herself as very strong Max but she is exactly the opposite. She is so fragile...so breakable." She began to cry. "And now you are in the position to do the most damage."

"I'm sorry." I wasn't sure why I apologized, it just came out. Lucy wiped her eyes, smearing her heavy makeup in the process.

"I don't like that!" she grumbled.

"I know this won't make you feel any better but I do love her." She stepped backwards from my words. "So much that it scares me sometimes."

"Me too Max...me too," she sulked. I felt terrible now and wanted to run in the opposite direction. Maybe if I changed the subject...

"I hope to see you at the concert Friday night." I wasn't sure if I really meant that but for some reason I wanted her to like me. She shrugged her shoulders in indecision and turned to walk away. Just before I turned away too, her eyes locked onto me from behind those bright blue bangs.

"And the blonde?" she cursed. I froze with my legs ready to buckle and she nodded.

"That's what I thought."

4:01 p.m.

After school I found myself in Kai's garage in a daze. Asia was by my side again and she could tell that something was bothering me. She never asked me what was wrong; she just gave me my space but seemed to be dissecting every word that I would say, which wasn't very many in the mood I was in.

"Give me a minute guys," I said setting my guitar down.

"No prob," Marcus sang into the microphone in front of him.

"Good...I could use a drink anyways," Kai said as he headed for his house. "Anyone else need something to drink?"

"We're fine." She answered for both of us without even the slightest glance his way. Kai smiled and waved for Marcus to follow. He did quickly.

"Asia can I ask you something?"

"Anything," her voice was as sweet as her smell.

Ember

"Are you happy?" The thunder grumbled far away. "I mean...are you happy with me?" I asked and a single slice of lightning flashed above us.

"Take it easy," I warned.

"Why would you ask me that Max?"

"I don't know," I was lying.

"Yes, you do." She was upset now.

"Because of your actions," I spit out bluntly. "One minute you're by my side and I feel safe and complete and the next minute you're gone and you show up when it's right for you," I yelled. Her brow creased with frustration.

"You're questioning my feelings for you?" she was furious.

"No, not at all." I turned from her angry stare.

"Asia, our time together has been the best and when we hold each other and kiss each other..." I turned back to her hurt face. "My heart screams."

My warming hand found her soft cheek. "But I think I need more than that."

"What more is there than the way we are together?" she asked worried and the rain fell with full drops. It soaked us both in seconds.

"I think I need you to tell me. I need you to say it." Her eyes stared at mine. "I know the way I feel for you and I know the way you feel for me. Even if you won't let yourself say it." I pulled her against me and inhaled the deepest of breaths.

"I love you Asia." There, I said it. No turning back now. "I've loved you from the first moment I saw you."

"At the beach," she whispered a little dazed.

"No, the morning I first arrived, when you almost ran me over with your Jeep." I smiled but she only looked more upset. So much for being honest.

"Max, I'm not good at this," she said coldly and pulled herself away.

"Yes, you are!" I said upset. It had been a stressful week and it wasn't going to take much to light my fuse.

"Why won't you tell me how I make you feel?" I shouted over the crackling rain.

"Max you know I hate being pushed!" she warned and the storm overhead backed up her every word.

"Tough!" I spit out. That was a bad idea. She stormed off toward her truck and the rain fell even harder. As she started the engine up my anger got the best of me.

"Fine! Leave!" I screamed with a smile. She paused for a moment behind the wheel as her eyes filled with tears. She scratched them away and then she was gone. I dragged my angry feet back to the garage.

"Love huh?" Kai asked from behind me. Marcus was at his side too.

"Ain't it a bitch?" Marcus chuckled and handed me a bottle of water.

"How much of that did you guys hear?" I asked taking a sip from the bottle.

"Too much," Marcus smiled.

"Oh." I leaned against my amp that she had bought me.

"You're screwed," Kai teased. He smiled and clinked his bottle against mine, making a little chime sound with his mouth.

"I know."

Ember

~After Tonight: Justin Nozuka~

Kai drove me home later and I cleaned up and settled into my room. Just Oz and I. I was happy to be alone again. I took out my cell and dialed Sam's number again. It went directly to her voicemail without even ringing. That was a good sign that she was officially done with Max Valentine. I leaned over and patted Oz's head, letting out a giant sigh. The rain pounded against my house until I fell asleep.

Friday after school – 3:35 p.m. – September 1ˢᵗ.

The excitement of the upcoming show had my day fly by restlessly. Sam had officially taken the whole week off and was nowhere to be seen. That's good though because I had no idea what I would say to her if I saw her anyways. I wasn't even sure I wanted to talk to her anymore.

The four horsemen were back together today. Brian, Jason and the Hansen twins were trying their best to pick up where they left off but you could tell it was hard for them without their fearless leader, Devon. Eddie, the twin I had lost my temper with and slammed against the truck, looked bad. His chest was wrapped up, along with his arms and hands. He tried to cover his torso with clothing but by now everyone in school knew he was anything but okay. I only saw him for a moment but I was surprised he came to school as bad as he was.

Most of the gossip today was about the show tonight and if there might be some form of retaliation from the horsemen. By the way they were keeping their distance I wasn't too worried. That only left my nerves about performing tonight. As I made my way to the parking lot Asia pulled in quickly and her Jeep looked different. She had attached the trucks soft top on; it was as black as the rest of the truck. I found that strange because she seemed to enjoy the wind through her hair. I opened the door and slid my body inside and she greeted me with a kiss.

"Hey sexy," she cooed.

"You talking to me again," I snapped annoyed. She deflected my anger with a shy smile.

"No more fighting. Let's start over." Her tone was demanding. I pouted and looked around silently.

"What's with the Jeep top?"

"Just trying something different," she smiled. I glanced behind me and noticed half dozen shopping bags.

"You've been busy I see."

"Just a few things for the show tonight," she said biting her lip. I found my eyes trapped in hers.

"And for later." Her eyes sparkled as the wind picked up. She was forgiven.

In my room I found myself spending more time flirting with Asia than preparing for the show. I just couldn't resist her velvet soft lips and cooling embrace. After a few hours of play we were interrupted by my uncle. He gently tapped on my bedroom door.

"Hey Max...got a minute?" he asked and offered Asia a polite smile. "Hello Ms. Michaels."

"Please, call me Asia," she demanded in her softest tone. "I'll start getting ready," she said as she stood up with a few of the designer bags in her hands. She blew me a kiss and slithered past my uncle.

"I need to talk to you son," he said serious. My cell phone rang and I hesitated before answering it.

"Go ahead. I'll be in the kitchen when you're done."

"Okay uncle." I looked down at the incoming number and froze. It was Sam. I slowly brought the phone to my ear and answered it. "Sam?"

"Max..." she was very quiet. "Can we talk?"

"Now is not the best time. I have a gig tonight." It was still hours away but I was stalling. I didn't want to have this conversation, especially with Asia in the next room.

"Maybe we could talk at the show? Maybe before you go on?" she asked worried.

"How about after? I can't guarantee my undivided attention but after the show...I'm all yours." I tried to calm my nerves in my tone but I don't think it worked.

"Okay," she said.

"Sam?" I asked quickly.

"Yes Max."

"Are you okay?" worry filled my voice. She said nothing for a long second.

"We'll talk." She hung up and I tossed my phone on the bed and headed for the kitchen. My head was beginning to throb a little.

"Hey uncle." He was waiting at the table with his arms crossed.

"Max, I need to know what you know about the accident that happened Monday." He shifted his weight in the chair. "I need to know how you were involved."

"Uncle...everything's okay now." He did not like my answer.

"Samantha's parents asked me how you were doing after the accident. They wanted to know why you refused medical attention on the scene when all the other boys were so badly hurt," his tone was dreadful. "Let's hear it."

"Devon and his friends crossed a line. A line they will not cross again," I said smugly.

"Max you know better!" He was so mad.

"Do you realize it took Samantha and her family two days to convince the Wahlberg's not to press charges?" It hurt to hear that.

"I didn't mean for this..." He cut me off.

"They are still thinking about a lawsuit."

"Really?" I felt horrible now. My uncle didn't deserve this...not because of my stupid temper.

"I can't afford legal fees Max. If the courts get involved, that's it...you're done. You do not have anywhere else to go." He started to choke up a little.

"Uncle..."

"I don't want to lose you," he said flustered.

"Uncle...I'm sorry. You're right, I have to be smarter than I have been," I agreed filled with gloom. "I won't let you get hurt by this."

"Max, don't you understand? The only way I get hurt by this, is if I lose you," he said proudly.

"I understand." I was a bad person.

"Don't sweat the legal stuff," he said as Asia walked up.

"Legal fees will not be an issue," she said coldly but with a warm smile. Frank disapproved of her comment

272

but I barely noticed when Asia's web caught me in it blindly.

Her hair was pulled up loosely and her makeup was flawless. She stood in my kitchen smelling like heaven. Her floral scent sent dizzying waves over my senses. A tight metallic blue dress of Asian design was painted on her hourglass. It was deadly short and her long legs were wrapped in black stockings with strappy matching heels that made her six feet tall. But not even her beauty could sway my uncle's anger. She realized that before I did and pulled me from the table quickly.

"We're going to be late Max," she winked at Frank and dragged me to the door. I fumbled along behind her like a brainless zombie, with my mouth wide open. My hands popped with excited heat.

"Be good Max," Frank called from the kitchen and his voice sounded hurt. That hurt stung me back to the living and guilt washed over me thick. My uncle had done nothing but sacrifice for me and I was treading all over that. I needed to be better, at least for his sake. My head pounded harder as we pulled out of the driveway.

"I can't wait for tonight Max!" she said full of sin. The clouds filled in the darkening sky and my heart kept pace with the growing thunder. My chest filled with nerves as my eyes fell to hers in the rear view mirror. She smiled with her eyes and I cleared my throat nervously.

"Asia...you are my kryptonite," I sighed helpless.

MADISON DANIEL

Crashing_26

~Mouth (The Stingray Mix): Bush~

Friday night – 7:40 p.m.

It was less than twenty minutes until show time and I should have been ecstatic about our first concert. Club Tsunami was smaller than I expected but still big enough to hold 300 screaming bodies. That's 600 hundred eyeballs, Kai warned me earlier. It was open floored with a tall ceiling and a mid-sized stage, which was covered by a thick red curtain that smelled of mold. A dozen tinted windows surrounded the venue, letting in no light at all.

The crowd was much larger than I expected and the venues lone security guard was on edge because of it. He was a heavy set gentleman with a giant flashlight and extremely bad breath. He paced the perimeter of the place every 15 minutes nervously.

I found my stress overwhelming as I set up the last few things on stage. My mind was racing with thoughts of how I let Frank down or how scared I was to talk to Sam. What was I thinking letting myself get so close to two different girls? How could I be so stupid?

"Max you are going to be amazing!" Asia whispered in my ear as she cozied up from behind me. Her fingers traced my arms down to my hands and she pulled them up to her mouth. With the softest of breaths she began to blow on them, it felt sweet and cool. It was scary how well she understood how I worked.

"Thanks," I said distant.

"What's wrong?" she asked.

"Nothing. I just feel bad for the way I left things with Frank," I sounded depressed. Her eyes looked deep into mine.

"This is your night," she whispered into my ear.

"I guess."

"Just let the music speak for you." She slowly began swinging her hips to the music playing over the speakers and my mouth grew dry instantly.

"You're right." Giving in I kissed her.

I could hear the crowd growing restless from behind the giant red curtain that separated us and my heart sped up. Asia's hand found my chest and rested itself over the pounding and I quickly calmed down. Marcus strolled up with his instrument in hand. He began tuning his green and black bass. Things were going to be okay, I thought to myself. That was until the curtain in front of us parted just enough for a single body to slip through. When Sam's golden curls fell into view, I thought the thunder outside would shatter the windows.

She was wearing a little green dress that exposed more of her skin than I was used to seeing. Her makeup was fancy but still natural looking and she was wearing high heels, another first for her. Her hair was curled and cascading down her curvy little body. She held her camera close to her stomach and smiled lightly at me.

"Hi," she was so nervous. Asia stepped forward, marking her territory. I tightened my grip on her hand and gently pulled her to me.

"My night...right?" I spoke calmly. Her eyebrow raised and a pout formed on her lips.

"Let me handle this." I kissed her cheek and Sam looked away when I did.

Ember

"I'll grab you some water," she said with the emotion of a robot and walked away angrily, never taking her eyes off the competition.

"I go on in less than ten minutes. Can't we talk after the show?" From behind me a symbol crashed and Kai smiled at us.

"Seven minutes bro!" he called out.

"Kai gimme a sec," I shot back. He winced and nodded in agreement.

"This can't wait...we need to talk," she managed to sound calm.

"Then talk," I said impatient. She stood her ground clutching her camera and watching me closely.

"I see you've made your choice," she scolded.

"Wait a second! You made yours first!" Now I was mad. "So you made my decision a whole lot simpler." I stormed off to the side of the stage but she followed close behind.

"We're not done Max!" She grabbed my arm. "You owe me an apology." My mouth flew open in disgust.

"What?" She was talking crazy.

"And a thank you!" she added with venom.

"For what?" I almost screamed.

"For cleaning up your mess!" Now she was up on her toes, pushing her emerald eyes into my face. Kai smacked one of his drums and she lost it.

"Kai! Not now!" Her curls were shaking. Kai's eyes were sad and he stumbled off stage, throwing his sticks to the floor.

"Devon and his buddies got exactly what they deserved! And for you to stand at his side when I needed you most is unbelievable!" I stepped back from her.

"Max...please..." She reached for me.

"And after the night we spent..." My hands flared to life. "Sam, please leave," I begged through my teeth.

"No!" she snapped. She was so damn stubborn. "I'm not done with you yet."

"Yes, you are," Asia said walking up. She had a bottle of water in one hand and my guitar in the other. Sam stood her ground even though her confidence was fading now.

"Max..." Sam begged.

"Don't make me say it again!" Asia warned. The thunder pushed itself against the walls, making the kids in the audience nervously cheer. My head was spinning as my inner core came alive. I wanted to run outside into the rain and scream.

"Don't push me away," Sam pleaded as her hand found mine and when she felt the heat it was generating, she pulled hers back quickly. She was still scared of me...and with that, I snapped.

"Leave!" I yelled so loud that everyone back stage turned and looked at us.

"Bye bye Goldie locks," Asia smirked. I gave her a dirty look and she gave it right back to me. Then I saw the fear and hurt wash over Sam's face and my inferno engulfed me.

"Ahhh!" I screamed. I swung my guitar around my neck and twisted the volume knob to the max as my lips pushed against the cold steel microphone. Kai and Marcus were caught off guard and ran for their instruments.

Ember

Lightning crashed outside when I grabbed the mic and howled.

"...ALL YOUR METAL ARMOR!"

The crowd was taken by surprise and so was the young man running the giant curtain. The crowd roared to life as the curtain stuttered open. My hand came down on my strings, unleashing a gut wrenchingly loud chord that split the air.

"...NOTHING HURTS..." My eyes caught Sam's. "...LIKE YOUR MOUTH!"

The audience screamed holding their arms in the air as the green and red lights from the stage washed over them. Kai's drums came crashing in behind me. My chest thumped with every beat. Marcus and his bass crawled across the stage and slid to life, filling everyone's ears with the pulsating hum of the music. The groove was undeniably sexy and my guitar cried to the rafters. The music was born from us and the crowd bounced with every twist and turn of its rhythm.

Sam disappeared off the stage clutching her camera and crying. I pulled my eyes from her tears because it hurt me too much. Asia danced near the end of the stage, never taking her eyes off of me. I was raw and breaking but she was my rock in this sea of pain. I used her strength. I used her beauty to not fade into this abyss of doubt. My eyes locked with hers as she moved to the music, mesmerizing me. I sang to her. I sang for her.

Halfway through our set I spotted Lucy in the crowd. She was dancing and swaying at the back of the theatre. She genuinely looked happy in the moment; even though I was sure her first priority was Asia. She had spotted Lucy seconds after I had and the rain slashed at the venues dark windows.

We finished our set after about an hour and it took another hour for the crowd to fade to about twenty kids, the band included. Some kids wanted autographs and others just wanted to talk and we obliged as best we could. It felt good to be adored for the music we loved. My body was spent when we started to pull our gear apart.

"You guys were so good!" Asia said sweetly as she snuggled around my left side. She kissed me hard and inhaled the heat coming from my body.

"Thanks," my voice was scratchy and fading. "We'll probably be another twenty minutes or so."

"No hurry," she purred and walked away from me quickly. All three of us watched her hourglass slither away and for about half a second I was happy; completely content in the satisfaction that we put on a phenomenal show. That was until I saw whom she was heading towards.

"This is going to be a beautiful disaster," I whined in a gravely voice. Kai and Marcus exchanged worried glance.

~Walking After You: Foo Fighters~

"Why did you come tonight?" Asia's voice was cold. Her body blocked the lens of Sam's camera that she was holding to her face.

"You almost ruined Max's night."

Ember

Quickly dropping her camera from her face Sam's defenses went up. "I don't have to explain my actions to you."

"You're hurting him!" Asia's hands found her hips as she accused Sam.

"Am I? Or am I just hurting you?" she asked, standing her ground. Her eyes were on fire.

"Not possible, Blondie." Her lips pouted as the thunder rumbled much closer to the windows; making a handful of people nervous.

"Do you even love him?" Sam fired back. "Because I do. Completely." Sam stepped into her. Asia's eyes flared with rage.

"That's none of your business." She leaned down towards Sam. "Besides, how could you possibly love Max when you're scared of him?" Asia's remark cut through her defenses a little and Sam hid her face and spoke softly.

"Not of him." She looked my way and I pretended not to notice.

"Just what he's capable of." Her eyes whipped back to Asia's. "And I think you make things worse."

"His powers ARE who he is. Max IS fire." Asia wasn't holding anything back now. "Don't you get it Samantha? You run from what and who he truly is."

"You're wrong!" Sam shouted but deep down she knew Asia was right. At least partially right. Her thoughts filled with guilt and she began to shrink away from Asia's assault.

"And I don't make things worse...you do." Asia pointed her black painted finger nail in her face.

"But I think you know that," Asia scolded as a lone thought bloomed inside her, causing her to relax her body a little. "If I hadn't shown up during that fight and calmed him down...I...I..."

She turned back toward me with her eyes breaking, "I might have lost him."

Asia fell quiet. She had spoken this as if the words were meant for herself and not Sam. Outside the rain raged on.

"I could have lost him too," Sam said with a new confidence. "But I won't. Not again."

"It's my turn Sam, you had your chance," Asia said bluntly.

"You never answered my question..." Sam continued with a smile and to make a very tense moment even worse, Lucy walked up to them. Sam ignored her and added more fuel to the fire.

"Do you love him?" she asked again. Asia groaned through her teeth. Lucy stepped in with her own worries.

"Asia, I was hoping we could talk tonight," Lucy said in shambles. Asia only looked at her coldly and then turned her anger back to Sam. She couldn't shake Sam's last question from her mind.

"Lucy this is not the time or place," Asia declared.

"Please?" Lucy begged. Asia ran her hands up to the sides of her face and rubbed her temples as if she were fighting a headache. With her eyes closed she folded.

"Okay Lucy."

"I'll leave you two alone," Sam said readying her camera in her hands. "Think about your answer Asia,"

Sam ran off towards me and the boys. She quickly clicked off a picture as she did.

"Lucy...this isn't going to work anymore," Asia said with steel in her tone.

"What are you saying? There has always been a you and me!" Lucy said shocked. Asia shook her head and placed her hands on Lucy's petite shoulders.

"I know but I think that is part of the problem. We haven't been happy in a long time," Asia said softly and then looked over her shoulder at me. "It's time to move on."

She gently raised Lucy's face with her finger, "Both of us Lucy."

"No!" she stomped her combat boots like a spoiled toddler. "I won't! I can't!" Tears rolled down her white cheeks.

"You are the most important girl in my life and always will be." Asia's eyes fell cold again. "But we can't keep doing this, it's time to move on." Her eyes found me again.

"It's time for me to heal. It's time for me to be truly loved." She paused and inhaled a shaky breath.

"But I've always loved you!" Lucy sobbed.

"And I have you but we've done it all this time...broken," Asia's voice barely spoke above a whisper.

"I don't believe you!"

"Both of us. I didn't realize how broken we were until recently." A flood of memories hit her forcing her to stop talking. Memories of her family. Of meeting Lucy for the first time. Of the day on the beach when she woke in my arms.

"Stop saying we're broken damn it!" Lucy spat with hate.

"You know it's true but it's time to heal." She wiped the tears from Lucy's face. "It's time for you to find the one that heals you."

Asia walked away trying not to cry. Lucy's hands reached out for her but slowly fell down to her sides.

"I already have," Lucy whispered. She stormed out the venues doors, into the pouring rain and ran down the street crying.

"This was the best night ever!" Marcus cheered as he slammed his bass into its case.

"We were pretty awesome," Kai agreed while twirling his drumsticks. "Especially me." We all laughed and for a second I was happy...again.

"Sorry for the attitude guys. I almost ruined a great set with my pouting."

"It's cool. We're used to it," Kai teased as he tossed a stick at me.

"Besides, that whole attitude thing worked tonight. Did you see how the crowd reacted to you? To us?" His eyes widened. "They would have done anything we told them to."

"Yeah...we could have marched them into the sun and they would have gone with smiles on their faces," Marcus laughed.

"Thanks guys but I think you're exaggerating a little."

"You were amazing man," Kai said before softening his tone. "And I completely understand the drama." He pointed towards Asia and Sam arguing. "But this isn't gonna go away Max. You're gonna have to make some kind of decision."

"Soon," Marcus added.

"For your own sanity," Kai said before he nudged me with his elbow.

"I know." I glanced at the girls talking. "What would you guys do?"

"I look at it this way…you have two amazing girls fighting for you. Whoever you pick…you win," Marcus said as he tossed me a loose chord to roll up. He added with a grin.

"Personally…I vote for tall, dark and mysterious."

"And you?" I shot Kai a quick glance.

"I wish it were that easy brother. Only you know where your heart lies," he smiled. I let out a tired breath. He sounded like a fortune cookie.

"I'm kinda partial to blondes myself," he pushed.

"Kai…Marcus…after tonight I officially consider you two my brothers." I smiled at them. "We are blood now." We shook each other's hands.

"But boy do you guys suck at advice!" I laughed and they joined in. We would have probably still been laughing had Sam not walked up.

She snapped a quick picture and smiled nervously at us, causing my hands to sweat immediately. As she took a step closer to me, Kai and Marcus turned away from us awkwardly.

"Max, can we start over?" her voice was soft and sweet. I could feel my anger rising like a beast inside again. Obviously I wasn't done pouting.

"Sam I'm tired," I was but it was just an excuse and Kai knew it.

"Let's give them a minute." He nudged Marcus then pulled him off stage.

"You sounded great tonight…I think I got some really nice pictures." She was stalling. My temper kept rising and as I glanced over at Asia with her hands on Lucy's shoulders, the two year old in me escaped.

"Say what you need to say Sam!" I snapped coldly.

"I need you to understand that I am not giving up on you." She reached for my bangs but I stopped her hand just before she touched them.

"On us," she added with her rock solid confidence.

"What if I give up?" I said a little defeated. Her eyes pulled together in determination and her nose wrinkled slightly as she pushed her body into mine.

"I won't let you." Her green eyes searched mine for any sign that I still cared.

"Is that so?" It took every bit of strength I had to fight back the truth.

"Matter of fact," she said still searching. The truth was I wanted her to reach for me. I wanted her to push her sultry little frame against me. I wanted to kiss her and I wanted her to kiss me back. But more than anything else...I wanted NOT to feel this way about her. About us.

"I'm done talking," I said quietly. As I stared into her eyes I wanted to hate her for not standing by my side when I needed her most. I wanted her to feel bad for the nights she spent at HIS side and not mine. I wanted to be stubborn.

"I'm not," she paused. "We'll get through this Max."

"Not tonight," I said angry. I swallowed everything I felt for her and pushed her away.

"Not ever." I couldn't believe how cold it sounded as I said it. The rain outside scratched at the walls as Asia walked up slowly. She glared at Sam as she walked up behind me and slid her arms around me. I had to look away from Sam's face as the pain hit her.

Ember

Sam nodded in defeat slowly, at least for the moment but her eyes seemed to say that she wasn't done yet. She carefully placed the cap on the lens of her camera and walked away without another word. But she did give Asia a curious glance as she left. It felt like I was missing some kind of inside joke between the two. What had they talked about? It was probably best that I didn't know.

MADISON DANIEL

Forbidden_27

~Love Bites: Def Leppard~

11:22 p.m.

Driving home with Asia I felt guilty and I didn't say much as we drove. She was just as quiet. Half way home I could tell that she was just as uncomfortable as I was. The rain was still falling but much softer now. She pulled the Jeep over to the side of the deserted road we were on and I became very uneasy. The rain intensified as she sat quietly for a minute with the radio serenading us.

"What's going on Asia?" I asked but I was scared to hear the answer.

"Max I ended it with Lucy tonight."

"Ended what?" I didn't quite understand.

"Everything." She pulled her warm curls of hair back behind her shoulder and peaked at me. "Her friendship...our sisterhood."

"I never meant for you to do that," I spoke concerned.

"I didn't do it for you." Her eyes smiled at me with the pouring rain reflecting in them. "I needed to let go of her. I had held our relationship in this weird sacred box of emotions. In the past I had needed Lucy's strength and I will always care for her because of that." She paused and looked at me petrified. Lightning flickered outside, stealing the dark away and burning every beautiful line of her face into my memories.

"Go on," I said mesmerized.

"But we have only been hurting each other by the bubble that we had built around ourselves." She began to shake. My hands closed around her perfectly smooth jaw.

"What are you trying to say?" I asked.

"I don't want to be alone anymore." The rain was falling so hard now on the Jeeps roof, that I could barely hear her next words.

"I want to be happy. With you," she said as a tear ran down her cheek. I took a deep breath and leaned in and kissed her.

"I want that too," I whispered and continued to kiss her. I kissed her hard and long, with every bit of energy I had left. The storm outside had now grown so heavy that the visibility was zero and the heat I was giving off made the Jeep feel like a sauna.

I had so much to say to her, so much I wanted to hear her say to me but I couldn't stop kissing her. The fire in my chest was filling my head with wicked thoughts and my hands started removing any piece of clothing that was in their way. My skin was on fire and her cool skin seemed to call to me on an instinctual level. I was beginning to expel heat much too hot for this confined space but she didn't seem to notice. She was too busy ripping my shirt in pieces as she climbed on top of my lap. The radio filled with a pulsing fuzz, drowning out the music.

I had to get myself under control before I hurt her but my mind ran from that thought as my hands found the lines of her bare back. My head felt fuzzy and a dizzying wave overcame me as the thunder shook her tiny truck. Asia felt it too as both our ears filled with a deafening ring and the hair on our bodies stood on end. The cab of the Jeep filled with white light that strained our eyes. My head was buzzing like a fire alarm now as she held me tighter. The truck started to shake like an earthquake when our eyes finally focused on the giant blinding arc just outside the driver's side window. It vaporized the torrent of rain all around us and cut through the asphalt violently. Twisting and buzzing right for us so fast that I barely had a chance to understand what was happening. A giant twister of lightning was shredding right toward us.

"Asia!" I yelled and her fingers slid into the hot flesh of my back. As fresh blood trickled down my skin she closed her eyes and exhaled. In a split second the light vanished, leaving only the sound of pouring raindrops on the roof. The radio was silent now too and my head was still spinning. Thunder laughed in the distance and we slowly caught our breath and said nothing.

"Well, that was...intense," I finally spoke. She quietly looked at me and then down at herself. She was almost completely exposed as her dress lay on the floor of the truck. She was bare from the waist up with her lower half only covered by some lace and stockings. I couldn't take my eyes off of her shape. She didn't seem to mind though; she was too concerned with my back. As she leaned herself into me, my chest heated rapidly out of control from her touch.

"Easy Max," she warned. Her cool fingers found the gashes in my back and they had already begun to heal but she still seemed to be upset with herself. She softly blew her soothing breath on the disappearing wounds.

"I'm sorry," she said mad at herself.

"It's okay," I said laughing lightly. That didn't go over so well.

"I don't find this funny," her voice cut through the sound of the storm.

"I do." I pulled her hands to my face. "My back's fine. I can handle that." I turned slightly to show that I was good as new.

"See and the tattoos fine too," I said. Her eyes softened when she saw that.

"You're right Max," she whispered.

"Now as for that giant freaking bolt of lightning that almost split us in two...that might have been a little bit trickier to fix." My laugh returned and so did her smile.

"That's never happened before...I don't know what..." she trailed off embarrassed.

"Well then...I'll take it as a compliment." I put my arms around her and she fell into my still hot chest and giggled softly. It hit me right then just how tired I was and if it hadn't been for her half naked body I might have passed out right then and there.

"So do you think that will happen every time?" she asked nervously.

"Nah...just once or twice more," I said and she pulled herself away a little. Her face filled with a puzzled look as she bit her bottom lip slightly.

"Why's that?" she asked.

"Because we'll be dead," I said dryly and her eyes rolled around her head. Her body tightened up on top of me.

"Come home with me Max." There was no more joking in her eyes, only waves of blue passion.

"I better not." I couldn't believe the words came out of my mouth, but they did. She pushed her body into me even harder.

"Why not?" She tilted her face and ran her finger along my lower lip.

"Because as much as I want this...as much as I want you..." I swallowed nervously. "I want something even more." I needed to hear those three little words. I wanted her to not be scared of the way I made her feel and by the look in her eyes I could tell she knew exactly what I meant.

"I'm trying." Her eyes watched me cautiously.

"I know." I kissed her softly, letting the taste of rain trickle along my tongue. My heart started to pound again, which filled my hands with heat once more.

"We'll try again tomorrow," she said as fact and climbed back into the driver's seat. She turned the key and started to pull back on the road. The rain had calmed itself again and I rolled down the window to inhale its sweet smell. My eyes caught the flickering gleam of the trucks side mirror. From behind us smoke still spun up to the night sky from the revenge seeking lightning burst. A long charred black scar was etched along the scenery. I leaned back in my seat exhausted.

"Thank you Max," she said suddenly. I looked at her lost. She smiled and her hair fell along her shoulders.

"I'm so happy to be…yours."

"Mine?" I asked under my breath. She nodded yes.

"Always Asia…always," I said trying not to sound too sappy. She wiped a tear from her eye and smiled.

~Breakdown: Tom Petty & the Heartbreakers~

Saturday morning – 9:16 a.m. – September 2nd.

I knew it was going to be one of those mornings when the music came floating through my bedroom door. It was loud, it was laid back, and it was old. My clock read 9:16 a.m. but it felt like 5:00 in the morning.

"Rise and shine!" Frank sang from the living room at the top of his lungs. I loved my uncle like my own father but when he started singing like this, I felt like moving out.

"I'll be right out," I called back to him. After about fifteen more minutes of procrastinating I stumbled into the living room. As the morning sun filled the room with warm light my eyes took a second to adjust. As they did I was surprised by what I found waiting for me. On the living room table was a large basket of flowers. Every color and every kind you could possibly find on the islands. There must have been at least ten dozen.

"What the..." I grumbled. Oz was rummaging his little nose inside a couple of red roses when I startled him. He barked sharply and bounced over to me, wagging his tail.

"They were delivered about an hour ago. There's a card but no name," Frank said sipping his morning coffee.

"Thanks for being nosy uncle," I said sarcastically.

"Easy grumpy," he warned. I smiled apologetically. "So...who are they from?" he asked wearily. I snatched up the card and the scent of cherry blossoms hit me. I didn't even need to read the card...I knew exactly who had sent them. On the card was my proof; it was blank with only a pair of red lips smack dab in the middle. Asia's familiar shade of lipstick.

"They're from Asia," I said quiet.

"I thought so," Frank didn't approve. He slowly paced around the living room with his face all bunched up.

"Isn't the boy supposed to send the flowers?" he joked.

"Be nice uncle. She's important to me," I warned. A quick chill ran down my exposed back and I realized

294

that I was standing in the living room in only a pair of beat up jeans. As goose bumps filled my chest, my heart beat a little harder with the thought of Asia's cool kisses. Frank finally noticed the new tattoo along my shoulder but kept his thoughts to himself. He managed a small smile though.

"Sorry son, I didn't mean to rain on your parade," he said. I looked up at him with a smile, tickled with his choice of words.

"There's so much that you don't understand about her." Maybe I should just tell him her little secret. I knew he would understand but I kept my mouth shut and he noticed I was wrestling with something inside and eased his tone.

"Maybe you're right. I'll try harder," he smiled.

"Thanks," I said and walked to the kitchen and grabbed something to drink.

"How did it go last night?" Frank asked from behind me.

"It went well."

"Well? That's it?" He knew better.

"We were fantastic and the crowd was amazing," I bragged and I thought I was done but he sensed a 'BUT' in there somewhere.

"But?" he asked with a goofy smile.

"But what?" I tried to hide it.

"Max, I can see it in your face...what happened?" He won.

"The girls had a few words last night," I winced.

"Ahh...to be young again?" he laughed.

"Something funny?" I snapped at him. I was still very grumpy this morning. I felt stupid for losing my temper with him though.

"Don't get upset with me son. You did this." He was stern but still sweet Uncle Frank.

"You're the one that continued pursuing these young women even after it became complicated. Things were bound to get messy."

"Messy..." I agreed under my breath. "I know."

"Do you?" he challenged. I looked at him hard for a moment.

"Uncle, can I be totally honest with you?" My throat felt dry.

"Of course, always."

"My first weekend here, when I first met Asia...there was an accident." He looked at me worried. "She was hurt pretty badly."

"How bad?"

"As bad as it gets. So I did what I could," I said calmly.

"You healed her."

"Yes and ever since we have had this connection," I said.

"Connection?" he asked.

"She calms the fires inside of me," I paused. He stepped closer to me and almost knocked over a vase of daisies as he did.

"And that same fire seems to call for her, like it needs her...like I need her," I said with my eyes wide. "Is that crazy?"

296

"Yup," he quickly said. He laughed making me feel a little silly. I reached down and slid my hand over little Oz's furry head. His tongue darted out surrounded by a wide smile. I thought we were finished and turned to walk back to my room, when he asked me a question I wasn't ready for.

"And how do you feel about Samantha?"

"I love her." It just came out. I didn't even have to think about the answer...it was just there. Frank choked on his coffee.

"So, I was right," he said satisfied. I turned back toward him.

"Everything's just so easy with her. It feels natural to talk and laugh with her. She makes me feel like a better person when she's around. I can see myself growing old with her." I felt an ache in my chest and stopped.

"Is it possible to be in love with two people at once?" I asked desperately.

"I don't know Max," he said. I was overcome with doubt again and rubbed my brow in frustration. "But I know you should do what's best for you." He smiled at me and I felt a little better.

"I just wish I knew what that was."

"What's the plan for today?" he asked glancing over at the explosion of flowers in his living room. Asia deserved a thank you.

"I think I need to go shopping," I said watching those flowers too.

"Can I borrow the truck today?"

MADISON DANIEL

Wicked Game_28

~Wicked Game: Chris Isaak~

Saturday evening – 6:47 p.m.

The wind was cool and moist as I drove to Asia's house with the windows down in my uncle's truck. The rushing wind helped ease my growing fear of tonight's date. Asia was expecting me to stay the night and I was sure when I found myself staring into those eyes, I wouldn't be able to leave this time. But was that a bad thing? If I was going to make any sense of my feelings I had to give everything to her. I did that with Sam and got burned. It was time for me to be happy. If Asia would let me in completely and not run from her feelings, then I think I could be truly happy.

So here I was driving to my possible future with the sun setting, making the air crisp and the colorful sky beautiful. Vivid orange bursts faded into dark blue and purple clouds as I got closer to her house. The smell of rain was everywhere as I turned onto her road and up her immense driveway. I had been here before but I was still taken aback by the sheer size and beauty of her house.

I parked the truck next to hers and tried to shake off any nerves I had left. I was wearing some clothes that she had bought me just days before. She had left the designer bag on my desk. They were expensive and stylish but totally not me, and I felt uncomfortable in my own skin now. I rang her door bell trying to ignore how awkward I felt in the clothes. She didn't answer, leaving me one option, enter at my own risk.

I walked in and the smell of cherry blossoms swallowed me. Music was playing upstairs and there was no sign of Asia; only a trail of flower petals that scattered their way to the bottom of her staircase. There were no lights on and the last of the suns light filtered through her gigantic windows. Sprinkles of rain gently began to pepper the windows as I made my way up the steps.

I followed the music to the large balcony on the third floor when I was stopped dead in my tracks. Lightning flashed on the horizon, leaving the unmistakable outline of Asia at the far end of the balcony wall. Her hair was pulled up behind her with some of it trailing down over her shoulders. It gently swayed in the light breeze across her face. She was tightly poured into a stunning red dress that looked as expensive as any one of the dresses you'd see the latest Hollywood starlet wearing on Oscar night.

The rain fell softly on the glass awning above us; rippling its way down to the sides and dropping over the edge of the house. Between us was a small intimate dining table set with our dinner. From across the balcony I smiled and held up my hand, revealing a small box covered in shiny silver wrapping and curly black ribbons. She glanced down at it and back at my face motioning with her finger for me to come closer. I shook my head no and waved for her to come to me. Her eyes squinted and thunder quietly rumbled above us.

"Grump," I said with a shy smile.

"Is that for me?" she asked slyly.

"Nah," I teased as I set it on the dinner table and slowly walked up to her. "Asia, you look simply stunning."

"Thank you, Max. I see you found the clothes I bought you." She ran her fingers down my shirt. Maybe these rags weren't so bad after all. She kissed my neck gently, sending my hands to her waist and she shivered slightly from the heat radiating from them already.

Ember

"What's for dinner?" I asked.

"Nothing too fancy." She kissed my neck again. She had better knock that off before my head catches fire. She sensed my wave of anxiousness and walked me to the dinner table. As we sat down she carefully picked up the small present I had bought her.

"You didn't have to do this," she said as her fingers tangled themselves in the black ribbons.

"Just wait until you open it. Then we'll see if you still feel that way," I said smiling. Her eyes lit up and she started to tug at the ribbons when I stopped her.

"Not now...later." I grabbed it from her hands and placed it on the edge of the table. The thunder spoke for her as her face looked annoyed. The silvery wrap dared her to touch it.

"I hate waiting," she pouted.

"It's worth the wait." I reached for her hand and slid my fingers inside of it. "You were worth the wait." She blushed at my words and squeezed my hand. The wind picked up, sending her scent through my senses and making me dizzy for a moment.

"So are you." Her eyes saddened slightly. "I've felt alone all my life. I don't want to be alone anymore," she said cautious. Her other hand slid itself over my other hand.

"Then don't be." My words hit her hard and for a second I thought she might pull away from me but she didn't.

"Are you staying tonight?" she asked with confidence. The fact that she was even giving me the option was a surprise but then she shifted in her chair and let her hair down making the wind entwine with her curls and I was paralyzed. She wasn't asking at all. Steam

301

floated up from my collar and her eyes focused on mine when it did. She had me exactly where she wanted me.

"Well?" She was so impatient but I found her voice hypnotizing.

"I'm scared to stay." I turned serious. Her eyes fell away as she wasn't expecting those words.

"I don't understand." She sat nervous.

"I'm scared that if I stay the night Asia, I might never leave." I tried to pull my eyes from hers but it was impossible. Her eyes had swelled with hope.

"Promise?" her breath stuttered.

"Asia..." All right, this was it. Time to put everything out there.

"I love you," I said the words as honest and full of passion as I possibly could. I was completely exposed. This was my everything. She hesitated and my chest felt as if I couldn't breathe. She stared at me frozen, her blue diamond eyes never broke their hold but she never spoke. So I spoke for her.

"That's what I thought...it's getting late." I tore my hands from hers. "I better get going," my voice sounded pathetic and broken, which filled my head with anger. How could I possibly stay any longer this open and raw? I stood up and turned to leave when the thunder crashed against the glass awning. The balcony shook as her hand caught mine. Asia forced her body in front of mine, blocking my escape.

"Max no!" she shouted.

"Asia please move," my voice cracked with frustration but she only pushed herself harder into me.

"You can't leave!" Now she was angry.

302

Ember

"Why should I stay?" I was yelling too easily. "Tell me! Tell me why I should not regret my honesty?" I challenged her. She began to shake with tears streaming down her cheeks.

"I may not be able to say it..." her lips crashed into mine. "But I can show you." Her kiss devoured me as the room and world started to spin. I pushed her away with all my might but it was no use, the inferno inside was in control now. I said that she was my kryptonite and tonight she was going to prove it.

"No!" I pulled my lips from hers but my arms only held her tighter. The storm outside pushed even harder and began to bury the house in blackness. Lightning flashed everywhere, blinding us every other flash. Fire engulfed my body and my new clothes caught fire as steam billowed everywhere. That was warning enough for me.

"Asia I think we better stop," I gasped over the pounding rain.

"No," she said angry.

"We obviously cannot go about this without some control..." I still felt light headed from her taste. "I mean we'll crack a hole in the Earth," I laughed at the ridiculous idea but then remembered the deadly arc of light that severed the ground the last time she let herself go.

"You are not leaving tonight," she was absolute.

"Okay...but I would like to live through the night!" I was kidding but she wasn't laughing.

"Maybe if we calm ourselves down and start at square one, take it slow and concentrate." I had barely finished my thought and she was kissing me again. This time soft and sweet.

"Let's try it your way," she said as she walked away from me, dropping her dress to the floor. Silently we walked to her room.

"Okay," I whispered as my heart was telling me to leave. If she couldn't say those three little words now, then she would never say it. I squashed the thought instantly. Outside the thunder had all but stopped and I hadn't seen a single flicker of lightning since we stopped. The rain was still falling but I found the sound extremely calming.

I glanced down at my charred clothes and felt guilty for ruining them.

"I think I ruined the outfit you bought me. Sorry." I grinned nervously.

"Don't worry about it." She grinned and raised a single eyebrow. Her bedroom popped with a building electricity and heat.

"Now can we try this again?" she asked with a pout.

"Definitely." I gave in.

Here we were, two opposites being pulled toward each other by some unnatural force and when we came together it was like a national disaster. Maybe this wasn't meant to be no matter how much I cared for her. Then I caught a glimpse of her as she slid onto her bed and I didn't care about anything but this moment. The thunder knocked at her window and I gave her an awkward glance.

"Take it easy," I said playfully. She stuck her tongue out and smiled. The lightning returned as the rain filled with new life.

Ember

Our passion built quickly with our pounding hearts. The thunderstorm outside built even quicker, shaking her room lightly. As I enjoyed each one of her curves my heat began to rage out of control again. I was in heaven but was starting to get scared now. If I got any hotter I would definitely hurt her. She pushed harder and I felt helpless in her arms.

Just as the moment approached where our two bodies would become one, the signs fell dark again. The hair on our bodies rose at attention and my head filled with a dull hum. My thoughts were fuzzy and I felt weak. Asia was covered in sweat...too much sweat. I was dangerous this close with her. My fires spun out of control while the thunder became deafening. Her breathing was much too heavy as tiny bits of static popped off her body. I was too hot now and the fire was only moments from being let free. I was petrified I might kill us both.

A deep pop filled our ears as a bright flash of light blinded us from outside her windows. The power went out as I fell into her arms. We should have stopped at that moment but we didn't. Her arms tightened around me as my eyes caught two giant arcs of light outside her windows. They weren't as big as the one from the night before but they seemed just as angry with us. They were about 100 feet from the house and moving our way quickly. The two bolts of fire twisted and twirled in some evil dance, never touching one another, but increasing their fury.

"No!" Asia screamed.

"We have to stop!"

Through her teeth she cursed, "Not again!"

I felt so dizzy and hot that it took a second for me to realize that she had pulled herself from me and was running toward the window. Her palms slammed against the glass with a slap. Her silhouette taunted me as the approaching lightning glowed in front of her. I ignited into flames and rose from the bed. She saw this in the reflection of the vibrating glass and closed her eyes. She began to cry and leaned her forehead into it.

A low growl rose from her chest as she tensed her body, flexing every muscle she had against the cold window. The two bolts were only feet away now and their sound was ferocious. Her house shook violently as the lightning screamed like two locomotives out of control.

"Asia you can do this!" I yelled from behind her. She trembled against the glass and in the blink of an eye the two arcs of fire were gone, almost like they were never there at all. The room fell into blackness as my ears still hummed from my burning torso. She quickly pushed her window open and the ice cold rain showered us instantly. The sound of it burning as it hit my flames brought her back to her senses. She turned to me with eyes full of terror and I pushed the fire back down inside of me. She ran and embraced me as the flames fell away.

"Are you okay?" I asked brushing her wet bangs from her sobbing face. She looked devastated and broken.

"Damn it!" she cursed. "The one thing I wanted more than anything…" Her eyes found mine and I tried to smile for her. "I can't even show you what you mean to me."

I kissed her forehead, "We'll figure this out." She only looked at me with disappointment. I held her for the next few minutes, making sure to keep my temperature strong enough to keep her warm while she sulked.

"Will you still stay with me?" she finally asked defeated. A thousand fears stood up inside of me and my stomach knotted up. It had been an emotionally long night. I lifted her head and kissed her gently.

Ember

"I'm not going anywhere."

Sunday morning – 7:09 a.m. – September 3rd.

I awoke in a fog with my throat dry and my head a little fuzzy. Even as groggy as I was from the explosive night before, it only took a moment to realize that I was alone. The sun was shining brightly through Asia's room, illuminating every corner in a warm peaceful glow. There wasn't a cloud in the sky and the breeze fell softly around me. I could smell the tray of breakfast before I even saw it and my stomach rumbled to life. My batteries were running low after last night's events.

I stretched with a long yawn, reaching for the tray of food and froze in mid reach. A small yellow piece of paper was neatly tucked under a single rose. My appetite vanished as I forced myself to grab the note. Her scent was all over the piece of paper, making my heart sink into my stomach. I had given her all of me and she had left. I swallowed deeply, letting out a nervous sigh and opened the note.

"DONT FREAK OUT...I HAVE TO THINK ABOUT SOME THINGS. PLEASE DON'T TRY AND FIND ME. I NEED TIME. I'LL FIND YOU. PROMISE...XOXO."

"I'm such an idiot," I crumbled. First Sam, now her. Sadness climbed up from deep inside of me and choked away my inner heat. I felt cold as I sat surrendering to the over powering sadness. It began to smother me and I didn't think I could take much more. I slowly gathered my things and left.

307

MADISON DANIEL

Ember

~Strong Enough: Sheryl Crow~

Sunday – 8:19 a.m.

Why is it when your heart is breaking, every song on the radio seems to exploit that pain? Driving back home from Asia's, I found that my one constant friend music, had become my enemy. I was already numb enough from the past twenty-four hours to take the truths the singer on the radio had waiting for me. I clicked the stereo knob off and drove the rest of the way home in silence.

As I pulled into our driveway, safe and sound, I was glad to be home. That sliver of happiness cracked into a thousand pieces when my tired eyes focused on the tiny silver car parked next to the house. What was Sam doing here first thing in the morning?

"This morning just keeps getting better," I pouted.

I reached down inside and found what lingering courage I had left and stepped from the truck. Sam had slowly walked out the front door to meet me half way between the house and the truck. As I walked up I noticed Frank peering from behind the curtains in the living room. I shot him an awkward glare and he took the hint and disappeared. Without missing a beat, Oz's furry head popped up and his happy little face almost made me smile.

"Do you have a sec?" Sam asked politely. I could only stare at her, as my overnight bag fell to the ground next to me. She smiled but her confidence was shaken.

"I'll take that as a yes."

"Why are you here Sam?" I was annoyed.

"For you."

"It's too late," I grumbled. Deep down though, I didn't believe that. She shifted slightly and ran her hands along a large manila envelope. In my misery I hadn't even noticed it in her hands.

"It's never too late Max."

"This isn't the best time to talk." I was surprised at how defeated I sounded.

"Long night?" she asked with hesitation.

"Sam...please. I don't want to do this right now." I grabbed my bag and started to walk toward the house. Her hands reached for me and her small 5 foot frame felt like a 20 foot wall. I slowly turned to her again, trying my hardest not to look in those big green eyes. I couldn't afford to let her in again...not now. My fragile heart just couldn't take anymore.

"Let me have my say..." her eyes seemed to ease my pain a little. "Then I'll go."

"Okay," I agreed. Inside I tried to put up my walls as fast as I could.

"Devon and I are done. For good." Damn it, there was his name again! I hated when she spoke it. "I've known for a long time we were over. I just let my fears cloud that truth for a while." She reached for my hand but I pulled it behind my back.

"Sam...stop," I begged.

"Devon is gone. There is only you Max. You are the one I love," she smiled. My eyes closed as the first swing from her wrecking ball smashed into my new walls. Another hit like that and I was done for.

Ember

"We've been through this already and you chose him!" I yelled.

"No, I didn't!" she said defiantly. "I was afraid that after your fight that he would retaliate in some way. With the police or some expensive lawyer...or worse," she trailed off.

"I can handle that," I said shaking lightly.

"That's not what I was afraid of Max. I was afraid of you leaving if any of that happened." Her eyes caught mine. "I was afraid of you...leaving me."

"Oh," I whimpered.

"I will love you forever and a day...if you let me," she said as her eyes filled with tears. My walls fell from her latest swing of the wrecking ball of truth. I was drowning now and my knees felt like they would give out.

"This can't be happening," I whispered through my teeth.

"Max, I need you to tell me the truth now." She was so beautiful when she let her natural confidence shine.

"Tell me how you feel about her. Tell me how I make you feel." Her hand ran through my hair, "Tell me everything."

And with that the world cracked open and the heavens shook. My last little thread of sanity I had left...snapped. I lost it completely and threw my bag away from me and into the nearby bushes.

"Ahhh!" I screamed. My inferno was back and I embraced the heat.

"Fine! You need the truth." My hands ignited in two bursts of flames, twisting and twirling around my fists. Tiny embers sizzled and dripped to the bare ground.

"This is me Sam!" I yelled again but I couldn't stop myself. "Look at me! This will always be who I am." The flames crept up my fore arms. She stared at me hard.

"Do you really want to love this?" I said and my voice felt thick with pain.

She stepped towards me with no hesitation, "Yes."

"Damn it Sam..." I cursed throwing my arms in the air in frustration, extinguishing the flames.

"Fine," I took a deep breath and let her know everything.

"I feel like a candle burning alone and all this craziness surrounds me, spinning and spinning. It takes everything I have to not let my flame burn out and the best way to do that is to just be still and let everything else pass," I said calming down. She stepped closer to me.

"Alone." I leaned against my uncle's truck and continued.

"I know you don't want to hear this but Asia is a part of me," I checked to see if this hurt her at all but her face stood strong. "On some crazy level she feeds the fire inside of me, making me feel whole. I love her."

That did it; her face broke and filled with pain. I couldn't stand to see her like that. I pushed my body closer to her.

"And there's you..." she looked up at me, clutching the envelope tighter. "I think you're my soul mate," I whispered. Her eyes focused on me heavily.

"Max..."

"I don't know how it's possible but I do. I've tried to deny it. I've tried to fight it. I feel as if were supposed to grow old together." A smile returned to her flushed face but my face fell sullen.

"What does this mean?" she asked quietly.

"I love you too. I don't know how that is possible." I was heating up again. "How selfish is it that I think I can love both of you?"

The world fell silent as I let my misery wash over me.

"I don't deserve your love Sam. I'm sorry for hurting you," I said through clenched teeth. "You deserve better."

She stood quietly thinking for a moment before she spoke. She looked so vulnerable. I wanted to reach out and hold her but I thought it would be better if she just left. Leave me behind and find someone that truly deserved her but she wouldn't leave. Instead she walked closer to me, sliding her falling hair behind her ear.

"This is for you," her voice was soft. She handed me the yellow envelope and gently caressed my hands as I took it from her. "Please don't open it yet, okay."

"What is it?"

She pulled her body into mine, staring up at my hurt eyes. One of her hands slid along my cheek as the other one brushed my bangs from my face. She really enjoyed doing that and it seemed to make things better every time she did it.

"I know you blame yourself for your family, for your sister," she paused then continued cautiously. "But it's not your fault Max. The pain you carry is not for you."

She lifted her lips to my chin and kissed me gently, "Not anymore." My face filled with a rush of heat.

"Your sister would want you to move on," she whispered. Her head tilted to the side as a tear fell from my eye. "It's time to let Mia go. It's time for you to be happy." She kissed me again and I felt my chest cave in under the sheer torture of her words.

"It's time for you to be with me," she said crying. Her hands fell from my face and she walked slowly past me toward her car. I couldn't move. I couldn't stop her. I was devastated.

"Make me a promise Max," she insisted.

"Anything," I barely spoke.

"Don't open that until you are ready to forgive yourself," her little voice cracked. "Okay?"

"Sam…" I couldn't find any words. The world was spinning too fast again. I wished that someone would stop it though; I was ready to get off.

"Promise me." She was crying fully now and it killed me to hear her that way. I looked down at the envelope and traced my finger along her hand writing on the face of it.

"I promise," it barely came out of my mouth. I was so confused by her request but I would honor her wishes. She nodded quickly and climbed into her car and drove away. I stood alone, clenching her gift in my overheating hands. After what felt like hours, I found enough strength to walk into my house. I avoided my uncle and barely acknowledged little Oz as I stumbled inside. Frank watched me as I wiped my eyes dry and fumbled to my bedroom but he did not follow.

In my room I sat staring at Sam's gift and my mind fell numb. Oz curled his long body up against mine and I managed to pat his head gently. There we sat for hours, not moving an inch. I sat replaying the last day's events over and over again in my head. It was slowly driving me insane but I was determined to make some kind of sense of what was happening. But I kept coming back to the fact that I was in love with two amazing girls and I think it was killing me.

I managed to climb in the shower for at least an hour, letting the running water wash over me. It soothed my tired body as I drowned in my own self-pity. When I finally finished Frank was waiting for me with a smile and a handful of photos. He held them out to me and I reluctantly took them.

"Sam thought you might like these. She has a great eye," he spoke softly.

"Some say she has two of them," I joked half-heartedly.

"Good one," he said laughing politely. "If you need to talk son..." I cut him off.

"I know where to find you. Thanks," I actually managed a smile.

"Take all the time you need," he said as he patted me on my back and walked away. "Oh yeah, I almost forgot. I won't need the truck tomorrow. Roger from work needs my help with something and offered to pick me up early. So, if you want her, she's all yours," he winked.

"Okay. Thanks," I smiled.

I settled onto my bed and spread the handful of pictures along my blanket. As I fumbled through them my smile grew. There was one of Kai, Marcus and me at the barbecue and another couple from our concert. There was one that I took of Sam at her house and that one hurt to look at. To my surprise, there was one of Asia and me together. But the last shot seemed to rattle me the most. Sam and Asia were sitting side by side on the living room couch with flowers in their hair. The ones my uncle had given them the day of the barbecue. They both looked happy next to one another, almost like long lost sisters. It was crazy but there they were.

"Oz, I think I need to get away." He groaned back at me as I rubbed his belly. His eyes rolled in the back of his head as he rolled over and fell asleep. I sat the stack of photos on my desk, leaving the one of the girls exposed on top.

"What the hell am I going to do?" I asked disgusted. I glanced down and watched Oz as he drifted away to sleep and my head felt like bubble gum. I stretched out beside him and waited for the darkness to overtake me. When it finally did, I surrendered to it completely.

~Rain: The Wreckers~

Monday morning – 9:44 a.m. – September 4th.

I awoke with a peaceful feeling and recharged sense of purpose. I had slept through the afternoon and night without waking up once. I had forgotten to set my clock alarm again and was late again for school. I didn't care though; I needed to get away. That's when I saw my uncle's truck parked outside the window and remembered that he didn't need it today.

"How about it Oz, you up for another adventure?" He yipped loudly at me. His tiny tail wagged so hard I thought it might break off.

"Then it's decided...let's go."

We drove as far as we possibly could on the island. The two of us: man and his best friend. We found a peaceful patch of land with plenty of trees and vegetation. The ocean was close and filled the place with sticky freshness. We spent the morning playing guitar and

316

chasing butterflies. It was the perfect day until my cell phone beeped to life. I should have left it at home.

"Oh no..." I huffed staring at its screen.

At school, my non presence was becoming an issue. Sam waited in the parking lot nervously until the last bell, for me to show.

"Max, where are you?" she mumbled to herself. From behind her Kai walked up with a smile.

"Still no Max huh?"

"Nope," she said frustrated. "Do you know where he is Kai?"

"I haven't heard a peep. I called him this morning but it went right to his voicemail," he chuckled. "I don't think he's in the mood to talk."

"Yeah, I've been calling his cell phone all morning," she started to give up.

"We're gonna be late...come on," he tugged at her shirt. She resisted at first, glancing around one final time but found no sign of me. Her shoulders fell slightly in a hunch and she walked to her first class. Just before she reached the door of first period she was stopped by Lucy.

"Morning Samantha," she said as politely as possible but Sam didn't trust her.

"Morning Lucy...if you don't mind, I'm going to be late if..."

"No Devon today?" Lucy watched with wide eyes. This caught Sam off guard.

"I don't know. I haven't seen him in a couple days," Sam said annoyed. "What do you need Lucy?"

"Oh that is too bad," Lucy said sarcastic. "And Max?" she asked as her purple eyelids slid together. That was enough for Sam.

"Goodbye."

"No, no, no. I'm sorry. I was just being nosy." Lucy quickly pulled a folded piece of paper from her belt and flapped it in front of Sam's face.

"This is for you," she smiled like an alligator.

"What's this? Who?" Sam was confused. As she held the paper in her hands she realized that she didn't recognize the hand writing on it. Two words were written in a beautiful handwriting...

"FOR SAMANTHA"

"I don't know," Lucy giggled. "I'm just the messenger," she added with a bite. She let a sigh slide from her mouth and turned and disappeared down the hallway. Sam ignored her rude messenger and raced into her classroom and sat down. The teacher made sure that she knew that she was upset with her tardiness but Sam didn't care. Her sweaty hand gripped the note tightly as she decided that she couldn't wait any longer and opened it up.

It only took a moment to read what was written on it and when she was done she tucked it inside her school folder and sadness gripped her face.

Outside Lucy whistled as she walked to the parking lot. Her lips filled with a black lipstick pout as the air pushed itself out, louder with each breath. She walked up to a shiny new blue car, clicked her keyless entry button and slid in snug as a bug. She tossed her little black purse on the passenger's seat, right next to an envelope with hundred dollar bills falling out from its belly. She quickly dialed out on her cell phone.

"It's done," she said with an evil smile and clicked her phone off. She inhaled the new car smell and caressed the curve of the steering wheel before racing out of the parking lot.

MADISON DANIEL

Falling_30

~Sign Your Name: Terence Trent D'Arby~

Monday night – 7:53 p.m.

Tiffany's Bar and Grill is one of the local hangouts that has been around for years. It's a little restaurant bar that features live bands and karaoke in a small comfy atmosphere. I had never heard of the place but my uncle filled me in on all of its history. This is where Asia had asked me to meet her tonight. This night would either be the beginning of our lives together or our last dance. Sitting quietly in Frank's truck I stared at the bright colorful screen of my cell phone and read Asia's text for the 100th time.

'2NITE AT 8:00.

TIFF'S BAR & GRILL.

PLEASE COME.

XO....A.'

I sulked looking around the half full parking lot I rallied all the courage I could. I was parked right next to Asia's Jeep and my hands warmed at the thought of walking in. When I heard the faint sounds of someone singing a pop hit from the eighties inside, I settled into a quiet calmness. I used the word singing loosely, the poor man sounded as if he were in pain.

I walked toward the entrance, watching the clouds above me. They were dark and still but they seemed safe and peaceful. As I prepared my restless nerves outside the front door I found myself singing along with the poor soul on stage. He was giving it his all but I was sure the owners had one of those giant canes at the ready, to yank him from the stage. The image brought a much needed smile to my lips. With a nervous fire in my throat, I walked inside.

The place was bigger than it looked from the outside. There was a small bar to the left with only a couple people sitting along its counter. A dozen small tables scattered throughout but most of them were empty. That was probably normal for a Monday night. A small stage with a DJ close by filled the back of the place. The smell of fresh food filled the place as my feet fumbled through the door.

Asia spotted me from the front of the stage as the tone deaf patron finished his song and quickly rushed back to his table. She watched me with a delicate smile and wide eyes. She was wearing a white tank top with jeans and sandals. It was the most relaxed I had ever seen her. Her intoxicating scent only took a moment to reach me and overpowered the smells from the kitchen.

"Aloha," she quickly motioned with her mouth. Her hand waved to me but I was instantly distracted by what she was holding in her opposite hand. A shiny black microphone.

Before my mind had time to process the information my eyes were pulled away toward the side of the restaurant. Sam's nervous eyes called to me, watching every little move I made. Her hair was pulled up in a tight pony tail, exposing the lines of her neck. She sat fidgeting in a white summer dress with her hands stirring a drink with one of those tiny umbrellas. She waved at me and then glanced toward Asia and back at me. I froze in confusion of what my next move should be. What was going on? Why was Sam here too? Why didn't Asia seem upset by this?

I slowly stepped forward, not sure of where exactly I was heading and my palms flared with hot anxiety. Asia never took her gaze off of my face, even when Sam rose from her seat and started walking my way. She just casually walked forward in my direction. All three of us met in the middle of the room and there we stood for what seemed like an eternity, saying nothing. The thunder woke from its slumber and rolled softly outside. A small family gathered their things and ran out the front door, leaving the place looking almost empty now. My hand ran itself along the back of my neck nervously as I decided to break the ice.

"The gangs all here," I joked. I sounded absolutely desperate when I said it but neither one of the girls seemed to care.

"Thank you for coming Max," Asia said sweetly. Something was different with her but I couldn't quite put my finger on it yet.

"Aloha," I returned.

"It's nice to see you too Sam," she said softly. Now I was really worried. Asia sounded almost like she was glad Sam was here. She seemed...happy. My shirt filled with heat as my chest heated up.

"I wouldn't have missed this for the world," Sam said protective. Her body leaned into mine, sending me into complete confusion. Asia stepped in closer, ignoring Sam's advances.

"I need to tell you something," she grinned. Her eyes were alive and Sam pushed in closer again. I just stood there waiting for the first shot. Surely this was some sort of elaborate charade to get me back for my indecision with them.

"But first..." Asia nodded to the DJ and he pointed a finger back her way. "Tonight I sing for you Max."

She turned and walked back to the tiny stage, never even giving Sam a second glance. The DJ started the music and I knew the song instantly. My scattered thoughts settled themselves and I realized that this was her way of telling me how she felt about me...about us. Asia Lyn Michaels really did love me. Sam's hand found mine and grasped down tightly.

"And tonight, I am here for you," Sam said with the confidence that I had grown to adore. I had no idea what to say and stared at her beautiful face. We both grabbed a couple chairs at the nearest table and sat down. She slid her chair as close to mine as possible, never surrendering my hand. Asia began to sing and everyone left in the room stopped.

"...Fortunately you – have got someone who relies on you...We started out as friends but the thought of you just caves me in..." Asia sang sweetly. To my surprise her voice was quite lovely. It was sultry with a hint of sweetness that was totally unexpected. My hands burned hot causing Sam's hand to squeeze even harder.

Asia's eyes watched me like laser beams as she sang and strutted around the stage. Her stare was so powerful and captivating. Sam's glare was now filling with tears.

"...Stranger blue – leave us alone...We don't want to deal with you...We'll shed our stains – showering...In the room that makes the rain..." she sang with all her heart. My chest pounded and the room began to spin.

324

Ember

Sam's sad eyes saved me from complete shut-down. I focused on her hurt face. Why would she put herself through this? I gripped her hand tighter not sure what to do and finally gave in to her suffering.

"Sam...why would you come here tonight?"

"Because she told me to," her voice broke. Why would Asia want her here? It didn't make any sense.

"She said tonight would be the end of all this. We would all have closure." She wiped her eyes as I sat in silence.

"...Sign your name across my heart...I want you to be my baby..." Asia sang to me. I felt far away inside...I felt lost.

"She wrote me a note," Sam said handing me the piece of paper from her shaking hand.

"See," she scolded. I felt panic rush through me as I opened it. Asia noticed my discomfort and the rain started to fall outside.

"Sam, who gave this to you?" I asked in a panic. My anger welled up inside of me and she looked at me confused.

"Why?"

"Because this isn't Asia's hand writing," I warned. My eyes caught Asia's as I quickly scanned the room and she knew something was wrong. The ends of the paper caught fire in my hand and I let it fall to the table. My search continued until I reached the corridor to the entrance. There I found a curious shadow watching us. My hands grew tighter with fury and I accidentally burned Sam's hand in the process. She pulled it away in pain as I jumped to my feet and ran for the entrance.

"Max!" she shouted holding her hand. Her eyes then saw who I had seen.

"Lucy?"

Asia rushed to our table in a rage.

"What did you do? What did you say to him?" she accused. Sam stood up and shoved the note in Asia's face, still caressing her tender hand. It only took a moment for Asia to read the message and fill with confusion. Her hands crumbled the paper into a ball as her eyes filled with ice.

"Lucy," she gritted through her teeth.

"What's going on?" Sam demanded. Asia sucked in a deep breath as the thunder crashed outside. A single bolt of lightning flashed and forced the power to blink off and on for a second.

"I don't know..." Asia said looking at Sam scared. "But this is bad. I can feel it." Asia's hands began to shake. Sam pulled her own hands to her chest, rubbing softly the one I had burned. A few seconds later both girls jumped at the sound of the first gunshot.

They ran for the door.

OUTSIDE...

As I ran outside chasing Lucy, I was taken off guard at how dark it had already become. The rain wasn't helping the visibility much either. Lucy was in a full sprint now and if she hadn't fumbled to get her keys out of her pocket, I might not have caught her.

"Lucy!" My hands caught her by the wrist. She screamed in surprise.

Ember

"Leave me alone!" she hollered.

"Why did you write that note?" I said holding her wrist tighter. I didn't care if I burned her, I just wanted an answer.

"Let me go!" she struggled in my grasp.

"Not until you tell me what this is about. Why did you write it Lucy?" I demanded.

"Because he paid me to!" she cursed. My hand let go of her arm as the rain fell heavy.

"What?" I said dazed. She opened her car door and jumped in quickly.

Crying now she whispered, "I'm sorry." She slammed her door and drove off in a fury. I was so confused now. My eyes whipped around my surroundings, circling my position. Finally I saw him standing not twenty feet from me and it was too late to react.

Devon stood hunched slightly with the rain pouring off his grimacing face. The lightning flickered and exposed how bad he really looked. He was very pale and hadn't shaven in a while. His burn scars looked horrible. They surrounded his neck like a withered serpent. His eyes were pools of liquid hate, burning against my stare. My instincts kicked in and my body began to steam in the rain. Devon's motionless shadow came alive and his arm rose with a shiny gun as he screamed through his clenched mouth.

"Not this time Valentine!"

BANG!

The sound of the bullet sliced through the air and the fire in my chest seemed to fade, leaving only pain. I fell backwards still in shock from watching the bullet tear into my chest. I managed to only fall to one knee as I gripped the open wound with my hand. I could barely feel my chest and the pain was radiating everywhere. I tried to focus and let my fire heal me but the wound was massive. At the range he had fired, the bullet went right through me and I couldn't ignite now, no matter how hard I pushed. Devon laughed wickedly and stormed toward me with the gun pointed straight at me.

"Heal from that freak!" he spat. His eyes were possessed as his hand flexed around the handle of the gun. Its reflection blurred in the falling rain as I tried my hardest to focus. He was barely ten feet from me and I figured I had only enough energy for one shot at an attack. I concentrated every ounce of will I had left on my hands and they stuttered to ignite but they did. I lunged at him. His eyes grew big as he watched in shock as I came to my feet.

I had almost reached him with my hands sizzling in the fat drops of rain when he squeezed the trigger again. Two shots this time but I only felt the first one. Lightning curled itself along the nearest power lines, cutting the power out and leaving us in darkness. The girls screamed from the doorway and I tried to turn to them to show them that I was all right but I couldn't. My legs gave out and I fell to both knees this time. I hunched over with both arms crossed over my chest, gasping for air. I waited for the heat to return to me and fill the nothing in my chest but it never came.

"Why aren't I healing?" I gasped as blood filled my mouth. He was too close. Why can't I feel my fire? The wounds were too big. I tried again in vain to heal but it was no use, I didn't have the energy and the rain was falling much too cold now. Damn it Asia...please my beautiful rainmaker...turn off the waterworks.

Ember

"Don't come any closer!" Devon warned the girls. They froze in shock trying not to scream. Sam reached for Asia's hand but found a balled fist and the thunder shook the ground.

"This is what you get Valentine!" Devon screamed from above me. His shadow towered over me from the moonlight as my body began to shake uncontrollably. He spit on me and cracked the bones in his neck with a quick jerk of his head. He leaned down only inches from my face.

"This is what you get for mutilating me!" he growled. He rubbed the still warm barrel of the gun against my cheek.

"For destroying my reputation!" he smashed the gun into my eye and I fell back but he caught me by the neck and pulled me back toward his words.

"And for stealing my girl," he said seething. My lips pulled apart to reveal a bloody grin that dripped down my chin. The sight made him shake with anger.

"You're smiling?"

"Ha, ha, ha, ha, ha..." I laughed choking slightly.

"What?" he couldn't believe his ears.

"This doesn't change anything Dev..." I coughed up blood but the drenching rain washed it from my mouth as quickly as it came. "You're still a spoiled brat..." my hands reached for his collar.

"...And...Sam...still...picked...me," I cursed with a dizzy smile.

Devon's mind snapped and he broke my weak grasp from his neck, rising quickly above me again. With no hesitation he unloaded the rest of the clip into my body, screaming like a banshee with every bullet. The world stopped spinning and faded to black as my body fell backward into a puddle. The rain was still there but I could no longer feel it. I could no longer feel the coldness. I lied motionless.

Blackened_31

~Shame: Stabbing Westward~

It only took Devon a moment to come to his senses and realize what he had just done. Panic gripped him and he began to shake. The rain fell down on him as he quickly gave my broken body one final glance. Sam and Asia ran toward him but he turned and fled. He ran to his motorcycle that was parked against the back wall and mounted it, revving the engine. He disappeared into the darkness with the tail lights flickering in the falling raindrops.

Sam collapsed at my side and Asia slid herself under my head. The shock had melted away any strength they had left and they both cried out loud. Sam's hand traced my wrist and neck looking for any sign of a pulse. Her head rested inches above what was left of my chest and she listened patiently for a heartbeat. Her golden ponytail fell to my bloody body and filled with red blotches that washed away in streaks just as quickly from the storm.

"I can't find a pulse..." Sam said shaking. Asia ignored her words and continued wiping the blood from my head. "His heart isn't beating either," Sam continued. Asia kept up her invisible wall and rubbed my face even harder. She tried to look into my eyes but found them rolled back in my head and she screamed, making the thunder crack around us.

"Power up Max! Now!" she screamed holding my cold face tightly, but my color had faded to a ghost white.

"Max!" she screamed again, along with the fiery strips of lightning in the clouds. In the distance the sound of approaching sirens could now be heard.

"Wake up!" Asia's voice cracked.

"He can't!" Sam finally snapped. "Not with all this rain!" she was screaming now too. They stared at each other angrily for a moment before wiping the rain from their faces.

"He's so cold. What do we do?" Asia barely asked.

"Nothing," Sam answered in pain. "He's not breathing...there's too much blood..." she choked a little. "I think he's really gone."

"No!" Asia bellowed and dug her nails into my bloody shirt. She rose to her feet staring up into the rain and the wind swirled out of control. Her hands closed into fists as the winds rushed through the streets, in the direction that Devon drove off. She ran to her truck, quickly revved the engine and screeched the tires as she tore out of the parking lot.

Sirens filled the air just as the rain began to fade and Sam cradled what was left of me, in her arms. She folded under the weight of her misery and tears streamed down her face. My body lied still and cold as the wind died down to nothing.

THE CHASE...

Asia's eyes were two balls of steel fire as she gripped the steering wheel. She pushed the truck to its limits as the scenery flew by at a dangerous pace. Faster and faster she forced the Jeep forward. The clouds followed at the same quickening pace, morphing themselves into black walls of fire. Lightning chased through them as they grew and stretched along the sky. The wind barreled forward like a freight train, leveling any brush or tree that lied in its way.

Ember

Her tears began to sting from the icy rain that had engulfed her maniac hurricane. She didn't care and pushed her hate forward even harder when she finally saw the flicker of a tiny tail light up ahead. Her teeth smashed together and the sky split apart with a dozen streaks of white fire. The thunder had reached the point of a small earthquake, shaking her and the truck like a toy. Power lines blew as she passed them and her heart raced out of control.

Devon didn't have time to see what was quickly clawing its way toward him because of the pounding hail. He could barely keep the bike upright as the storm fell down on him so hard it hurt. By the time he managed to see the building Armageddon behind him, it was too late. He just didn't know it yet. At this speed, the slightest wobble would send him crashing so he eased his speed just enough to turn off on a mysterious path up a near-by mountain. He pushed the bike to its limits, even though it wasn't made to travel off road and the giant black mass followed. He felt a rush of panic but never stopped as the bike made its way up the mountain, through thick brush and scattered rocks.

Asia was close now and the clouds moved even faster as she realized that he had made the worst possible choice he could have, turning off the main roads. She knew all the back roads of every island and this particular one was one of her favorites. It was the same one she had brought me to that led to the ridge over the ocean, where we shared each other's secrets. The thought was too painful and made her sick to her stomach. She gritted her teeth together and closed the gap between her and the bike.

Devon's eyes burned from the stinging wind and he couldn't see where he was going anymore, it was too dark. The smell of the ocean was close and that confused him as he made his way through a clearing and realized that he was running out of road. There were cliffs up ahead and nothing more as he shivered from the ice cold wind. The moon slipped from behind the black and menacing clouds over him, making him ease up on the throttle so he could get a better look of what lied ahead. Big mistake...

Asia plowed into him and his bike with a gut wrenching scream. He flew from the bike, twisting and tumbling with the sounds of bones breaking. She slammed on the breaks sending her truck into a long skid, that she jumped from before it came to a complete stop. Devon's body came to an abrupt halt against a medium out cropping of rocks sticking from the ground. He was only thirty yards from the edge, the same edge where Asia stood testing me. Where I healed her scar on her hip. His bike crashed against the very same rocks before slowly scraping over the edge, falling away.

Asia stormed forward as he regained consciousness. The wind and thunder caught up with them and stabbed him so hard that he could barely breathe. The sound bled from the sky like a war zone. Lightning swarmed all around filling his body with static and a tingling that eased his pain for a moment. Waves crashed from below the cliff as the ocean seemed to reach for the sky. Spouts formed from nowhere in the clouds and reached down for the thriving waters. Funnels danced above the growing sea like serpents. The ground shook and he tried to focus his eyes on the approaching silhouette.

"Please help me!" he screamed as the icy hail shredded his open wounds. "I'm hurt bad!" he begged. The haunting shadow never answered his calls for mercy. He began to cry uncontrollably. Lightning flashed, revealing Asia's vengeful face and he realized that all his begging was in vain.

"Why?" her hands squeezed into fists. "Why?"

Ember

Devon started to go into shock and he was losing too much blood now to think straight. She kept stomping forward with the wind swirling behind her and the thunder rolled steady until something stopped her in her tracks. The shiny barrel of Devon's gun gleamed back at her from the wet ground and she froze still. The wind seemed to circle the clearing and the rain faded to a drizzle. Devon instantly found it easier to breathe again and slowly tried to get to his feet. He only made it as far as his knees when the bones started popping and sending pain down his back. His eyes watched Asia frozen in front of him and he wondered if he was in some bizarre dream.

Her eyes would not move from the gun even as the lightning flickered inside its reflection. Her mind drifted away. She drifted back to the night in the Jeep when she first asked me to stay the night. Then her mind rushed her back to the afternoon on the beach when our eyes first met. Then back to her house when she gave everything she could to me. Everything except the words that I wanted to hear the most, the words I deserved to hear. In her mind a single image appeared. One single flame flickered to life against a black background of clouds. It danced back and forth beautifully until the sound of a gunshot echoed everywhere. The flame disappeared into a trail of smoke followed by blackness.

Asia's eyes flew open with icy tears along her cheeks. Her hands grabbed the sides of her head as she screamed with the force of the surrounding storm.

"I won't lose you!"

The sky became white with the fire of a thousand lightning strikes. Too many of them slicing right through the ground around them. The wind slammed back into Devon and his crippled body, bringing him to his feet. His oxygen pulled from his lungs and his head was spinning from the lack of blood. The funnel clouds finally stretched their revolving arms to the water, sending the waves smashing into the rocks against the cliffs.

"Max!" she screamed until her mouth tasted like blood. Devon reached out as she fell to her knees and a single arc of lightning cut through his torso. She buried her hands into the ground and pushed with everything she had left. The wind rushed past her, carrying hateful debris and rocks that slammed into Devon, spinning him through the air and over the cliffs edge. His body tumbled along the wall of the cliff and fell into the raging water. A barrage of lightning bolts crackled over the tops of the violent ocean, sending it into a steaming boil and the thunder shoved its force against the side of the mountain in a deafening parade and then fell silent.

The tornadoes disappeared into vapor and the black clouds parted, exposing a blanket of stars and the full moon. The waves swished back and forth, quickly falling to a calm again and the rain shrank to a drizzle.

Asia took a deep breath before wiping her eyes. A long slow moan crept from her chest as she reached for the gun in front of her. As she climbed to her feet she threw the weapon over the edge and turned to her truck. The radio was on and in mid song when suddenly the local station cut to breaking news. She walked up exhausted and turned up the volume. The local reporter was talking about a terrible accident that had occurred earlier in the evening at a local restaurant. She held her breath already knowing what the voice was about to say. There were shots fired and one known death but details were still coming in. She clicked the knob off and began to cry as the skies above her cleared and filled the night with bright dancing stars.

Ashes_32

~Love Is Dead: Kerli~

Breaking Samantha...

Max felt so cold in my arms. He was so pale now but I thought that if I just held onto him tight enough and long enough, he would wake back up.

"Please wake up Max."

Wake up and I'd never let you hurt again. But he didn't wake up, he didn't even move. He only grew colder in my arms, even as the rain stopped and the temperature rose back to normal.

Two paramedics hopped from their ambulance and looked at us with weary eyes. They had obviously done this a million times and knew that this was not going to be easy; dealing with this silly over emotional girl and her dead boyfriend. They walked up with their medical gear in hand and placed their equipment beside me. One of the men sighed and I could have sworn that he rolled his eyes at the situation. How dare they stare at us like that.

"Excuse me miss," the first paramedic said softly. "We need to help him now," he tried his best to be polite but I knew better. They both knew there was no helping him but still they pretended that he was fixable.

"Miss?" the other paramedic asked. He was less polite and my eyes filled with rage.

"Don't touch him!" I cried. "He's gone and you know it!"

"We're here to help," the kinder man said. It took a moment but for some reason I believed him. Slowly I let go of Max's body and stood up, nervously taking a few steps back. I couldn't stop shaking as they began to check his body for signs of life and just how much damage was done. They knew immediately that he was long gone and one of them called the hospital to let them know the situation, while the nicer paramedic came up to me quietly.

"Miss?" his voice was soft.

"It's Sam...Samantha Summers," I tried not to sound rude.

"Miss Summers, we have to move him now," he said. In a daze I watched from behind him as the other paramedic had Max's I.D. and was giving out his information over the phone. My heart sank thinking of the call that Frank would soon be receiving. A sad fact washed over me as they prepared Max's body to place on the gurney, this was my fault. I should have seen this coming. I knew Devon better than anyone. I could have stopped this.

The gurney with Max's lifeless body clanked against the side of the ambulance as they loaded him in the back, snapping me out of my fog. With little hesitation I climbed in the back too. One of the men tried to stop me at first but I just pushed passed him and snatched up Max's ice cold hand.

"I'm riding with him." I wasn't asking and I didn't acknowledge their presence when I spoke. They nodded to each other reluctantly and shut the doors.

As the ambulance pulled onto the road my stomach filled with knots and a wave of nausea hit me.

"This isn't fair," I cried only loud enough for me to hear. My tears were back and I couldn't have stopped them if I wanted to. My head felt dizzy and I think I was beginning to run a fever. I wasn't about to mention it to the paramedics, they would just take me away from Max and that wasn't even an option right now.

After a few miles a call came over the radio about our situation and I did my best to ignore it. That was until one of the men made a joke about the way I was carrying on about someone who was so far gone. He said something about a high school crush and I snapped.

"How dare you," I screamed. It scared the driver so bad that we almost ran off of the road.

"Miss Summers!" he called out. My hand reached out for the nearest thing to me and I whipped it at both of them with the last bit of strength I had. A little blue container flew open in mid-air and connected with the head of the rude paramedic. The contents of the container spilled open, dropping several sharp objects into his lap, one of which cut his arm open. Blood rushed from the scratch and he turned to me upset and shocked.

"What the hell are you doing princess?" he scolded. He called me princess and if I had anymore strength I would have throttled him. But I couldn't, the truck was spinning too badly now and I felt my fever breaking. My eyes concentrated on Max's face but it was all blurry.

"Oh no Mike...I think she's sick."

"It's probably just the shock finally kicking in," Mike said distracted.

"Why is it so hot in..." the other one started to say but that was all I heard before I passed out over the top of Max's body. Just before the blackness swallowed me whole I could have sworn that Max felt warm but how was that possible?

"Max..."

MADISON DANIEL

Blackness.

Breaking Asia…

I killed a boy. He was awful and took away the one thing good in my miserable world, my beautiful Max. It was an act of revenge, but I still ended this horrible boy's life. I'd kill him again if I had the chance.

"Ouch," I said as I looked down at my hands. They were filled with many gashes and scrapes. Standing at the door of my beautiful empty house, I couldn't care less about those scratches. They were filled with dried blood and mud from the clearing but my eyes focused on the inside of my home.

The rain fell soft and steady behind me and I didn't even realize that I was still crying. I slowly walked inside, staring at all the things that used to mean something to me. Now they were just things, empty stupid things. I stood in the middle of my over-sized living room feeling cold and alone.

"Why didn't I tell you how I feel Max?" I said to no one. I could feel my legs weaken and they gave out shortly after, bringing me to the floor in a cross legged position.

"Why didn't I say those words?" I cursed at myself. He did nothing but love me for everything I am and everything I was afraid to be. Why couldn't I tell him the truth, that I loved him heart and soul? I felt it the second I saw him watching me from the beach. I even felt something the day before, driving past his uncle's place. I just didn't let myself think it back then…how dare I run from the truth. The one and simple truth that…

"I love you Max," I whispered. I had hoped to say those three words one day and they would blanket me in

340

warmth and hope. Now as I spoke them out loud, my heart completely broke.

The storm started growing again outside and the wind blew cold through the front door, but I no longer cared. It blew pictures from the walls and smashed expensive vases onto the floor, but I didn't move an inch. My eyes looked around the room at all the things I couldn't care less about. My anger welled up inside of my chest leaving nothing but the pain as I began to die inside.

The lightning came again as my hatred filled my lungs, closing my eyes as the thunder called my name. My house was surrounded by a hurricane and it pushed against its walls, smashing every window and screaming through my house. As I opened my blurry eyes the first thing I saw was the half million dollar painting my parents had bought me for my sixteenth birthday. It was hung across the wall and I had always truly hated it. It was extremely beautiful but it symbolized everything I had grown up despising.

My weary body rose from the floor with the wind filling my ears. I ran to the painting and drove my fingers through the canvas and ripped it from the wall. It shredded as it fell to the floor but I wasn't done. I grabbed the frame and began to smash anything in sight. Glass shattered all around as the storm rebelled with me. We worked together in a painful dance of destruction. I screamed as I destroyed anything in sight. The storm screamed along with me filling my living room with rain and the smell of the monsoon.

After twenty minutes I could taste the blood in my throat. I stopped in front of the bare wall, exhausted and wheezing. I dropped what was left of the frame in the water along the floor. As I caught my breath again, I spied one of my tubes of imported lipstick lightly floating past my feet and picked it up. It was the blood red color I loved to wear for Max. Ever since the beach when we made that connection, I just knew it was his favorite shade. At least on me it was.

Staring at the blank wall I felt my second wind and slammed the lipstick into the empty space. In a fit, I began scraping five words that summed up my feelings for this house and for my dying soul...

...LOVE DON'T LIVE HERE ANYMORE...

"I'm so sorry Max," I whispered. Then as the tears came rushing from my eyes again I ran upstairs to my room. I grabbed the first bag I saw and threw a handful of clothes and personal items into it. I couldn't stop the tears and that made my temper flair red hot. As I lost control again I caught a quick glimpse of myself in the mirror along the wall. My reflection was distorted by the spider webs of broken glass crossing it but I could see what stopped me so suddenly...the tattoo on my right shoulder.

It made me feel so close with Max but now it would only be a reminder of how badly it hurt to lose the one thing I truly ever loved. The lightning crashed outside my window, startling me back to life. I reached for the mirror and slammed it to the ground and ran out of my room. When I made my way to the stairs I ran right into a small silver box with black ribbons trickling down its side. I picked it up carefully, holding it to my chest gently. I thought about opening it but was terrified at what might be in it. Something amazing that would surely paralyze me for eternity. So I carried it down stairs and placed it on the kitchen counter. The image of Max handing it to me stole my breath from me. I closed my eyes, running from the kitchen and left my house in ruins.

Ember

As I drove away with the rain on my face I made one final decision. It was the easiest of them all...I would leave the islands and never love anyone again.

So I did...forever.

Breaking Max...

The ambulance came sliding into the ER parking lot with its sirens on and lights flashing. Both men jumped from the vehicle in a panic, calling for assistance. They were covered in sweat and their faces were as white as ghosts.

"It's not possible! I checked him myself," Mike said dazed. More of the hospital staff rushed to help them and another paramedic threw the back doors to the ambulance open. A cloud of steam billowed out from the back and everyone gasped.

"This cannot be happening..."

"I thought you two said he was dead?" a nurse accused.

"He was!" they fired back.

Sam was lying across my body and she felt extremely hot. I prayed that I had not lost control and hurt her. I couldn't see anything but I could feel her and I could smell her sweet scent of strawberry conditioner. Her embrace felt comforting in this weird darkness. I couldn't figure out where I was; only that it hurt like hell to breathe. A thousand tiny daggers would greet me every time I inhaled.

I pushed for my eyes to open as I felt Sam's weight leave my body, scaring me in this darkness. I could feel hands touching me all over and then nothing but a blinding pain. It felt like a million exposed nerves and I thought I was screaming in agony. I wasn't out loud, only in my head. I felt a shock of electric fire pulse through my body, slicing every vein and making my muscles feel like jelly. Then I felt another pulse and another. My mind fell into a dark fuzz as the silence came back.

"We've got a pulse!" the nurse screamed. They rushed both Sam and me into the ER. The two paramedics stared at each other, one of them clutching the cut Sam had given him. When he looked down to check it he fell backwards to the concrete. The wound was gone now. He passed out and his partner pulled him into the hospital speechless.

Rising_33

~Say (All I Need): OneRepublic~

Tuesday morning – 10:01 a.m. – September 5th.

The softest of rain woke me as it tapped against the glass of my hospital room window but it wasn't the rain I had come to know and love. It was quiet and soft and didn't call to me whatsoever. It didn't even smell right.

A fuzzy white light filled my blurry eyes as I tried to focus them and that's when I felt my hand being squeezed tightly. My eyes set themselves to the biggest smile I have ever seen and the glowing green eyes above it. Sam was at my side and she looked glorious. She quickly moved the hair from my eyes and tucked it behind my warm ear.

"Hey there hero," she whispered.

"Sam...are you okay?" I asked finally waking up fully.

"Max, don't worry about me..."

"Sam," I caressed her cheek.

"I'm fine...just had a bad case of shock and dehydration. I can thank you for that!" she smiled.

"The last thing I remember is you leaving me," I said worried. Her hand tightened around mine as she leaned into my face.

"I'm all right." She kissed me softly. "Now."

"Good," I said tired. She saw this and stood up quickly.

"I should probably go find your nurse," she said but I pulled her closer to me. I sat up in bed and pushed her hand to my chest, sliding it along the places that I had been shot. Now there was only fresh new warm skin that heated her fingers. I smiled as she understood.

"Good as new but it might be hard to explain," I kissed her softly.

"They had already written you off as a miracle," she slid next to me on the bed. "You were gone only ten hours ago," she said cautious.

"Gone huh?" I felt speechless. Had I come back from the dead? Was this just a sick dream? Was I some kind of zombie? Suddenly I felt her lips on mine and I didn't care if I was dreaming or not. That's when the hospital door flew open and Kai, Marcus and Frank rushed in.

"See! I told you I heard him talking!" Marcus yelled. Frank's eyes were huge and filled with tears.

"Shhh! We're interrupting the love birds," Kai laughed and Sam blushed.

"You big dummy," I shot back. Kai shook my hand and patted Sam on the shoulder.

"What did I tell you, you can't keep a good man down," he said into her ear.

"How are you holding up son?" Frank asked quietly. He pushed through Kai and Marcus and stood next to me with a smile.

"Strong like bull," I teased and pounded on my chest. He laughed lightly but his eyes didn't. They were filled with uneasiness. He exchanged a quick look with Sam that confused me a little.

"Here my boy, I brought you a change of clothes," he said as he dropped a brown duffle bag at the end of the bed.

"A change of clothes?"

"I figured you might need them if we needed to get you out of here in a hurry." Frank winked at Sam. I was lost.

"What do you mean?" I felt a little scared.

"The police are here Max," he said quietly. "They are very eager to talk to you and Samantha." She squeezed my hand tighter.

"None of this is making much sense to the authorities. They have been here for the last two hours waiting to talk to either one of you."

"About last night," Sam added.

"They brought you in as a D.O.A. but as we can all see, you are anything but," he laughed.

"Dead on arrival..." I mumbled.

"So they need to be told something and I figured if you were in your street clothes and not that hospital jump suit, you could explain that this was all a mistake."

"Why didn't any of you tell them that?" I asked.

"We did but they wanted to hear it from the source. Besides the hospital staff didn't want them poking around in here until they could figure out what was going on," Frank smiled at me.

"Max the doctors have been going crazy about your...um...condition," Sam added.

"Yeah, they're calling you some kind of miracle," Marcus said.

"Well, what are you two calling it?" I asked Kai and Marcus worried.

"Uncle Frank has filled us in on all the gory details about your little secret brother," Kai said softly. "I know Marcus and I don't look it but we're smart enough to put the pieces together. We love you bro."

"Your secrets safe with us," Marcus chimed in.

"Thank you. So what are our options?"

"Frank and I have discussed our options too and we think it would be best if I went out and talked to the police first...by myself," Sam whispered knowing I wouldn't like the idea. "It'll buy you some time to change and get our stories straight."

"What's the story?" I asked anxious.

"We'll fill you in son," Frank said and pulled Sam from the bed. "Go ahead, we'll be right out," he assured her. She kissed me again and left slowly, closing the door behind her.

"What's the story?" I asked again.

"This was all a silly prank that Devon had made up to get back at you and Samantha." I looked at him with doubt. "He came and made a scene, causing you two to come to blows. Then he ran and you were reported as being hurt, but you weren't and the hospital was just being extra cautious."

"Cautious?" I thought this was a pretty thin story. There was no way anyone would believe it but the look in my uncle's eyes made my nerves calm.

"Yes, cautious on behalf of my wishes," he smiled.

"Basically, you're saving my butt. Again." I smiled back.

"Always." We all laughed except Kai; he was distracted by the rain against the hospital window.

"Kai, what is it?" I asked. He looked at me and then back at Frank. They were hiding something from me.

"Tell me," I ordered. Though, I think I knew the answer before he said it.

"She's gone Max." Kai's eyes watched me carefully. I said nothing and glanced out at the drops on the glass.

"Asia left, nowhere to be found my brother," Marcus added seriously. I felt cold. I didn't want to believe it.

"It's true son," Frank said. "I even went by her place this morning."

"And?" I couldn't even look at him.

"She's gone."

"Gone..." I whispered to myself.

As I stood at the window pulling my shirt over my head, I couldn't help but feel scared. Scared of what I was about to do. I wasn't sure if it was the right thing to do but I knew that it had to be done. They would all probably think I was crazy but they would all just have to accept it. Frank wouldn't take too much convincing, that I was sure of. But the little angel outside my hospital room door was a different story all together.

"Thank you Frank." I turned to shake his hand. "For everything." I tried to smile without looking sad.

"You've always been like a father to me...but..." my voice cracked.

"But you're leaving," he said sharply. He always knew me better than I did myself.

"I have to go," I continued.

349

"You're leaving?" Marcus asked worried. I looked at him and Kai.

"Yes."

"But..." Marcus trailed off defeated.

"I have to brother, for my own sanity. Things have gotten way out of hand. It is time for me to grow up and make things right," I took a deep breath.

"This is about Asia," Marcus accused with a hurt tone.

"You don't have to explain son," Frank said as he stepped toward me. "We understand. I understand. You need to find your answers." His smile returned.

"Yes, I do."

"You will always have a home waiting for you son," he said choking on his words. "But I'm afraid a handshake's not gonna do." He pulled me toward him and embraced me tightly. I hugged him back not sure what to say but then I saw the look on his face and I knew I didn't need to say anything.

"What about the band?" Kai asked nervously. "And school?" I knew he didn't care about my schooling but he was genuinely hurt about the band.

"I won't be gone long Kai...I promise you that." I grabbed his hand and shook it hard and he pulled me in for a hug. Marcus wiped his eyes and ran his hands through his bright red Mohawk.

"Ah what the heck..." he grunted and closed his arms around both of us. Frank rolled his eyes at us with a sigh. I pulled myself away from my brothers and found Frank's weary stare.

"And I will finish school," I assured him. He said nothing but nodded as if he wasn't worried.

"I promise."

Sam's faint voice bled through the door and caught me off guard. I listened carefully before turning to Kai.

"My brother…you helped me find my music again. Our music," I said smiling. "I will forever be in your debt for that but I need one more favor from you."

"Anything, just name it," he said standing up a little straighter with a proud smirk on his face.

"Take care of her for me," I was serious. He didn't seem to understand at first. I nodded to the sound of Sam's voice outside the door and his eyes filled with fear.

"Oh," he cringed.

"Don't let anything happen to her. Please," I sounded like I was begging now.

"Okay," he agreed but I could hear the uncertainty in his tone. My eyes caught Frank's again and he knew exactly what I was thinking.

"She's going to hate me." I felt my chest burn at the words and I found it harder to breathe. "That's okay, just keep her safe."

"I won't let her hate you," Kai promised. I nodded and turned to my uncle again.

"Thanks," I said. He smiled as he tossed the duffle bag to me and gave me a wink. I slowly made my way out the door.

Sam's eyes fell on me immediately as I walked through the door and her eyes filled with happiness. Her hand found mine and I wasn't sure if I had the strength to do what I was about to. It felt right standing next to her yet I was still being pulled in another direction. I ran my hand through my messy hair as the two police officers stared at me in amazement.

"I guess you were telling the truth Ms. Summers," one of them said. The other officer grunted with disapproval as he looked me up and down. I cleared my throat and shook both of their hands.

"I've heard that there were some crazy, outrageous rumors going around and I'd like to cooperate in the fullest to get to the truth," I was laying it on pretty thick and to my surprise it seemed to be working.

"Well, since there doesn't appear to be any victims in this case anymore, I guess we just have a few follow up questions," he paused. His partner looked on irritated. He obviously knew we weren't telling the truth.

The two police officers asked me about the whereabouts of Devon and Lucy. They also asked about the report of shots being fired. I stuck to Uncle Frank's story and Sam squeezed my hand so hard it hurt. Their questioning only lasted for a few minutes and when I thought they were done, they asked me the last question I wanted to hear.

"Just one more thing Mr.Valentin, Asia Michaels was reported to be at the disturbance but now she has seemed to left town." Sam leaned into me and her hands began to sweat. "Do you know where she might have gone?"

The seconds ticked away as I struggled with my answer. I didn't want to hurt Sam any more than I had to and she waited patiently silent, not even breathing.

"Sorry, I have no idea." I felt a wave of nervous dizziness but it passed quickly. The officers searched my face before giving up.

"Well, Mr. Valentine, Ms. Summers, thank you for your time." He folded up his note pad and slid it inside his shirt pocket. He shook both of our hands.

Ember

"If we have any other questions, we'll call," he said smiling politely but his partner only glared at us. One of the officers handed Sam a card with their contact information. As they turned and made their way down the hospital hallway, a relieved sigh escaped from my mouth. Sam threw herself into my arms, squeezing so hard that it hurt. My arms fell around her and I lowered my head, inhaling the smell of her hair.

In her arms I remembered everything about our time together. The honesty we shared in her bedroom. The laughs we had in school together. The night we had spent together on the beach. We had shared a closeness that I would never forget and maybe one day I would find again...but for now...

"I have to leave Sam," I said quietly.

"Alright," she smiled. "Let's go."

"No...I...have to leave," I was forceful and her smile faded. Her eyes fell to the floor.

"Why?"

"For my own selfish reasons." I was telling the truth, just not the whole truth. She looked up at me angrily.

"I need to figure some things out and this island is making it impossible. Things I should have figured out before I ever moved here," I said.

"You're going after her," she scolded.

"I don't know," I paused and swallowed my tongue a little.

"Then why does it feel like I'm stuck in second place again?" she whispered. Ouch, that one hurt.

"All I seem to do is hurt the ones I love the most and now I am hurting you. Again," I said with my hands burning. "I don't want to do that anymore."

Her arms surrounded me with tears welling up in her eyes.

"Don't leave me Max," she pleaded. "Please."

"I have to Sam," I said trying not to break under the weight of her stare. My hands held her face and she blushed from the heat they were generating.

"No, you don't," she whimpered.

"I still haven't opened the envelope yet. I don't think I'm there yet." Her head tilted and she seemed to understand.

"Oh," she looked away.

"I want to get there. I want to forgive myself." I ran my hands down the lines of her neck. "But I can't do it here."

"I love you with all my heart," she sobbed.

"I love you too," I whispered.

"Take me with you."

She kissed me softly, sending a slow burning across my body and my hands began to shake. I pulled her as close as possible and kissed her long and passionately. Her embrace felt as strong as steel. If I stayed in her heaven any longer I wouldn't be able to leave. She knew that and used it to her advantage. I had said it was so easy to fall in love with her and I was right. It took a moment but I found the strength to pull my mouth away from hers and brought my lips to her ears.

"I'll be back," I promised in a whisper. She stared at me upset but with understanding breaking through. It was comforting to see but I still felt like a big jerk.

"Promise?" she asked wilting.

Ember

"Hand on heart," I said as I lifted her hand to my chest. She kissed the tops of my hands and found my brooding brown eyes for a moment.

I took a deep breath and turned quickly from her. I could still taste her lips on mine as I walked away. The sound of her crying made it feel as if I was walking in slow motion. Just before the hospital entrance I turned to look at her one last time. She hadn't moved an inch as her tears fell like rain down her flushed cheeks. Her devastated face would be burned into my dreams for the rest of my days. Just like my little Mia had been before her.

With a final sigh I turned and walked out the hospital with my bag around my right shoulder.

"Goodbye Sam," I said to the passing wind.

MADISON DANIEL

Hope_34

~Starlight: Muse~

Back at my uncle's house Oz greeted me with an extra giddy up in his step. I let him jump on me continuously and I tickled the fur on his belly making him crazy. After a few minutes of hellos and a quick game of fetch with his favorite stuffed animal I realized just how much I would miss him.

"I'm gonna need you to look after the old man. You up for the challenge?" I teased him. He barked with confidence and I patted his head.

Inside my bedroom I gathered a handful of clothes and my mp3 player. Oz watched curiously with his tongue half hanging from his mouth. When I was done I looked around my room, studying every inch of the place I had called home, even though it wasn't for very long. When my eyes finally made it to the picture frame faced down on my dresser, my heart skipped.

I slowly reached for it and turned it to my nervous eyes. Mia's little eyes stared back at me, book ended by two long pigtails with red bows. A smaller, happier version of me was sitting behind her with a goofy smile painted on my face. I touched the glass, running my fingers along her cheek and then tucked the frame inside my bag.

As I removed my hand it grazed a fat white envelope sticking out from a pair of jeans that Frank had packed for me. I walked to the kitchen as I opened it. Inside was a stack of money, mostly hundred dollar bills. Almost $7,000 all together. I stood at the table shocked. He had packed me get away money, even before I knew I would need it. I stared at it for a long time. I almost left it on the table feeling like there was no way I could possibly take it. In that moment two things occurred to me, it would hurt his feelings if I didn't take the money and that amount of cash wouldn't get me too far in the big bad world.

My mind was racing so I grabbed a pen and paper and quickly scribbled a few last words for my uncle. It was the least I could do for him. How could my life change in such a short amount of time? When I finished I looked down at Oz one last time, tossing him one last treat. He ate it with his tail wagging and I felt lucky that he had found me. He was destined to find my glowing burning embrace. His home. Now it was my turn.

"Lions, tigers and bears." I slid my guitar around my back and snuck out the front door to start my long journey but first I had one last stop.

Tuesday afternoon – 1:03 p.m.

Standing in the mess that used to be Asia's beautiful home, I fell silent. My eyes scarred by the giant red letters carved into the wall. I was only able to look at them for a second. The thought of how much pain she must have been in to write them, choked me. I felt numb thinking that she was out there thinking the worst, that I was dead and she was alone.

I made a lap through the house and almost every step was met with crunching glass and damp footprints. In her bedroom I sat thinking of the last time I was in her bed. A smile fell across my face at the thought of how sad it was that we couldn't even consummate our relationship. Her scent was still all through the house, even with the blowing wind rushing inside all the broken windows. That made my heart beat quicker.

Ember

Downstairs in the kitchen, I wondered just how she left. Her boat? Her helicopter? Her private jet? As I pondered such ridiculous questions, my eyes came to rest on the gift box I had left for her. It was unopened and still in remarkably good condition. The one thing to survive her hurricane. Without even thinking I picked it up and placed it in my bag.

A horn beeped from out front, signaling that it was time to go. I had called the cab company an hour ago but I was happy it took so long to get here. My eyes glanced around the broken house one final time before I quietly left. Outside the impatient cab driver honked again just as I walked up to the car.

"To the next ferry," I said climbing in the back seat. A pair of familiar eyes glared at me from the rear view mirror. The cabbie that had first picked me up from the airport the day of my arrival and again he said nothing. He just shook his head in some weird "I told you so" mannerism and drove off.

On the way to the pier I watched the scenery drift by and I quickly filled with an overpowering sadness. I reached in my pocket and pulled my headphones out and placed them in my ears. Turning my mp3 to something hopeful, I closed my eyes and let the music soothe me.

3:33 p.m.

Frank walked into the house, tossing his keys on the table by the door. He could hear a tiny whine coming from the kitchen and quickly went to find Oz. He was curled up along the letter that I had left on the edge of the kitchen table and whimpering lightly.

"I guess he broke your heart too, huh little man," Frank said with a small smile and rubbed the top of his

359

head. As he picked him up he read the words that I had left.

"Frank...I'd be lying if I said I wasn't scared – so I won't say it. You know me better than that anyways. I really don't know where I'm going or when I'll be back. Just know that I'll be okay and that I will be back...it just may be a little longer than I was letting on. (But I'm sure you knew that too!)

Now I know I am capable of some amazing things – the fact that I'm here now, writing you this letter is proof of what I'm capable of. But the one trick that I haven't been able to figure out yet...the one miracle that escapes even my gifts is...

...How do you heal a broken heart? I don't think there is a magic out there that can fix that. I'll check in on you every chance I get. Don't let the little guy sulk too much...and you either! I love you old man...Max."

He folded the note and tucked it in his pocket with a tear in his eye. He walked to the living room and turned on his stereo. To his surprise I had replaced his usual selection with one of my favorites. Something that would leave him with a smile on his face. Frank fell back in his chair as the song started and he laughed until he cried.

"...Far away...This ship is taking me far away..."

5:51 p.m.

Aboard the ship I found my mind at ease and I shakily felt happy. My guitar felt right at home across my back as the breeze swept through my hair, making me smile.

360

Ember

"Hope you enjoy the music Uncle Frank," I thought to myself.

Now came the scary part. The future was mine. Whatever I wanted to do, all I had to do was do it. Surfing in the Bahamas, sky diving in the desert, or chasing a falling star across the ocean. I pulled out the large manila envelope that Sam had given me and ran my fingers along the edge of the seal. I wanted to open it so badly but I had made her a promise that I wouldn't until I was ready.

"I will keep that promise Sam," I said to the ocean. And I'll keep the one that I had made to her hours ago...

"I will come back."

As I stuck the package back into my brown bag the shiny silver paper from Asia's gift winked at me. I pulled it out, gently brushing the curly black ribbons on top of it and held it in my hands. The mirrored paper reflected the distant shades of the sunset. I watched the colors mesmerized. Would I be able to give her this one day? I scratched my hand through my hair and caught a familiar scent. Just past that sunset a tropical storm was fading away.

Behind me the island shrank smaller with each passing wave.

"Far away...fade away," I sang. "But with hope I'll be back one day."

"Hope. What a crazy word...hope." I turned the volume up on my music and gently leaned against the railing.

"With hope..." I smiled.

THE END?

MADISON DANIEL

Ember

~With Or Without You: U2~

Monday morning – 10:33 a.m. – October 23rd.

This was it. I had spent over a month in a zombie-like crippled state. Well, 48 days and counting. It made me so mad that he had brought me to this pitiful level, counting the days without him.

I think I was starting to lose my mind a little and my health was not far behind. I had cut my long hair to just above my shoulders and dyed the naturally blonde locks to a dirty brown, chestnut shade. My way of rebelling against him...I guess. I had lost a little weight and I was starting to have a hard time keeping food down now. It began about a week ago and mentally I knew that was messed up but it only seemed to happen in the mornings. This new side effect to not having him around was enough to kick me in the butt and start making things better.

So here I was...at her house. My first step to freedom, confront your worst fear. I had driven past Asia's house a couple times before but never found the courage to actually stop. The front yard was a mess with the landscaping a wreck and covered in overgrown brush. Most of it was beginning to wilt and turn a dying shade of brown. Her once lovely home missed her daily torrents I guess. The front door was completely open and exposed. The emptiness invited me in.

As I walked through the archway my eyes were amazed at the destruction before me. It looked as if a tornado had smashed through the home. It was hard to tell if the damage was intentional or just from the month and a half of exposure to the elements. My nerves began to get the best of me as I stood motionless in the foyer.

"Alright Samantha...you can handle this," My stomach felt sick and full of knots.

As I pushed my feet forward and into the enormous living room, I couldn't have been more wrong. My heart sank as I read the giant red words that looked to be dripping down the wall.

"Love don't live here anymore," I whispered under my breath. I stood there for what felt like hours just staring at those five words. I couldn't remove my eyes from them. In an instant, something broke inside of me and a flood was released.

"Ahhh!" I cried out from my soul. I screamed again and again until it felt only natural to do it. My hands reached out around me for anything they could find and hold. I started to throw every piece of junk around me. Trash, debris, and broken furniture took the brunt of my tirade. Kicking and screaming I unleashed all that I had left. Those words! I hated those words that she had written. I despised that she had written them for him! For my beloved! For my Max!

My stomach cramped as my mind folded under the anguish. I felt like this hell would go on forever when my own blood splattered across the wall, stopping me in my tracks. The blood painted the five horrible words in a deep crimson flood. I had crushed a wine glass in my hand as I threw it at the wall. It tore a huge chunk of my palm open, making my stomach turn over again, as the blood poured from the fresh wound.

The gash smiled up at me about three to four inches long and at least half an inch deep in the center of my right hand. At first the blood showed no sign of stopping and sent me into a panic. Quickly, a nervous calm over powered the panic as a new fact had my mind racing. It didn't hurt. Not one bit. It hurt the moment it happened but not now.

I pulled my hand closer to inspect it and realized that the pain should be fantastic. Maybe I had cut it deep enough to cause nerve damage but I was moving it just fine. No pain...only heat.

Slowly the gash faded right before my bulging eyes. The pieces of skin pulled together like a zipper as the faintest trail of smoke twisted off my palm. My eyes blinked not believing what they had just seen. Frantically I wiped the excess blood on my pants and shirt to get a better look. Unbelievably, I found my hand completely healed...good as new.

I was stunned. I was confused. My eyes glanced back at the words on the wall and then back to my warm hand. A soft breeze slithered through the house, messing my hair. How could this be? How was this possible? I racked my numbing brain trying to process what had just happened. My stomach rolled over again and I felt close to losing my breakfast. As my hand slid to my stomach and filled with a familiar heat...I felt at peace...

"Max."

MADISON DANIEL

"Thank you so much for taking the first step in Max's journey. I hope you choose to follow his next step. It is filled with much more adventure and heartache. Keep an eye open for the next book in the series... 'Downpour.' Remember, music is life and love never dies..." - Madison Daniel.

ABOUT THE AUTHOR:

Madison Daniel is new to the literary world. He hopes to exist in that world by bringing something exciting to it. A literary soundtrack is woven into everything he writes. Combining the love of music and the written word with the latest technology is his passion.

We live in an "instant culture," lets embrace it.

A SPECIAL THANK YOU:

Sometimes you dream of what could be and sometimes you run away from it. This goes out to the quiet force that made me believe in this series completely. Thank you Court.

~LITERARY SOUNDTRACK~

Ember is a living, breathing work of entertainment. It is meant to be enjoyed and consumed with a musical playlist. Each chapter is bookended by a song that resonates with the story and its characters. I have enclosed that musical playlist. Feel free to follow my lead or download your own playlist. Support the arts and the artists. Don't illegally download.

Look, listen and fade away...

~Chapters and Playlist~

Prologue - NIGHTMARES "STOP CRYING YOUR HEART OUT" - Oasis

SAVIOR - 01 "CRUEL SUMMER" - Bananarama

2000 MILES - 02 "(SITTIN' ON) THE DOCK OF THE BAY" - Otis Redding

BROKEN - 03 "TIME IS RUNNING OUT" - Muse

MORNING GLORY - 04 "AMBER" - 311

NEW KID - 05 "ISLAND IN THE SUN" - Weezer

JADED - 06 "DIG" - Incubus

IRON JAW - 07 "SOMEWHERE I BELONG" - Linkin Park

DARK SKIES - 08 "MONSOON" - Tokio Hotel

CRUSH - 09 "#1 CRUSH" - Garbage

TEMPTATIONS - 10 "FLUTTER GIRL" - Chris Cornell

RAINMAKER - 11 "CAUGHT IN THE RAIN" - Revis

BAD MOON - 12 "PARALYZER" - Finger Eleven

HIGH TIDE - 13 "BREAK THE ICE" - Britney Spears

SUNBURN - 14 "SUNBURN" - Fuel

"DAYS OF THE WEEK" - Stone Temple Pilots

BREATHE - 15 "OXYGEN" - Colbie Caillat

TRUTH - 16 "POLICY OF TRUTH" - Depeche Mode

KRYPTONITE - 17 "I DON'T TRUST MYSELF WITH LOVING YOU" - John Mayer

TRIAL BY FIRE - 18 "BEAST OF BURDEN" - The Rolling Stones

UNDER PRESSURE - 19 "UNDERNEATH IT ALL" - No Doubt

DESTINY - 20 "DESTINY" - Zero 7

SPARKS - 21 "ARE YOU HAPPY NOW" - Michelle Branch

WILDFIRE - 22 "I DON'T CARE ANYMORE" - Phil Collins

"OUT OF CONTROL" - Hoobastank

INFERNO - 23 "24" - Jem

CRAVE - 24 "CRAVE" - Nuno Bettencourt

NUMB - 25 "STRAIGHTJACKET" - Alanis Morissette

"AFTER TONIGHT" - Justin Nozuka

CRASHING - 26 "MOUTH (THE STINGRAY MIX)" - Bush

"WALKING AFTER YOU" - Foo Fighters

FORBIDDEN - 27 "LOVE BITES" - Def Leppard

"BREAKDOWN" - Tom Petty & the Heartbreakers

WICKED GAME - 28 "WICKED GAME" - Chris Isaak

SUFFOCATE - 29 "STRONG ENOUGH" - Sheryl Crow

"RAIN" - The Wreckers

FALLING - 30 "SIGN YOUR NAME" - Terence Trent D'Arby

BLACKENED - 31 "SHAME" - Stabbing Westward

ASHES - 32 "LOVE IS DEAD" - Kerli

RISING - 33 "SAY (ALL I NEED)" - OneRepublic

HOPE - 34 "STARLIGHT" - Muse

EMBER - 00 "WITH OR WITHOUT YOU" - U2

Made in the USA
Lexington, KY
16 March 2012